GALBA'S MEN

The Four Emperors Series

GALBA'S MEN

Book II of the Four Emperors Series

L. J. Trafford

First published in 2016 by Karnac Books.

This edition published in 2018 by Sphinx, an imprint of
Aeon Books
12 New College Parade
Finchley Road
London
NW3 5EP

British Library Cataloguing in Publication Data

A C.I.P. for this book is available from the British Library

ISBN-13: 978-1-91257-326-4

Typeset by V Publishing Solutions Pvt Ltd., Chennai, India

Printed in Great Britain

www.sphinxbooks.co.uk

For DD
1944–2007

CHARACTERS

On the Palatine Hill
Servius Sulpicius Galba—the new emperor*
Icelus—Galba's freedman, now his secretary*
Cornelius Laco—Galba's man, number one*
Titus Vinius—Galba's man, number two*
Marcus Salvius Otho—a wannabe Galba's man*
Statilia Messalina—a wannabe Otho's woman*

Felix—head of slave placements and overseers
Straton—Felix's enforcer
Artemina (Mina)—Felix's merchandise
Alexander (Alex)—ditto
Lysander—an announcer
Daphne—a seamstress
The Galli of the Magna Mater—a group of whirling eunuchs*
Sporus—a eunuch of distinctly anti-whirling sentiments*

On the Esquiline Hill
Tiberius Claudius Epaphroditus—Nero's ex-secretary,
    now in retirement*
Claudia Aphrodite—his wife
Silvia, Faustina, Pollus, Perella, Claudia, Julia,
    Rufus—their children
Callista—their slave

vii

On the Viminal Hill

Antonius Honoratus—Praetorian tribune*

Lucullus—a dim Praetorian guard

Proculus—an equally dim Praetorian guard with a facial wound

Teretius—a builder

Pompeia—his wife

Teretia—their teenage daughter

Tiberius Claudius Philo—their lodger and the emperor's private secretary's secretary

* Historical personages

Rome AD 68

It was generally agreed that the palace ran far better without an emperor. Six months had passed since a spectacular coup organised by the emperor's own Praetorian prefect, Nymphidius Sabinus, had dislodged the imperial throne from beneath the fleshy buttocks of Nero Caesar and handed it to the Spanish governor, Servius Sulpicius Galba.

Fleeing the city Nero faced a stark choice: capture and sure humiliation at Sabinus' hands, or an honourable Roman death by his own hand. He'd chosen neither, his secretary Epaphroditus taking the knives in his hands and performing one final service for his master.

The furies soon had their vengeance on that arch-traitor Sabinus. Flabbergasted to discover his patron, nay his hero, Galba to be distinctly less heroic than he'd been led to believe, the prefect felt compelled to remove another unsatisfactory emperor.

The Praetorian Guard, previously unknown for their great political insight nonetheless recognised Sabinus' declaration as not so much veering towards insanity but crashing straight through it leaving nothing but a pile of rubble in its wake. Plus, deposing two emperors within a year somewhat undermined their primary duty as the protectors of the imperial family. It would, they agreed, be a bit of an embarrassment.

Showing a rare independence of mind, they parted company from their prefect by parting him from his life, dragging his body down to the forum as a unique show and tell. No doubt, they reasoned, exactly the sort of action Galba would appreciate and reward accordingly.

They'd have to wait for their reward. Galba was dallying in the provinces, clearing up the mess the army free-for-all Nero's death had caused. Stamping out dissent and putting the boot into the legions who had failed to support his bid for the throne; calling it conciliation rather than revenge. He seemed in no hurry to return to Rome and claim his prize. Which left a palace without an emperor.

Galba, an experienced statesman, had not left Rome completely unmanned: somebody needed to look out for any other would-be Sabinuses. It took the palace staff but a morning to realise that Galba's appointed man, Icelus, was as useless as a eunuch in a brothel. At least Nero, they moaned, had been raised within Caesar's family. Which meant he understood the duties and responsibilities of emperorship, even if he were happy to outsource the lot to his staff.

Accustomed to a household of only a hundred slaves, Icelus floundered in the complicated palace structure; unable to distinguish even between a secretary and a scribe. Baffled by the terminology used in the myriad of committees, he struggled to pass decisions on issues he had no hope of understanding.

Humiliated by his ignorance, Icelus began to lean more and more on his assistant, the palace-trained scribe Tiberius Claudius Philo. Slowly and effortlessly Philo absorbed Icelus' workload, taking responsibility for facilitating committees, ensuring paperwork was promptly signed, and gently manoeuvring his boss into decisions. Such efficiency had not been seen since the days of Augustus and the staff began to enjoy this peculiar state of affairs. It was found that the wheels of imperial bureaucracy ran so much smoother when freed from the whims of an emperor. Plus, with no imperial head to impress, the fierce and often deadly competition which characterised palace politics was suspended and a spirit of co-operation reigned.

Of course it could not last. The new emperor would eventually claim his crown. Few in the palace had even heard of Servius Sulpicius Galba before the events of the spring. Nobody seemed sure of his character, nor his intentions towards Rome. Or indeed towards the palace itself.

GALBA
AUTUMN AD 68

"So long as he was a subject, he seemed too great a man to be one and by common consent possessed the makings of a ruler—had he never ruled"
—Tacitus, *The Histories*

ONE

Somewhere behind the huge pile of wax tablets and a pyramid of scrolls sat Tiberius Claudius Philo. All these documents demanded his attention and they all required Icelus' signature; only Icelus was not around as usual. Luckily Philo had a workaround, having fashioned a copy of Icelus' signet ring which he used to stamp into the wax. This saved him the chore of searching the endless entertainment suites of the new palace trying to locate his boss.

It should be stressed that this was no fraud since Philo had put the idea to Icelus himself as a time-saving efficiency. Anything that enabled Icelus to spend more time with his masseur was warmly welcomed and Galba's official had eagerly embraced this innovation.

Quiet and studious, Philo had risen through the scribe ranks by sheer efficiency and intelligence to his current post as the emperor's private secretary's secretary. He'd worked briefly for Nymphidius Sabinus and before that far more happily for Epaphroditus, Nero's wily and devious advisor, a man whom he respected and admired above all others. Of Icelus, Philo, ever fair, was reserving judgement. The delights offered by the hospitality team had often turned men's minds from their duties. Icelus, he felt, would soon grow bored of all that banqueting and run out of fan boys to pleasure him.

It did not occur to him that some people will always prefer pleasure to duty and will wheedle out of any work given the opportunity, particularly if they have a very efficient and capable assistant. Philo's pleasures were few. He liked tidying things, he liked reading, and he was very fond of the spiced almond cakes his landlord's daughter Teretia baked for him each day.

He was nibbling at one of her cakes now, catching the crumbs in his cupped hand as he scanned the document stating Galba's progress. According to the author the emperor was now approaching the Alps. Philo swung round to check the map tacked to the wall behind his chair. He stood and traced his finger along Gaul until he located the town mentioned in the scroll.

"Hmm," he murmured, his mouth full of Teretia's delicious cake.

Two days riding perhaps? Nearer even. Time to check on the progress of Code Purple.

Code Purple was Philo's master plan for the arrival of Galba in Rome. Icelus, perplexed by the imperial court protocols, was more than happy to leave all of the arrangements to Philo. These dictated everything: the standing positions of slaves in alternately shaped rooms; the seating at every meal, be it a supposedly informal breakfast or large banquet; all the varied and particular greetings for the many ranks of slaves, servants, officials, and courtiers. Philo had applied his customary meticulousness to the task. He had spent days in the musty archives reading up on every previous ascension to emperor and the resulting grand events of thanksgiving.

He'd quizzed Icelus thoroughly on Galba's character in order to match his ceremonies to the new emperor's temperament. As he suspected, Galba was no Nero in his tastes.

Code Purple was to be a dignified, official welcome. A show of loyalty from the palace staff to their new emperor.

Philo tucked his papers away in his battered leather satchel, his most prized and practical possession, swinging the strap over his head as he trotted off with his tick list.

The small antechamber that served Philo's office was located in what was generally referred to as the old palace. This was the palatial residence built by Emperor Tiberius, improved upon by Caligula, and then near burnt to the ground under Nero.

The destruction of the imperial family's living quarters had given the flamboyant Nero the excuse to build a new home. This residence, known to the staff as the new palace, to the plebs as the golden house, and to the senate as an unjustifiable waste of funds, took up one hundred acres of the city and was spectacular in its design. Yet it lay unfinished and indeed unpaid for, as demonstrated by the builders' huts still standing on the Oppian Hill side of the new palace grounds.

Such a grand scale of a project made it an irritatingly long walk from the old palace. Still, it was a trek Philo enjoyed since it allowed him time to formulate his thoughts. His concern was one particular paragraph in his Code Purple master plan. This detailed the movements of the empress, Statilia Messalina, and her attendants. They were to attend Galba's welcome banquet, involving a short walk from the empress' apartments in the new palace to the octagonal dining room in the summer pavilion where the feast was being held. However, to Philo's over-analytical mind this short passage was fraught with potential mishaps and he wanted to drill the attendants again. Really this should involve the empress and this was the point which was causing Philo a knot of anxiety in his stomach.

Empress Statilia Messalina was a very spiky woman. The fact she was still referred to as empress despite being merely

Nero's widow attested to this. Nobody dared to address her by anything else. In a high fury that noble woman was known to fling her footwear at the source of her displeasure. When sanguine she was haughty to the point of rudeness and could reduce the most stoic of patricians to gibbering apologies by one hard glare from those wide-set eyes.

Her apartments, a rich array of rooms, lay in one of the new palace buildings. A separate building, it should be noted, from the emperor's suite which Icelus was minding. They were placed on opposite sides of the lake with their own gardens and private courtyard, a colonnaded walkway leading back to the main palace complex. Philo nipped along this path wondering whether he dared suggest to Statilia Messalina that she partake in his drill.

For thoroughness he felt it was necessary: Statilia's independent mind might have the whole party walking in the wrong direction. Her slaves would be unable to correct their mistress and they could wander the corridor all evening trying to locate the banquet. That wouldn't do. That would, thought Philo, be just awful.

He entered the building by a side door, passed the Praetorians on guard with a nod, and had just navigated round a corner towards the entrance to the empress' suite when he spied a large shape in a sludge-coloured tunic standing outside. Philo walked briskly back round the corner and pressed his back against the wall.

Straton. What was Straton doing in the empress' apartments? He was the last person Philo would have expected to encounter on this particular route; in fact he had taken this particular route to avoid bumping into the slave overseer.

He felt a familiar race to his heart and a tremble begin in his hands. He dared a darting glance round the brickwork in the forlorn hope that he had imagined Straton's presence, the result of the long hours he was putting in at work. But no, it was definitely the overseer. A man as large as Straton could not be imagined. A good six feet of bulk with huge muscled arms and a chest broader than three average-sized men. He was less of a man and more of an outbuilding: a granary or a summer house. Bristled hair matched the whiskers on his chin and beneath that a thick neck with a raised, white scar which dissected his throat. This injury had sliced at Straton's vocal cords and left him with impaired speech.

Philo, in common with everyone else in the imperial household, owned a healthy terror of Straton. It was not just his fierce exterior that frightened. As a slave overseer Straton had complete command over the imperial slaves: they were but his toys to amuse himself with. Philo, unfortunately for him, amused Straton more than anybody else.

If Philo had thought that his newly purchased freedom would save him from Straton's enforced embrace he'd been cruelly disillusioned. Free will, Philo had discovered, was harder to practise than he'd anticipated, especially when faced with Straton's black eyes boring into him.

He had only one method of dealing with this unpleasant situation: avoidance. A tactic that was wearing on his nerves as well as being generally ineffective, for Straton seemed to possess some strange inner homing signal that located Philo wherever he was.

Oh gods, thought Philo, daring another glance round the corner and noting Straton's immovable form patrolling outside the door, holding his cudgel on his shoulder like a spear. He had to see the empress; he needed to test her on her role in Code Purple. But there was no other way to get to her rooms without passing Straton. This set off a flutter of anxiety in Philo's chest. He leaned back against the wall, paralysed with indecision.

"PHILO!"

He jumped a clear foot in the air.

"Gods, Philo, what's got into you?" asked Mina, approaching with a pile of towels in her arms; the tools of her trade as one of the empress' bathroom attendants. "You look like Europa surprised by a randy bull."

Philo managed a polite but rather squeaky, "Hello." Before pulling himself together and stating more professionally, "I'm here to see the empress in regards to Code Purple."

Mina groaned, "Juno! We're all Code Purpled out."

"Nevertheless," insisted Philo, thinking that if he could get Mina to escort him to the empress Straton could not touch him. He pulled his satchel round and rummaged within, producing the tablet that contained his master plan. "There are a few details that need clarification."

"We're only walking down the corridor. I can see the door from here."

A head popped round the corner, large and bristled. "Hey," growled Straton in his usual hoarse whisper.

The tablet flew out of Philo's hands and hit the wall opposite, slamming onto the floor. He scurried to collect it, taking care to retrieve it without turning his back on the overseer.

"You're very skittish today," observed Mina.

Philo hugged the retrieved tablet to his chest. "I need to see the empress," he said, avoiding Straton's black eyes.

"Awright, awright," soothed Mina. "We're being purpled again," she said for Straton's benefit. "Thirteen times we've pootled down the corridor for his benefit," she moaned. "We could do the thing blind, we could do it drunk, we could do it blind drunk! In fact I may suggest that to the mistress, it might enliven the event for her." She smiled wickedly at Philo's horrified expression.

"There is no alcohol until the banquet," he stressed.

Statilia Messalina was abrasive enough sober; drunk she could give the Dacians a run for their money. "And then it will be properly rationed."

Mina rolled her eyes at Straton. To her surprise the overseer took Philo's side, emitting a hoarsely insistent, "Code Purple big deal. Should practise." He nodded at Philo who hugged his tablet tighter and took a step towards Mina, asking, "Take me to the empress, please."

"Fine, fine. Let us be purpled again." And then to Straton, "You on for later?"

Straton gave a grin, "Yerrr."

"Excellent," she clapped. "Come on Philo, stop gawping like a fish and let's go get purpled again. Though I should warn you that the empress is about to take her bath and so will probably be naked."

Mina kept one eye on Philo and noted with amusement the tension in his jaw. Still, Mina thought, that was surely an advantage. For naked, the empress had no footwear to fling at Philo when he suggested yet another run through of Code Purple.

TWO

There lay beyond the Viminal Gate into the city a large wall, several feet high. It was a compact square of brick with sharpened stakes discouraging any would-be intruder. Discouragement was not needed; anyone scaling this particular wall had to be insane or suicidal or had reached an extraordinary scale of drunkenness. For beyond this wall lived 8,000 heavily armed men: they were the Praetorians and this was their camp.

The Praetorian Guard was the emperor's elite troop of bodyguards, as they saw themselves. Or whoremongering bully boys, as everyone else saw them. At any one time there was a single cohort of 800 men on duty at the palace; another cohort might be on duty keeping the crowds under control at the games or theatre or circus. Had this been a military legion, the remaining guards would no doubt have been out building bridges across rivers, mending roads, and having a good old march about. However, the river Tiber was already well bridged, the roads were maintained by an army of public slaves, and the city streets were far too narrow and crowded to enable any serious marching.

Thus there were 6,400 men with an awful lot of time on their hands. Inevitably this led to trouble and everyone knew to avoid the Viminal bars from the kalends to the ides, which was all the time it took the guards to drink and whore away their inflated wages.

They had in recent years been stamped into a near respectable force by their dictatorial but energetic prefect Nymphidius Sabinus. However, since they hacked him to pieces back in the summer after he made a foolhardy attempt to declare himself emperor, they had fallen back into their usual louche ways with the added arrogance of having saved the throne for Galba.

Today on a bright September morning two guards were leaning against the wall by the main barrack gates. They were on official guard duty but their attitude was casual as if they had personally decided to put on their uniforms and gather there. One was big and beefy and went by the name of Lucullus. The other, Proculus, was slimmer with a red diagonal line that ran from his forehead, across his nose and onto his jaw, the result of a run-in with Straton some months back. These two were viewing the passing citizens with lax diligence, searching the crowds for any pretty girls they could leer at or any passing citizen whose appearance was worth insulting.

A few feet away from them tottered a large litter with green tasselled curtains borne upon the shoulders of eight Ethiopian slaves. Though they trotted along easily enough, the precarious bending of their poles suggested a great weight within. Proculus looked at Lucullus and raised one eyebrow; it arched high and was accompanied by an angling of his narrow head. Lucullus gave a snort and then a nod. As the litter approached Proculus slipped out a leg.

The first Ethiopian stepped over it. His colleague behind was less fortunate and stumbled. He automatically threw his arms out to break his fall, thus releasing his grip on the pole. The litter lurched violently to the left, the remaining slaves frantically trying to right it, yelling commands between themselves. Alas, the weight within was too much and the litter

12

slipped further to the left depositing a rather startled man on the cobbled street. Sat on the ground, he was immediately surrounded by the desperate apologies of his bearers and a dozen of his other slaves vying with each other to help him up.

Proculus and Lucullus doubled up with laughter, Lucullus slapping a palm against the wall in merriment. The man was now on his feet, the grimy remnants of the type of substances that fell onto the Viminal streets quickly removed by his wardrobe slave who rushed forward with his clothes brush at the ready. He was tall with a protruding belly, which made him near spherical, hidden beneath a green tunic. No doubt in previous years his height had masked his increasing waistline. Now there was no hope unless he took to walking on stilts. Red fleshy lips and hooded eyes lay beneath heavily oiled black hair which was slickly reflecting the morning light. Recovering himself from his unexpected descent he approached the still-snickering guards.

"And you two are?" he asked lightly in a well-bred accent, surrounded by his slaves who seemed far more indignant than he was from his recent experiences.

Lucullus recovered himself into an upright position, pointing his spear straight at the stranger and replying, "What's it to you?"

The man, unfazed, clicked his fingers and a slave shot forward with a scroll. He played with the scroll in his hands, rolling it round so they could both see the seal. Imperial.

Seeing the bravado slip from the guards, the man smiled and told them, "His Imperial Majesty Galba has sent me. My name is Cornelius Laco and I am your new Praetorian prefect."

A greater contrast to the last could not have been found.

The Praetorian tribune Antonius Honoratus was a seasoned veteran of the legions and a great organiser; it was he who had assisted Nymphidius Sabinus in the reform of his guards. It was also Honoratus who had ordered the murder of the insane Sabinus. That he had no choice in the matter did little to alleviate his conscience. He was a haunted man, lacking his previous drive. His one joy in life was Alex, a young imperial slave who acted as his messenger and to whom Honoratus had formed a great, and wholly innocent attachment.

Today Alex was assisting him in prepping the daily roll calls, rolling up the documents and sealing them with wax. These Alex would deliver to the imperial treasury for calculation of the individual guards' monthly pay. Any failing to achieve full attendance would be docked money, one of Sabinus' reforms which had been particularly effective in tackling absenteeism and the peculiar tummy bug that always ravaged the barracks after festivals.

The door swung open and Proculus announced, "Cornelius Laco, Praetorian prefect."

Then he stood aside to allow a full vision of the new boss. It was not Honoratus' job to make judgements. He quickly saluted and kicked his heels together, briskly barking, "Honoratus, Praetorian tribune, sir!"

Alex, ever in awe of soldiers' ways, copied the move, though with less distinction.

Cornelius Laco gave a crooked smile, his eyes amused. "Excellent," he drawled. "Now if you would be so kind as to direct me to my quarters."

Quarters was overstating it. Nymphidius Sabinus had taken but a single room in one of the stone barracks' huts. Although Honoratus had returned Sabinus' sparse personal possessions to his mother, there remained a lot of the fallen prefect's personality in that square room. It was barren, stern, and basic. There was a low camp bed, and a bulky chest of drawers on which sat a bowl for washing. Laco's nostrils twitched. His slaves sized up the space and exchanged knowing looks. Laco scratched his ear. "I'll go up to the palace I think, tribune. Check in with Icelus and that. Perhaps you could drill the men or whatever it is you do."

"Yes, sir," concurred Honoratus.

Laco's slaves moved closer to him: none of them wanted to be left behind. Not when there was a palace to explore.

"How is it that your rooms are so much better than mine?" asked Laco, running a finger along a huge water organ.

Icelus, propped up by seven fluffy pillows and being fanned by five loinclothed boys, opened his arms. "I am sorry, Laco," he smarmed. "Did Sabinus not leave his quarters tidy?"

"Tidy is not the word for it. They are Spartan." Laco gave a shiver. "I've seen comfier stables. And given what they did to their last commander, I decided I would not stick around. Can you imagine trying to sleep surrounded by those brutes, knowing that they were fully armed? I should have bags under my eyes. Tell me, how did you bag this luxury?"

Icelus smiled toothily. "I have an excellent little secretary. He sees to all my needs."

"Wow, you are a quick worker."

"Scraping the barrel, Laco, as always."

"Seriously though, can your little secretary sort me out something as downright imperial as this?"

A fan boy gently wiped away the moisture from Icelus' brow. "No go, Laco. Get your own assistant. Philo is far too busy."

"Busy arranging this for you?" Laco fingered a marble column representation of Priapus, the god's erect phallus pointing directly at the freedman.

"I like it," Icelus justified.

"Galba will not."

"Is there something you wanted? Apart from criticising my décor."

Laco flopped into a chair, arms hanging over the sides. "I wanted to ask about your senatorial friends."

Icelus clicked the fan boys away. He watched their departure with a sigh.

"Don't trust the staff?" queried Laco.

"Who knows where their loyalties lie. It is the same with the senate. I think Galba's actions in the provinces may have unnerved them."

Laco chewed a fingernail. "Necessary, if unpleasant. The legions were out of control. It was necessary to stamp on them. You can only buy a man so far. At some point you have to at least attempt to win his respect."

"It is not the strictness with the legions that is causing the worry," Icelus told him. "The consensus seems to be that it is fine to remove traitors but not to take their wives and children with them."

Laco crinkled his nose. "That was the legions again. The order was to execute certain individuals."

"Without trial!"

"Without trial," confirmed Laco. "We couldn't have them making some great deathbed speech that could appeal to the masses."

"And their families?"

"The soldiers got carried away," Laco shrugged. "I don't like it any more than you do. But these are crazy times and if anything that justifies Galba's harsh regime for the army."

"It has created great anxiety both in the palace and in the streets. The senate is most upset."

"They are upset because they thought themselves in control and they have learned that Galba is his own man."

"I have a deputation visiting if you want to sit in. I am sure they would love to hear all the news."

"Is it worth my while?"

Icelus smiled. "Oh yes. Since they heard of the massacre, they have been paying homage to me. They hope I can put in a good word with Galba."

"And will you?"

"If the price is right."

"I am also very friendly with the emperor," Laco pressed, eager to share in the good fortune to be had.

"You will not go short," Icelus promised him. "And I will get Philo to look into your accommodation."

"Thank you. Can I ask where one goes for a little comfort?"

"That depends on your tastes. Zosimus deals with the catamites. Diomedius, I believe, deals with comfort of the female persuasion."

"Good?"

"They breed them for attractiveness and train them in certain skills I have never come across before."

Laco leaned back in his chair and closed his eyes, saying, "I have the itch for a black beauty with tits the size of melons and a tongue the length of my cock."

Icelus clicked his fingers. "It shall be so."

THREE

"He's not even a proper solider!" huffed Alex. "You should have seen his hair. It was oiled and it smelled like, like, like flowers," nose crinkling in disgust.

His companion Mina, sprawled out on his bed, blinked and enquired, "That's a bad thing?" Thinking of the lice infections that caused havoc in the slave quarters on a regular basis, a bit of flowery hair oil might well solve that problem.

They were both off duty, and as was their habit they had holed up in Alex's room to dissect the day's gossip. Mina took the bed, considering it her right as a girl. Alex sat cross-legged on the floor, his back against the wall.

"And!" continued Alex, stabbing a finger in the air. "He took one look at his quarters and demanded to be put up in the palace. What do you make of that?"

"Seems a sensible move to me. Who'd want to lodge among such brutes?" was Mina's response.

Though best friends Alex and Mina disagreed on the subject of the Praetorian Guard. Alex admired their discipline, their camaraderie, their grave duty to protect the imperial family from threat. Mina thought they were drunken animals who were the key threat to the imperial household. Their many stinging arguments on the subject concluded generally with

Mina deploying her most effective tactic: a two-fingered nipple pinch which had Alex gasping in pain and conceding at least momentarily that her view was the correct one. In remembrance of this lethal weapon, Alex quickly changed the subject.

"What's new with you?"

Mina laced her fingers behind her neck. "Not much," she confessed. "I managed to completely humiliate Philo with the empress' help, which was most kind of her. What is it with him? You'd think he'd never seen a naked woman before when all the while he's banging away at that Teretia freebie-girl." *Freebie*, palace slang for the free born.

A thought suddenly struck her, visible by her widening eyes and the arm that reached out and grabbed at Alex's wrist.

"Hey, is this Laco attractive?" she demanded.

"No, not at all," he said, loosening her fingers off, one by one.

Mina thought for a moment and then asked, "Is he bearable?"

Alex shook her off. "Why? What do you care?"

Feeling a sting of jealously from even this short exchange.

"No reason," sighed Mina. "I could do with a hobby. Some out of hours action. It could be useful to have a lover on Galba's staff. I deserve a promotion."

She went quiet, staring at the ceiling and then said softly, "I miss Epaphroditus."

Epaphroditus, Philo's former boss, private secretary to Nero and the man Mina had slept with to secure her job as keeper of the empress' towel. She possessed a mercenary attitude towards sex, using it as a bartering tool. Unfortunately for Alex he had nothing to offer in return, so had been forced to settle for friendship. He used to consider it a consolation, now it was sheer torture.

He adored Mina, loved her entirely but had yet to tell her this; fearful of losing the one connection he had with her. So he suffered through her affair with Epaphroditus in all its graphic detail which she shared happily, ignorant of Alex's fingernails digging into his palms. Ever the friend, he reached over and took her hand. She gave a sad smile of gratitude.

"I still can't believe he's dead, and Sporus."

Here she gave a choke, her eyes moistening. Alex knew exactly what his role was: he sat next to her on the bed and hugged her close.

"It's not the same without Sporus," she cried. "He should be here, sitting there," she pointed to the other end of the bed, the spot where Sporus had always sat. "He should be divulging his gossip. Juno knows it would be better than ours!"

He hugged her closer murmuring, "I know, I know."

Sporus had been the third member of their group; a painted eunuch of indeterminate duties. He'd been Nero's lover, fleeing with the emperor and Epaphroditus the day Sabinus had taken over the city. None of them had returned.

"I can't believe they're both dead!" Mina wailed.

The thing was; they were not. A fact Alex through his Praetorian connections was well aware of. Nero might have opened his veins but Epaphroditus and Sporus were still pumping blood through theirs. As to why he'd failed to inform Mina of her lover's and her friend's fate, he was justifying it as essential to their safety. Both Epaphroditus and Sporus playing dead meant avoiding retribution from Galba's new regime, a very real threat. Certain favoured freedmen and confidants of Nero had already met a bloody end on Rome's streets, and lynchings were common.

Late at night, lying on his bed alone, staring up into the darkness, Alex allowed his real motives to be revealed. He wanted to split Mina and Epaphroditus up. He couldn't bear for her to jump back into her passionate affair with the secretary. And as for Sporus … Well, the eunuch had taken against Alex most violently for his support of the Praetorians and Nymphidius Sabinus. He seemed to suppose that Alex should have warned both him and Mina about the coup against Nero when anyone else would have understood such information was classified!

Tempered into this was the feeling that Mina might agree with Sporus. Alex couldn't bear for her to think badly of him. So he remained tight-lipped as Mina mourned, taking on the role of supportive shoulder. A state he secretly enjoyed.

Mina used the sleeve of her gown to wipe her eyes, clearing her throat before enquiring, "Laco, is he married?"

"No idea," yawned Alex. "Probably. Most of that class are. Though I pity his wife, the pillows must get awfully oily."

Trudging home through the Viminal streets, Philo barely noticed the street hawkers, the priests, or the stallholders pulling their wares to their storage holds. He was reflecting or rather dwelling on his interview with the empress, feeling distinctly peeved towards Mina. When she had shown him into the empress' private dressing room, Statilia Messalina had been sat clothed in a green robe with one foot outstretched for the maid seated on the floor painting her toenails.

"Imperial Mistress," Philo had greeted her properly, keeping his head low and his eyes averted as protocol dictated.

"Oh it's you," had been her Imperial Mistress' response. "What it is?" she demanded tetchily.

Past exposure to Philo had taught her that his appearance rarely signified anything entertaining or diverting; generally it entailed paperwork.

"There are a few matters to discuss regarding Code Purple, empress."

Statilia would have had something to say about that had Mina not crept forward and whispered something in her ear. The empress' lips twitched into a smile and then she regally pulled herself to her feet, pushed back her shoulders, and let her green robe slide off onto the floor, telling Philo, "You'll have to talk as I bathe."

Walking past him she made sure her naked arm brushed his, Philo squirming backwards in response.

He'd tried to keep it professional, standing beside the sunken bath with his note tablet but his words came out stammered and stuttered. The empress, sitting waist-high in her bath, taking an inordinately long time to oil up her breasts, addressed his points straight-faced; unlike Mina who stood beside him holding her signature towel, shaking with laughter at his discomfort. Which he felt was jolly mean of her.

Mina seemed to delight in embarrassing him. He still acutely recalled the previous year when she'd appeared in his office, slipped her dress from her shoulders and thrown her naked body full pelt into him, knocking him back into a corner. Philo was very particular about his person and he did not enjoy his genitals being grabbed by such a firm and determined hand.

In fact he had been greatly distressed and upset by the whole incident. Even more so when Mina had related the entire, excruciating episode to most of the palace, adding that her conquest only failed because he was impotent. Which was most unfair. Philo maintained that no man taken so unawares could respond in anything but a limp manner.

He climbed the stairs to the first floor apartment where he rented a room from a local Viminal family: Teretius, his wife Pompeia, and their teenage daughter Teretia. The family were in the kitchen, seated around the wooden table that took over most of the room. The look that Teretia gave Philo on his entrance was the reason everyone at the palace presumed they were sleeping together. A gaze of total adoration. "Philo!" she breathed, her cheeks colouring.

She was very pretty, with a round friendly face, two light blue eyes, and golden hair that when loose fell to her waist. In the last year she had filled out into a plump, curvy girl with large melon-shaped breasts which she generally kept hidden behind a tightly knotted shawl. Had it not been for her sweet, kind disposition and the heavy chaperoning of her devoted parents, those melons would have led her into many difficulties of a male kind.

She was now fifteen years old and unmarried. A rare situation in her neighbourhood where most of her contemporaries were beginning their families with gusto. Pompeia was of the view that Teretia was far too good for the local Viminal lads, whom she considered grubby and loutish. Teretius, a protective father, was in full agreement and they vowed to wait a few years before beginning the search for a suitable husband for their beloved daughter.

Then ten months back, in he had walked, the perfect son-in-law: salaried, meek, clean, polite, educated, and well-spoken. They agreed that Philo's good points, his kind, shy manner and well-paid job, outweighed the deficiencies in his background. Pompeia's aunt, after all, had married an ex-slave and that had been a very happy marriage. But of course Philo was an imperial freedman which was much more suitable, distinguished even.

That was back when they had thought their unassuming lodger to be a petty clerk in the palace bureaucracy, before they'd discovered just how highly he ranked: the emperor's private secretary's secretary no less! Then they were in full and unequivocal agreement that Philo and Teretia should marry. A point Teretia, dreamily in love, fully concurred with.

So a wedding would take place but with Philo lacking any family to speak for his interests, Teretius and Pompeia could only wait for the young man himself to come personally to them to make the necessary arrangements. Which he had not done.

Teretius, seeing his daughter gaze so adoring at their lodger, had attempted to speed up the process by dealing with some of the concerns he felt Philo might be wrestling with. Bringing up the subject of Teretia's dowry, assuring the bewildered Philo that she was taken good care of, he talked at length about the successful construction business he had founded, dwelling upon its annual income and increased productivity, mentioning casually his membership of the Viminal branch of the highly regarded Builder's Guild. He then threw into conversation Pompeia's brother-in-law, a highly successful merchant with a large villa further up the Viminal Hill, as evidence of the good standing of the family. He had even somewhat obliquely raised the issue of Teretia's assured virginity by way of underlining the special care Pompeia had taken over her daughter.

Yet still no date had been set.

There was one very simple reason for Philo's dallying: he was genuinely unaware of Teretia's devotion to him. He might have been clever and quick of mind when it came to filing, translating, and scribing, but Philo possessed a peculiar denseness when it came to women. It would never occur to him that any woman could hold feelings of attraction towards him.

Tonight as usual Philo completely missed Teretia's devoted gaze, his eyes taken by their empty bowls.

"I've missed dinner again!" he wailed.

He looked so distressed by this that Pompeia rushed to the steaming cauldron on the stove, reassuring him, "There's still some left, Philo. I'll get you a bowl."

Philo's shoulders relaxed and he slipped off his satchel and sat down beside Teretia on the bench. She quivered with excitement as the cramped space meant that their thighs were pressed together. Philo gave her a small smile. Teretia took in every detail of that greeting to note down in her journal later; a document in which Philo featured extensively.

Teretius sat opposite, picked at his teeth with the point of his knife asking, "Good day, son?"

Philo did not want to repeat his embarrassing nude meeting with the empress, nor his escape from Straton's clutches that evening, and he didn't think that Icelus' and Laco's requirements from the entertainment committee were a suitable topic for the dinner table.

"The emperor is only two days away," he settled on, causing a flurry of "ooohs".

They were all extremely impressed by Philo's imperial connections. Pompeia used them in competition with the other Viminal housewives. Corsica's tale of Emperor Nero's chariot running over her foot paled into the inane anecdote it was by Teretia's attendance at an actual palace banquet with Philo. There she had met Emperor Nero and Empress Statilia Messalina and many of the ladies of the court. She had also met Sporus, Nero's eunuch consort, whom she determined was a great friend.

In his attempts to engage his lodger in conversation, Teretius made a catastrophic error when he remarked amiably, "There must be lots of plans for the emperor's arrival."

He had meant it as a rhetorical statement or perhaps the opening of a brief description of the festivities to occur. Philo, however, had lived and breathed Code Purple for two months. It hung in his mind during breakfast, his walk to work, any brief breaks he took to the privy, and was a useful mental distraction when Straton had sex with him. He therefore launched into the entire Code Purple master plan: every movement of every slave and every freedman/woman on that day. It was descriptive, it was meticulous, it was a very long monologue that soon had Teretius and Pompeia glaze-eyed. Only Teretia listened to every word, infected as she was by the strange (and easily disproved) view that nothing Philo uttered could be dull.

"That sounds magnificent," was her bright comment when Philo finally reached a conclusion with the timings and exhaustive guest list for the evening event. Philo was momentarily stunned by the comment and then decided that she was right. It was going to be truly magnificent.

Concentrating on his stewed cabbage, Philo did not notice Teretia staring at him, watching his every mouthful and sprung into nervous anticipation for any further words he might speak to her. Her parents locked hands under the table, Pompeia whispering to her husband, "He'll be waiting till after all this hoo-ha for the new emperor. Then he'll ask us. When it's quiet. You can't expect him to think about a wife when there is all this going on!"

She was unaware that Philo's only post-Code Purple plan was a thorough review and evaluation of how the events had gone. He rather thought he might issue questionnaires for the staff to fill in.

FOUR

The messenger cantered through the streets, kicking at his horse to go faster, the hooves pounding on the cobbles. As he reached his destination he pulled at the reins and leapt off before his steed had come to a full halt. His state—he was covered in mud with dark lines under his eyes—suggested he'd ridden through the night, as did the sweaty sheen on the horse's flank. He ran from his horse to the gate, his mouth in a hard determined line, his brown eyes resolute. He clearly had an absolutely vital message to deliver.

This did not mean, however, that Proculus and Lucullus were going to let him pass. They crossed their spears to block the gate and perfected their best "like I give a fuck" faces. The messenger, holding one hand across his stomach, told them, "The emperor is coming!"

Proculus blinked and replied, "Yeah, we know."

The messenger's eyes bulged.

"He's been coming for days."

"He's on his way!" insisted the messenger. "Emperor Galba is on his way!"

"Yeah, so you said," Lucullus weighed in, using his spare hand to scratch at his groin.

The messenger began to stutter, struggling over alternative words that would clarify matters. He settled on a strangulated, "Today!"

Proculus looked at Lucullus and asked in a whisper, "Do you think this is Code Purple?"

"Hang on, let me check my note thingy."

Lucullus handed his spear to Proculus and then fiddled behind his leather breastplate producing a small, square piece of wood. Written in Philo's neat handwriting was the following:

How to spot Code Purple

1. A dirty, tired messenger will arrive at the palace gates.
2. He will tell you that the emperor is on his way.
3. He will offer you a timescale of when the emperor is to be expected.
4. If he says "today" or measures the emperor's arrival in hours: this is Code Purple.

Lucullus looked at the exhausted scout and his sweating horse, telling Proculus sagely, "It's Code Purple alright."

According to Philo's exhaustive notes on Code Purple, Proculus should have dashed off to tell the Praetorian tribune on duty, who would then pass word to Felix the head of slave placements, who would then get the overseers organised to move the slaves into their positions. From then onwards every-one should know what they had to do and where they had to do it.

However, Proculus broke protocol entirely. With the scout following wearily behind, he entered the grand Palatine side entrance hall to the old palace. Seeing the night slaves quietly sweeping the floor and mopping the marble columns, he merely yelled at full volume: "CODE PURPLE!"

The slaves on duty instantly dropped their dustpans and jumped to their feet, staring in panic at each other. This was it!

Felix, head of slave placements, chief overseer, and possessor of the greatest bushy red beard this side of the Danube, stood behind his desk and gave his knuckles a quick crack before asking, "You sure, Lysander?"

The blond announcer nodded. "I heard it from Daphne, who heard it from Mina, who was told by Cassandra whose brother runs the cleaning section, and he was told by one of his operatives who was actually there when the guard yelled it."

Lysander, happy with this conclusive evidence, crossed his arms, hoping to gain points from Felix for being the bearer of such momentous news.

Felix scratched at his red wiry beard. "This is it then. Fucking Code Purple," he murmured to himself and then turning his gaze to the smug announcer yelled at eardrum-piercing volume, "WHAT THE FUCK ARE YOU DOING HERE? FUCKING CODE PURPLE! GET TO YOUR FUCKING POSITION!"

Lysander, so quickly out of favour, legged it. Felix opened the drawer of this desk and pulled out a scroll as thick as his wrist. He unwound it and read from Philo's neat handwriting: Code Purple: Action Number 1.

There were seventy-two items of direction on Felix's Code Purple sheet. He hadn't read any of them, nor would he now as he rolled up the scroll and threw it in the bin. Felix had better things to do, like get his lazy-arse slave overseers up and taking control.

Swinging open the door to his office, he noted the panicking slaves running in disorientation down the corridor. The sooner he got Straton onto this with his sturdiest whip the better. Right now Felix bellowed, "CODE PURPLE!"

Which caused a momentary hiatus in the chaos. Grabbing a white-clad slave by the nape of his tunic, lifting the unfortunate lad off his feet, Felix yelled in his ear, "GET PHILO!" Then he let him go, giving him a shove in the back to move him quicker.

Well, thought Felix, this will be the fucking making or breaking of Philo. Secretly, and this was a thought he would never express publicly, for Felix had a reputation of hairy scariness to maintain, he hoped it would be the former. The little freedman was one of the best investments he'd ever made. What Philo paid for his freedom being many times his original purchase price. Felix liked those kinds of sums: it had certainly made up for that dodgy Dacian he'd spent far too much money on and who'd died without putting in a single hour's labour. Dacians had gone on Felix's list of nationalities he considered useless. So far the only country missing was China: he'd never bought a Chinese slave. Instead he mentally tallied the Chinese as *probably useless.*

Teretius' response to someone banging on his door in the middle of the night was brisk.

"I'm armed and I'm mad" he yelled through the bolted door to the unseen disturber of his sleep. "So don't even think about it. We don't tolerate thieves in this street. We dispose of them!" With the spade he was currently clutching in his hands if necessary. Teretius had a wife and daughter to protect after all.

Alex on the other side of the door called out, "I'm not a thief. I'm from the palace."

This seemed a likely opening for a complicated ruse, being just the sort of statement that would cause star-struck Viminal residents to fling open their doors to a band of lying, stealing, grubby thieves.

"Yeah, right," sneered Teretius. "Now get away with you before I unbolt this door and give you a right whacking."

He banged the spade against the door to illustrate the point. Alex, who had his ear pressed against it, jumped backwards with a yelp.

"I'm here to see Philo. I have a really, really important message for him," protested Alex, thinking of the chaos that would reign without Philo at the helm of Code Purple. He heard the bolt slide back, the door opened, and Teretius, spade still in hand, regarded his visitor with suspicion.

True, he was wearing a palace uniform, but that was easily faked. And true, he did have that posh accent all the palace staff possessed, but again that could be faked. For a thief though, he didn't look like he'd be terribly capable; he was a gangly youth, all hands and feet. No match at all for Teretius' burly builder's strength.

"You here for Philo?"

Alex nodded, gazed back over his shoulder to the deserted stairs behind him, and then whispered, "It's Code Purple."

Teretius was familiar with Code Purple, far too familiar after Philo's exhaustive description the night before. He stood back, holding open the door.

"You'd better come in then. Philo's in bed."

Teretius led him down the corridor, stopping before a door and then rapping on it with his fist. "Philo. Code Purple," he called out, thus stealing Alex's mission.

This, however, brought no response so he rapped again. "Philo! Code Purple!"

Then he stood back, Alex beside him hearing a mumbled and dazed, "What?"

And then a lock slid back, the door opened, and a sleepy Philo stared at Alex through slit eyes, his hair peaked above his forehead giving him a surprised air. He was wearing an oversized sleeping tunic that fell far beneath his knees making him seem even smaller than usual.

"Alexander?" he murmured, puzzled, his sleepy brain trying to make sense of this unusual interruption to his sleep.

"Code Purple, sir," announced Alex proudly. "You are needed at the palace."

A pause and then Philo's eyes opened wide. "Code Purple? Code Purple? Gosh," he flustered. "I must get my master plan."

His eyes twitched from side to side as his brain whirled through the many tasks that needed accomplishing. "The piglets," he burst out. "They need to go on now otherwise they'll not be cooked!"

He pulled a hand through his hair.

"Ah, son, it'll be fine," soothed Teretius. "You just need your plan."

"Yes, my plan."

Philo disappeared into his room, Alex and Teretius hearing a frantic scrabbling from within. Teretius looked to Alex and angled his head towards the door.

"I'll go help him," agreed Alex.

Philo was on all fours on the floor, the contents of his satchel tipped out in front of him. Alex knelt beside him, picking up a random scroll and asking, "Is this it?"

Philo looked up, shook his head and turned back to his pile. Alex's attention was drawn to the bed. He was surprised to see it was empty. Where was his girlfriend? The busty blonde that all the palace were talking about? Didn't they sleep together?

Philo jumped to his feet crying, "Ha!" His master plan clutched in his hand. "Let's go!" he said, restored to his usual efficient self.

"Err, sir, don't you want to get dressed first?"

Philo looked down at his nightgown and bare feet. "Oh. Good idea. You wait in the kitchen and I shall join you when I am ready."

Then he hurried Alex out and shut the door, the bolt sliding across.

Teretius smiled. "Shy thing, ain't he?"

FIVE

There was still a gloom when Straton awoke, light enough to see but leaving everything indistinct and fuzzy. The overseer gave a stretch, extending his large, muscled, hairy arms to their full reach above him. It was many years since Straton had been to a gym. He found his daily routine of hauling slaves about kept up his strength. He cleared his throat, with a wince, for his wound was always at its most painful in the morning, and rubbed a knuckle across the scar. He felt pleasantly refreshed and just a bit horny.

Luckily for Straton he had anticipated this very mood and picked up a wee companion the night before. He rolled over to the edge of the bed, peered downwards and noted happily that his new friend was just where he had left him: curled up naked on the floor, one arm pulled backwards by the belt that was looped around the bedpost to his wrist.

The boy fulfilled Straton's very particular tastes in that he was small and toned with brown skin and dark hair. However, Straton was not wholly satisfied with him: the boy had been difficult, snuffling and crying, keeping the overseer awake. Which was why he had damned him to the floor rather than the comfy bed.

In truth Straton had been hoping for a night with Philo. Only a disruption in the slave complex (a presumed runaway who'd later been found drunkenly slumped under a plane tree in the new palace grounds with an empty wine skin) had delayed him. When he'd finally got to Philo's office the freedman had already gone home leaving the overseer bereft. Which when he had picked up the boy.

Gazing down at him Straton decided that the boy had been unsatisfactory. He was attractive enough but he was no Philo. Straton wanted Philo. Straton loved Philo.

Love was an emotion that hit the overseer periodically every few years and always culminated in an absolute disaster that had Felix threatening to slice off his penis with a meat cleaver. Not this time though. This time Straton was firmly of the belief that his love was returned.

It would be incorrect to describe the sound as a knock, it was far too loud. It was more of an explosion. A fierce bang that had the door pounding against the frame.

"Oi!" came a yell from behind the door. "Get the fuck up you big fucker!"

It could only be Felix, nobody else would dare address Straton so disrespectfully. The overseer stepped over the tethered boy and ambled over, unlocking the door, swinging it back on its hinges.

Fifty years of imperial service and twenty-plus years married to the fearsome Vallia meant that Felix was unfazed by the truly extraordinary sight of a naked Straton. His huge belly sat beneath his muscled chest, cock hanging loose between thighs the size of tree trunks. All of it covered in thick dark hair that made him less of a man and more of a gorilla—the nickname that Empress Statilia Messalina retained for him.

"Fucking Code Purple," he told Straton. "We got fucking work to do!"

There was a muffled cry from within the room. Felix's eyes narrowed.

"You got one of my fucking slaves in there?"

"No," lied Straton.

"You'd better fucking not!"

"Haven't," protested the overseer.

"Coz I don't want none of them fucking broken again," warned Felix. "I had to write off three hundred sesterces' worth of goods last month coz of your fucking lechery. It ain't fucking on, Straton. I can't take any more out your fucking wages coz you're in fucking negativity. At this rate it's gonna take you a good decade to get fucking even with me."

"Haven't," persisted Straton, slightly offended by Felix's deserved lack of trust.

Felix hmmed and crossed his arms. "Get your kit on. Code Purple. Didn't you hear? Fucking Code Purple! Get to it!"

He clapped his hands to hurry him on. Straton grabbed his tunic off the floor and threw it over his head, utterly ignoring the tethered boy.

"AND!" called Felix. "Bring your fucking elephant hide whip. I don't want no fucker out of line! No excuses! We ain't gonna be the department that fucks this up. No way! I couldn't take Philo's disappointed little face!"

Straton didn't want to disappoint Philo either. He wanted everything to go perfectly for his beloved.

"So," began Teretius, elbows resting on the kitchen table. "Which way is the emperor coming into town?"

Alex, biting into an apple he had been given, replied breezily, "Milvian Bridge way, then down the Via Flamina."

Teretius hummed, a thought forming in his mind. "You a messenger then, boy?" he asked politely.

"I usually work for the Praetorians," said Alex proudly. "But with Code Purple I've had to diversify."

"That so."

"Oh yes. I have several important messages to deliver across the Palatine Hill," said Alex. "All crucially important to Philo's plans."

This was a bit of bluster. Alex's role in Code Purple was distinctly minor. Teretius would have queried further but there arrived in the doorway the busty blonde that everyone at the palace was talking about.

"What's going on, father?" Teretia asked, stretching back her arms and yawning. A movement that thrust forward her best assets.

She was not Alex's type. His tastes ran to tall brunettes, infuriating yet beguiling (Mina in other words) but this did not stop him appreciating Teretia and his mouth fell slightly open.

"It's Code Purple, love," her father told her, kissing her on the top of her head and putting a paternal arm around her.

"Ooh," breathed Teretia. "Does Philo know? He's got such a terribly lot to do. The pigs have to begin roasting or else they won't be done!"

"Right. I'm ready," said Philo, appearing in a pristine blue tunic, his hair sensibly brushed down excepting the small curl that was ever untameable on the nape of his neck. His satchel was thrown across his shoulder and his master plan was held firmly in his hand at page one. Alex shot to his feet.

"Good luck, son," smiled Teretius.

"He doesn't need luck, father," smiled Teretia. "Because Philo has it all organised."

She gave the freedman an adoring smile and he gave a shy smile back of his own.

"Come on, Alexander, we must get to the palace and get those pigs on."

Alex trudged after him, mentally noting that the supposed lovers didn't even kiss each other goodbye. Something to share with Mina in their next session.

Back in the kitchen Teretius hugged his daughter close and said, "How's about we go greet this new emperor?"

Teretia's response was a shrill squeal of excitement.

SIX

All was madness at the palace. They'd been practising Code Purple for two months with daily drills. The drills had been dignified, calm processions with everyone moaning that they knew what to do and did they have to go through it all over again? Now when the real Code Purple was announced, it was pandemonium. Nobody could find their instruction sheets and panic had caused memory blanks with slaves dithering back and forth trying to remember where they were supposed to be.

The banqueting hall was awash with slaves dashing hither and thither. Midas, the head of catering, stood screeching in the midst. "No, no, not silver. Code Purple is Gold! Gold I say! Take it back, back!"

Philo stood watching them, his arms crossed. "Hmm," he muttered and then quietly took control.

"Midas, can you send a boy to check on the pigs please. Diodorus, you're not meant to be here, you are in corridor three."

Then to Alex, "Do you know where you have to be, Alexander?"

Alex gave a toothy grin. "Message to the temple of the Magna Mater and then in the line-up."

Philo let out a small breath. "Excellent," he commended the messenger.

Alex, proud to have earned such praise, clicked his heels together and saluted before dashing off to complete his next mission.

There was one group of people who were thoroughly enjoying Code Purple. They were the overseers and they were in their absolute element. Stalking the corridors for any slaves that looked vaguely lost and inflicting their own unique way of memory improvement. Straton was particularly exacting, using his rod to flick passing shins and buttocks.

He was still suffering from Felix's intrusion into his anticipated morning satisfaction. Normally Straton would not interrupt his pleasure for anyone or anything, but Felix was his boss and Code Purple was a big fucking deal. Straton was therefore frustrated, extremely frustrated, and itching to take it out on someone, presenting a real danger for anyone within whipping radius of him.

He was aware that he'd left the boy tied up in his room. He didn't think it was a major aberration though. He had left a bowl of water within reaching distance. That should keep him alive until after Code Purple was completed. Anyway, it was only a serving slave worth a hundred sesterces maximum, Straton calculated, and with his current debts to Felix exceeding the hundred thousand mark, one hundred sesterces was mere chicken feed.

The joke doing the rounds was that Icelus was greasing himself up in anticipation of Galba's arrival. It was not far off the truth: he was being smeared with oil by Hesiod the masseur.

"Is there something we should be doing?" he asked Laco, lain out on a table beside him.

"We'd just be in the way," he said, groaning as his own masseur released a knot in his shoulder blade. "They are used to organising this sort of pageantry. Let your little fellow deal with it."

Icelus thought of the complicated plan Philo had put before him, the sides and sides of wax containing figures and timings and areas and support staff. Icelus had nodded in approval, though in truth his eyes had merely skimmed over the words.

"Yes, he is very capable," he decided, flipping up an oiled leg for particular attention.

"Hmm. I'll maybe go see the Guard before they assemble. Sort of thing I should do, being their prefect and all."

"Isn't your tribune arranging that?"

"Honoratus? Probably. I wouldn't want to tread on his toes. He is a remarkably sound chap. Perhaps I will just wait here until everything is ready."

"Excellent plan, Laco. I think I shall too."

"It will be good to have Galba in Rome," murmured Laco. "I am even looking forward to seeing dear Titus."

Titus Vinius, the third member of Galba's advisory committee.

"Really?" gulped Icelus in a high pitch. "I thought you loathed the grass he walked on."

Laco gave a chuckle. "So I do but I find our dear colleague excellent for straightening my thoughts."

"How so?"

Laco smiled, showing two sharpened incisors, "Because they are always the very antithesis of Vinius'!"

Then he lowered his voice, his tone growing more serious as he said, "Can I count on your support, friend?"

Icelus turned his head on the table. "Of course, Cornelius," he soothed.

"Even if it is contrary to Titus Vinius?" he pushed.

"Laco, I am the emperor's personal advisor. I will always advise him to the truest course."

Laco gently switched the subject. "You must be looking forward to seeing him," he suggested gently.

"Of course," said Icelus, turning his head the other way.

Laco fell silent. Everyone knew what Galba's and Icelus' relationship was, though he had never spoken of it to either of them. It was an entirely private affair, its secrets hidden behind doors. Galba had never shown any special regard or affection towards Icelus in public. So cool was his manner that Laco had speculated that such coldness continued into the bedroom. However, Icelus' devotion to Galba was held less in check; the freedman unable to remain neutral when his lover was present. His expression adoring, his words unmeasured, and his whole being waiting for affection that would never come.

Did he hold sway over the emperor, Laco wondered. Or was he a mere toy? Either way it did not matter. The emperor had three special advisors: himself, Vinius, and Icelus. Laco was determined that it should be he that the emperor minded. He that the emperor listened to, promoted, rewarded. One more voice on his side and Titus Vinius would cease to have influence. A shouting voice in the fog as Laco reaped the benefits. No, Icelus must be truly won.

Having doled out what he felt were foolproof instructions, Philo was very surprised when he was plagued by requests for clarification.

"When it says I should bow when the emperor walks past me in the atrium, what does that actually mean?"

"It means as he walks past, you and everyone else in your line should bow."

"When you say bow what do you mean exactly?"

"You bow."

"But from our heads or our waists? There is a pointed difference. Bowing our heads is simply averting our eyes from

His Imperial Majesty but bowing from the waist, that implies something very different. Do you see the distinction?"

Clutching his stylus between clenched fists, Philo fought back the urge to stab the slave between the eyes with it. Instead he took back the instructions and inserted the word "heads" before handing it back. The slave nodded approval and exited.

Page fifteen of his master plan told him he should be in the banqueting hall checking on the arrangements. He had fallen very far behind. Also according to his schedule, Icelus should be here addressing the heads of department, except he was nowhere to be found.

He felt a fleeting panic in his chest which was when Lysander drifted back in, pondering over the wording of his announcement of Galba. "Philo, there is loads of stuff in here about wishing for best health towards Your Imperial Majesty's glorious family and mother. Galba doesn't have a mother does he? He's about ninety, she'd be ancient, we'd never get her up the palace steps."

"Omit it."

"Yeah, but then it doesn't make sense because there is all this stuff about the Great Mother and motherhood and fertility and—"

"Just make something up! You can do that can't you? Nobody is going to be listening anyhow!" burst out Philo, crashing onto the floor.

Lysander sat down beside him. "You're quite stressed, aren't you?"

Philo lobbed a tablet across the room, hitting the door with a thud.

"Where's Icelus?"

"I don't bloody know, alright! I don't know where in Jupiter's knackers he is. He should be here. I shouldn't be doing this. I shouldn't have had to arrange all of this. I'm just an assistant. If it goes wrong it'll all be my fault." He took a noisy inhalation before muttering, "Epaphroditus would have helped out."

Lysander was rather staggered by this outburst. He'd shared a room in the palace with Philo since they were boys, right up until his friend had purchased his freedom earlier in the year, and he'd never heard him use anything stronger than the occasional, "Gosh."

Rubbing his arm supportively he told his former room-mate, "It will go fine, Philo, honestly it will. If it doesn't then, yes, officially you might be blamed but unofficially we'll all know whose fault it is."

The door opened. "Philooo," whined Mina and stopped as she saw them sitting on the floor. "What's happening here?"

"Philo's stressed," Lysander explained.

"Are you? I've never seen you stressed before. Is this what it's like?"

Embarrassed, for he had always found Mina an intimidating presence, he stood up and addressed her formally, "What is it, Artemina?"

"A message from the empress. She is concerned about her positioning. She thinks she should be nearer Galba at the banquet."

"Technically she is not the empress any more and she is not related to Galba and so she ranks lower than family and lower than the senators and their family and so she is placed with the nobility."

"That's the bit she doesn't like."

Philo looked helplessly at Lysander. "It's too late to change the seating plan."

"OK, OK, don't panic. Mina, can't you explain that to the empress?"

"She won't like it," Mina warned. "But I'll hang around here and help you guys. That way, when I go back, it really will be too late and she'll have to lump it. I'll just wheel her out for the grub before she can protest."

"Thank you," said Philo quietly, looking down and spotting a thick black mark across his formerly pristine tunic, no doubt from lugging boxes about. "Oh gods."

He wet a finger and attempted to wipe it off.

"No stressing allowed," Mina told him, waggling a finger. "Do you have a spare tunic?"

"Not here," he replied miserably.

"Lysander will have a spare uniform."

"I can't wear white. It breaks the etiquette. I'm not a slave."

"OK, let us dispose of that suggestion," she said calmly. "Are you wearing a toga?"

He nodded.

She clapped her hands. "Well, there you go, we'll just drape it over the mark. Nobody will ever know."

"Really?"

"Absolutely. Pass it here and I'll have a go."

Mina fussed with the draping of the toga. "Aah," she said.

Philo looked down: the mark was fully on display.

The door swung open again. "Philo, I want to talk about my position in the line up."

The freedman sighed, slipping off the toga. "What is it, Apollodorus?"

"I'm next to the overseers," he complained. "I am a professional. I don't see why I have to stand next to them. It looks bad. The emperor will think that I am one of those fat bully boys. They shouldn't be in the line-up anyway, best to hide them away. We don't want to frighten the new boss."

"Everyone is in the line-up. I need them in the line-up so they can slip out easily if there is a problem with the other staff in the line-up. I can't move anyone now, sorry."

Apollodorus crossed his arms, "Where is Icelus? I demand to be moved."

"He is looking over the gardens in the new palace, by the lake."

"Fine, I will go talk to him there," and he stormed out.

"Is he in the gardens?"

"No idea," shrugged Philo, "but that'll keep him out of my way for a bit. What am I going to do about this?" He fingered the mark.

Mina snapped her fingers. "I'll get Daphne, she's a seamstress. She'll whip you up something."

"There's no time."

"Nonsense, her fingers move like dizzy mice. I'll go get her."

Lysander sat at Philo's desk and began revising his announcement. The sound of his deep voice rolling the words round his tongue as he worked them out.

SEVEN

The rumour started in the morning. A drover coming down from the hills reported hearing the clamour of hooves and marching feet.

"Reckon it's the new emperor."

That nothing was planned for the route showed he was not expected. The people thought it rather a shame. Many remembered Nero in his golden chariot trundling down the road waving and smiling. They had thrown rose petals and cheered until their throats were raw. It had been a big old party: sacrificing thirty goats for the emperor's safe keeping, banqueting on the sweet, crispy meat in the evening, and toasting Bacchus in some style.

In the aftermath nobody recalled who first made the suggestion. It was just decided that they would wait on the Milvian Bridge for the new emperor. Once word got round there became quite a gathering. People travelling for miles, eager to witness the excitement. Others came ready with their petitions for assistance; wishing to catch the emperor before he was subject to all those other petitions waiting for him in the palace.

A whole gang of navy men turned up from the fleet at Miseum wanting Galba to officially recognise them as a legion; Nero inconsiderately dying before all the forms could be filled in. They looked frighteningly tough with their rippling biceps and shaven heads, but they soon entered into the spirit and joshed and joked alongside the locals. Hearing the distant clump of boots the crowd jostled for good positions, the sailors better equipped to do so.

"Oh father I can't see," Teretia whined, standing on her toes and seeing only heads.

Teretius patted her arm. "When the emperor comes by I'll lift you up, love. I hope you haven't been hitting the pantry."

She slapped him on the arm with a smile.

"Well, I don't think I'll be able to deliver my petition today. Not with all these other folk," he sighed.

He was in dispute with a senator whose bathhouse he'd renovated but who was now quibbling over the cost. It was an affair that had dragged on for months; Teretius' burly work-men failing to unnerve the senator when they had been sent over en masse. The senator responded in kind and the whole thing was beginning to gain a nasty edge to it.

"Could you give it to Philo? He could deliver it personally to the emperor."

"Truth is, love, I didn't want to bother him with it. He has a lot on."

They had all noticed Philo's increased hours, hearing him come home after they had retired for the night and seeing him but briefly in the mornings. Some nights he didn't come home at all.

Had he not been so grey of face, Teretius would have suspected Philo had a woman at the palace. But the little freed-man looked so drained and downcast that he had rejected this thought happily. Teretius, who'd loved his wife deeply throughout their long marriage, was unable to imagine any woman causing such dismal feelings.

A burst of trumpet rang out. Teretia bounced on her feet. "I can see their helmets," she told Teretius. "Oh and the standards, father, I can see the standards. How will I know which one is the emperor, he hasn't got any coins or statues yet?"

"He'll be the one on the best horse," her father joked.

What Titus Vinius was most looking forward to in Rome were the baths. No, scrap that. The bars of the Subura where the wine flowed and the girls danced. No, it was catching up with old friends, perhaps in the bars of the Subura. Actually, he thought, it was just the damn city itself. That swirling mix of noise and dirt. Rome. His city. He glanced over to Galba riding beside him on a white steed.

"Not long now, sir," Vinius grinned.

Galba turned his thin features on his aide. Eyes a cold grey above an imposing hooked nose, giving him the stern look of a republican general. His thin lips twisted into a smile. "I wonder what welcome we shall receive."

"Icelus said the city was calm," said Vinius. "Now that Laco is in control of the Praetorians there should be no problems. Of course Nero was very popular with the people," worried Vinius.

"The people are irrelevant," snapped Galba. "They are impressed by trickery and gimmicks. These I will not stoop to," he declared, tugging at the reins of his horse.

They were interrupted by cantering hooves as a horse pulled up alongside them. Its rider was smiling widely, his cheeks ruddy, his blue eyes sparkling. Marcus Salvius Otho was governor of Lusitania, the lesser province that neighboured Spain.

"Nearly home chaps!" he exclaimed, rubbing the mane of his horse. "Good girl," he soothed. "Been a bloody long way, hasn't it?"

The horse whinnied in reply and gave a snort.

"The men are in good spirits?" Vinius asked.

"Legionary Taurus certainly is. I just settled my gambling debts with him!"

He raised his eyebrows and grinned; an infectious, easy smile that had Vinius grinning back. Galba, however, was made of sterner statesman material. He was not so easily swayed by the charm of Otho, replying tersely, "I do not approve of gambling."

Otho ignored the rebuke. "You would if you diced against me! You'd have three hundred sesterces of approval like legionary Taurus!" he laughed and slapped his horse on the backside, cantering ahead.

Galba narrowed his grey eyes, "I do not trust that man."

Vinius was shocked. "Otho? He was the very first to our cause. For a while the only support we had. If he had not declared you emperor nobody else would have dared. He is sound."

Galba looked ahead to where Otho had drawn alongside the standard bearer, leaning over. Whatever he was saying, it was clearly amusing for the standard bearer was tickled, grinning away. That was not the way to treat soldiers, they needed discipline. But despite this, Galba could not fault Otho. His cheery disposition had improved the men's morale immensely over the long trek from Spain. His unflappable spirit and friendly ways had rallied them and the other provincial governors to Galba's side. Vinius was right. Otho had been essential. Otho had made Galba. Yet Galba could not bring himself to trust the governor of Lusitania. There was his background for one thing. The years he'd spent as Nero's partner in vice, the debts and dishonour he had brought to his family's good name, and then there had been that ill marriage to Poppaea Sabina.

They said it was Otho himself who introduced Poppaea to Nero as a potential mistress. What sort of man procured his own wife for imperial favour? Though that had backfired. Nero deciding he wanted Poppaea as more than just a bed partner, determined to make her his bride. Had Otho objected? No one knew, except that it had been deemed necessary for the cuckolded husband to be absented from the city and the newly happy couple. That Otho had not been murdered, as so many had, but merely forced into the governorship of Lusitania had most supposing he'd been in on the affair from the start. Such morals left ashes in Galba's mouth. It was all that Rome and Roman virtue had sunk to under that effeminate, spendthrift wastrel, Nero. And though Otho, to everyone's surprise, had turned out to be an efficient administrator, Galba could not let his feelings slide. A man who prostituted his own wife was capable of anything; no matter how charming he appeared.

Vinius interrupted these thoughts. Gazing ahead across the heads of marching soldiers, he told Galba, "Quite a crowd."

Galba put a hand to his lower back with a wince.

"Are you alright, Caesar?"

Galba gave a terse nod. "I'll be glad when I'm off this horse."

"Too right," agreed Vinius. "Let's hope the palace has a decent bathhouse. Hey up, what's going on?"

The sailors had pushed themselves to the front, beseeching the passing soldiers with yells and waving fists.

Vinius signalled to a cavalryman who trotted over. "Firmius," he said and pointed to the sailors.

Firmius returned some moments later. "Sir, they wish to petition the emperor."

"I will hear no petitions," said Galba. "It is not the place."

"They are from the Misenium fleet," Firmius continued, addressing Vinius. "They want the emperor to declare them an official legion. They have no quarters and they haven't been paid in months."

"It is not the place," Galba stated, staring straight ahead. "Tell them so. There are official channels, procedures they must follow. They must petition in Rome."

Firmius trotted off. Vinius watched his exchange with the sailors. They did not look happy. Some shouting took place. Seeing Vinius' expression, Galba turned just as they were passing the point. Despite his age Galba had quick reactions. He saw the sailors waving fists, shoving at Firmius' mount and then he saw what he assumed was a flash of a knife. The emperor raised his index finger.

Vinius caught the gesture but was too late to prevent what followed. The cavalry shot into action ploughing their way into the crowd, swords drawn. Vinius impotently shouting, "No! They're civilians!"

The crowd parted ahead of Teretius. A discord of screams and yells battering the cool autumn air. A horse galloping full pelt, scattering the people. Its rider grasping a sword and liberally slashing at the terrified fleeing men, women, and children. He was heading straight for an open-mouthed Teretia.

Teretius threw himself at her, shoving her aside as the horseman passed. She hit the mud with a thud, feet kicking at her as people ran for their lives. Curling herself into a ball, hands held over her head she tried impotently to protect herself. Some feet away lay Teretius bloodied and unconscious.

EIGHT

"It is wholly unacceptable!" snarled Galba.

A sweaty and tired Titus Vinius rubbed his cheek. "I know, sir," he placated him. "But we really must move on from here."

Here was the home of Aulus Gemmellus, a comfortable dwelling close to the Milvian Bridge. Gemmellus had offered hospitality to the new emperor after the incident on the bridge. No doubt the canny aristocrat hoped to be the first to win imperial approval. It had been a fortuitous refuge. Galba settling in Gemmellus' lounge while Vinius had checked on the casualties, daring the angry crowd. Had it not been for the 3,000 legionaries present, Vinius would have seriously feared a lynching. Not an auspicious start to Galba's tenure in Rome.

Otho was still out there, offering sympathy and distributing alms; a role he fitted into surprisingly well. Vinius watched him sit beside a new widow, holding her hand, and speaking in a low voice, quite as if he were a firm friend to the family rather than the passing governor of Lusitania.

Otho aside, the mood was turning distinctly ugly. Faced with a superior force of heavily armed soldiers, the citizens had taken a more novel route for revenge; raiding the baggage trains and looting the backpacks, knowing that losing such vital equipment was a disciplinary offence. The tribunes were just about keeping the rank and file in order but the longer they stayed, the higher the chances of another unfortunate incident.

Foolhardy young boys were seemingly eager to egg on such a possibility by standing on top of the bridge ramparts and waving the stolen articles in full view of the legionaries.

"Caesar," pressed Vinius.

Galba pinched his lips together. "The behaviour of those sailors is unwarranted. That they should petition me in such a manner shows their ill discipline."

Vinius' eyebrows lifted. Had Galba not a thought for the dozens of corpses currently lying in the streets outside?

"We cannot let such indiscipline pass, Titus. Control of the army is crucial at this time. The legions in Africa and the East have not yet offered their full support to my reign. If they hear the merest rumour that the soldiers in Rome itself are not showing full respect, then this whole venture is in jeopardy."

He was right. Clodius Macer, governor of Africa, with the support of Nero's ex-party planner Calvia Crispinilla was blockading the grain boats from sailing from Egypt to Italy. In the Western Empire, there were dire stories concerning the hardened Germanic legions. And in the East, those client kings of Rome were openly mourning Nero. So when Galba said, "They must be punished," Titus Vinius was in full agreement. Dissent was not acceptable in these dangerous times. Only Galba's idea of a suitable punishment went far beyond anything Vinius envisaged. The new emperor poked his bony hand from his sleeve and told Vinius stonily, "Decimate them."

It was a punishment that had not been employed for over a hundred years. It was archaic, it was brutal, and it had only ever been used for extreme acts of cowardice on a large scale. A cloth bag was filled with white and black balls; each soldier dipping in his hand and selecting a ball. Choose a white ball and you were safe. Choose black, and you had a one in ten chance of doing so, you were marked for execution.

Your fellow legionaries; your comrades in arms; the men you had slept, eaten, and fought with for maybe your entire twenty-five years of military service, were handed nail-studded clubs to accomplish the task.

So it was not surprising that Vinius gawped. "Decimation, Caesar?"

Galba faced Vinius, his grey eyes uncompromising. "We need to assert our authority," he stated evenly.

"All under control," Midas assured.

Philo was not convinced. There seemed to be a great deal of movement but very little happening. Slaves dashing back and forth empty-handed, couches and tables stacked at one end of the octagonal dining room yet to be positioned, the coloured ribbons that were meant to be hanging from the ceiling sat in a tangled heap. In Midas' eyes there was the manic glint of a man about to break.

Philo pulled out a list. "Read these again, familiarise yourself. I'll go get an overseer to assist you."

Midas pawed at Philo's arm. "Thank you, thank you."

Disengaging himself from Midas' disturbing strokes, Philo trotted off to find Felix.

Icelus smoothed down the covers of the bed, the bed which would be Galba's bed. Their bed (on the occasions it suited the emperor). He gazed at himself in a full-length bronze mirror, running a hand across his bald pate. Sniffing, he decided there was something missing. Clicking fingers, he told a slave, "Fetch me rose water. Oh, and some wine." Settling himself down on a chair, cocking his feet up on the bed, "Snacks too!" he yelled at the departing slave.

Having got the banqueting preparations running smoothly, checked on the 300 roasting piglets, and given the major domos a quick recap on how they should greet the now-arriving guests, before nipping out to see whether the Praetorians were coping with the gathering crowd outside the palace, Philo now headed back to his office to see how his tunic was coming along.

Daphne held it up for his inspection. "Ta da," she announced "Do you like?"

He felt the braiding round the neck.

"Try it on," Daphne told him.

He looked round at Mina, Lysander, and Daphne. "Could you just …?"

Mina laughed, "Gods Philo! We won't look. It's not like it's anything I haven't felt before." Seeing Philo flush she added, "And as I recall you have nothing to be ashamed of." Though they both knew that wasn't true.

Looking up from his speech Lysander said, "Guess who she's feeling now?" Keen to share the astounding and utterly false gossip that was doing the rounds about Straton and Mina's kinky, twisted sexual liaison. It was a piece of gossip that would have cheered Philo in his present frazzled state, offering as it did a get-out clause of his wholly unhappy acquaintance with the overseer. Only he never got to hear it because Mina interjected,

"Oi, Lysander, butt out! Do I interfere in your love life? No I do not. Because you do not have one."

Lysander puffed out his chest, "I've stuffed more girls than anyone else on Apollodorus' list."

Apollodorus was the head of the breeding section, the man in charge of ensuring a steady supply of little slaves. Lysander was his top breeder, a man of legendary potency.

"That's work. It does not count. You may as well say all the girls had terrific love affairs with the guards after Nero died. Does not count."

Daphne, rubbing her pregnant belly, the result of such an enforced encounter, started to cry. An apologetic Mina put an arm round her and shot Lysander a furious look.

Philo grabbed his new tunic off the seamstress and fled into Icelus' office.

56

NINE

Alex trudged across the Palatine Hill, gazing down to the forum below. The temples were being draped with colourful banners; the Praetorians assisting in the construction of wooden barriers to keep the expected crowds under control. The senate was convening. Alex watched the gaggle of togas disappear into Senate House no doubt to argue over who had been the first to declare his loyalty to Galba. He had given his loyalty to Galba earlier than they had, way earlier. They had still been crawling to Nero when he had been helping Nymphidius Sabinus and Icelus to take over the city.

Alex had no respect for the senate: they were pointless in his view. He didn't have much of an opinion of emperors either. Sporus had fed him too many stories about Nero for him to have much respect for the position. Most had been weak, ineffectual, bullied by their secretaries. Galba would be different. As a general he was able to process information with speed and act decisively. He wouldn't be bullied by any pasty, devious administrator. Nor would he be fooled by the senate's ingratiating cowering.

Alex couldn't wait to meet him. He had never even seen Nero, not alive anyhow. But Philo had him in the line-up of palace staff, somewhere between the barrel boys and the laundry girls. He imagined Mina would have a much better view attending the empress at the banquet.

He weaved through the bulk of white-clad slaves running about their tasks with ill-disguised hysteria. He had instructions to deliver to the Temple of the Great Mother. It wasn't a great assignment, for they were a weird lot.

Nipping down the tunnels that linked the different parts of the palace, he emerged the other side strolling up to the three temples dedicated to Apollo, the Great Mother, and Juno. Climbing up the steps of the Temple of the Great Mother, he banged on the great bronze door. It creaked open slowly to reveal one of the Galli dressed in saffron robes and laden with a heavy chain necklace which fell to his ankles. He regarded Alex suspiciously.

"I have instructions for your ... erm ... leader?" He waved the scroll as proof.

"You'd better come in," squeaked the eunuch holding the door open. Alex entered cautiously.

The Gallus led him through the temple to the private area at the back, his long black hair swishing above a suggestively wiggling bottom.

The Galli, the eunuch priests who ran the cult of the Great Mother in Rome, were heavily restricted in their movements; allowed out only once a year for the Megalesian Games in April. After that they were locked back behind their gates and not seen again until the following year. You could hear them though, practising their strange wailings and beating their tambourines.

Alex walked uncomfortably through the unfamiliar surroundings. He was only allowed in because he was a slave. Roman citizens were strictly prohibited from the building. And from participating in the goddesses' more interesting rites lest they suddenly be infected and commit the ultimate act that one Gallus initiate undertook each year: a very public self castration with sharpened tongs. The very thought of it brought water to Alex's eyes.

He was led to what looked at first appearance to be a huge, fat white slug lolling around on the floor. On closer inspection Alex could make out two small eyes and a piggy nose squished into its features. The Gallus prostrated himself before the slug, kissing two slippers which poked from beneath the folds of his orange gown.

The slug wriggled his feet with a giggle, rippling his chins.

"A visitor, a visitor!" he clapped, wobbling.

"He has instructions, Arch Gallus, for the procession."

"Goody, good. Hand them here, boy. I must gather my girls."

Alex handed over the scroll, noting that the Galli lounged around the room painting their nails, braiding each others' hair, and staring at him as if he were the odd one. They were being allowed out to greet the emperor. Well, not exactly greet but rather stand outside their complex and allowed to watch the emperor's procession. There was to be none of their excitable dances or enthused music and certainly no orgiastic rites. However, the high priests of Rome had confirmed that it did not pay to upset any of the gods at such an important moment, so behind their high walls they could go all out nuts for the Great Mother.

Alex, waiting for a response, became aware of movement behind him. Turning his head he saw some of the Galli crawling towards him on all fours. He took a large step forwards.

"Don't mind them, boy," laughed the Arch Gallus. "They are just curious. They don't see many Roman boys."

Alex lifted a leg up to dislodge a hand that was stroking his ankle.

"Your response?" he asked hastily as hands caressed his feet.

The Arch Gallus stood, his acolytes falling to the floor before him and wailing. "Tell your master that all is fine and that we shall perform the necessary rites that will appease the Great Mother." He gave an odd smile leading Alex to wonder exactly what the rites involved. Nobody knew what the Galli got up to when they were holed up in their annex. Alex was not in the slightest bit curious.

"Good, sir." Then looking round nervously, "How do I get out of here?"

In the far corner of the Galli's room sat a single eunuch dressed in red. His hair was dark and curled to below his shoulders, his eyes painted extravagantly. He sat fiddling with a bangle, viewing Alex's back with ill-disguised loathing.

"Sister, sister, what ails you?" asked one of his fellow Galli in heavily accented Latin.

The red-clad acolyte shot a withering look at the Gallus who simpered under his gaze. "I've told you before I am not your fucking sister!"

Alex was extremely keen to escape back to the normal world outside those iron doors, where men were men, women were women, and the eunuchs of the palace were practically minded and had formed their own guild. He was at the door, one hand on the iron ring when a voice cried out.

"You treacherous, duplicitous, lanky, freckled, ginger bastard of Cronus!"

Such a charge could not be ignored, especially when it had been delivered with such heartfelt venom.

Alex spun round to see a Gallus dressed in a red gown, loose black curls falling unevenly towards his shoulders, two large golden hoops hanging from his ear lobes. His hands were on his hips. His mouth twisted against his teeth. He looked distinctly pissed off, furious even.

"I'm sorry?" blinked Alex.

"You scum of Saturn, you froth of Poseidon's cast-off faeces, you pathetic excuse of a slave," continued the Gallus, marching towards him with considered strides. "How dare you stand there! How dare you have the nerve! The audacity! The cheek!" squeaked the eunuch.

As he gained ground, Alex noted the exotic slanting dark eyes, the manicured fingernails, the womanly mince of his walk; and the name fell from his lips.

"Sporus?"

For indeed it was him: Sporus. Nero's lover. The spare empress when Statilia Messalina couldn't be bothered. The only eunuch to be excluded from the palace eunuchs' guild for letting the side down. The singularly most showy, infuriating creature on earth. Alex's former best friend.

The intervening months had not lessened Sporus' anger with Alex. If anything, they had increased it manifold. Epaphroditus' genius idea of hiding him among his fellow eunuchs had seemed almost fun at first. They were a sparkly lot, fond of bracelets and bangles and fully appreciative of a good nail varnish. He had even joined in their silly whirling and wailing, learning to bang the tambourine in time and chime the cymbals in the proper manner. It had been rather a lark.

But as the weeks passed, Sporus found himself heartily sick of all the noise. The pretty chimes set his teeth on edge, the tambourine gave him a headache, and the whirling dancing simply made him dizzy. His companions, he grew to despise. They were vain and self-centred, obsessed with their dresses, of which they had a veritable rainbow collection. They delighted in only the exterior. The high squeaks of their voices annoyed him as did their posturing, sister this and sister that.

Centuries later some wise man would comment that, "Hell is other people." Sporus had discovered that hell was scores of mirror images of himself. Among the exotic and the alien, Sporus did not shine, he did not radiate, there was no one to wonder in his light. He was horrifyingly ordinary.

He grew petty and bad-tempered, snapping at the Galli and increasingly sitting alone, ignoring their colourful swirls around him. Now, finally, was his chance for revenge.

"I ought to gut you with a fish knife right where you stand," he snarled.

Alex, recovered from the shock of seeing his pal, enquired lightly, "Do you have a fish knife?"

"No, but if I did I would gut you. Right there." He pointed a taloned finger at Alex. "In your stomach up to your neck so that all your innards slithered to the ground in a plopping mess like uncut sausages. And then I would jump up and down on them in my bestest heeled sandals until there was nothing but a pile of bloody goo. And then I'd collect up that goo in a pail and take it to the city cesspit, where I'd throw your remains on the stinking shit of the city. Because that is all you deserve."

This was quite an invective and it took a moment for Alex to appreciate the entire image painted before him. Then he blurted out a hurt, "I saved your life! If it wasn't for me Sabinus' guards would have killed you!"

"If it hadn't been for you I wouldn't have been arrested in the first place," yelled Sporus in his high eunuch voice. "You were supposed to be my friend," he protested, furiously pointing his finger. "And you knew. You knew there was going to be a coup. You knew Sabinus was going to snatch my beloved Nero's throne. You fucking knew and you didn't tell me."

Sporus choked on the words, seeing his adored Nero with a dagger sticking from his neck, the blood gushing on the ground. Remembering the sound of running feet as the Praetorians dashed to intervene. Sporus draped across the emperor, kicking at them. Tears formed in his kohl-ringed eyes as he rubbed at them with a fist, smearing black across his cheek.

Alex stared at the floor, shuffling his feet, biting at his lip. "I had no choice," he mumbled. "The situation … I wasn't allowed to say. It was restricted. Confidential. Sabinus wanted to carry it off smoothly so there would be no great loss of life."

"There was a great loss of life!" cried Sporus. "There was Nero!"

He began to sob, his small chest pulsating with hurt. "And there would have been me," he interjected, cutting off Alex's words. "You say you saved me. You didn't. You didn't at all. Lie to yourself all you like but it was Epaphroditus who talked them round from killing me. It was Epaphroditus who put me here in safety."

It was also Epaphroditus who had stabbed Nero in the throat, but Sporus failed to mention this.

"What does Mina think? Does she think you're a hero?"

Alex's response was uttered before he could edit it. "She thinks you're dead."

Sporus froze and there fell a silence, a state that was highly unusual with that eunuch present. He swallowed a few times, his lips parting, his mouth falling open, before a shriek of: "The Sporus is not dead! The Sporus did not die! The Sporus lives!" His gesticulating arms had his bracelets clanging together.

This heartfelt cry drew the attention of the temple priests, who gathered in the hallway. Even the fat grotesque Arch Gallus managed to waddle himself to the scene of the action.

"Ooh!" he cried, clapping his palms together, flesh slapping against flesh. "Will there be a fight?"

Sporus was certainly up for one. Casually forgetting his utter lack of brawn, he pulled off one of his bangles, sliding it over his wrist, and flung it at Alex. It missed him entirely, flying over his head and hitting the door with a clank.

Alex watched the bangle spin on the ground before retorting, "Well, that was pathetic. You've always been rubbish at ball games."

"Oh so wrong, Alexander," crowed the eunuch. "I am highly proficient in the only ball games that matter. Nero himself was beguiled by my gaming."

He pulled off another bracelet and slung it at Alex. This one hit him on the shin. The messenger jumped, yelping and rubbing at the injury.

Sporus smiled serenely, held out his arms and gazed at the eight remaining bangles that were threaded onto each brown limb. Then he looked back up at Alex, his eyes narrowing.

"You wouldn't dare!"

Sporus slowly slid off another bangle, showing very clearly that he did dare. The Galli stared wide-eyed at this spectacle. Their lives were generally rather dull and this was most intriguing. The Arch Gallus grinned and chuckled, his chins wobbling.

"Let's expel the Roman invader!" he declared impulsively.

He then attempted to remove one of his own bracelets to offer as ammunition. His podgy wrist thwarted this attempt, the flesh having long grown over the gold. His attendant priests, however, followed the order and began removing their jewellery.

They were a flashy lot and Alex's keen eyes took in what an arsenal they owned. Faced with such huge odds he had but one recourse: retreat.

He turned round and frantically twisted at the door's iron ring. A bang by his ear alerted him that the assault had begun; a further hit to the back of his knee hurried him on. Twisting the handle, he pushed open the door with such eagerness that he fell fully forward. He landed with a crash on the steps, grazing a knee. A rather nice ankle bracelet in the shape of a snake bounced past him and rolled down the steps. Alex scrambled to his feet and followed it downwards, hearing Sporus' high-pitched giggle behind him.

The world is neatly divided between those who can make an amusing anecdote from being chased out of the Temple of the Great Mother by a dozen Syrian eunuchs armed with costume jewellery, and those who prefer to bury the story in red-faced humiliation. Alex fell firmly into this second camp. Hurrying back to the palace thoroughly ashamed as the Galli priests stood in the temple doorway bouncing up and down and yelling at him in their strange native tongues.

"Don't you scrub up well," Felix told a toga'd up Philo, natty in his new green tunic, as they walked to inspect the practice line-up. "There has been a slight hitch," Felix began with uncharacteristic calm. "Diodus is out of action."

"Diodus? He has a key part."

"Yeah, well, there was a mishap." Felix scratched an ear. "Straton got a bit overexcited, gave him a quick whip for speed, and got him right across the face."

"His face doesn't matter so much to his duties."

"The fact is the fool didn't blink in time and it caught him right across the eyes. I'm thinking his eyes are important for his duties."

"I have a back-up that can take over."

Felix grinned. "The organising spirit of Epaphroditus lives on," he declared.

Philo allowed himself a small smile as he went to check how his master plan was holding together. He had just reached the far end of the line-up when Icelus came running across the hall, his eyes rolling left and right as he asked, "Is he here? Is he here?"

"Final practice," Philo told him.

Disappointed, Icelus made a florid hand gesture. "Of course. I knew that. You best talk me through the arrangements."

"Sir, this boy says he knows you," interrupted a guard. Beside him stood a wan youth whom Philo vaguely recognised as one of Teretia's many cousins.

Those in the line-up (the undistinguished middle part; the beautiful being presented on the steps, and the useful, body slaves and the like, being present at the other end), were able by leaning forward to see the boy evidently explaining something. Whatever was said it caused a very definite reaction in Philo, the colour draining from his face. Then he muttered something to Icelus and an almighty argument kicked off.

Icelus was yelling at Philo, who stood open-palmed, appeasing. Gesturing at the boy with anger, Icelus had the teenager escorted out by a guard. Smugly satisfied he crossed his arms and pointed into the hall, Philo meekly shuffling in.

Faced with such an intriguing altercation, it was inevitable that those nearest the quarrel would whisper along the line. It became rather mutated as it passed from slave to slave but soon the entire hall was in possession of the facts: Philo's girlfriend had been seriously injured, she might even die, and that bastard Icelus was refusing to let him rush to her bedside.

Icelus walked along the line, inspecting the arrangements. Nothing seemed to satisfy him: the line-up was uneven, the décor was crude, the roasting piglets were overdone, the golden plates were smeared, the entertainment disastrous. An extremely upset Philo tagged along behind him as his hard work was publicly pulled to shreds.

"No, that is no good at all," yelled Icelus, his voice echoing off the ceiling. "I am surprised that you ever thought that would be suitable for an emperor."

Philo scratched out a line of his precious plan with a shaking hand. If he had looked up he would have seen the laundry girls shooting sympathetic looks his way. For though they possessed bulging biceps and coarse natures, they were a soppy lot and were fond of a good love story.

Halfway down the line-up, Icelus telling him how disappointed he was with him, Philo halted. Then he turned and walked back in the other direction towards the doors. Icelus, walking several paces talking to thin air, noted the smirking faces and spun round.

"Philo! You get back here. You do not have my permission to leave. I order you back here."

Philo did not look back, leaving Icelus red-faced and screaming as the barrel boys sniggered at his humiliation.

TEN

The shutters were closed and it took a moment for his eyes to adjust to the gloom. When they did he saw a pale-looking Teretia lying under a blanket. Her eyes were closed, her chest gently rising and falling. A young girl sat on a chair beside her, another cousin he supposed.

On seeing him she smiled. "You must be Philo. She has been asking for you."

"How is she?" he asked the girl.

"She was lucky. She took some pretty nasty kicks. Her hand is broken most probably but nothing else we think. I'll leave you two alone."

He knelt beside the bed. "Teretia?" he asked gently. Up close he could see her cheek was bruised and cut. She opened her eyes and looked at him vaguely.

"Teretia, how are you?"

"My father ..." She tried to sit up.

"No, no, stay where you are." He pushed her gently back onto the bed. "You need to rest."

"How is my father?" she asked tearfully, her chest rising quicker.

Philo had briefly looked in on Teretius. It did not look good.

"There's a doctor coming," he told her.

Philo had avoided the palace doctors who had but a single remedy for all afflictions: to drain a good armful of blood. Instead, he had sent for the Praetorians' own doctor who was army trained and experienced in patching up recruits after Sabinus' drills, which possessed a tendency to go awry.

"He is the best doctor there is. He will take good care of your father, I promise." She looked tearful. "I'm staying with you," he told her. "I won't leave."

This calmed her a little. Biting her lip she said, "I don't understand. We were watching the soldiers march and father said he would lift me up to see … to see the emperor and then …"

Philo didn't say anything. He held her swollen hand extremely gently in his and wiped a stray strand of hair away from her face. She began to drift off again.

Pompeia's elder sister Pompeia Major had filled him in on the events at the Milvian Bridge. It had, according to her, been a total massacre. "The emperor set the soldiers loose on the crowd. My brother-in-law was trampled by a horse we think. He hasn't woken up yet. Luckily Manius from down the street was there. He spotted Teretia crouching over her father and pulled them both out from the chaos."

Privately Philo hoped Galba had a damn good explanation. You could write endless death lists of senators, wipe out your entire family, but if you started on the plebs, Jupiter help you.

He wasn't sure how long he sat there. He heard a commotion of sorts in the room next door, voices and groans. Thankfully Teretia slept through it. Sometime later a shaven-headed gruff-looking man who could only be the doctor slid in quietly. Philo removed Teretia's hand from his own and placed it by her side. She did not stir.

Standing by the door he asked in a hushed whisper, "How is he?"

"I've seen worse," the doctor told him. "He took a direct hit, it shattered his left thigh. I've splinted it up. It'll heal but he'll limp; how badly I can't say. The left arm I've had to splint too. His fingers on the right are fairly mashed and I can't say if he'll ever be able to bend them properly again. There are some facial injuries: they'll sort themselves out in time."

"He'll live though?"

The doctor sighed. "I'm not going to say yes and I'm not going to say no. I've patched him up but I've seen this sort of thing before. You sort them out, bones ready to knit and then they just drift off anyway. He's not woken which is not pleasing. I prefer them screaming and hollering."

Philo looked back at a peaceful Teretia.

Guessing his thoughts the doctor told him kindly, "Tell her the truth. It will prepare her if the worst does happen. Do you want me to examine her?"

"If you could, please. Her hand is broken I think and she seems to be having difficulty breathing."

They woke her gently. The doctor prodded her carefully, enquiring where it hurt. Philo sat on the end of the bed reassuring her. The doctor bandaged her hand and poked at her ribs.

"I don't think you've broken any of those," he told her. "It hurts though?"

She nodded and gave a little whimper, Philo rushing to comfort her.

"I think you've bruised yourself, miss. You'll go a range of lovely greens and blacks but it will heal itself. Just rest and be careful. Let Philo here take care of you."

He stood up, packing away his equipment.

"Thank you. If there is anything I can ever do for you …"

The doctor gave a grim smile. "You're well placed to the emperor. I reckon we might all need a favour soon."

There was much debate by the slaves as to whether they would comply. The idea of deliberately ballsing up the entire ceremony was extremely tempting. But then as someone pointed out, if it all went tits up Icelus would blame Philo, and if it went smoothly the bastard would claim the credit for himself. It was a win, win situation.

A tactful agreement was therefore reached with the catering staff that they would all gob in Icelus' food. That way they were all in a position to impress the new emperor who alone had the power to influence their present and future.

Mina, keen to impress, had dared to add a little red to her lips. From what she heard about Galba it would be a wasted effort, but you never knew. Maybe he had an attractive right-hand man she could flash her eyes at. The empress would be officially introduced to all the top men in the new emperor's staff. Mina would be standing behind her so there was ample opportunity for silent flirting.

The afternoon dragged dreadfully as they waited for the trumpets that would announce Galba's entrance to the palace. Lysander paced back and forth perfecting his announcement; trialling different pitches for the words and alternative stresses until he felt he could improve upon it no more. At that point he sweet-talked one of the wine waiters into giving him a draught, claiming it would preserve his voice if he could merely gargle with it.

Icelus was the most nervous of all. He twittered around the palace screeching orders, dashing off, and then returning at a sprint to reverse them. Laco, patting his shoulder told him, "Calm yourself. It will all run fine."

"If he shouldn't like …" Icelus rubbed a sheen of sweat from his brow.

"Nonsense. He will be impressed by the level of effort you have put into the arrangements."

Felix, who happened to be passing, laughed all the way down the corridor muttering, "Your effort? Your fucking effort?"

At a little past dusk the clear sound of trumpets rang out. Without Philo present there was no one to give the order for the staff to take their places. But they had been drilled and tested and practised all day. There had also been a hefty amount of sacrifices and small prayers offered to the gods, who must have decided to lend a hand since they all floated to their exact positions without panic.

Midas, hot and sweaty from his efforts, clapped his hands together. "Boys, boys. This is it! He will be doing some mad religious crap on the steps; auspices, etc., etc. The senate will do a bit of crawling; blah blah blah. Lysander will give his little ditty. Galba will then pass through the palace, past the line-up until he reaches our door. He will be announced and we kick into gear. I want food flying about the place. I want no spillages, no breakages, and no guest with an empty glass!"

They could hear the crowd cheering outside. A chant of, "Caesar, Caesar," yelled with increasing volume. Alex, midway through the line-up, fiddled with his sandal strap. Others were smoothing down curls, straightening hem lines, and making exploratory sniffs down their tunics.

The palace doors were thrown open. Imperator Servius Sulpicius Galba Caesar Augustus entered his new home. Tall, hook-nosed, with thinning grey hair and cool grey eyes, he surveyed the entrance hall. Icelus, head bowed, greeted him. "Imperator Caesar."

Galba smiled, two teeth hanging over his lips giving him a wolfish appearance. "Icelus, good to see you. It has been quite a journey. I am looking forward to a rest."

"Caesar, there is a banquet to be held in your honour."

Galba frowned. "Must I? I am very weary."

Laco intervened. "A brief introduction to the important players, Caesar?"

"Very well," he grumbled.

Head bowed, all Alex saw of Galba was his feet rapidly passing by. Though quick moving he noted dispassionately the emperor's twisted toes and bunions. Then he was gone.

Heads up, they began breathlessly gossiping about what they had just seen.

The banquet was in full swing when the emperor was announced. His five hundred guests stood to attention. Icelus, sensing Galba's impatience, ran through the introductions quickly.

"Statilia Messalina."

"You are being treated well, I hope," said Galba as a statement rather than a question. A fact Statilia learned when she opened her mouth to complain loudly, only to find Galba had moved on to greet another guest.

"Well," she hissed, outraged.

"May I say how attractive you look tonight?" came a melodious voice.

Its owner was not a handsome man. He was bulky with bowed legs. Yet he was rewarding her with the most charming smile. Statilia felt almost giggly under his appraising eyes.

"Sir, you flatter me."

"I should hope so. I was going to compare you to Venus and wilt you with my elegant prose as I listed your glorious attributes one by one. But then you seem like the sort of woman who wants it straight, so I am obliged to tell you that you are incredibly beautiful, lady. And I say this not because I have been travelling from Spain with 2,000 men for weeks and weeks without sight of a woman but because you are the most attractive female I have ever seen in my life—and I do have a great number of sisters."

She was both charmed and amused by this bewildering speech.

"And you are, sir?"

"Marcus Salvius Otho," he smiled. "I do hope that we shall get to know each other better, madam. I wish to try out some of my more ponderous compliments on you. I shall experiment to see which pleasantry will weaken your knees to the best effect."

Mina, standing to one side, watched with amusement as Otho effortlessly disarmed her usually barbed mistress. Mina liked him immediately: he was fun and jovial compared to the tight-lipped Galba. She attempted to throw him suggestive glances but he only had eyes for Statilia, leading Mina to wonder if he was actually sincere.

Failing on that score she eyed up Galba's advisors. Icelus, no way. Laco, too podgy for her tastes plus she had heard stories about his peculiarities from his chosen bedfellow the night before. Her eyes fell on the sturdy, dark-haired man standing beside Laco. Passably attractive with a kind smile and easy manner. Not as easy as Otho's but genial all the same. His proximity to Galba suggested an important man.

Galba was never going to marry Statilia. Surely he would pack her back to her parents, which meant Mina would be unemployed. No way was she going back to the nursery so she raised her eyes and threw the look that had secured Epaphroditus straight at Titus Vinius.

Vinius smiled back.

Necessary pleasantries dispensed with, grim politeness achieved, Galba strode down the corridors. "My rooms?" he barked to Icelus.

"This way, Caesar."

As he led him into Nero's old chambers, the body slaves snapped to attention.

"Caesar," greeted Theseus, head bowed respectfully. "Do you wish to change?"

A nightgown was laid out ready on the bed. Galba looked to Icelus. "Who is this?"

"We are Caesar's personal attendants. To serve as Caesar sees fit."

"I do not need help to undress. I am not a child," he barked. "Icelus, dismiss them."

The freedman nodded to Theseus who slid out with his two associates.

Galba lowered himself carefully onto the bed, his face taut with pain as he did so.

"Help me."

Icelus began unbuckling Galba's armour. "We heard there was trouble."

Galba clicked his tongue. "Wilful fools. I will not have such disobedience in the ranks."

Icelus took the breast plate, laying it to one side. Kneeling before Galba he began to remove his shin guards.

"We heard there were deaths."

"They wished to be proclaimed a legion and then demonstrated their unsuitability for such an honour. I needed to make an example of them, to show them that I will not tolerate such behaviour from the forces."

"Was it necessary to decimate them?"

"You doubt me?"

Icelus sat back on his heels. "Of course not. Never. Others will ask though."

"Let them ask." He patted the space beside him, Icelus taking the spot.

"Are you sore? A bath might relax."

Galba gave a tight smile. "I must smell of horse."

"Sweet as roses."

Galba nodded to the door.

"They won't come back unless you summon them," Icelus told him.

"Good, my hands, Icelus."

The freedman took hold of Galba's left hand, bent and twisted. Slowly he massaged it finger by finger, releasing the painful spasms that held them. He did the same to the right hand, the emperor visibly relaxing under the smooth movements.

"I have no desire to return to this function," he told Icelus as the freedman removed his tunic for him. "I am no Nero. I will not entertain for them. If they have business, let them petition the correct way."

"Quite, Caesar."

Devoid of armour he was a slight man, white hair lightly covering a concave chest, his lower back and stomach hidden beneath a cloth girdle.

"Do you wish me to remove it, Caesar?"

Galba nodded, cracking back his shoulder blades. "Only way I kept on that damn horse," he said. "I shall sleep now."

Icelus stood up, head bowed, waiting for dismissal.

Galba painfully climbed between the sheets. "You may stay with me tonight," he told him, their eyes meeting with understanding.

Icelus stripped off quickly and positioned himself as required in the imperial bed.

Across the city, curled up on the floor by Teretia's bed, Philo was awakened by a wail from the room next door signalling that Teretius had died.

ELEVEN

The first day of the new regime started for many of the imperial household with a sore head. Empress Statilia Messalina was particularly badly affected. One arm draped over her eyes groaning, "Juno, have mercy on my head, urgh my head," as her attendants squawked out a series of conflicting hangover cures.

Mina, who should have been there with the towel, as was her role, and with her own proven cure of turnip juice mixed with three eggs, was absent. She awoke draped across Titus Vinius' hairy chest. Leaning her chin on his breast bone she smiled, "Morning."

For Vinius, who had spent many weeks travelling on a bony horse surrounded by only men and not terribly attractive ones at that, this was the best possible wakening. A thought he expressed by rolling Mina onto her back for a fresh rutting to add to the four they had enjoyed the previous night.

Mina quietly congratulated herself on her rapid insinuation into the new elite. Titus Vinius, she mused, was but two fucks away from the emperor himself. Though she might wait until the one after Galba, whoever he might be.

It was in fact Icelus who awoke in the prime position beside the emperor himself. Something that should have pleased him immensely for he was often relegated to a separate room once the act had been committed.

However, this morning Icelus had but one thought: "What does the emperor's private secretary actually do?"

Icelus had no idea. Philo did all that stuff. He sat in the meetings his assistant told him to, barely listening because he knew Philo would be taking notes. Since Philo produced a duplicate seal, he hadn't even looked at any of the paperwork. He had absolutely no idea what the work involved.

This terror stayed with him over breakfast as Galba said, "Arrange a treasury meeting. Let us see how the finances stand. We have much to accomplish."

Icelus gave an efficient nod and left immediately to fulfil this order. Standing in the antechamber that passed for Philo's office he picked up random scrolls reading paragraphs that made no sense to him and throwing them back down again onto the desk.

He had no idea how to set up a meeting with the treasury. He didn't know who ran the treasury. Or even where it was situated. The palace was corridor after corridor of offices and departments. None of which, barring his own, Icelus had ever explored. How did one go about setting up a meeting? Who should be there? The head of the treasury and the emperor obviously, but what of the scribes and admin staff who seemed a permanent feature of such meetings discreetly working at the back? Where did they come from? And chairs? They would need chairs to sit on: where did one find chairs? And refreshments. Galba could not be left without wine and nibbles.

Icelus rubbed a hand across his sticky brow. The thought of displeasing Galba terrified him. When he had been that man's slave he had endured more than one whipping. But even worse was suffering a stern glare from those ice-cold eyes.

He needed Philo. He needed Philo back now. Only then could he hide his deficiencies from Galba.

A barked, "Sir," from the doorway alerted Icelus to the presence of a young messenger boy.

"Yes?"

"A message from Miltiades, sir," Alex informed him.

Icelus took it, having no idea that Miltiades as head of the treasury was exactly the man he wished to speak to. Alex made to leave. "Hang on, boy. I have a message for you to deliver."

Icelus grabbed a tablet and wrote three lines on it: "Hope girl is well. You are required. Icelus."

He then handed it to Alex, telling him to deliver it to Philo.

By bawling at every slave who passed, Icelus somehow managed to arrange the meeting. It was at this first budgetary meeting between the new emperor and the treasury that Laco brought up the subject of the Praetorians' promised bounty.

"I have been asked about it several times with much mention of how they saved your throne from Nymphidius Sabinus."

"Actually, Caesar," interjected Vinius, "Whilst we are on the subject of bounty, the German legions are clamouring for recognition of their services."

Galba looked down his long patrician nose. "The Praetorians are overpaid as it is. I see little evidence of their deserving such an additional payment. As for the German legions, are they soldiers of Rome? I levy my troops, I do not buy them."

"Quite, Caesar," said Icelus smoothly, giving the other two a hard glare. "The state of the treasury is next on the agenda. Miltiades has looked into this."

Given his cue Miltiades stood up, cleared his throat, and read from his tablet. "There is currently 20,000 sesterces in the imperial treasury," and sat down again.

Galba leaned forward on his throne. A sum of 20,000 sesterces would buy a moderately good meat carver or a third-floor rickety apartment in a dubious area of the city. "What! That cannot be right. Was not Nero building a huge palace?"

"He had to stop," admitted Miltiades. "Lack of funds."

"No, it is not possible," insisted Galba, seeing his grand plans for Rome disintegrating. "There is trickery involved here. Have you checked these figures?"

"Yes, Caesar, I had it checked and double-checked and triple-checked. And then I checked it again," said Miltiades.

"Right. We need money then," said Vinius, ever the pragmatist. "How do we get money?"

"Sod that, Vinius. Where did all the money go?" Laco aimed this at Miltiades.

The head of the treasury took his time answering, trying to work out the best way to phrase it.

"Nero was rather extravagant and generous."

Vinius clicked his fingers. "There's your answer. Generous to whom?"

"It would solve one problem, Caesar. The amnesty towards Nero's favourites is viewed with suspicion. If we could be seen to take back some of the money which rightly belongs to the state …"

"How much did Nero spend in the last year? Do we have that figure, Icelus?"

Icelus turned back to Miltiades who said quietly, "A thousand million sesterces were rewarded last year."

Vinius whistled. "We could pay all the bounties out of that."

Galba turned his gaunt neck and snapped at Vinius, "I told you. I don't buy my men."

"I am sure it was far jollier without the emperor," said Mina.

She was holed up in Alex's room enthralling him with tales from the banquet.

"The empress certainly had fun."

Indeed she had. Flirting shamelessly with Otho and hitting the wine with gusto, drinking even Vinius under the table. Gleefully she told all she met, "Of course I am a prisoner here," embarrassing many a senator who did not know quite how to respond. Mina helped hold her mistress upright and ensured that the drink remained in her hand and not over any of the distinguished guests.

"How did the emperor look? I only saw his feet."

Mina crinkled her nose, "Old. Really old."

"As old as Epaphroditus?"

"Epaphroditus wasn't old. He was in the prime of life," she insisted, a shadow crossing her face.

Alex distracted her with another question, "How old then?"

"Wrinkly old. Old man old. Old enough to be our great-grandfather old. If he lives till the end of the year it will be quite something."

"He doesn't like parties then?"

"Apparently not. Gods, it will be so dull if there aren't any parties. Where will I get all my gossip from? People rely on me for top tittle-tattle."

Alex wasn't sure what to think of Galba. Sabinus had built him up as the saviour of Rome, as the great distinguished man of the empire. But then Sabinus had become disillusioned before even meeting him, and what Alex had heard of Galba so far was not encouraging.

"Rude, very rude," Theseus complained. "He yells and yells and nothing I do is satisfactory. The only one who can do anything right is that Icelus. He actually dresses him. Can you imagine Epaphroditus dressing Nero?"

Icelus, unbeknown to him, had crossed important palace boundaries. Jobs were heavily demarcated and by undertaking Galba's toilette he had simultaneously stolen four slaves' positions as well as undermining the dignity of the role of private secretary.

Icelus was not popular with the workforce who looked down on him as an inferior. He might be a freedman but he was not an imperial freedman. He had stumbled into a job which he'd no training in, a position he had no right to inhabit, just by way of whose slave he had once been. It was well known that it was

Philo who had done all the actual work and Icelus' behaviour towards him the day of Galba's arrival had been noted by all and not forgiven.

Then there was the business at Milvian Bridge. Vinius tried his best to underplay its significance at the party: "An unfortunate matter. Some troublemakers made a run at the emperor. It is sad that innocents were caught up in the trouble but Caesar lives and that is the most important thing."

"Alex, are you alright?" Mina asked, seeing his troubled expression.

"I was thinking of Philo's landlord."

It had been poor timing for delivering Icelus' message. The apartment full of wailing relatives returned from the funeral. Philo tight-lipped and pale. Reading the tablet but refusing to give a response, saying only that Teretia needed him.

"His girlfriend is alright though?"

Alex briefly glimpsed Teretia, sitting quietly on a bench, evidently in some pain. Her face bruised and her expression infinitely sad. Alex attempted empathy but he had never had a father. Nor a mother either. He was a foundling child. An unwanted addition to a family. Left to die on a rubbish heap until Felix had picked him up and taken him to the palace. It was an extremely cheap way of replenishing the palace slave stock. Though Felix maintained foundlings were only such, "Because there was something fucking disposable about them!"

He couldn't even imagine what it was like to have a father. The slaves were fed from birth that Caesar was their father, Caesar was their family. Any other tie, blood or otherwise, was void.

His sad thoughts were interrupted by a thump of boots coupled with scattering feet.

Mina sat up listening and then she broke into a grin. "It's Straton!"

The scattering feet were those of slaves sensible enough to get out of his way.

Straton had never mastered the art of knocking. His presence needed no polite introduction. Reaching Mina's room he merely kicked in the door. It spun back, smashing into the wall with a cloud of plaster, Straton's bulky form taking up the entire doorway.

Alex automatically nudged backwards on his bum. The hairs on his arm standing up, a sudden lump appearing in his throat.

"Hullo," said Mina cheerfully.

Straton gave a thin grin. He looked genuinely pleased to see Mina, his black eyes sparkling. For one brief moment Alex felt a pang of jealousy, until he reminded himself that all those Straton and Mina stories were just to cover up what they really got up to in those hours they spent together.

"Lesson," growled Straton.

Mina was on her feet. "Absolutely," and then to Alex: "Gotta go!"

Left alone in Mina's room, a bored Alex buggered off to the Praetorian camp to see Honoratus.

He found the tribune sitting on the steps outside the Praetorian mess hall quietly whittling at a piece of wood. Alex sat down next to him. Honoratus handed him his own piece of wood and a penknife.

"They are good, very good," commented Honoratus, pointing with the blade of his knife at Alex's creations: a wooden elephant and a camel. Alex, shavings forming at his ankles, waved a block. "This one is going to be a tiger. The stripes are going to be my finest moment!"

He had certainly come on from his earlier attempt, a brittle misshapen pole that he had imagined was a sword. Time, patience, and more than a little talent had aided him.

"I find it calming," he told Honoratus, working on a leg with deft strokes.

They spent a lot of time together doing this. Just whittling, talking quietly, calmly. He liked spending time with Honoratus and it was here that Alex had an epiphany. He might not have a father but he had Honoratus.

"Have you ever thought of becoming a carpenter? You have a talent for it," Honoratus was asking him.

Alex blinked, not understanding. "I'm a messenger," he said.

"You like being a messenger?"

"Not really. Once," he admitted.

He had, in the early days when he imagined his quick promotion up the ranks. Not any more though. Well aware that he was never going to reach the high placing he once dreamt of. He didn't have the right mix for the palace higher rungs: he was a foundling. The exalted positions went to the vernae, palace-born slaves carefully bred for optimum looks and brains by Apollodorus.

Mina, Lysander, Phaon, Epaphroditus, and anyone of any note were vernae. Though not Sporus, who claimed to be the most expensive item of slavery ever purchased by the palace. "I'm worth five thousand camels!" he boasted. "Or a herd of elephants; really large ones with flappy ears. Or a great big boat filled with wine amphora. It's because of me that they had to raise the taxes on the provinces. That's how expensive I was!"

The prejudice against the non-vernae was strong, especially when some of the palace workforce were of third or fourth generation in imperial ownership. They considered themselves very much part of Caesar's family and looked down on those they considered interlopers, unwelcome additions to the household.

As they monopolised the departmental head roles they tended to employ those who most closely matched their own backgrounds, leaving foundlings like Alex distinctly unlikely to ever make a success of themselves.

"I'd rather do this." He waved the lion. "I like it. You get something at the end of it, better than a scowl and a rude message to deliver back."

"You couldn't be a carpenter?"

"They don't let you change careers at the palace. They decide what you're going to be."

There was a silence. Honoratus put down his knife and asked, "What if you didn't work at the palace?"

TWELVE

The beaker wobbled on the shelf and then fell, smashing into pieces on the stone floor. Mina squealed and jumped into the air.

"Result!" she cried, the whip bouncing in her hand.

Straton patted her on the shoulder, walked over to the wall, wrenched the shelf out, and then moved it up to the next set of brackets, placing an unbroken beaker on it.

"Try that," he commanded and stood out of the way.

Mina narrowed her eyes, assessing the distance and height. She pulled back her whip and cracked it forward with a jerk. It hit the wall beneath the shelf with a slap. The vibrations travelled through the stone, jiggling the shelf above, and the beaker fell forward onto the ground.

"Result!" Mina crowed and looked to the overseer for approval.

Straton, his huge arms folded across his chest, slowly shook his head. "Not near."

"It broke the cup," protested Mina, gesticulating with her hands.

"Works on cups. Not men," was Straton's sparse reply. "Lesson over."

Mina began to protest again. "Oh come on. A bit more pleeeease. Three more goes and I'll hit this height. I will. You'll see."

Straton was immovable. "Lesson over," he growled. And then added with something that might have been excitement, it was difficult to tell with Straton's ugly features, "Got something to show ya."

He gestured her over to a large wooden trunk from which he pulled out a smaller wooden book which he handed to her with gentle care.

Mina stared at the oblong box in her hand and slid off the lid. Inside were three gleaming steel stylos, a metal pen with sharpened nib, and a small sealed pot of what Mina assumed to be ink.

"Nice, hey?" It was more a hopeful question than a statement, Straton looking at her imploringly.

"It's lovely," smiled Mina. "For your friend I take it?"

Straton nodded, taking the stylo set from her. Rubbing a thumb across the lid he told her, "Gonna be a plaque 'ere. Engraver got it. Gonna pick up later."

This was quite a speech for Straton. It made his throat sting and his face crinkled in pain.

A sympathetic Mina grasped hold of his arm and linked hers in. "What's it going to say?"

Straton cleared his throat a couple of times before managing to expel, "His name," in little more than a whisper.

"Well, that's a lovely thought. He's going to love it."

"Think?" asked Straton earnestly.

"Know," replied Mina.

And this was how Mina and Straton spent the time that had generated so much gossip. It was a straightforward deal. Straton was teaching Mina the art of cracking a precise whip and in return Mina was assisting Straton in his romancing of Philo. Of course she didn't know it was Philo who was Straton's very special friend. Such gossip would have whipped its way round the palace in no time and Philo would have doubtlessly hanged himself from the nearest available rafter or tree. No, all Mina knew was that Straton was deeply in love with an unnamed male who was clearly literate since Mina had spent a great deal of time copying out Catullus love poetry on behalf of the illiterate overseer.

Mina hoped that Straton's friend appreciated all the effort he was making. Mina wished someone would shower her with such nice gifts. Perhaps Titus Vinius would in time. Once he realised how special she was.

Overwhelmed with excitement, Sporus had not slept at all. Since Alex's noteworthy appearance in the temple the previous day, he determined that he must leave the Galli and their maddening whirling ways. That the world believed him to be dead was a burning injustice to the eunuch. He feared for those poor heartbroken souls who were out there mourning his demise.

No doubt there had been a lavish funeral for him. Mina he was sure would have done his memory justice. She would have employed the thousand or so professional mourners to mingle with the crowd of proper mourners. He imagined it had been difficult to round up the necessary zebras but Mina was not the sort of girl to cut corners and paint stripes down mules instead.

He licked his lips when he thought of the handsome, young, oiled male slaves carrying his coffin. And he pondered as to which of his admirers had thrown themselves onto his funeral pyre in unutterably tormented grief. He supposed that they must have held at least a day of games for him: the people would have demanded it. This so-called new emperor Galba could not afford to upset the populace by denying them such an outlet for their grief. Think how happy they would be when they discovered that the Sporus was not dead at all!

And here Sporus smiled and clasped his hands against his heart. What an entrance that would be! To come back from the dead! That would outclass anything anyone had ever done before! They'd write plays about him: *The Eunuch Who Lived*! A great tragedy of dramatic proportions. They'd have to stage it twice daily with additional performances on festival days.

Such thrills grew in Sporus' rather self-obsessed heart and he danced to see the Arch Gallus first thing the next morning. The chief priest was relaxing on a couch tethered to the ceiling by golden chains; two of his acolytes on hand to gently swing him. On hearing Sporus' request he shook his fat head.

"Cannot be done, young Gallus."

"What?" spluttered Sporus. "You cannot keep me here a prisoner!"

"You are not a prisoner. You are our sister. Our sister Gallus. And the Galli serve the goddess all their lives."

"But I am not a Gallus. I'm a Sporus!"

The Arch Galli looked puzzled. "But we are family," he said. "You are our sister. You are a Gallus now. You have been initiated into the secret rites of the Great Mother."

"What secret rites? Oh you mean the whirling and that weird dance round the black stone and then that chant that starts—"

The Arch Gallus was shocked. "Hush! You must never speak of the secret rites. It is forbidden."

Sporus pushed a finger to his lips to demonstrate his trustworthiness. "I won't tell a soul," he promised. "No one will be in the slightest bit interested."

The chief priest shook his head, his chins wobbling. "No one has left the priesthood of the Great Mother before."

"I could be a pioneer," suggested Sporus.

"No. It cannot be done." He was resolute. "You must stay here, with your sisters."

And then that final word uttered firmly in a tremulous pitch that struck terror into Sporus' mincing heart, "Foreverrrrr."

THIRTEEN

Epaphroditus, former secretary to Nero, was engaged, highly engaged, and was in no mood for an interruption from his slave.

"Not now, Callista," he barked with ill temper.

"Master, there is a gentleman to see you."

"He can wait."

"He says his name is Marcus Salvius Otho."

Epaphroditus' head sprung up, "Otho?"

"Yes, master."

"Show him to my study."

"Yes, master."

"Oh no you don't," protested his wife Aphrodite. "You get back down there and finish what you started." She pushed his head down between her thighs.

Though he called it his study there was not much to distinguish it as such. There was a big imposing desk but there were no books, no tablets, nor any busts of Cicero or other literary giants.

This study had one very particular function that had nothing to do with poetry or rhetoric. Epaphroditus possessed five daughters, and whenever the fighting over clothes or wailing over curling tongs got too much, this was where he would retreat. Occasionally he was kind enough to allow access to his son Pollus.

Otho was casually examining the contents of Epaphroditus' stern-looking desk: an apple and a jar of pink ointment which he gave an exploratory sniff.

"Otho."

Holding the jar up he asked, "What is this for?"

Epaphroditus, cricking a pain out of his neck, hurriedly shut the door and snatched the jar from Otho. "Nothing to concern you."

"For a *nasty* then."

Placing the jar back in the drawer he looked pointedly at Otho's thick locks, commenting, "Weren't you bald the last time we met?"

Settling himself on a chair Otho told him, "You know how you always claimed that entreating the gods was a waste of effort? Turns out it isn't. I sacrificed a load of cattle and behold, my barber invented this ingenious toupee. Wonderful isn't it? Not a slip, I can even bathe in it."

"I am very happy for you. What do you want, Otho?"

"I've been up at the palace. Apparently you're dead. I came to pay my respects to your widow, and your doorman suggested I come and talk to you personally. You can imagine how surprised I was."

"A necessary fiction."

"Quite so," smoothed Otho. "Especially if Galba should wish to crack down on all those men who flourished under Nero."

"Well, you would know more about that than I," stated Epaphroditus coldly.

Otho raised his black eyebrows. "You're mad at me, aren't you? Is it because I declared for Galba?"

Epaphroditus didn't answer.

"He's a fine fellow. Full of reforming zeal and old school discipline."

"I wouldn't have thought that would appeal to you. I seem to remember that you could outdo Tigellinus in the fornication stakes."

"Don't mention that name to me, Epaphroditus, please."

It was Tigellinus, the former Praetorian prefect, who had pushed for the Nero/Poppaea marriage. Otho who had been married to Poppaea at the time had never forgiven him for it. Smoothing down his toupee he asked, "How is it that your lovely wife has failed to notice you have a *nasty*?"

"I do not have a nasty."

"You should always go for virgins. That was what Nero used to say. That way you know they're clean and you can train them up to your own particular standards. Talking of which, I met the very wonderful Statilia Messalina."

"Statilia Messalina is not a virgin, trust me on that one."

"I liked her. She has a certain," Otho paused, gazed up at the ceiling and then concluded, "gleam."

"Gleam?" queried Epaphroditus, who'd always found the empress cold.

"Yes, gleam," he sighed. "I might have to marry her."

Epaphroditus threw himself onto his chair and regarded Otho with a wry smile. "So now we come to the crunch. This is all some twisted revenge on Nero for Poppaea isn't it? Declaring for Galba, interesting yourself in his widow."

"Not at all. I happen to believe Galba is the best guy for the job and all."

Epaphroditus frowned and asked suspiciously, "What are you up to, Otho?"

His companion beamed, took the apple from the drawer and threw it into the air, catching it in his palm. "Never could get anything past you, could I? Tell you what, I'll do you a deal."

"A deal?"

"You tell me how your wife doesn't know you've caught a nasty and I'll tell you about my scheme."

Epaphroditus thought hard. Though he'd enjoyed his break spending time with his family, he was starting to get just a little bored. An Otho scheme was always worth hearing, if only for the sheer level of preposterousness it invariably held.

"Deal," he said and shook on it.

"So?"

"I am distracting her with other methods of pleasure while things clear up."

"I am sure she is glad of the break. Don't you have a ridiculous number of children?"

"Your scheme?" insisted Epaphroditus, who disliked having his private life dug into in such a fashion.

"Galba is an old man, right?"

"Positively ancient."

"And he is childless, right?"

"Oh gods no, Otho, you're not?"

Otho smiled happily. "I am going to convince Galba to adopt me as his son."

Once Epaphroditus had swallowed this idea he asked, "Why would Galba adopt you?"

"Why so sceptical? I can't see why he wouldn't. My own father was exceptionally fond of me."

"He had more time to adjust to your eccentricities."

"Galba is very old. He has no children and is unlikely to have any. He has quite spectacularly become emperor of most of the world. Which is quite an achievement. He is not going to want his legacy to die with him. He will be looking for an heir."

"And you think he will naturally choose you?"

"Not at all, you misunderstand."

"I do?"

"Obviously it is an aim that will need work. It will need a plan, strategic thinking and all that. I thought you might like to join the team."

Epaphroditus laughed, hard. Actually, he thought, it was worth the discomfiting disclosure regarding his inflamed genitals. "You are insane. You'll never do it. Galba's not daft. And by your own admission, he's old school, whilst you are …?" He finished by raising an eyebrow.

Otho rubbed his hands together. "But surely that is the fun of it? How utterly unlikely that I, Marcus Salvius Otho, should become emperor-in-waiting. It will blow the senate away."

"That it will. Gods I wish Nymphidius Sabinus were alive to hear this."

"Will you do it?" Otho asked eagerly. "Come on, it will be fun like old times."

"Yes and I remember all the trouble you got me into back then," commented Epaphroditus. "Besides, I have retired from politics."

"What a waste!" exclaimed Otho, leaning forward. "When these are such interesting times. Think about it. Some old fart who everyone thought had died years ago comes from Spain with nothing but his name and destroys a dynasty that had lasted a hundred years. Juno, Epaphroditus, if that's possible, anything is possible."

"Otho for emperor."

"Otho for emperor," he agreed. "So what do you say? Will you be my campaign manager?"

Otho could sell sand to a Parthian camel merchant. He had a knack for making even the most ludicrous idea seem plausible. His enthusiasm was infectious and Epaphroditus began to sway. Aphrodite would hate it. He wouldn't tell her.

"I know that I am going to regret this."

"Trust me, you won't. Remember when you told me that I would make a lousy governor?"

"I will confess you surprised me on that score."

"Quite, and remember that wonderful girl you said was way out of my league?"

"You married her."

"And remember that time when we were at that hellish dive in the Subura and you said that pickled egg was off and would make me sick to my stomach?"

"It was off, Otho, it stank. It had mould on it. Even the damn rats were turning their noses up at it."

"But," smiled Otho, "I was not sick."

FOURTEEN

The Arch Gallus danced naked in the pit, his flesh rippling and rolling as he did, arms snaking in the air. Above, his acolytes whirled ecstatically, their distinctive warbles filling the air. "Ellalalalalahhhh," they cried, crashing cymbals and whipping themselves into a frenzy.

Sporus was leant against a wall banging a tambourine half-heartedly as the rites reached their crescendo. He was dwelling on his incarceration. Forever was a long time. It was a longer period than Sporus could envisage, so he cut it down in his mind to a single month.

Thirty days. Thirty more days of the sisters and their preening. Thirty more days of getting dizzy from whirling. Thirty more days of cymbals chiming and that high pitched wailing which grated on Sporus like nails on iron. Thirty whole days. He couldn't take it! He literally couldn't bear it! He had to get out! Escape. Yes that was it, he must escape.

At the point it seemed that the Galli could go no faster, sing no louder. When it looked as if they might ignite from the sheer energy emitted, a single Gallus took hold of a knife and slit the throat of a snow-white bull. The blood gushed from its neck onto the Arch Gallus below, who met it with eyes held upwards. The Galli ceased their singing and stood in silence.

"Thank fuck," thought Sporus, his head pounding, watching the Arch Gallus bathed in blood and grinning like a madman.

Seeing his fellow acolytes distracted by the immense amount of cleaning required, he whipped forward and nabbed the sacrificial knife, hiding it within the folds of his gown. Then he serenely trotted back to his quarters.

"What did Otho want?" Aphrodite asked from the doorway of the study.

"A chat."

"A chat?"

"Yes, a chat. I haven't seen him since he took up his governorship so there was plenty to catch up on."

"Such as?"

"Rufus, Claudia, and Julia for starters."

"You discussed our children with Otho?"

"In passing."

"In passing," she repeated suspiciously.

"I don't know why you are looking at me like that. It was wholly innocent. A chat between friends."

"Nothing Otho does is wholly innocent," she told him. "I suppose he is dragging you into whatever daft scheme he has dreamed up now."

He walked over and kissed her. "There is no scheme, darling."

"Otho is trouble. He always was, no matter what they say about him now."

"You don't believe him a reformed character?"

"Not him, I don't. I know him." She looked at her husband seriously. "Better than you do."

Epaphroditus shifted slightly, uncomfortable at the way the conversation was heading.

Sensing his discomfort she stroked his hair, telling him, "I don't forget. Even if you choose to."

"Dite, don't," he pleaded, and then feeling an acute burning sensation in his groin excused himself with urgency.

Unaware of his malady Aphrodite thought his sudden exit due to her words, which she immediately regretted speaking. He didn't like to talk about before: the before they were freed, when they were both imperial slaves. He liked to pretend it had never happened and that everything that mattered had taken place in the years since they had been manumitted.

Aphrodite did not participate in this selective amnesia. She remembered it all. The shadow that hung between them, the issue Epaphroditus did not wish to recognise concerned Silvia, their eldest child. Aphrodite had been eight months pregnant when she was freed, Epaphroditus rushing through the paper-work so that the child would not be enslaved. They married the very day the final documents were signed. Both of them knew there was a good chance their first freeborn child might not be his.

They talked about it a lot in the early days. Aphrodite terri-fied that he might have the baby exposed if he doubted its par-entage. She had handed over four children to the palace. Three died in infancy. The fourth, Iugarthus, had fared better. They spent as much time as was permitted with their son, fitting it around their duties and the watchful eyes of the overseers who were suspicious of familial links. Iugarthus had been a hand-some lad whose future looked bright. His father secured him a good position within the administration for when he left the imperial training school.

Only the boy had never taken up the job. He drowned in one of the palace bathhouses shortly before his sixteenth birthday. Aphrodite did not rate the palace's child rearing skills and she did not think she could bear to lose another of her babies.

The thought of exposing the child had never crossed Epaphroditus' mind and he spent much time reassuring her that he would love the baby regardless. After Silvia was born the subject was not raised and they didn't talk about it again, ever. That Otho and Epaphroditus had become buddies was testament to his ability to block out any unpleasantness.

Aphrodite did not like Otho. He was charming but reckless. If an idea struck him he would follow it foolishly without thought to the consequences, leaving a trail of destruction in his path. She did not want her husband to be one of his casualties and she viewed their renewed acquaintance with trepidation.

FIFTEEN

The freedman is an odd position. The change from property to family is a strange one. However, such creatures can prove useful. They are tied to your name as are their children and any slaves they may purchase and free. Which means you can command quite a retinue should you need some crucial votes in an election or a ready-to-hand angry mob. They are also duty-bound to you financially should your sesterces and denarii run low.

Of course, the most prolific collector of freedmen in the empire is the emperor himself. Thousands of wealthy, well-connected ex-slaves to support his every whim and protect his person. Emperor Galba Caesar didn't know it, but he was about to gain his first imperial freedman.

Lysander, sat opposite Felix, asked the crucial question. "How much am I worth?"

Felix fingered his beard. "Bit of a rhetorical question, isn't it? How much would I pay for a man with a nice voice? Dick all! I don't need anyone to tell me when my dinner's ready. I can fucking smell it."

Lysander sighed but persisted.

"Oh well, market forces and all that. Five thousand and that's my final offer."

"I have that," said Lysander dropping a heavy purse on the desk with a thud.

"Good, good. You know you can't be an announcer when you're free, don't you? Not a suitable position for a freedman. We will have to find you something else. What can you do apart from talk fancy?"

"I could train announcers. I'd be good at that. I know all the proper diction and I have a secret recipe of herbs, wine, and vinegar that preserves the voice. Nero used it before his singing competitions. He complimented me on it more than once."

"I'll look into it," promised Felix. "When are you thirty?"

"The day after tomorrow."

"We'll do the paperwork then. You'll have to get your stuff out of the complex. Do you have somewhere lined up?"

"Not yet."

"I wouldn't wait, Lysander. Rome's a hard city to get decent accommodation. You don't want to end up in some fucking pleb ghetto. Still, I suppose you could stay with your ma should you get stuck."

Lysander cleared his throat. "Probably not. Her new husband doesn't like me much."

Felix raised a bushy eyebrow, telling him, "Apollodorus will miss you. You're his top breeder. You fucking amaze me. You just walk past a woman and bam, she's stuffed. Sure you don't want to squeeze one more out? They're about to start another set."

Lysander shook his head. "I've done my bit."

"Well, watch it. Out there you stuff some girl there are consequences to be had. You'll find yourself forced into marriage by some slab-faced pleb; her muscle-bound father and sturdy brothers making sure you don't bolt for it."

"I really don't think—" began Lysander but he was cut off by Felix.

"How do you think I ended up married? Yes, let my lovely wife be a lesson to you. Keep your legs crossed or pay your way. The alternative is a lifetime of sheer horror."

Having met Felix's wife, Lysander knew the truth of that statement. She resembled a marginally attractive orangutan.

Apollodorus' top breeder for the last thirteen years was going to be put out to pasture finally. The announcer was secretly relieved. Although publicly he crowed his successes to anyone who wasn't fast enough to flee; privately he had found it more and more dispiriting to have sex with girls who clearly didn't want to have sex with him.

He attempted some out-of-hours action but this had been robustly rejected by all for fear his potency would ruin careers and upset Apollodorus. His promises that he would pull it out in time were viewed with the scepticism they deserved. Rather than putting down his lack of success with the opposite sex to anything he was doing wrong, he had decided that it was their fault: slave girls.

Freebies, as the announcer always referred to freeborn girls, were different to Lysander's mind. If they slept with you it was because they wanted to, not because they'd been told to or because of what you might be able to secure for them. They would be soft and willing, and Lysander could not wait to try one out.

That Philo of all people had already bagged a freebie seemed ludicrously unfair to Lysander who spent their mutual adolescence tormenting his room-mate on the subject of girls. Philo never retaliated to such gibes. He simply rolled over to face the wall, pulling the blanket over his head, which was all the more infuriating for Lysander. He was wondering whether Philo's girlfriend might have a freebie friend when the door opened and in walked a Praetorian.

"What the fuck do you want?"

Honoratus, unsettled by this welcome, said stiffly, "I want to buy one of your slaves."

"Buy this one if you like." He thumbed at Lysander who interjected angrily.

"Hey, I'm buying myself."

"Not if he outbids you, you're not."

Honoratus, taking in Lysander's superior poise, high cheekbones, nicely manicured nails, and precisely arranged wavy blond hair, could not help asking, "What does he do?"

"Announcer," Felix told him. "Could be useful round the camp. You could announce the drills, couldn't you, Lysander?"

He fell into laughter, picturing the immaculate slave surrounded by muddy Praetorians as he elegantly counted in their marches.

"My purchase," interrupted Honoratus.

Felix gave him a hardened glare. "I don't sell to guards. My stock is far too precious to be wasted on you fuckers. If you want a bum boy, go down the market and get some diseased Gaul."

"Now look here, slave."

Felix pulled at his tunic. "Am I wearing a fucking uniform? Is this a uniform? No it is not. So I am not a fucking slave, all right!"

Lysander, seeing Felix going rapidly purple thought it might be a good moment to slip out before there was a full-on explosion. He'd almost made it to the door when Felix yelled, "And you get back here!"

Honoratus' hand was on the hilt of his sword. Felix was on his feet, fists clenched. Lysander slid back in and sat meekly between them.

"Now then, guard."

"Tribune."

"Tribune is it? You the tribune that totalled Sabinus?"

Honoratus stiffened, recalling the moment he'd thrown the javelin that felled the Praetorian prefect Nymphidius Sabinus.

"You put me in a dilemma now, tribune," Felix, certainly no fan of Sabinus, told him. "I don't know whether to kiss you on both cheeks or kick you out my office."

Lysander breathed easy. Felix blew down as quickly as he blew up.

"You wanted to make a purchase, though," he smoothed, pulling out his inventory.

Honoratus, puzzled by Felix's sudden geniality, commented, "A boy."

"Yes, I have boys. Many boys. They don't come cheap though. Do you have any preferences?"

"Can I go now?" persisted Lysander.

"This one's not a boy." He thumbed at Lysander again. "But I can do a very good price for you, tribune. One must reward valour."

Honoratus eyed up Lysander who sat nervously playing with his fingers. "I don't think so."

"You sure? He's a great breeder: keep your stock levels high."

"No."

Felix dropped his stylus. "Awright, Lysander, you can go now." The announcer sped out.

"So, a boy?"

"Alexander."

"You can call it whatever you like when it's yours."

"You misunderstand. I wish to buy the slave Alexander. He is sixteen or seventeen, red hair, freckles."

"Oh him? Really? Him? If you're looking for entertainment, he ain't trained. You'd be better off buying one of my catamites, they retire about that age."

"I want the boy Alexander."

Felix flicked through his inventory looking for Alex's name. "Yep, here he is. We have them valued on a yearly basis," he told Honoratus. "10κ."

"Ten thousand sesterces? That seems a lot."

"I have to factor in the years of service that I won't get out of him now."

Honoratus shuffled awkwardly. "I don't have ten thousand sesterces."

Felix slammed his tablet shut. "Shame," he said with a sneer.

Honoratus left disheartened. It would take years to save up that sort of money. Unless, he thought, Galba paid him the bonus of 30,000 Nymphidius Sabinus promised the guards for overthrowing Nero. That would buy Alex and set them both up very nicely.

Philo walked through the palace corridors, satchel slung over his shoulder. Despite Icelus' note, he was not convinced of his welcome. However, he needed the money, so what choice did he have?

The apartment on the Viminal was rented and without Teretius' wages that rent was impossible to meet. A fact their landlord was well aware of, turning up the day after the funeral demanding upfront payment. He had been chased away by two of Teretia's burlier cousins but it would be a temporary relief.

Philo, infected by Pompeia's anxiousness, handed over his whole month's wages. Apart from food which he could always nab at the palace, Philo did not have any material needs. His precious tunics were wearing well and he lacked any hobbies or women which might dent his salary. Pompeia stared at the bag of coins and gave it straight back to him with a sharp shake of her head.

"Now then, Philo, I'll not take your money."

But Philo, somewhat out of character, had insisted forcefully and would not back down. Pompeia burst into tears and told him that he was the kindest soul she had ever met.

Philo was rather impressed by the solidarity of the family. The way all the aunts and uncles had rushed over to help, taking turns by Teretia's bedside, lending a shoulder for Pompeia to cry on, and turning up with pots of food at just the right moment. If you fell ill at the palace, people just came to gawp and enquire if they could nick your bed when you carked it.

The family support and his money would save them for a while, but it would not last. Philo would have to return to work, but he waited several days to show Icelus that he could not be pushed around.

"Philo!"

"Hello Daphne."

"How is your girlfriend?" she enquired eagerly.

As far as he knew he didn't have a girlfriend. A very big, scary boyfriend: yes. Girlfriend: no. So he looked at the seamstress blankly.

"Teretia?" she prompted.

"She is not my …" he began, stopping when he saw Daphne's evident concern for her plight. "She is much better," he told her. "Very bruised and sore. She can't use her hand yet. I have been helping her with her hair. She always has a plait when she sleeps but with only one hand she can't manage on her own. It is surprisingly difficult to accomplish."

He smiled at the memory. He, sitting behind Teretia with three strands in his hand as she instructed, "Left over right first and then the right over the left and then …" getting in a terrible muddle. Teretia looking in her hand mirror and giggling at the result.

"I shall have to practise," he told Daphne, who hugged this tale to her heart and dashed off to repeat it to the laundry girls who were itching for news on Philo's great love.

"Morning," he muttered to Icelus as he quickly sat behind his desk.

"Good morning, Philo," returned Icelus coolly. "I have left some things on your desk that need attention."

"Of course, sir. I shall see to them."

As Icelus went to walk through to his office, he stopped short of the door. "Your girl is faring well?" he asked.

"She is recovering slowly but grieving for her father," Philo reported, hoping it would get passed on to Galba so he would understand the consequences of his actions at Milvian Bridge.

"I am pleased to hear she is better."

"Sir, I was wondering if I might employ some help."

"Help?"

"A scribe to assist me. I believe we could get a small desk over by that wall." He stood, demonstrating the width and position of his proposed addition.

"You think this would be a help to you? Would ease things?" Icelus asked carefully,

"I do, sir."

They looked at each other. Icelus did not apologise for yelling at him and he did not apologise for walking out.

"Very well," said Icelus. "Employ whoever you think is suitable."

SIXTEEN

Relaxing later in Laco's ample new quarters, Icelus stretched himself out on a couch and helped himself to a slice of flamingo.

"I hate my assistant," he told Laco.

"Philo? I thought he was a walking marvel? He sorted me out with these rooms for which I am indebted to him." Laco stretched out his toes and wiggled them.

"He's so, so …" Icelus struggled with his words. "So bloody perfect."

"What a bastard."

It wasn't just what happened before Galba's welcome ceremony; the way Philo humiliated him in front of everyone. Although he still smarted from this: the sniggering looks from the line-up, the jokes he knew were spreading at his expense. It had been from that point that Icelus began to notice how the staff treated him. There was never outright defiance, unlike Philo that day who had disobeyed him in such a public manner, but rather slights, small but noticeable.

That rude red-bearded man telling him that he was clean out of fan boys, his body attendant who was so slow at getting him dressed, the kitchens whose food was beginning to taste distinctly odd to him. Walking into a chamber filled with imperial slaves he could feel their hostility, see their eyes roll when he gave them orders. He was the emperor's private secretary: they should respect him.

They respected bloody Philo though. Since the freedman's return to work, their office had been plagued by people dropping in to ask how Teretia was doing.

Until Icelus with increasing rage had yelled at Theseus, "She is fine. There is nothing wrong with her. Now get out of my office!"

Theseus, taken aback by this ungraciousness, recovered himself quickly telling Philo he'd catch up with him later and exiting with a distinct smirk.

He was the emperor's private secretary, he was the important man. Yet in meetings and seminars the participants looked to Philo for confirmation of any decisions. They asked him to clarify points and talk on the feasibility of any initiatives. Of course he would have the answer instantly, quoting statistics and figures as if he'd memorised the entire imperial archive.

Even Galba turned to Icelus one night when he was unlacing the emperor's girdle and said, "That Philo, he's a capable sort. Diligent. I like him."

Icelus would have screamed had he not been able to salvage his pride and claim points from Galba by saying it was he who had spotted the freedman's talents and promoted him to his role.

"Icelus," prompted Laco. "You could always have him removed if he annoys you so much."

"Oh no I couldn't." He gave a bitter laugh. "They wouldn't let me," he said thumbing to a white-clad slave standing to attention by the door.

"There is still a vacancy for a Praetorian prefect. It's a good position if you fancy it."

"And let that little bastard slip into my job. No way."

"Well, the offer stands if you change your mind."

Icelus stood up, angrily wrapping his toga around him.

He stormed down the corridors, his attendant running behind him trying to keep up. Bloody perfect Philo with his talents and skills, his perfect nails and dapper tunics, his perfect hair (at this point Icelus ran his hand across his bald head) and good looks, with his no doubt perfectly beautiful girlfriend who he went home to every evening to make perfect love to.

He burst into his office prepared to assign the most tedious task he could think of to bloody perfect Philo, only to find the single inhabitant of the antechamber was the greasy little boil that his assistant had hired.

"Sir," said Talos, jumping to his feet, head bowed respectfully.

A deference which went some way to soothing Icelus' delicate sensibilities.

Philo sat in the atrium of Epaphroditus' luxurious Esquiline house. Usually when visiting he liked to examine the death masks lit by lamps that lined the walls, or let the red fish swarming in the central pool nibble at finger tips; an odd tickling sensation. Today he ignored entirely Epaphroditus' and Aphrodite's made-up relatives and even the opportunity of a bit of fish tickling, troubled by a very particular problem.

He had long recognised that Teretia was a beautiful girl. Much as he recognised that a sunset was beautiful or a chair was particularly well crafted. Since her accident though, he found himself dwelling more and more on those attributes he previously so dispassionately noted. Those warm blue eyes, that long golden hair, her rather plump rounded bottom.

At night he was bombarded with dream after dream about her, all of them distinctly erotic in character. To his shame he found these thoughts drifting into daylight hours. At breakfast time sitting opposite Teretia, he was hit with a potent image of her clad in the two-piece leather bathing suit that was a persistent feature of his nocturnal fantasies.

That poor girl, who had endured such a horrific experience and lost her beloved father, and here he was inflicting his perversions onto to her. Philo was finding it increasingly difficult to look her in the eye, convinced she could read his pornographic thoughts.

It was wrong. It was obscene. It was using up exhausting levels of self-control. It had to stop.

"Hello, Philo," said Silvia, standing by the pond. "What are you doing here?"

A question that stumped him since he wasn't entirely sure. Her father had sent him a note requesting he came. To distract her he said, "I hear you are getting married. Congratulations."

She made a face. "I am going to call it off," she told him. "Don't tell my parents though. They don't know yet."

"Oh," he said, uncomfortable at this confession.

Silvia had always made him feel awkward. Even as a child she was alarmingly self-possessed, projecting a strength he almost envied. From what Epaphroditus told him, she owned a fiery temper and lived only to make life difficult for everyone around her. Philo had never seen that side to her. To him she was a remote, cool statue of a girl, though, he computed inwardly, not nearly as beautiful as Teretia.

"Silvia, haven't you got anything better to do than pester Philo? Your mother wants to talk weddings," said Epaphroditus shooing her away. Silvia shot Philo a knowing look as she departed.

"Sorry, sorry. I don't know why they left you out here. They should have seen you through." He gripped Philo's hand. "Come on in. Let's have a drink."

Settled in the study Epaphroditus failed to get to the point of his summons, talking at length about Silvia's impending (or so he thought) marriage.

"He is from a good family and has decent manners according to Aphrodite. I couldn't get a complete sentence out of him. I think he must be a bit slow in the head. Jupiter knows what Silvia sees in him. He has far too many moles. One really big fat brown one on his cheek, right there." Epaphroditus shuddered. "But she likes him so …"

Philo kept his peace.

"And then Faustina is jealous of all the attention and storms around the house complaining as to why she doesn't have new dresses like Silvia and why Silvia is allowed to go to the coast with Martinus' family while she is kept prisoner here, though why anyone would want to hit Baia at this time of year … You would not believe the dowry his parents are demanding. It would buy a sizeable country estate. Once all this is over I shall have to get a job, lest I have Faustina whining that her wedding isn't as fancy as Silvia's." He sighed before telling Philo, "Children are a trial. I prefer them young, preferably before they learn to talk. Rufus and I spend many a happy afternoon together. Tell me, how is work?"

Catching Philo's dismay he added, "That bad?"

"I don't think Icelus likes me."

"Not like you?"

Epaphroditus was stunned. Philo was singularly inoffensive. He was the perfect receptacle for all musings, mainly because he never interrupted but listened intently before politely pointing out the fatal flaw in your scheme.

"He is very short with me," Philo explained, "and mean. I don't seem to be able to do anything right. He let me have an assistant though." He brightened as he told Epaphroditus all about Talos. "Lysander says he's arrogant."

Felix had had some choice words for him too. "He's a clever little fucker. No friends mind coz he's got fuck-all personality to attract them. Still, I don't suppose you care about his character. Fucker can read and write and all that. Just as fucking well coz he ain't going to win any prizes for his fucking looks either."

All of which had been said in front of an increasingly red Talos. Philo sympathised, he keenly recalled Felix describing

113

him to Epaphroditus. "We all thought he was a fucking mute but apparently he can talk. Just ain't got nothing to say have you, Philo?"

"He is a good transcriber. A great help to me."

"Well that's good," responded Epaphroditus trying to place Talos before hitting a mental image of a spotty youth with flaring nostrils. "And the new emperor?"

"He's OK."

He'd been determined to dislike Galba after what had happened to Teretius but the emperor was refreshingly straightforward to deal with. There were no hysterics, no walking on tiptoes in case of an outburst, none of mollycoddling or coaching that had been necessary to get Nero to do anything official.

Galba sat in on all the departmental meetings, absorbing the facts, breaking for discussion with his advisors before presenting his decision. Sometimes these breaks could go on for hours and contained heated exchanges between Laco and Icelus versus Vinius but no one had to be bribed an allowance to chariot race the afternoon away and the orgy quota had dropped to zero.

"He has lots of plans, I imagine," Epaphroditus threw in casually.

"Oh yes." Philo took a sip of wine. "Lots to do. The city is bankrupt."

"I heard about the recovery plan."

"You're not on the list," Philo reassured him.

"No, I know. Phaon is, though. He came round earlier in the greatest temper. He has to sell his villa to make the payments but nobody will buy the thing: they all think it is haunted by Nero's unhappy spirit."

"Gosh."

"Surely that won't bring in all the necessary funds?"

"Well, no," admitted Philo. "They have other plans."

"Really?" Epaphroditus said silkily before effortlessly steering Philo into revealing all those plans as well as the happenings in all the meetings of any note.

Philo didn't ask him why he was interested. It wouldn't occur to him that Epaphroditus wasn't merely making small talk. A fact his former boss was aware of. If you asked Philo a question he would always answer it to the best of his abilities. He had the fastest shorthand of all the scribes in the palace and was heavily in demand, minuting everything of any importance. Which meant that he was staggeringly well informed. A fact that Icelus found so belittling. He was trusted and he was liked and had he but realised it, he could have been the most powerful freedman at the palace. As it was he was blissfully unaware of the esteem he was held in.

Having secured the information he needed to pass on to Otho, Epaphroditus changed tack from the professional to the personal.

"Tell me, how is Teretia?"

"She is much better. Her hand is healing well. The swelling has gone down much. It still hurts her, but she can bend her fingers a little and it is a more normal colour, so I think it will be alright eventually. Her thumbnail is very black and she will keep accidentally banging it on things and then yelping. She should get it bandaged really, it would protect it better, but she says that a bandage would get in her way with her chores. But really she shouldn't be doing chores. I told her that. I said I could help but she wouldn't hear of it."

Epaphroditus listened to this speech with amusement. When Philo finally reached a conclusion he said, smiling, "You like her, don't you?"

Philo looked away, chewing on his lower lip.

"Are you two intimate?" he asked, pouring more wine into Philo's cup.

Though he would answer any work-related question, he was more tight-lipped over his personal life. Liquid lubrication was required so Epaphroditus gave him a hefty refill before prompting, "Well?"

Philo shuffled awkwardly on his chair, replying primly, "We're friends."

"Only friends?"

"Friends."

Some years prior when Philo was a shy young man (as opposed to the silent teenager he had been and the quietly competent adult he was to become) he developed an infatuation with one of the empress' junior correspondence clerks, a rather serious-looking girl named Cassandra.

Epaphroditus, noting his assistant's yearning looks whenever the girl was present had done his best to encourage him. Sending him off to the correspondence bureau with ever more pointless and unnecessary messages, gratified when the deliveries took longer and longer to accomplish.

Then something happened. What exactly Epaphroditus had never got to the bottom of. But returning to work after a bout of illness, Philo had refused to take a missive. Naturally it was a politely worded refusal requesting whether it would be possible for someone else to deliver the note since he was rather busy at that moment, but it was a refusal nevertheless.

When forced to be in the same room, Epaphroditus could not fail to notice the very conscious way Philo did not look at Cassandra. He wondered whether the nerves that had so afflicted his assistant in the breeding programme had led to the rift.

However, a careful investigation by Aphrodite, who retained good contacts in the correspondence bureau, revealed that the relationship had never progressed beyond some rather earnest comparisons of filing systems. Cassandra confided to Aphrodite she was as perplexed as they were by Philo's sudden change of attitude.

They had, she told her, enjoyed a very nice chat over breakfast and arranged to meet for lunch in a quiet part of the palace grounds that Philo knew of. Only he failed to show up. Hearing he had fallen ill she attempted to visit, only to be denied entry by his smarmy room-mate (Lysander, Aphrodite translated).

Seeing Philo some days later sitting quietly at breakfast she sat herself opposite, only for him to abruptly stand up with his dish of porridge and walk off. Since then, any attempt to talk to him had been met with the same response. She was confused and bewildered as to what she had done to upset him.

Epaphroditus attempted to talk to Philo about it, bringing the matter up gently and with concern. But he was greeted by a stubborn silence leaving him none the wiser as to what had gone so terribly wrong.

In retrospect he regretted not pressing the matter further, especially on seeing Philo's distress when Cassandra took up with Lysander shortly afterwards.

It was with this sad little tale in mind that he said, "Well, it seems a waste to me. There's Teretia completely besotted with you and here's you mooning over her …"

"She's not besotted with" Philo replied automatically, for the thought was ridiculous.

"Philo, I've met her. I saw the way she looks at you. Aphrodite saw the way she looks at you. Everyone at that party from Nero downwards saw the way she looks at you."

Epaphroditus watched Philo's eyes shift from side to side as he struggled to process this surprising information.

"No, that's not right," he concluded.

"Philo, trust me on this. I know women. Teretia loves you."

Epaphroditus, seeing his confusion, fixed him with a meaningful stare. "The question is, what are you going to do about it?"

"No, no I couldn't. It wouldn't, it wouldn't be right. To inflict that on her."

Epaphroditus, wondering at Philo's choice of words, gently persisted. "I rather think that Teretia would like you to inflict yourself upon her."

"No, no." A frantic shaking of his head. "No, it wouldn't. I couldn't …"

He was saved from further discomfiture by the entrance of Aphrodite.

"Hello, you two."

Epaphroditus was determined not to let the subject go. Smiling, he said, "Hello, love, I was just about to invite Philo and Teretia to Silvia's wedding."

"Excellent idea. You'll come?"

Recalling Silvia's confession, the freedman nodded anyway.

"Wonderful," smiled Aphrodite.

"It's a good excuse to buy Teretia a new dress," Epaphroditus pushed.

Aphrodite, looking harried, said, "Just don't let her outdo the bride please."

SEVENTEEN

"So there's not going to be a wedding?" Teretia asked, wide-eyed with horror.

"They've got it all planned as well," Philo told her, recalling Aphrodite's long account of the complicated arrangements.

"Oh, but that's dreadful! You don't think she'll wait for the actual day to call it off? With all the guests waiting and her poor parents."

Philo, dragging his eyes away from her heaving bosom, where they had developed a natural tendency to stray, assured her, "I am sure it will work itself out. Perhaps Silvia will change her mind again, decide she does like Martinus after all."

They were sat side by side on Philo's bed, their knees lightly touching. Since Epaphroditus' amazing claim that Teretia was in love with him, Philo had kept a very close eye on her, trying to ascertain whether there could be any truth in that extraordinary statement.

The problem was that Philo did not know what he was looking for. It was true that Teretia always smiled when she saw him but she was a very cheerful girl. He was almost ninety per cent sure Teretia wasn't in love with Tadius the butcher, yet she

119

always gave him one of her widest and loveliest smiles. Philo wished there was some kind of tick list of symptoms that he could compare with.

She did ask him lots of questions about his work and his day and seemed genuinely interested in his replies in a way that no one else ever had. It was this that pressed him into an experiment as he asked tentatively.

"You will come though? If there is a wedding. With me? As my guest?" he added shyly, avoiding her gaze, waiting anxiously for rejection.

"You want me to come? Of course I will," she exclaimed excitedly. "Will it be terribly posh? I suppose it will. Should I wear the dress I wore to meet the emperor? But then Epaphroditus and Aphrodite have already seen me in that one!"

"I thought," he interrupted, "I thought that I might buy you a new dress."

"You can't do that."

"You don't want a new dress?"

"No, yes, no, but," she stuttered.

"I'd like to buy you a nice dress. We could go shopping tomorrow. Unless you'd rather go with your mother. I don't know a lot about dresses."

There was something else that Philo didn't know much about that Teretia was soon to discover. Overcome with excitement she threw her arms around him, telling him, "Thank you so much. We shall have such a lovely time." She willed Silvia to keep her word to Martinus, otherwise it would ruin everything for her.

With Teretia's body squished against him Philo's first thought was, "Gosh, she's all soft." It was quickly followed by, "And she smells so nice, like … like …"

Here it was necessary for him to nuzzle into her neck to identify the scent of fresh bread. Though Philo was surprised at this discovery it was not that strange since Teretia had spent her morning making dough, rolling it out, and baking it in the stove. Philo's rigid self-control began to wobble. An instinct long suppressed reasserting itself. He held her tighter, pressing against her, nuzzling further into her white neck, one hand working its way down towards her plump bottom.

Feeling his hot breath on her neck and a hand squeezing at her bum Teretia tensed, alerting Philo with cold horror to the great impropriety he'd committed. Here he was with a single, unchaperoned girl, in his room, on his bed, and he had embraced her, rubbed himself against her, and touched her bottom! He flew back on the bed, wide-eyed and apologising profusely.

"I am so sorry. I shouldn't have done that. It was … it was wrong and unforgivable and … obscene. I'm sorry. I don't know what came over me," he stuttered. Ending with a pleaded, "Please don't tell your mother. I promise it won't happen again. I swear."

For almost an entire year Teretia had waited for Philo to seduce her, and OK, it wasn't quite what she had envisaged. In Teretia's daydreams Philo had been holding her hand gently and confessing undying love in a picturesque setting before moving in for a kiss that would tremble her to her toes. Nowhere in her fantasies had such an inexpert groping featured. But it had been nearly a whole year and she was not going to waste the opportunity.

Her response therefore to Philo's rather clumsy fondling was to grab the neck of his tunic and pull him in, delivering him a kiss enthused with all the passion a romantically minded fifteen-year-old girl can muster. If Philo had been wearing socks they would have been blown clean off.

When they came up for air some time later both rather red in the face and breathing heavily, their eyes met. Philo managed to squawk out a, "Wow," before she pulled him in for another session. Teretia was pleased to note that her toes were indeed trembling, in fact she felt hot and wibbly all over.

And although her Philo-themed dreams always culminated in the kiss and never any further, she knew what was required. When they broke apart for the second time she began to unlace the leather ties that held her dress together.

"We don't have to," interjected Philo hastily. "Not if you don't want to. You know it's, erm, it's OK, if you don't want to. It's fine. I won't mind, honestly." He took her hand and squeezed it. "I can wait."

This was palpably untrue. One more touch of Teretia's wonderfully soft body and Philo feared he might explode all over her. "We could just kiss," he suggested. And then blushed at the presumptuousness of that statement.

"I want to," said Teretia quietly. And then added, "If you want to."

Seeing the rounded tops of her breasts through a gap in her dress, he felt his mouth go dry. He did want to, he really did. In a rather shaky voice he said, "If you are positive it is alright with you."

"It is, I am sure," Teretia said and continued to undo her dress.

She went to push the material down over her shoulders when he felt he had to interrupt. "Teretia, I need to say, I need to tell you," he began self-consciously, staring down at his hands, feeling more uncomfortable than he had ever felt before (which was quite an achievement, for Philo spent his life in a permanent state of mortification). "I haven't," he continued awkwardly, "I haven't before. With a woman. Done this before. Sorry."

He didn't dare look up at her, staring at the floor hearing his heart thundering in his ears, convinced she would lace up her dress, stand up, and leave.

No doubt she was disappointed, assuming him to be a man of great sexual experience, because at his age you would, wouldn't you? Probably she'd been looking forward to some expert love making. Whatever that was. Philo wasn't too sure on the details. He once heard through palace gossip that Epaphroditus could make a woman's toes curl using just the tip of his tongue. A statement he had found sufficiently intriguing to raise with Lysander. His room-mate's response was a singularly withering look and a statement that if he didn't know about that then there really was no hope for him.

Contrary to Philo's expectations Teretia didn't leave. Philo's confession of his virginity (or so she thought) was a huge relief to her. She knew about sex. Her mother had told her all about it. Warning her that the first time would hurt but you just had to grit your teeth and get through it because with time and practice she would learn to enjoy it.

It was good, Pompeia had said, that Philo was considerably older than her. A man of experience would make it easier for her, would initiate her gently. Secretly Teretia was unsure about this, fearing comparison. What if she wasn't as good as the other girls he had bedded? What if they had been prettier? What if when he saw her naked he thought of those other girls instead?

That he had nothing to compare her with was a huge weight off her mind. "I don't mind about that."

Philo dared a glance upwards. "You don't?" he asked incredulously.

"Not at all." Taking hold of his hand, kissing his knuckles. Then she slipped off her dress, standing up to kick it from her feet and sitting abruptly back down again on the bed, trying to repress her natural instinct to cover herself with her hands.

There was housed in the old palace a statue of Venus rising from her bath. Philo often mulled over it as he waited to be called in to meetings and now he was presented with the real-life image of that goddess (though considerably better endowed in the bust region). She was to his mind the most stunning, beautiful, amazing thing he had ever seen. He gazed longingly at her large, globe-like breasts and then looked down at his small hands, feeling distinctly inadequate. Teretia, misunderstanding his look of consternation asked anxiously, "Is it alright? Am I alright?"

"You're beautiful," he breathed and then asked politely, "Could I kiss you?"

Teretia, happy with this compliment, smiled and folded into his arms. It was a softer kiss this time, more tender, gentle, exploratory. Philo was enjoying it immensely and was surprised and a little worried when Teretia pushed him away.

"Was that not right?" he asked, his forehead crinkling. "Did I not do that right?"

The reason for the break was revealed when Teretia reached over and began to unbuckle his belt.

"Oh," exclaimed Philo as she placed the belt on the floor beside the bed and bent over to do the same to his sandals.

He'd half hoped he could keep his clothes on: it would save on the inevitable question. But he couldn't really, could he? Not when Teretia had so shyly displayed that wonderful body to him. He knew he'd have to strip. She would feel awkward, embarrassed if he didn't. She might not even notice, he thought hopefully, as he pulled his tunic over his head, if he kept to a certain angle, a certain position.

Tunic disposed of in a heap on the floor, he made sure he sat directly facing Teretia. She placed a palm on his narrow chest, feeling the light covering of dark hair, still too embarrassed to look downwards to where a certain part of Philo's anatomy was rigidly pointing to the ceiling.

"Well," he said, conscious of this hardness, "I should, erm … probably, you know. Put it in."

Then cringed at such a graphic description.

"Should I lie down?" Teretia asked.

Philo supposed that she should. It seemed that was the way things were done. She settled herself back onto the pillows, getting comfy and then parted her legs. It was the sight of those soft, inner, oh-so-white thighs that caused Philo to forget all about angles and positions.

A gasp, then Teretia was upright, pawing at his side, turning him round and exclaiming, shocked, "What happened to your back?"

Philo flinched from the prodding fingers, Teretia tracing the criss-cross of scars: some raised, puckered; others mere light brown lines against Philo's dark skin.

He'd always been a lousy liar, but then Teretia was a rather credulous young girl. So his garbled explanation, regarding a cart running over him when he was a boy, was fully accepted by her. She ran her finger lightly along one particularly vicious scar from his shoulder blade, across his back and down to his left buttock. This had him fidgeting, bringing forth an image of a huge sneering face that had no right to be there, not now, not at this moment, his moment. Keen to change the subject and force all thoughts of Straton away, he grabbed Teretia rather quickly and planted a long and lingering kiss on her lips, gently manoeuvring her backwards.

It would be nice to report that the earth moved for them both, that it was a beautiful conjoining of bodies, but it wasn't. It was as awkward, stilted, and brief as all such first encounters are. Philo, assailed by a whole series of anxieties he'd never experienced, was apologising before he'd even finished.

Afterwards, lying side by side, he stared up at the ceiling miserably and wondered if there was anything he could do to salvage the situation. So he hadn't messed it up as badly as before when he'd been entered in the palace breeding programme; Apollodorus having to send for Epaphroditus to come and calm him down. But she hadn't liked it. He'd hurt her, he could see that as she lay beneath him biting her lip and staring at some point beyond his shoulder.

He would have to move out, that went without saying. He may as well go live with Straton, give up completely on the idea that something nice might actually happen to him. He was wondering whether Straton would allow him a rail to hang his clothes on when Teretia said quietly, "Philo."

He propped himself up on an elbow. "I'm sorry," he muttered. "I shouldn't have taken advantage of you like that. It was wrong. I was wrong. And I'm sorry about … about what happened." In ten beats flat. It had taken him longer to undo his belt.

Really he had no excuse, having grown up in Nero's court surrounded by naked writhing bodies most of the time. He didn't pay much attention to them, so frequent were they. He walked around them much as he had the furniture.

Assigned to the breeding programme, he'd taken a brief interest in the hope of learning something useful but he hadn't even got close to putting any of it into action.

Then there had been Cassandra. He'd sort of liked her and he'd thought that maybe she sort of liked him too. Though he never got the chance to build up any lusty thoughts about her. Straton, viewing their cheery breakfast discussion on date versus subject filing, and filled with a seething jealousy, enacted a searing brutality on him that had laid him up for days, leaving him with some nasty scars. To remind him, the overseer had hissed in his ear exactly who it was he belonged to.

That had been so thoroughly unpleasant, so nasty that it had put him off looking at girls entirely. At least until a certain blue-eyed, golden-haired one had unexpectedly entered his life and now he had gone and messed that up too.

Seeing his attention waning Teretia sat up in the bed. "Philo," she said again, leaning into him and brushing her lips against his. "I love you."

EIGHTEEN

In contrast to the damp, mizzly October weather, a sunny Otho skipped up the palace steps accompanied by his freedman dwarf Onomastus, whose unenviable task was to keep his master's thoughts in order.

Otho paused to talk to a guard on the gate.

"Aah, Proculus."

"Sir," barked Proculus crisply.

"No need to 'sir' me, guard. Otho will do fine. I have great news for you."

"For me?"

"Only you. Remember that little problem you were telling me about?"

"My ma's farm?"

Otho beamed, turning to Onomastus who handed him a scroll. He gave it to Proculus. "You'll like this."

Proculus unrolled it, responding amazed, "It's the deed to the neighbour's land."

"Should sort out that dispute you told me about."

"How much do I owe you?"

Otho waved a hand. "Nothing, nothing."

"No, seriously, sir, sorry, Otho, this is a lot of money."

"Not for a man in my position it's not. Let me do this for you, Proculus. I like you. I like your ma from what I've heard about her from you. I couldn't bear to think of her fighting such a petty man when I have the means to resolve it. Take it as my gift. Allow me to be generous, guard."

Proculus, touched by this speech, nodded and gave Otho a particularly crisp salute.

"Good man," said Otho dancing through the gates.

Lucullus, marching past, cast back a look at him. He thumbed at Otho in query.

"Great guy that Otho," said Proculus in response.

It was a sentiment rapidly spreading. On the journey from Spain, Otho's high spirits, generosity, and fun nature enlivened the trip for many of the legionaries. That he kept in touch, popping into their camp to check on Titus' bunions or Decius' mother or to join in their nightly dice games, betting large and laughing when he lost, was winning him many friends.

He'd taken a similar attitude to the Praetorian Guard. There was in Otho's view, bribery and bribery. He was far too savvy and well bred to hand over wads of cash to secure their favour. The whole idea left a bad taste in his mouth; it was common and belittling. However, giving Proculus money to save his ma's farm or clearing poor Salustus' debts with that baying moneylender and his bully boys, well, that was different. You couldn't buy friendship, but you could encourage its growth with a little well-targeted financial assistance.

That he was having to borrow the money himself from lenders to pay off other moneylenders on behalf of his new chums was not something that concerned him. He'd been up to his neck in debt since he was a pimply adolescent; it was his natural state. It probably explained his generosity: unused to actually having money to touch, Otho tended to distribute it quickly away.

Walking through the palace he greeted the slaves by name. "Morning, Julius, you are looking very brisk today."

"Theseus, stylish as ever."

"Lysander! You've lost the uniform. Congratulations and welcome to the free world. It's a great place to be."

"Straton, how's it going, pal? Is that a new whip at your belt? Can I have a feel? Blimey, fabulous quality. It must make your work a lot easier."

"Felix, you should put some conditioner on that beard, make it lush."

"Fuck off," responded Felix, but he did so almost jovially and walked down the corridor stroking his face fur, considering the advice.

"Artemina, now I have heard lots about you," he beamed.

"The empress is not ready," replied Mina.

Statilia, on hearing Otho outside her quarters, had squawked and dashed off to her dressing chamber with a hit squad of beauticians.

"Mind if I come in and wait?"

Mina held the door open for him. Sitting on a chair, with Onomastus standing upright (or as upright as he got) beside his arm, he gazed at her dreamily. "Epaphroditus was right, you are a peach."

The former secretary had said no such thing; he was close-lipped about his dalliances. Onomastus, that all-round wonder dwarf with a prodigious memory for slave names, also provided the details he needed on Mina.

"I know that he was very fond of you," said Otho to Mina, who was beginning to waver on her previously held opinion that Otho was full of bull.

"He wrote some lovely letters to me about you. Perhaps I could show them to you some time?"

Mina nodded, feeling unaccountably emotional. "I would like that," she said, wiping away a tear. "I do miss him."

More and more since she had taken up with Vinius. A decent, honest bloke certainly, but he mated with her as if he'd never had a woman before and this was his only chance before facing imminent execution. She spent a lot of time pressed against walls as Vinius quickly relieved himself in her before sending her away with a peck to the cheek and a muttered, "Thank you."

But the alliance paid off; Vinius helping her promotion to a more senior level of attendant. No more towels for her: now she got to open the door and dash about the palace with her mistress' latest insane requests to the bureaucrats and to Galba, neither of whom had any intention of honouring them.

"How is Epaphroditus' wife taking it?" she asked.

The automatic response in Otho's head was, "Every which way she can." Earlier, sitting in Epaphroditus' study, he had distinctly heard her cries of pleasure. To Mina he said solemnly, "She is very brave."

"Marcus."

"Statilia Messalina. What a vision!" he exuberated at the pink-cheeked empress dressed in her very finest clothing: a yellow floating dress studded with jewels that rose decently (but only just) across her bosom (the bosom having been freshly powdered and perfumed by her attendants—it was the sort of attention to detail that would secure many a man).

"I am so glad that we are chaperoned, madam, for I fear I would not be able to control my manly desires." He let out a small groan beneath his breath.

Statilia giggled, her hand to her mouth.

"I am afraid, madam, that I cannot stay long." Her smile faded. "Unfortunately I am summoned by the emperor but I just could not resist the opportunity to pay my respects to you." He took her hand and kissed it. "I hope that I shall have the pleasure of your company again."

"Later? Today?" Statilia asked quickly. "If you are available that is," she added more smoothly.

"I would be delighted," he said, kissing her hand again. "I shall take your smile into my meeting with Galba. When they start talking budgets I shall bring it to the forefront of my mind to cheer me."

Statilia Messalina gave a longing smile. "Marcus," she simpered, "please have dinner with me."

"How could I resist such a sweet invitation? I shall be there."

He gave her another chaste kiss to the hand before he took his leave. Turning once at the door as an afterthought he gazed at her, a sweeping gaze that brought goose bumps to her arms and a shiver down her spine.

Following him out Mina said, "Sir, those letters. I would really like to read them. It would mean a lot to me."

"Of course, Artemina. I shall have Onomastus deliver them to you."

Walking down the corridor Otho muttered out of the side of his mouth, "Onomastus, do you think you could put something together?"

"Composing the sentiment already, sir."

Icelus pottered around the room moving chairs and overwhelming Talos with orders. He greeted Otho with clear dislike, a curl forming on his thin lips.

"What are you doing here?"

"I'm here for the budgetary meeting. Can I sit here?" he asked Talos. "This looks the most comfortable chair, or does the emperor get the comfy chair? I confess I am out of touch with palace etiquette these days. Under Nero we'd all lie on couches and naked girls would whirl round dear old Seneca as he read his reports. I can never think of that great man without recalling those twirling tassels."

Talos, a teenage boy with all the interests that entailed, was fascinated by this tale. "Did they really sir?" he cooed, thinking it was just his luck to be born ten years too late.

"Oh yes, young laddie, it's all true. Happy days," he mused. Then he clapped his hands. "So when does it begin because I could whip down and talk to Diomedius about the whirling girls?"

"You are not part of this meeting," said Icelus coldly.

Otho looked around him. "I sort of am, dear chap. I've brought my own scribe and everything." Onomastus waved a stylus.

Icelus attempted to contain his temper which was increasingly strained these days. "You are not part of the emperor's consortium."

"I am his number one fan," said Otho genially. "I think I should be here."

"You may think that. But facts are facts."

"Facts? I'll go see little Philo, he'll sort out this terrible error. It's probably all administrative-related stuff. No, don't worry, Icelus, I am sure it can all be sorted out. Laddie, can you save a seat for me?"

Talos, who'd not been exposed to Otho before, nodded eagerly and plonked himself down.

Pushing open the door without knocking, Otho walked straight in on a couple entwined in a rather passionate embrace. "Philo! You have a blonde hanging from your lip," he cried in mock outrage.

The freedman hastily disconnected from Teretia, retrieving a stray hand from her breast which it had been happily massaging. They looked extraordinarily guilty, like small children caught stealing food before supper. Otho would have laughed but Philo was a sensitive type and he could not afford to upset him. So he smiled understandingly. "Marcus Salvius Otho, delighted to meet you."

The little cracker was pink with embarrassment and mute, so he looked to Philo.

"This is Teretia. Teretia this is Otho. He was governor of Lusitania." Then realising this would mean nothing to her he added, "Otho was a close friend of Nero's."

"Before he stole my wife and had me banished."

"Oh, how awful for you," sympathised Teretia.

"Actually it was. She was a lovely girl, Poppaea. Full of life, spirit. I loved her very much. But that is all past now. I won't delay you two long. I am sure there is much you would rather be doing then talking to old Otho." He gave a saucy wink at the girl who giggled a little and lowered her eyes.

"How can I help?" asked Philo back in official mode.

"This consortium thingy, am I on it?"

"No."

"Why not? I think I'd be great at it. I have loads of ideas about rebuilding Rome. I could be a very positive presence."

"Sorry, but it's not my decision."

"Really? I thought you were the man with the plan. Everyone keeps telling me how important you are to the palace."

Philo blinked before answering, "Icelus decides."

"Urgh, shame. He says I'm not in."

"Sorry, Otho."

"I don't seem to be in on any of these meetings."

"Icelus' and Laco's orders."

"Oh. I wonder why. I can't think what I have done to upset them, apart from throw my time and money at making their master emperor." He pulled a hurt face.

"Philo, that doesn't seem fair," said Teretia, pawing at his arm.

Faced with Teretia's and Otho's sad looks, Philo folded. "Talk to Titus Vinius. He needs an ally. Laco and Icelus are very tight."

"Thank you, Philo and delighted to meet you, Teretia," beamed Otho.

Outside the door he turned to Onomastus. "Titus Vinius?"

The dwarf smiled, opened his cloak, and pulled out a scroll. "I have a full profile of him here, sir."

Teretia straightened her attire. She'd only popped in to show Philo the dress material for Silvia's possible wedding. Philo expressed a clear preference for the blue. Giving him a thank you peck on the lips developed into a full-on snog and then became rather more heated, and if Otho had not walked in …

"I like him," she said. "He seems a nice man."

"Hmm."

Philo possessed clear memories of Otho during the high (or low depending on your view) days of Nero's reign.

"So you like the blue for my dress? I shall take it to Canutus today."

"No don't do that. I'll get Daphne to make it for you, she is a whizz with a needle. She made this tunic."

"She won't mind?"

Daphne was a slave; minding didn't come into it. Actually Daphne was pleased with her assignment, touched by Philo's gentle fussing over Teretia. Requesting that Daphne bring the girl back safely after her fitting and that if he wasn't there she should get Talos to summon a slave to escort Teretia home.

Taking Teretia to the slave complex, Daphne was bombarded by questions as to when her baby was due, and was her husband looking forward to it, and did she have any names chosen? She was so well meaning that Daphne did not want to hurt her with the truth, so she swallowed the tears that always came when she thought about the baby and told Teretia that she was hoping for a girl.

Really it didn't matter what "it" was. "It" would be taken away the moment it left her body. In the early days of her pregnancy that had seemed desirable. Now she wasn't so sure and as the birth date came closer she became consumed by a growing dread.

"I would so love a baby," Teretia told her as Daphne measured her up.

"With Philo?" Daphne asked as she pulled a tape measure around Teretia's sizeable bust.

"Oh yes, of course."

Teretia bit her lip, worried that she'd revealed too much. Philo had been rather upset when he found out she'd told her mother that they had slept together.

"But I tell my mother everything," she'd said to Philo's horrified face. He mentally scrapped the request he'd been about to make regarding a certain two-piece leather bathing suit.

She didn't dare tell him that she, her mother, and her aunt had dissected the whole event over the kitchen table. Teretia was glad she'd told her mother, for both she and her aunt were able to offer her plenty of good advice regarding her new sex life. They told her which parts of him she should touch to encourage him and ways she could make it more comfortable for them both; tips which had made her and Philo's subsequent encounters less awkward and bordering on pleasurable.

"Is the dress for a special occasion?"

"A wedding."

"Yours?" squeaked Daphne excitedly, thinking the laundry girls would love this. "You and Philo?"

"Oh no, no, it is Silvia's wedding."

"Silvia?"

"Epaphroditus and Aphrodite's daughter. She is marrying Martinus. Philo and I have been invited to the wedding. It's going to be terribly posh."

"I shall make a dress to suit, don't worry," smiled Daphne, thinking that Silvia no doubt had to marry to secure her family in the wake of her father's death.

"Daphne, Daphne, emergency!" Mina burst in.

"Oh blimey. What?"

Mina looked Teretia up and down. Turning to Daphne she asked rudely, "Who is this?"

"Don't be nasty, Mina. This is Teretia and I am measuring her up for a gown."

"Terrreeetiaaa," Mina rolled the name off her tongue. "Philo's Teretia? Are you Philo's Teretia?" she asked, speaking to her as if she were a particularly dim-witted child.

"Yes she is, leave her alone. What's the emergency?"

"The empress' dress for her dinner with Otho; the beads have fallen off. She is going mental. She asked for you personally."

Daphne sighed and put her kit down, "I have your measurements, Teretia. When is the wedding?"

"The day before the nones," Teretia replied shyly, unnerved by Mina's brazen confidence.

"I will have it ready by then," Daphne smiled at her.

"Thank you. You have been so very kind. I am sure it will be just perfect."

Mina rolled her eyes. Gods, Philo's girlfriend was wet. Whatever did he see in this damp little thing? Especially when he could have had her. A fact that was ever so slightly denting her pride. Daphne, sensing her dangerous mood, tried to hurry Teretia out of the way of a Mina maelstrom.

"Come on, I'll take you back to Philo before I go and sort out the empress' dress."

"Why are you making a gown for her anyway?" Mina asked Daphne, snubbing Teretia entirely.

"She is going to Epaphroditus' daughter's wedding."

"Are you?" Mina fixed Teretia.

"I am," she said, uncomfortable under Mina's gaze. "If it goes ahead. Silvia keeps changing her mind."

"Oh dear," Daphne sympathised, imagining Silvia forced into an unhappy marriage because of their desperate financial circumstances.

Teretia, reassured by Daphne's comforting presence confided, "It has all been very stressful. Philo says Epaphroditus is very wound up about it. He is thinking of banning his other girls from marriage entirely."

Unaware of the great revelation contained within that statement, Teretia prattled on happily about the complicated wedding arrangements.

Mina butted in urgently, "What did you say?"

Teretia looked at her innocently. "About what?"

"About Epaphroditus? What did you say about Epaphroditus?" She grasped hold of her arm, Teretia wriggling to get away.

"Mina," warned Daphne stepping in between them.

"Ask her what she means."

"I don't know what I've done to make you cross," said a tearful Teretia. "I didn't mean to. I am sorry, Mina. I should go, Philo will be waiting."

"Teretia, it's alright," smoothed Daphne, putting her arm around her and sitting her down. "We are just a little confused. You say Epaphroditus is going to be at the wedding?"

Teretia nodded.

"You've seen Epaphroditus? Recently? Since Nero died?"

Teretia shook her head.

"But Philo has?" pressed Daphne gently.

Teretia nodded, adding quietly, "They meet most days."

Mina gasped. "Daphne! He's alive!"

NINETEEN

Mina sprinted to the Esquiline. Epaphroditus' home backed onto the new palace so she fled down corridors, across numerous courtyards, through the colonnade by the lake, past the huge golden statue of Nero that nobody had thought to remove yet, and down endless cultivated gardens until she reached the Esquiline exit. There she found herself on a quiet street facing the unobtrusive walls of his house.

From the outside it didn't look like much: drab, small even. But from the street you could not see the acres it backed onto, or the expansive gardens that were situated within its interior. It was the house that Epaphroditus had built for Aphrodite and it only just escaped annihilation during the great fire of five years previously.

Luckily Epaphroditus' coinage bought the attention of the vigiles who deigned to put out the fire. That disaster over, Epaphroditus then faced a determined Nero who wished to demolish his home and use the space for the new palace. It took a great deal of Epaphroditus' skilled machinations to save the house he so adored. Mina walked up to the grey door and banged on it with her fists.

Hearing from Callista that there was a girl asking to see him, Epaphroditus was both intrigued and worried. For his slave's disdainful tone informed him exactly what she felt about the visitor.

He told Callista to take her through to one of the public rooms at the front of the house, a room Aphrodite was unlikely to wander into. Callista, though stoic of expression, showed her disapproval for the order by asking, "Shall I tell the mistress to expect one extra for dinner?"

A sarcasm that caused Epaphroditus to have her soundly thrashed for insubordination.

Mina, pacing the small room, felt her heart beating at her chest. She shouldn't be here. The empress thought she was ill. If she checked her room, Mina would be for it. She'd told Daphne not to make excuses for her: in her condition she would not withstand a beating.

Under pressure from her room-mate she'd reluctantly apologised to Teretia, Daphne hissing to her, "If not for the fact that she didn't deserve your tongue then because she's Philo's girlfriend and I imagine he will be very upset at you if you upset her."

Philo's displeasure was not much of a threat but Mina admitted he was a decent sort and decent sorts were in short supply in the palace. Teretia wasn't so bad. Yes, she was a bit wet but on the walk back she showed herself to be extremely kind-hearted, apologising for shocking Mina with her news and hoping she would forgive her. Which she would of course, for it would be hard to hold a grudge against Teretia; like slapping a particularly cute kitten. They'd almost parted on good terms, though to Mina's mind she would have been the far better lay of the two of them.

No matter, Epaphroditus was alive, fully alive. Which he proved by entering the room, stopping, and asking, clearly surprised, "Artemina?"

She threw herself at him, alternately laughing and crying and kissing him all over his face. He held her in his arms automatically, a hand naturally straying to her rear before remembering where he was. He disconnected her arms from his neck and pushed her gently away.

"Artemina, what are you doing here?"

"I thought you were dead! We all thought you were dead," she cried, her nose running most unattractively. "I can't believe it. I have missed you so much. It has been so awful."

She attached herself to him, leaning her head on his shoulder, needing comfort after everything that had happened in the last four months.

He stroked her hair to calm her. "Artemina," he cooed quietly. "It's OK, it's all OK. We'll get you sorted and I'll get one of the slaves to take you back to the palace."

She snuffled into him and he rubbed her back, caressing a bit too low to be considered merely for comfort.

A cheery exclamation from the doorway interrupted them. "What is it about today?" cried Otho.

Epaphroditus gently removed Mina, sitting her down.

Otho grinned. "I walked in on your little assistant with his hand down some beauty's dress and now here you are fiddling with the staff. There is evidently some magnetism I am missing."

"You caught Philo with a girl? Well I hope it was Teretia."

Otho looked from Epaphroditus to Mina and then back again.

"You said he was dead this morning," Mina aimed at Otho.

"I don't think I did. I think I said I had some nice letters from him when I was in Lusitania. And I did, and here they are."

Onomastus handed over a pile of scrolls with a flourish and a grin. Epaphroditus looked quizzically at Otho who simply smiled. Mina, the scrolls piled up in her arms, told

Epaphroditus, "I shall treasure these, always," and kissed him on the cheek.

"Perhaps you should go back to the palace and read them there," he suggested, gently angling her out.

"You will come see me though?"

"I can't, Artemina, not at the palace."

"I could come here."

Epaphroditus, knowing how Aphrodite would feel about that replied, "Not possible."

Otho, watching this touching scene, said, "What you need is a place that is neither of your homes. How about my house? It is very conveniently located."

Epaphroditus shot him a glare for interfering; Mina thought it the best idea ever.

"You will send word?" she asked as he escorted her out.

"'Course,' course," he muttered.

Mistress safely disposed of, Epaphroditus asked Otho, "What is in those scrolls?"

"Some rather pleasing sentiment. She'll gush over them."

"I don't want her to gush over me. She is becoming too attached."

"Now that is heartless. Lovely girl like that. She's been devastated thinking you were dead. When I saw her this morning she was in tears, tears at your demise."

Epaphroditus walked him through to the study, Onomastus following at a discreet pace behind.

"Tell me how things progress," he demanded briskly.

Otho, unused to making reports palace-style replied dreamily, "I am having dinner with the empress tonight. I don't mind saying that I am pretty smitten. I could pass a message to Artemina for a proposed rendezvous if you like."

"I am not rendezvousing anywhere."

"Still sore is it? I brought this for you." He handed him a jar. "My doctor says it will totally clear it up, hundred per cent guaranteed."

142

"Your plans?" insisted Epaphroditus, taking the jar anyway.

"Progressing. I went to see Titus Vinius on the suggestion of Philo. I feel a bit sorry for him."

"Philo?"

"No, Titus Vinius. Philo is a very lucky man that Teretia is …" Otho licked his lips, sitting himself down. "They bully him, Laco and Icelus. They have formed their own pact and shout down any reasonable suggestion he makes. Of course Galba naturally sides with them as the majority. Poor lad. I rather liked him. He's a bit stolid but fair I think. A positive asset."

"Friend to Tigellinus," threw in Epaphroditus, watching Otho's expression fall.

"Oh dear, is he? Now that is a failing."

"He is useful though. How did you get on?"

"Great. Like buddies and, boy, does he need one. Though if I'd known he was buddy to that man, I would not have bothered. The upshot is that he is going to bring up the question of an heir to Galba."

"He is going to bring up your name?"

"No, I took your advice on that one. The thing has to naturally occur to Galba. He has to think it was his idea even if Vinius pushes a little on my behalf."

"Good, good. It would help if Laco and Icelus were discredited, then Vinius' lone voice would carry more weight."

"No doubt you have an idea," yawned Otho, stretching in his chair. "Personally I am fagged out by all this scheming. Mind if I have a kip here before I head out for my date with the empress?"

Epaphroditus wasn't ready to let him go. "What did you promise Vinius?"

"Who said I promised him anything?"

"Marcus," he smiled. "It is admirable that particular quality you possess; wanting everyone to be happy. 'Fess up. What did you promise him?"

Otho, eyes closed, said, "Apparently he has a very lovely daughter of marriageable age. She quite fancies being empress. All the pretty frocks and that."

"What about Statilia Messalina? I thought it was true love."

Otho waved a hand. "I'll sort it out later."

This amused Epaphroditus immensely. "And you mutter about my private life!"

"Are all matters concluded?" asked Galba, shifting uncomfortably on his chair.

His back was extremely painful today. His hands were caught in painful spasms. Both no doubt from the change in weather. Cold made his afflictions worse. If duty allowed, he would relax in a heated bath. That always soothed his aching limbs. He could sign papers then if necessary. The Emperor Augustus would work as his hair was cut or whilst enjoying the games: it was an example Galba was keen to emulate.

Despite his ailments, despite his age, he insisted on finishing things before he retired for the night, even if that meant but a few hours' sleep. Galba had been a soldier. Barbarians having no respect for tiredness he always slept on edge and was awakened by the slightest sound.

Things, he felt, were going well. The senate was a great support to him, regaining some of the confidence that had been knocked out of it by his predecessor. He allowed them to have their say on points even if he did not personally agree, and they were beginning to lose the obsequiousness that so disgusted him on his return to Rome.

A dignified, strong senate should not cause an emperor fear. They should be a team; a partnership in government. It helped that he had brought in his own advisors: Laco, Icelus, and Vinius; dispensing with the palace freedmen who caused so much trouble under Nero and whom the senate viewed with suspicion.

His plan was to recruit equestrians to the higher posts in the administration, fostering a spirit of cooperation between the ranks. He wanted those well-bred families to offer their sons as servants to the state, for it to be a respectable career once more. There was to be no more hotbed palace politics of shifting alliances and stabbed backs. Let there be open, honest debate. Laudable aims.

Galba was not to know that his well-chosen advisors sold his audiences to the highest bidder or that Icelus and Laco were busy appropriating the more glittering palace contents, ordering slaves to carry them to their private homes. If he had known, perhaps the world would have turned out a different way.

"There is one matter, Caesar," said Vinius, earning hard looks from his colleagues who had expected there to be no other business.

Avoiding Laco's and Icelus' glares, he looked straight at Galba. "There is the question of an heir, Caesar."

"Really, Titus," drawled Laco. "This is hardly the time. We have far too much to do in Rome. The issue can sit."

"Nero let the issue sit," persisted Vinius. "It led to plots. He wiped out his entire family lest some disgruntled louse see them as a replacement. Clarity is required, Caesar, for the senate and the people's peace of mind."

Vinius had practised this short speech several times before delivery. He knew his colleagues would be eager to spot and shout down any flaws.

"It is a fair point," said Galba slowly. "The position of Statilia Messalina also needs clarification. I shall give it my consideration. Thank you all. I shall be in my rooms should I be required."

Icelus froze. Surely he wasn't going to marry Statilia? It was the proper, dutiful thing to do, which would appeal to Galba's sense of decency. When he was a young man, Galba had been briefly married to the noble Lepida. She bore two sons, both of whom died, followed shortly after by their mother.

Icelus never knew Lepida, Galba having purchased him during his long widowhood. The other slaves told him that their master was so devoted to her that he could not contemplate marriage to another. It was a great line that had served Galba well.

From the age of twenty, Icelus had known it for the screen it was for his master's true tastes. Marrying Statilia Messalina would scotch those rumours, which since his return to Rome had begun to flourish again. Icelus was struck by a vision of being banished from Galba's side, hidden away to appease the gossips. It was not a happy thought.

"What do you think that was all about?" Laco asked, breaking into Icelus' thoughts.

"What?"

"Vinius, the question of an heir. Most unlike dear Titus. I doubt he has ever had an original thought in that wooden block he calls a head."

"What are you talking about, Cornelius?"

"I don't know yet," mused Laco. "I shall do a bit of digging and then you and I should meet."

A distracted Icelus waved him away, keen to follow Galba and cement his position in his favours.

TWENTY

"**A**nd you are?" the woman asked, peering down her nose at them.

"Philo."

"Philo works for the emperor," Teretia supplied.

"Oh, so you're a slave," the woman replied with a wrinkling of her nose.

A hot-faced Teretia had looked set to interject, had Epaphroditus not smoothed his way over and extradited them calmly. He took them to safety within a large dining room that was bustling with the rushing of slaves and a mingling of guests.

"Martinus' mother," he told them. "She likes my money well enough but she disapproves of the connection."

"What a rude woman," huffed Teretia. "How dare she?"

Philo stroked her arm. "Ignore it, it doesn't bother me, honestly darling."

Darling? Epaphroditus hid his smile. Teretia was positively glowing. Dressed in a beautiful sapphire gown that showed off her figure to its best advantage, her hair rolled up into a fashionable court style, a gold and bead necklace with matching dangling earrings completing the outfit.

But it was more than that. Epaphroditus had always thought her a rather sweet girl but today she was calmer, more polished. Somebody had turned her into a woman.

"Is everything set for the wedding?" she asked eagerly, her eyes sparkling, one arm linked onto Philo's.

Epaphroditus gave a wan smile in response. Though the majority of his life had been spent negotiating tricky politics, his daughter's wedding proved the most stressful settlement he had ever made. Frankly, he would rather have taken on the Parthians than Martinus' parents.

They'd demanded a wholly unreasonable dowry, reminding him of their name and what it would mean to his family. He talked them down a little but they were obstinate, stubborn snobs and he found them unwilling to fall for his charms. They saw both he and Aphrodite as some lesser species, a sentiment that grated. Each time they met for negotiations Epaphroditus had found himself grinding his teeth, returning home to Aphrodite with an aching jaw and palms littered with nail marks from clenched fists. Silvia and Martinus had better be blissfully happy!

"Is Silvia excited?" Teretia asked.

"She has been lording it over her sister all morning, rubbing in how her new status will elevate her. It has been rather trying." Epaphroditus rubbed a thumb across his forehead at the memory of having to physically haul an irate Faustina from the room while Silvia pulled faces at her.

A slave whipped round with a silver platter, angling it towards them. Philo and Teretia helped themselves to some morsels, Teretia unable to stop herself complimenting the slave who looked at her with shock.

The food was delicious. Small appetizers before the main wedding feast which was due to take place in Epaphroditus' large banqueting hall. Though Epaphroditus owned his own musicians, he'd hired in some additions to make a truly impressive-sized band that were due to play for the guests' pleasure later on. There were also jugglers, Silvia's request, some dancing animals to amuse the younger guests, and a poet for the more serious-minded.

Old Emperor Augustus had once limited the amount of money that could be spent on weddings to 1,000 sesterces. Nobody had paid much attention to the law back then. Epaphroditus had spent over ten times as much on Silvia and Martinus' wedding. The groom's family had contributed nothing, believing that the stature their presence commanded was all that was required. This lack of involvement also gave them free rein to criticise the arrangements, which they were already doing. Gathered in small groups, they were pointing and looking down long noses at Epaphroditus' younger children who were running around the guests in delirious over-excitement.

"Epaphroditus, chum." Otho bounded over full of enthusiasm, a serene Statilia Messalina holding onto his arm.

To Epaphroditus' joy he saw Martinus' parents exchange shocked but impressed looks which almost warmed him to the ex-empress.

"Statilia, you are looking very beautiful today."

"Isn't she just," burst in Otho with pride. "We've absconded from the palace for the day. It took all my ingenuity to get her out."

"It was a masterful plan, Marcus," smiled Statilia. "But we won't repeat it lest we need to employ it again." She looked pointedly at Philo as the sole palace representative.

"Not my department," he muttered under her gaze.

"So, Epaphroditus," she continued, "this must be hard for you, losing your daughter to marriage? She is your eldest?"

"Yes," he replied quietly, Statilia hitting several sore points at once.

"No doubt you have selected your son-in-law carefully. My mother is a very good friend of his mother's. I am so glad that Martinus has sorted himself out. He was such a worry at one point."

Bitch, thought Epaphroditus smiling genially nonetheless.

Otho, sensing the atmosphere took her arm. "Madam, let us mingle and make the most of your freedom."

He led her off, Epaphroditus' eyes boring into her back.

"Are you OK, sir?"

"Philo, you don't have to call me sir any more and I am fine. It's just …" he sighed, remembering the day Silvia was born.

She was such a small, pink thing. Aphrodite holding her up for his approval, he had felt a rush of love for her. They sat together staring at her for hours, marvelling over her tiny fingernails and the soft creases in her palms.

"It's amazing, how all this was going on in there," he had told Aphrodite, patting her stomach affectionately. Now that little girl, his little girl, was getting married, leaving his home, and moving in with her new family.

"He's a good boy, Martinus. He'll look after her."

"Of course he will," Teretia agreed enthusiastically. "They will be extremely happy."

He gave her an appreciative smile, "Thank you, Teretia." He reflected that this pleb daughter of a builder was a far better woman than the well-bred widow of an emperor.

Aphrodite swept in looking harried. She rushed over to her husband, kissing him on the cheek, and announcing, "It is all in hand. Silvia is ready. We should take our seats."

It was a short, simple ceremony. The bridal couple at the front of the room. Silvia dressed in traditional scarlet with her hair tied in plaits, looking round for her family who gave her supportive smiles. A pale Martinus standing stiffly beside her. They both looked so young, too young thought Epaphroditus. He should have waited a couple of years before looking into marriage. Aphrodite squeezed his hand, whispering, "It will be fine. They will be fine."

He nearly stood up when he heard Silvia's voice break on her chant of, "When-and-where-you-are Gaius, I-then-and-there-am Gaia," so desperate was he to offer her comfort, but

Aphrodite weighted him down by handing him Rufus to hold. And then it was over. She was married.

The libations to the household gods were completed, a sheep sacrificed, and the guests were led by slaves to the wedding banquet. The food that Aphrodite had fretted over was utterly devoured, Phaon taking the time to compliment her on the wine selection.

"Mamertine. Excellent choice, Aphrodite," he had smiled, ordering a slave to top up his goblet for more of that delicious nectar.

Faustina trudged around moodily, jealous of all the attention Silvia was attracting, before collapsing in her bedroom and declaring that it was just all too boring for her and could somebody wake her when something interesting happened.

Otho set to charming Statilia Messalina with outstanding success. This triumph being a little too easily granted, he turned his attention to Martinus' sour-faced mother. By the final course she was declaring him, "A very nicely brought-up boy," and discounting all those debauchery rumours linked to his name. She even went as far as to comment that she had one daughter as yet unmarried, earning a furious stare from Statilia who cuddled into Otho so that there could be no mistaking her territory. An action that Otho rather enjoyed.

Philo and Teretia sat discreetly holding hands under the table and talking exclusively to each other, seemingly with an endless list of fascinating topics to discuss. Epaphroditus, seeing his wife viewing this sweet little scene, snuck up behind her and kissed her on the back of her neck, wrapping his arms around her.

"Well, whatever you said to him seems to have worked. I counted two sweeties, three darlings, and four dears."

"And from Teretia?" smiled Epaphroditus.

A few days prior, Philo had appeared in their atrium. After holing up in his study, talking round subjects, Epaphroditus grew aware that his companion was clearly trying to build up to something. After a few glasses of wine the atmosphere was amiable enough for Philo to announce rather solemnly, "I want to make Teretia happy."

"A very laudable aim and one which I am sure you will achieve."

"No, I mean, I want to make her happy. In bed. I thought you would, you would know things."

He did indeed know things, soothing the embarrassed freedman. Epaphroditus gave a fairly comprehensive lecture on women and their physiology. Though Philo didn't quite whip out his note tablet, he could see the young man mentally recording each point.

From the way Teretia hung off his arm and from the small secret looks they kept exchanging, Epaphroditus guessed he'd put at least some of it into practice.

"It is rather cute, isn't it? Were we ever so soppy?"

"Never. You were a remarkably serious young girl."

"I was not!" she protested.

Her husband turned her round, giving her a peck on the lips. "I distinctly remember that when I suggested we could perhaps meet outside of work, you turned to me and said, 'Do you have prospects?'"

"I did not!" she squawked, though she knew it to be true. A fact she betrayed by adding, "I had heard an awful lot about you. I was on my guard."

It was partly because she was so singularly unimpressed by him at their first meetings that Epaphroditus pursued her so diligently. That and because he was utterly smitten by her.

Some hours later it was time for the happy couple to depart from the bridal home to the home of Martinus' family, their now merry and rather full guests following. Silvia was at the front of this procession: one boy holding her left hand, one boy her right, and a third boy walking in front of her holding the flaming torch that would be used to light the hearth of her new home.

Silvia's parents walked arm-in-arm surrounded by their children who bustled noisily alongside them. They earned a hard stare from Martinus' mother who glared over her shoulder at them. Rufus, held in Faustina's arms, stuck his tongue out at her, causing a fit of giggles among the girls. Epaphroditus slapped them across their heads, warning them to behave.

"I wouldn't do it," scorned Statilia.

"Do what, madam?"

"Sell my son and my name for money. They're strapped for cash, mother says. Of course, nobody has any money these days aside from the palace slaves. I do approve of these measures Galba is taking to recoup money to the treasury. It is time that our kind reclaimed our rightful position in the state."

"Quite," said Otho, adding cheekily, "Madam, I would ensure any son of ours was married well to a perfect little well-bred peach of a girl who will supply us with happy, bouncing grandchildren."

Statilia Messalina felt her heart quicken and her cheeks pinken.

At Martinus' family home, a much less splendid house than the bridal party's, there were a series of sad partings. Aphrodite, embracing her daughter, wept a little, as did Silvia. Epaphroditus held a check on his emotions, telling her, "I am so proud of you." Which prompted more tears from his teenage daughter.

"Just think," he told her. "You can come visit us in a couple of days as a married woman. It means we will have to wait on you. I could get Faustina to pass the nibbles."

Silvia laughed through her tears and hugged him tight. He let her go, handing her over to her husband under whose power she now sat.

It was a sad little procession back to the house, Aphrodite weepy and even Faustina unusually pensive.

"You look like you need a drink," Otho, walking alongside Epaphroditus commented. "Come to mine. We'll drink ourselves stupid and demolish the mother of the groom's character. I've extracted some juicy titbits for your enjoyment from Statilia."

Seeing a sad Aphrodite clutching a sleepy Julia tight to her bosom, Epaphroditus declined.

"Another time," suggested Otho. "I want to bring you up to date on some matters that concern us both."

"Otho for emperor," chanted Epaphroditus.

"Otho for emperor."

Mina was annoyed. She had hoped the empress would return with news of Epaphroditus. Instead she drifted in with Otho. Mina enduring a nauseating parting, all the more so because it was so chaste. The sauciest it got was Otho gently kissing Statilia's hand and declaring her to be the best of women. Then Statilia had sat on a couch staring dreamily into space, a smile on her face as her attendants undressed her. She went to bed without speaking a word. Mina kicked the leg of the bed in frustration before being dismissed.

She'd waited days for word from Epaphroditus, haranguing Otho for news, hoping that he was an intermediary, but he had nothing and Mina was not in the mood for his charms.

It was not just that she ached for him physically, though by lovely Juno above she did desperately, nor that she fancied herself in love. Rather, something important had occurred to her and she needed to talk to Epaphroditus about it. She was a little ashamed that she had not thought of it earlier.

She was halfway through Otho's scrolls, lying on her stomach and reading the most flattering descriptions of herself out loud to Daphne when she suddenly sat up. If Epaphroditus were alive, could Sporus be too?

A thought she raced down to share with Alex, who was not excited in the slightest and seemed displeased with her. But then he was always annoyed with her these days. If he wasn't grumbling about Straton or Vinius (oh yes, he had found out all about that) then he was hanging around outside the empress' quarters seemingly solely to bend her ear about what people were saying about her. Really she had much more fun with Straton these days.

Well, screw him. Epaphroditus clearly thought something of her: his words to Otho had greatly moved her. She had not thought him so romantic. He'd never brought her a present or even taken her out of the palace. But she knew now, thanks to Otho, this was due to his complete infatuation with her and how he had fought against his deepening emotions by engaging with her for only short periods of time. She was dying to see him to assure him that his feelings were very much reciprocated.

She itched for all this but she itched more for Sporus. Was he alive? Could it be possible? The thoughts tumbled over and over in her mind. Epaphroditus was alive but Nero was dead. Mina could well imagine her friend throwing himself onto the funeral pyre with his beloved, shrieking and crying in full dramatic fashion. Yet Epaphroditus had survived that final journey and that gave her hope. It also begged another question: if Sporus were alive, where had he been all this time?

TWENTY-ONE

In the end, it was so absurdly easy that Sporus kicked himself for not attempting to escape months earlier.

He chose the day the cloth merchant visited with his latest silks. The Galli rushed round him oohing and aahing at the floating fabrics, pawing at the material, and outbidding each other in squeaky, excited voices. Sporus, seeing them distracted, even the Arch Gallus who was having a whole roll of green cloth wound round him (it took that much), scampered to his room. He retrieved the sacrificial knife from underneath his pillow, threw off his red dress with a hint of regret, for red really was his colour, and pulled on the brown, itchy tunic he had arrived in. He fingered the material sadly, a spot of Nero's blood still evident on the chest.

Tying his long hair back, he snuck through the corridors to the garden. He ran full pelt through the pleasant shrubbery to the wall at the back. Catching his breath, he grabbed hold of the ivy that covered the brickwork and used it to climb his way up.

It was possibly the most energetic act he had ever committed. His arms burned from the effort and his feet scrabbled and scraped on the bricks. But the thought of freedom from those whirling nutters gave him the necessary spur. Reaching the top with grazed knuckles and knees he was horrified to find there was nothing to help him climb down the other side; just a straight drop to the cobbled road beneath.

Sitting on the edge with his legs dangling down, Sporus felt sure he would be killed from the fall. He looked anxiously about hoping for a passer-by to cushion his landing, but there was no one about.

Gazing upwards he intoned, "Mercury, messenger for the gods, you have those lovely winged sandals. It would be wonderful, really wonderful if when I jump you could whizz over, catch me, and gently lower me to the earth. In return I swear to make you my favourite god and I will sacrifice twenty pigs, fifty goats, and pour you a river of wine. Honest. Promise."

He took a deep breath, closed his eyes, and pushed himself off the wall.

From the point of view of Pompeia and Teretia who were walking across the Palatine after accompanying Philo to work, the boy dropped from the heavens with a thud and then a scream.

"Oh my word!" exclaimed Pompeia, gazing down at Sporus who was rolling on his back, clutching his leg and squealing.

She bent down and asked the somewhat superfluous question, "Are you hurt?"

"Mercury, you total bastard!"

Teretia, gazing down at the shrieking creature lying on the cobbles suddenly recognised him and pawed at Pompeia's arm. "Mother, mother, it's the Sporus."

The eunuch, with tears in his eyes, looked up at that serene countenance and cried, "Teretia, Teretia, help me please!"

"Oh come on, Philo," pleaded Lysander, his palms on the desk. "I just want to know what it's like."

Philo, piling up wax tablets, frowned and told his former room-mate for the seventh time so far, "No."

He handed the pile to Talos telling him, "Take these down to the archives please."

"OK, now he's gone you can tell me."

"I said no."

"I'd tell you."

"I wouldn't want to hear."

"Why not?"

"Because," Philo flapped his hands, "because it's private."

Lysander's obsession with freeborn girls had not diminished with his manumission. He'd been disappointed to discover that securing one was not as easy as he had supposed. He couldn't quite work out where he was going wrong. He'd rented a flashy apartment on the Viminal a few streets away from Philo. Astounded to find it near double the size of Pompeia's, Philo assumed that Lysander was up to something he ought not to have been.

Actually Lysander had discovered moneylending and had run up credit with a gaggle of bankers knowing he could pay it off once he acquired a large dowry. Except that was proving difficult. He'd talked up his association with the emperor in all the local shops, offered his most charming smile to all passing pretty girls and their mothers, and let it be known in the neighbourhood that he was a very important man. All to no avail. None of the girls even returned his smiles.

He just couldn't understand why. He was good looking. He had a good job. He even had a bit of money. All in all he was a damn good catch. They should be throwing themselves at him, their fathers should be tossing them his way.

Having been somewhat overused in the breeding programme, Lysander was finding celibacy hard. He had waylaid Philo for salacious details on Teretia to satisfy his more lurid fantasies as to what freebies were like. Only Philo was refusing to divulge.

"All I want to know is whether she's moist down there, because slave girls never are. They can't produce it. It's a physiological thing," he told Philo sagely before prompting, "Well, is she? Wet before you go for it?"

Philo busied himself stacking up scrolls, wishing Lysander would get bored and leave him alone.

"I need to know," pleaded Lysander desperately. "It's so bloody unfair that you should bag one. It should be me banging some big-titted freebie."

"Hey!" protested Philo, upset at having the best thing that had ever happened to him described as a big-titted freebie.

"OK, OK, sorry if I offended. Just tell me one thing. Is it different with a freebie than a slave? You don't have to tell me any details, just yes or no." He looked hopefully at Philo who turned away to concentrate on packing away some further paperwork.

Lysander sighed heavily and reminded him of all the times he had shared details of his conquests (much against Philo's will and solely in order to torture him).

"Don't you have work to do?"

"Not really. I've finished training my trainees for the day. They are absolutely hopeless. I couldn't take it any more. I packed them off to the slave complex to contemplate their pronunciation of Pontus Polemoniacus."

"Is that something they are likely to have to announce?" asked Philo.

"What if the governor of Pontus Polemoniacus made an unexpected visit?" suggested Lysander. "You have to be prepared, always. Crucially important in announcing."

Lysander was boastful. He was arrogant. He was conceited. And he suffered from a severe case of self-importance. But he was Philo's best and only friend since childhood. Philo felt duty-bound to like him, though even he admitted that some days it was a struggle.

He looked so sad this evening that Philo offered him a little piece of advice, saying quietly, "When you hang around the bathhouse winking, the local girls think you're some kind of pervert."

He'd heard so from one of Teretia's cousins. They even had a nickname for him but Philo felt Lysander did not need to hear that. He looked hurt enough already, his mouth opening in shock at this news.

"Philo, what is the meaning of this!" Icelus stood in the doorway of his office flapping a tablet. "Why is Otho's name on this list? He is not on that committee." He jabbed an angry finger at the relevant line. "He has no right being there. What is it with that man? Everywhere I turn is bloody Otho! I go to pay my respects to the emperor and bloody Otho is there sipping cordial. Laco and I inspect the Praetorians and bloody Otho is lounging around throwing dice with them. I go to the senate and bloody Otho is talking to Regulus like they're long-lost buddies. And now that bloody man is on the bloody committee. Is there no escaping him?"

Philo, glancing behind him noted that true to form Lysander had legged it at the first sign of unpleasantness, took a deep breath, and told his irate boss, "It was requested."

"Requested? Requested? Requested by whom? Requested by bloody Otho himself? Did he bribe you, Philo? Is that it? How much buys you?"

Oh the irony. Icelus with his home dripping with treasures that rightly belonged to the Caesars. However, it was not that which really upset Philo but rather the suggestion of corruption. The accusation that he could be bought stung him into a rare moment of, if not actual anger, then certainly heated annoyance.

"It was requested by Titus Vinius," he replied, voice raised. "I suggest that you take it up with him."

He stood his ground. His eyes meeting Icelus' directly and very obviously omitting the usual "sir".

"You do not work for Titus Vinius," shrieked Icelus, throwing the tablet onto the floor where it broke into several pieces. "You work for me!"

"I work for the emperor," corrected Philo stoically.

They stared at each other in silence. Icelus on the balls of his feet, absolutely enraged. Philo upright with a clenched jaw.

The stand-off was broken when the door flew open and in trembled three fan boys accompanied by Straton.

Icelus, breaking the gaze, admired the boys and rubbing his hands together told Straton, "Excellent. Show them in."

Straton gave a half-hearted flick of his whip onto the floor. The boys, naked but for their sparkly loin cloths, shivered their way into Icelus' office. This being late November Philo failed to understand the purpose of the boys, thinking you'd have to cook up a pretty good fire to make them useful today. Then he noted Icelus' lecherous gaze: here was the emperor's private secretary salivating over fan boys. It didn't show outwardly but somewhere deep inside Philo a sneer formed.

He bent down to pick up the broken tablet, his fingers hitting Straton's and their eyes meeting. Philo stood up with speed and whizzed behind his desk for protection. The overseer fiddled with his whip, saying almost coyly, "Been a while." Then, "Missed you."

There followed a deeply uncomfortable pause which Straton broke, staring at the floor rasping, "Love you," before glancing up to see how Philo had taken this declaration.

The freedman was frozen to the spot, clasping the broken pieces of tablet in his hand and sporting a distinctly green tinge.

TWENTY-TWO

"Then Nero looked at us all gravely and said, full of imperial dignity, 'What an artist dies in me.' Then he took a knife and he plunged it right here." Sporus pointed to his nipple. His audience hung on his every word and gasped on cue.

"He took one last breath and then … and then …" he broke off, sweeping an arm across his brow. A well-rehearsed pause later, he concluded with gravitas and tear-filled eyes, "Nero Caesar was no more."

The audience wiped away tears muttering, "Poor Caesar," and, "What a hero he was."

Sporus, blackened foot propped up on a pillow, took the sympathy graciously. Accepting squeezes to his shoulder, small hugs, and very happily the coins that were pressed into his hands.

This was the fifth time of telling, which he felt he was perfecting with each repeat. In his next version Nero was going to fall onto a sword with a, "Et tu, Nymphidius?"

Word spread quickly round the Viminal that there was a genuine celebrity under Pompeia's roof. Grocery shopping was quickly abandoned, local girls were left un-whistled at, and the local traders pulled down their shutters. The apartment was full to bursting with a healthy queue outside Teretia's bedroom door waiting for their opportunity to hear Sporus' sad tale of their emperor's death.

Starved of attention for so long, Sporus was absolutely loving it, even if he had broken his ankle. He consoled himself that it lent him a more tragic air which fitted with his sad tidings. Pompeia and Teretia sat beside him and cried at the end of each version, failing to spot the many inconsistencies. He was a little vague about what had occurred after the emperor's death, saying only that he had been in the most terrible danger and awoke each morning in terror of what the day might bring.

"You're safe now," Tadius the local butcher told him, flashing a cleaver. "We take care of our folk." Making it clear that Sporus now fell into this camp.

"Thank you. You cannot know what a relief that is to me."

"Tadius, out you go, he's tiring. Can't you see?" Pompeia swept them all out ready for the next batch to be delighted by Sporus' tale.

Philo had endured a crap day. Icelus had been short, bad tempered, and more than a little mean to him. He had become paranoid and obsessed with Otho which had become wearing. There were only so many ways Philo could think of to assure his boss of Otho's essential harmlessness.

Then when Philo had been about to leave, Icelus insisted that he rewrite the entire minutes of the emperor's consortium meeting, claiming they were unintelligible. He could have left it to Talos but it seemed unfair and so the two of them had worked on it together to speed up the process.

Walking through the freezing city all he wanted to do was to get home, enjoy Pompeia's warming meal, listen to all the day's news on how much Tadius had put up his prices or how there was a fabulous bargain to be had at the fishmonger's. Then he wanted to curl up in bed, Teretia there to keep him warm and tell him that everything was going to be fine and that she loved him. Which might just cancel out any thoughts about Lysander's unwelcome prying and Straton's definitely unwelcome announcement.

So when he walked through the door to find the flat full of noisy, gossiping Viminal residents, his heart dropped. He slipped through the crowd intending to grab Teretia and hide in his room. Unfortunately he was spotted almost immediately by Tadius who told him, "What a brave chap he is. Galba should be ashamed of himself persecuting him like this. You tell him that, Philo. You tell Galba he should be ashamed!"

Philo found the chap in question propped up in Teretia's bed, swooning to effect and accepting all the attention smugly.

"Sporus."

The invalid smiled but with a hint of some great underlying tragedy. "Philo! Thank the gods you're alive! I thought you might have perished, like, like …" He gave a sob and threw himself into Teretia's bosom, where she put her arms around him.

"What are you doing here?"

"He's in the most dreadful danger," Teretia told him, shaking eunuch at her breast. "He has broken his foot escaping from those horrible people."

Sporus raised his swollen foot slightly for inspection.

"And they could be hunting for him right now!" she exclaimed.

The thought of the Galli hunting down Sporus was outright ridiculous and he gave the eunuch a look he hoped conveyed these thoughts. Teretia, sensing his disapproval said breathlessly, "He has to stay here, Philo. Until it is safe."

"It was safe. He was safe."

"You have no idea what I have endured!"

"Yes I do. Epaphroditus told me," said Philo, arms crossed.

"He's had a terrible time," pleaded Teretia, the eunuch burrowing himself further into her cleavage and trembling.

Philo was not fooled by these antics but he didn't see how he could turn him out on the street in this weather with a broken foot and without upsetting Teretia.

"You can stay, Sporus, but only until I find somewhere else to put you. I'll talk to Epaphroditus tomorrow."

"I don't think we should move him so soon, Philo. Look at his foot, it's all black," said Teretia, who looked upon Sporus much like a pet cat she had once had as a child. She wanted to stroke and play with him during the long hours Philo was at work.

"We'll talk about it tomorrow. If he is so injured he should rest."

Sporus dutifully yawned, telling Teretia, "You should go to bed. Philo is right. I need my sleep. I hope I shall not have nightmares but if you should hear me cry out …"

"Oh, I shall rush straight in," she cried. "And I shall hug you and make you feel better."

Sporus relaxed happily into her. Philo could have punched him.

Mina could tell that Straton's heart was not in it. He failed to knock the chair over, whacking the wall instead with a heavy slap.

"Do you want a break?"

He grunted, flinging the whip down.

"Tough day?"

He didn't answer, looking towards the desk, Philo's desk.

"Trouble with your friend?" Mina asked with concern, sitting on the bed and spreading out her skirts.

When he didn't answer she told him with a sigh, "My love life is not going so good either. Otho showed me those letters Epaphroditus wrote to him when he was in Lusitania. There was all this stuff about me in them, how wonderful I am, and how in love he is with me. They really got me, right here," she thumped her chest. "But he hasn't sent for me at all and it's not like he has a job now or anything. So what was it all about?"

Straton sympathised and made an attempt to explain his situation, "Friend not stay. Say busy."

"Oh, that's too bad." She patted a space beside her and he sat down heavily, springing her into the air slightly.

Staring at the floor, arms hanging down loosely he told her, "Told him, loved him." He gave a cough, cleared his throat, and concluded, "Didn't say."

Mina rubbed his arm, "He didn't say it back?"

Straton shook his head miserably, recalling the long silence that had followed his declaration, broken only by a screech from one of the fan boys Icelus was enjoying. He didn't understand why Philo couldn't stay. Philo had stayed many times over the summer.

That summer had been the highlight of Straton's life.

Waking up with Philo in the morning. A bowl of porridge with two spoons. The long nights that the overseer had so enjoyed. Straton was finding he didn't sleep so well without Philo in his bed. He missed him.

"I'm sorry. Maybe he's thinking it over. It is a pretty big deal."

Straton looked up hopefully, "You think?"

"Could be. Don't give up, hey?" She held his hand and squeezed it. "Now let's crack open one of them wineskins you have over there and get raucously drunk. I promise I won't handle the whip intoxicated." She gave a tight salute.

Straton attempted a smile. He didn't succeed.

Icelus dashed off to prepare for dinner, the fan boys having distracted him longer than he intended. He mused over their tight buttocks as his body slave dressed him, arranging the toga around his shoulders. It was to be a private dinner. The emperor and his closest advisors: Vinius with his solid, plain wife; Laco and his latest floozy; and Icelus beside Galba. Nothing would be said. There would be no comments. Certainly no affection. But it would be clear to all in that room that Icelus was accompanying Galba.

It was an odd relationship, if it could even be called that. In all the years Icelus had shared Galba's bed and showered him with affection, the older man had never complimented him, never shown any weakness (beyond the physical), and always spoke to him as a master to his slave.

Nothing Icelus did or offered ever made an indentation into the formal manner Galba used to address him. Meaning the freedman was never quite sure where he stood with his lover. Which no doubt explained his jumpy paranoia and jealousy whenever a new friend beckoned on the horizon.

Otho, he knew, had in the past shown tendencies that way. He was alleged to have enjoyed Nero's favours if you believed the gossips. Icelus wouldn't put it past the unscrupulous senator to sleep his way into another emperor's affections.

So when Icelus entered the dining room to find Otho seated beside Galba, entertaining him with some anecdote, his heart gave a nervous flutter. As the slave showed him to a lesser position beside Vinius' horse-faced wife, Icelus's heart went from nervous to enraged. Otho, seeing Icelus, gave him a friendly wave. The freedman glowered back with itching anger.

TWENTY-THREE

Sporus awoke early the next day, his stomach rumbling. He waited patiently but no one seemed to realise he was hungry, which was most irritating. The Galli always fed him early, all the better for the morning's first whirl. He made some whimpering noises, then a louder moan, to no effect. Pulling himself to the edge of the bed he tested his foot on the floor, finding that, although it throbbed dreadfully, he could just about stand on it and even limp it behind him.

Dragging himself down the corridor to the kitchen he found it deserted and very cold. He sat down for a bit but Pompeia did not appear with his breakfast and it was boring sat all by himself. He felt sure that Teretia would feel awful if she knew he'd got himself out of bed with such a terrible injury. He decided to seek her out so she could lavish guilty attention on him, hopefully in the shape of breakfast and sympathy.

Holding onto a wall he pulled himself along the corridor, wincing each time he put too much weight on his swollen foot, marvelling at his own courage and resilience. In the old days Sporus could be laid up for three days with a lightly stubbed toe and for a day at least with a broken fingernail. Reaching a door he pushed it open with his elbow and limped in.

In the morning gloom he could make out a bed, a blanket, and a couple of lumps underneath it that were moving in an unmistakable rhythm. Starved of anything he would call entertainment for the last five months Sporus decided to stay for the show. He slid down the wall and made himself comfortable on the floor, his poorly foot stretched out in front of him.

He wished he had a bowl of honey-roasted dormice and a goblet of wine. He also wished the blanket didn't hide most of the action. Still it was most engrossing and it was all that he'd assumed Philo sex would be. There were an awful lot of whispered questions. Was it feeling nice? Was he hitting the right place? Should he go faster or slow down? Was it hurting? Was she getting cramp because he could stop if she were? Was it OK if he touched/stroked/caressed/inserted …?

Giving the impression of an interrogation rather than a bout of lovemaking.

In fact this was Epaphroditus' doing. His advice to Philo on the subject of women included asking them what they liked. A tip Philo had employed rather more vigorously than had been intended. Teretia seemed to enjoy it though, her feet showing at the end of the bed, her toes bending upwards. Sporus heard a distinct cry of, "Oh, Philo," that betrayed that something good was happening there.

As the motion became more pronounced he was tempted to shout out encouragements. Exactly the sort of behaviour that got him expelled from many a palace orgy. There came a guttural groan, followed immediately by an apology. Figures, thought Sporus. And then out loud, "Now that's done can I have something to eat? I'm perishing!"

Philo's head shot out from beneath the blanket. Sporus smiled sweetly. "I am very hungry. I think it would help my foot if I were fed."

Philo looked as if he were going to say something. His mouth opened and Sporus waited in great anticipation but nothing came out.

"Hang on, Sporus," said Teretia, fiddling about and then appearing clad in a heavy winter nightgown. "Oh you poor thing," she cried, seeing him heaped on the floor. "Did you get up all by yourself?"

Sporus nodded sadly, gave a whimper, and pointed to his foot.

"Oh, and you're so cold, you're trembling. Philo, pass the blanket here, he's shivering. You shouldn't be up, your foot is all mangled."

"Not so mangled that it couldn't get him along the corridor," said Philo, reaching out for his clothes and cursing Sporus inwardly in language he didn't know he possessed.

"Be nice," warned Teretia, collecting up the blanket as Philo frantically tried to get his tunic over his head in time. He failed.

"Jupiter, Philo! What happened to your back?"

"A cart ran over him when he was a small boy," Teretia informed him as she wrapped the blanket round his shoulders.

"Gods! How many wheels did it have?"

Philo ignored him, concentrating on buckling up his belt.

"Did it reverse back over you?"

"Let me help you up. Hold onto my arm."

Sporus looked beyond her at Philo pulling on a sandal.

"Was Straton driving it?" he asked innocently, noting the freedman tense in response.

"Who's Straton?"

"You wouldn't like him," Sporus told her. "He's a nasty ugly brute. Handy with a whip though, hey Philo?"

"Let's get breakfast," he said, helping Teretia get Sporus to his feet, or rather foot.

The eunuch hopped, hanging onto her for support. "You are such a kind soul, Teretia. Nero noted it, that final night. He said so to me."

"Really?" she asked wide-eyed. "He remembered me?"

"Absolutely. He asked me all about you."

She threw Philo a thrilled look which melted his heart and made him dislike Sporus all the more, for the story was likely rubbish.

They hauled him into the kitchen, the eunuch deliberately (so Philo felt) making the task difficult. He had hobbled into Philo's room quietly enough but now the eunuch oww'd and winced his way along, earning undeserved fussing from Teretia. Sitting him down Philo told her, "I'll not go into work today. I'll sort out the arrangements."

"Is that wise?" interjected Sporus. "Won't your boss get suspicious if you don't turn up?"

Teretia grasped his arm. "What if he guesses? What if he comes here for Sporus?"

"I doubt Icelus gives him much thought. I think he has forgotten all about him. I think they all have."

Sporus was simultaneously outraged and horrified.

"Caesar."

"Yes, Icelus."

"There is a subject I need to raise that I know you find unpleasant."

"Spit it out," instructed Galba as the barber neatly trimmed his sparse hair.

"The issue of an heir."

Galba sighed. "I am aware of it, Icelus, but I do not want to be rushed over it."

"There are mutterings, Caesar."

"Mutterings? I don't like mutterings. If someone has something to say I want to hear it to my face."

"If the matter could be settled decisively these mutterings would cease. Laco and I feel that Dolabella—"

"Dolabella?" interrupted Galba, waving the barber away.

"We feel he possesses many of the correct qualities. He is a fine young man."

"I had Vinius in here earlier saying much the same thing about Otho."

"Otho is nowhere near as distinguished as Dolabella. He was one of Nero's worst creatures. The stories I have heard about him."

"He was a very successful governor nonetheless."

"A fluke, nothing more. A man does not change so dramatically."

"You think our nature's fixed then, Icelus?" Galba asked.

Icelus had no great opinion on this. "Otho, though, Caesar? I don't trust him."

"Yet he was the first to support our claim. And speaking with him the other day, I noted that he shares many of our views. I am beginning to warm to him."

Icelus spluttered, "Caesar, Otho is a beast."

Galba lifted a hand to silence him. "His ideas for rebuilding this great city mirror our own in so many ways. He should be an ally and I order you to treat him as such. There will be no factions in my court."

Icelus sloped out back to his office. Talos was silently working at his desk, scribbling away industriously. "Talos, get me Cornelius Laco. I wish to consult him."

"Yes, sir."

Icelus slouched into his office, spreading out on a couch. Laco appeared shortly in full uniform, a special one he'd had constructed. It was midway between Praetorian garb and the sort of armour you might wear to a fancy dress party as Mars. It wouldn't stop an arrow assault but Laco felt it distinguished him and had it polished by a small team of slaves each morning. Icelus shielded his eyes from the gleam.

"You sent for me." Laco sat down easily in his adapted armour. It was one of his specifications that he be able to sit, lie, and screw in it.

"What in Jupiter's name is going on with Otho?" asked Icelus from his prone position.

"Popular fellow," quipped Laco.

"Popular with Galba too now."

"Now, that is interesting."

"He has impressed with his ideas, so close to our own apparently. Galba is beginning to see him as a kindred spirit. I don't like it."

Laco considered before replying, "Neither do I. I find it extremely hard to believe that Otho shares anything with our emperor. Two more different people I can't imagine."

"Yet Galba says he is bristling with zeal to rebuild the city and the populace."

"Icelus, what exactly are these grand plans of Otho's? Did Galba say?"

Something in his tone made Icelus sit up. "No, not specifically. Just that they matched his own."

Laco laughed. "Don't you see?"

Icelus didn't.

"He is saying exactly what Galba wants to hear."

"Evidently, but I don't see—"

Laco interrupted him. "Icelus, friend, someone is feeding him Galba's planned policies and he is feeding them straight back at him. Ingenious."

"Vinius?" queried Icelus.

Laco scratched his chin. "Perhaps, perhaps not. Let me do some digging. And don't worry," he told the anxious Icelus. "There's not a chance in Hades that Otho is talking his way into becoming Galba's son. Not on my watch."

TWENTY-FOUR

"I think I should stay here. Help mother with Sporus," said Teretia, washing up a porridge bowl.

A fed Sporus was encased back in Teretia's room. His theme today was betrayal and he was already enthralling Pompeias Major and Minor with Alex's brutal treatment of him. A subject they found suitably shocking. Philo could hear "Oohs", "Aahs", and "The beast!" floating down the corridor.

Taking a bowl from her and drying it he said, "I would like it if you came with me to see Epaphroditus."

He was anxious about leaving her with the eunuch. Who knew what kind of havoc he would reap in his absence? Plus he was acutely aware that Sporus possessed at least one bit of gossip regarding him that he was bound to pass on.

"I have things to do here. It is a very long walk," she protested. "I don't see why he can't stay here."

"There's not enough room."

"There is plenty of room. He can have my bed and I'll stay with you, like last night. He has suffered so. He needs us to take care of him properly."

"It could be dangerous. I couldn't put you and Pompeia in such a situation. It wouldn't be fair."

"We want to. Anyway you said Icelus had forgotten all about him."

Philo presented the crux of his objection. "Sporus is trouble. He always was. I don't want him here."

She flicked her plait over her shoulder. "It doesn't matter whether you like him or not. He is in need. He needs our care and we shall give it to him because that is the right thing to do."

At any other time he would have found this greatly admirable. Right now he had images of Sporus dishing the whole Mina disaster out to her.

"You never were run over by a cart were you?" she asked, handing him another bowl to dry. "You made me look foolish repeating that lie to Sporus."

"Sorry," he muttered.

"I'm not angry," she said, though she did look distinctly peeved. "We should tell each other everything. I tell you everything."

She did. She told everyone everything. It was both her most endearing and most irritating trait.

"It was all I could think of at the time," he told her, rubbing at the bowl ineffectually.

"I don't understand. Why couldn't you just tell me the truth?"

"Because, because ..." He put the bowl down on the side.

She was beautiful. Even in her nightgown with her hair tied back sensibly and up to her elbows in dirty washing-up water. He still couldn't quite believe she was his. That such a sweet, wonderful girl liked him. Nobody had ever liked him before. He couldn't bear to lose her, not now.

"Because it doesn't count," he said finally. Seeing her perplexed face, he extended his explanation. "Before. Before I knew you. When I was a ..." He forbore from mentioning the s-word. "It wasn't pleasant. I don't know why you'd want to know about that."

He was taken by surprise when she flung her arms around him, water dripping down his neck. "Oh, Philo, it's OK. It's OK with me if you don't want to talk about it. It's fine. I understand. I don't fully understand, but I can try." She kissed him on the cheek. "Some day though, when you're ready, when you can, I will listen if you want to talk about it."

Philo heard Sporus' high voice decrying, "My best friend in all the world handing me over to that brute Sabinus," eliciting shocked cries in response.

Seeing Teretia's expression he told her, "Go listen if you like. I'll finish up here."

Another hug and a kiss on the lips. "Thank you," she breathed before dashing off to hear chapter two of the continuing adventures of Sporus.

Epaphroditus laughed. "You have Sporus? That must be fun."

"What do I do with him?" Philo asked desperately. "He can't stay. I don't want him to stay."

Epaphroditus handed him a drink. He looked like he needed it despite the early hour. Philo drained it in one, telling him, "I can't stand it and he's only been there one night. Teretia thinks he's some maligned, injured bird that needs nursing back to health."

"I would say take him back to the palace. With Sabinus dead I doubt there's anyone who means him any harm. But if he is genuinely injured?"

Philo reluctantly confirmed that the foot was indeed damaged.

"Then Felix won't have much use for him."

Otho, reaching forward to help himself to a truffle enquired, "Who is Sporus?"

"Eunuch playmate of Nero's," explained Epaphroditus. "Troublesome, yet entertaining."

Otho pursed his lips, asking thoughtfully, "The one who dresses like Poppaea? Yes, that rumour even made it up to those of us in backward Lusitania. I could put him up."

"Could you?" said Philo eagerly. "Could you really?"

"I don't see why not. I have a lovely large house with plenty of space. He sounds an intriguing fellow."

"Won't win you any favours with Statilia Messalina," warned Epaphroditus.

A sentence that gave pause to Otho until he saw Philo's desperate, pleading look, much like the antelope in the arena just before it was well and truly javelined. Otho was a generous sort and he hated to see anyone suffer unnecessarily. Not when he could help.

"I'll take him."

Philo grabbed hold of his hands. "Thank you. Thank you. I owe you, Otho. I definitely owe you."

Otho prised his hands gently off. "No trouble. No trouble at all. Can I pick him up later?"

Philo nodded enthusiastically. "Whenever. I should go. I should go now. I don't like to leave them alone …" He stood up and was out the door before either man could interject.

"Will I regret that?" Otho asked, staring at the space where Philo had been.

"I think you'll like Sporus," mused Epaphroditus. "It will be interesting to see where your breaking point is. Philo was rather robust to last the night with him."

"Does he resemble Poppaea?" Otho asked casually, fiddling with his food. "Just out of interest, mind."

"I should put that interest away. It was that sort of interest that made Nero unpopular with the men that matter. You will not win favour with Galba if he suspects you of the same."

Otho pulled a face.

"I thought you were a reformed character?"

"I am. I am positively celibate. I spend my evenings politicking to your specifications."

Epaphroditus nodded his approval.

"You've no idea how exhausting it is to be this charming all the time."

"And I thought it came naturally."

"It does, but even Otho needs downtime. Can I have a night off? I want to wallow in self-pity and shout at my slaves."

"How is it going with Galba?"

Otho sighed. "Hard work. Very hard work. Sometimes I feel I have won him over only for him to appear suspicious of me the very next day. Jupiter knows why."

"Icelus no doubt." Philo had been most helpful on Icelus' growing paranoia.

"Vinius builds me up for Icelus and Laco to knock me down. I am not sure what else I can do to win him round. Now the war is over he has no need of my money."

"Your money?" Epaphroditus raised an eyebrow.

Another sigh from Otho. "One of my creditors had the audacity to bang on my door yesterday. He actually wanted payment in full. There and then. Onomastus had to have a little chat with him."

Though small, Onomastus could deliver a well-crafted threat with an exaggerated promise of violence.

"Antonius Honoratus," began Epaphroditus handing him a wax tablet.

"Go on, shock me. I would have thought him unbribeable. He stands up very straight. I envy his legs."

"Not bribeable but he has a distinct soft spot."

"I hope it isn't little boys again. I am beginning to despair of our political leaders. I don't see when they have the time to legislate."

"Says the man who is taking in a small, ball-less boy solely because he likes to dress as his ex-wife. Read it. It's not unpleasant. It is very nearly heart-warming."

"Father!"

"Silvia."

179

He stood up to greet his daughter, accompanied by her mother. She looked older he thought.

"You look well."

A little too well for Epaphroditus' comfort. He did not want to contemplate what had contributed to her serene state.

"I am well. Very well. Martinus is taking me to the theatre. Where's Faustina? I want to gloat."

She plonked herself down on the bench beside Otho.

Aphrodite grabbed her husband on the arm, whispering in his ear, "Otho is here again. What is he doing here?"

"Just a friendly chat, my dear."

Aphrodite looked unconvinced. "You're up to something."

"Not at all. I'm allowed to have friends aren't I?"

She would have made a pithy reply regarding Otho's suitability for that role when she froze suddenly. Concerned, Epaphroditus followed her gaze to where Otho and Silvia sat.

There was no reason why they should have noticed it before. Silvia was a child when Otho left for his governorship and at the wedding, the bride had been veiled for most of the proceedings. But sitting side by side there was no doubting the resemblance between them.

They both possessed the same blue eyes, long dark lashes, rounded faces and naturally ruddy cheeks. It was too striking to be mere coincidence.

Aphrodite knew her husband had noticed it too. For though he maintained his usual genial demeanour during Silvia's visit, allowing her to taunt Faustina a little but not enough to send her younger sister off in a strop, he never once looked at her, keeping his attention on his guests. It was an act he struggled to maintain. Aphrodite saw the tense line of his jaw, the heavily injected spirit in his conversation.

Once the guests departed Epaphroditus was on his feet, ordering a slave to bring his cloak.

"Where are you going?" Aphrodite asked, following him into their atrium.

"Out," he replied, fastening the cloak around his neck, refusing to look at her.

"Stay, please stay," she pleaded holding onto his arm. "Tiberius, please don't go. We need to talk about this. We knew, didn't we? We knew it might be the case."

He brushed off her hand and strode out without speaking. Aphrodite sat down heavily beside the fountain, gulping at air, feeling her heart beat rapidly.

Had he been a drinking man he would have holed himself up in some dirty Subura wine bar and drunk until he fell. But he'd never been one for excessive alcohol consumption. It dulled the senses and Epaphroditus led the kind of life where full command of his wits was essential for survival. Instead he jogged down the road and yelled at a departing litter, "Otho!"

The bearers ground to a halt and he moved alongside. Otho pulled back the decorous golden curtains, yet another reason for his extravagant debts.

"What's up?"

"Are you going to the palace?"

"You did just tell me to, chum."

"Can you get a message to Artemina for me? Ask her to meet me at your place. That's still OK?"

"Absolutely. Anything to smooth the path of true love."

Epaphroditus winced at this but continued, "Make sure she gets proper dispensation from the empress."

Otho smiled. "I am sure that I can talk Statilia into letting her have the afternoon off."

TWENTY-FIVE

Provinces have been conquered with a great deal less trouble than it took to move Sporus into Otho's house. What hampered the operation more than any other factor was the eunuch's own tongue.

Sporus spent an enjoyable morning enrapturing the Viminal locals with his daring escape from the Temple of the Great Mother. He related how the Galli pursued him down the garden wielding their sacrificial knives, determined to prevent his escape. And how he, a humble slave, had outrun them; bravely scaling a forty-foot-high wall!

"It's not just bulls they slaughter in that temple," he told them, voice lowered for an increased level of confidence. "That's why they sing so loud, it's to blot out their victim's screams."

"I knew it," stormed uncle Gnaeus. "Didn't I always say? Well didn't I?" he enquired of his family. "Knew them damn eunuchs were up to no good."

"Of course they cursed me," continued Sporus, surprisingly cheerful for a man supposedly in fear of his life. "In their evil Eastern ways. They'll be asking the Great Mother to remove my eyes with pincers or the like."

Teretia shuddered.

If it wasn't a band of killer eunuch priests after him, then Sporus was determined it would be the palace assassins ordered by Galba, or possibly Alex, to have him wiped out.

"And they are terribly efficient. I remember my dear Nero scribbling out a list of seventy names on a napkin over dinner and by breakfast they were all dead."

So it was not really surprising that the Viminal traders were ever so slightly jumpy. Determined to protect Sporus from those nasty men/women/eunuch priests that bode him ill.

A fact Onomastus discovered that afternoon. He found himself pinned to a wall by a mean-looking butcher when he innocently asked directions to Teretia's residence.

"What business have you?" spat Tadius.

Otho, sat on the edge of his flamboyant litter surrounded by burly tradesmen sporting a variety of home-made weapons, asked nonchalantly, "Is this really necessary?"

"State your business."

"Gentlemen, I have business with Teretia and …" He looked to Onomastus, who was kicking his little legs against the wall and turning somewhat purple, for assistance.

"Pompeia," the freedman choked from behind Tadius' arm.

"Teretia and Pompeia."

"Your business, senator?"

"I am here to collect a friend of theirs."

This produced a flurry of whispers. Tadius leant back to confer with his comrades. Decision made Tadius looked back to Otho with a certain amount of menace and enquired, "What friend?"

"Sporus."

Now there was a definite buzz. Sporus had clearly made his presence known in the neighbourhood.

"Why?"

Otho, tired of this charade and worried by Onomastus' increasingly desperate wheezes behind Tadius' arm, replied evenly, "Friends, we come here to take Sporus somewhere safe, somewhere comfortable, somewhere he can recuperate with all the luxuries he could ever wish for."

This calmed them until a voice piped up, "Hang on! That's what he would say. What if he's an assassin?"

There was a collective intake of breath at this plausible suggestion. "It would be a typically cowardly palace action."

"I reckon them litter bearers are eunuchs. They'll be working for the Arch Gallus."

"They are not eunuchs. Check if you don't believe me," said Otho, earning himself furious glances from his bearers. Opening his palms, he beseeched them, "Gentlemen, I am not an assassin. I am no murderer. I mean no harm to Sporus. I offer him a safe heaven. Philo asked me to help."

"Philo?" asked Tadius, narrow-eyed.

"Little Indian chap, works for the palace, shuffling papers and the like. Terribly useful sort."

"Teretia," prompted Onomastus hoarsely.

"Is courting Teretia. Lovely girl," concluded Otho.

"What do you think?" Tadius asked a comrade. The comrade regarded Otho's beaming face and purple striped toga. If he was an assassin he was a master of disguise.

"Legit," he said.

Tadius slowly lowered Onomastus to the ground. The dwarf bent over coughing and spluttering. The butcher patted him kindly on the back to aid his recovery.

Philo at least was pleased to see Otho. His mouth twitched into an almost smile. "Thank Jupiter, Juno, Vishnu, and Hanuman," he mouthed to himself.

Otho, flanked by Tadius and burly friend, greeted him cheerfully. "Where is he then, the eunuch?"

Philo led him through to Teretia's room. If Otho expected to see a mirror image of his former wife he was to be disappointed. He saw a soft, tawny-limbed boy of about fifteen with liquid brown eyes and curly hair that rolled onto his shoulders.

He was attractive but Otho failed to see anything of Poppaea in him. He sat down on the end of the bed, Sporus looking at him dubiously.

"Sporus, this is Otho," Philo introduced. "He has come to take you away."

Sporus scuttled back on the bed alarmed. "Take me where? Why do I have to go anywhere? I thought I was staying here? I like it here."

Teretia, sat beside Sporus a little too cosily for Philo's liking, cried, "He doesn't want to go. I told you he wouldn't want to go."

Sporus shook his head rapidly. "My foot, it's too sore to move me. I should stay."

"He should stay," agreed Teretia, looking to Philo for support.

He was unmoved. He'd been entirely correct in his worries about leaving Sporus unsupervised in his home. Returning home from Epaphroditus' house he had discovered Teretia looking rather sheepish and Sporus greeting him with an extremely wide grin. She had clearly let something slip she shouldn't have, leaving him tense all day waiting for the inevitable dig.

It came eventually, not from Sporus but from old uncle Gnaeus who, wrapping his arthritic hands round a beaker, announced in front of an entire room full of Teretia's many relatives of all sexes and ages, "So here, Philo my lad. Sporus tells me that my great-niece has relieved you of your virginity. Good for her, I say. Left it a bit late though, lad, hey? Want to get that sort of thing out the way years back. No one expects much of a boy, lets you get away with all that dreadful fumbling and poking till you've got enough experience to get it right."

Philo, to whom mortification was an everyday event, felt he had entered a whole new realm of humiliation.

He was firmly blaming Sporus for it, though retaining a little bit of annoyance with Teretia. Not a lot because he was far too devotedly in love with her to stay mad at her, but he was not going to lose any sleep over separating her from her new friend.

"Otho will take care of you until your foot is better."

"I shall."

"I don't want to go," he appealed to Philo and then Teretia, distraught on his behalf.

Otho, picking at his teeth, commented breezily, "I have a steam room."

Which was what swung it for Sporus.

TWENTY-SIX

Mina, dashing past Straton on her way to Otho's house, told him excitedly, "I've got a message from him!"

Straton, who was always pleased for her successes, unlike Alex, grinned and said, "Knew you would."

"I'm going to see him now!" she exclaimed and pelted down the corridor, Straton watching her go.

Let in by a slave she found Epaphroditus sitting morosely on the edge of the bed, head held between his hands. Hearing her enter he glanced up and fashioned a smile.

"Artemina," and rose to greet her.

They never made it onto the bed, which was a shame since lain upon it was a very expensive gold thread blanket that Otho had spent a great deal of someone else's money on.

It was a frantic ripping of clothes, bouncing off walls, slamming into furniture that should have been brief but somehow the passion was prolonged. A combination of Epaphroditus' enforced celibacy and Mina's series of dour Vinius encounters spurring them on.

Afterwards, lying on the floor, Mina cackled happily, "That was a-maze-ing."

Buttocks pressed onto the cold floor, back aching, and a sting to his groin indicating Otho's remedy was not quite as effective as he had been promised, Epaphroditus could not agree.

Blast, this could put him back days. Days before he could make love to Dite. Was she waiting for him now? Wanting to talk? What was there to say anyway? Silvia was Otho's daughter. Not his. How could that be?

"We thought it might be the case," she had said. He hadn't. Not after she was born anyway. He'd had no doubts at all. You couldn't feel that much love for a child that wasn't yours. Could you? It hadn't felt any different with Silvia than with any of his other children. If anything it had been stronger because she was their first freeborn and it was all new.

He'd been so sure.

He couldn't be mad at Otho. He knew that his friend didn't even remember sleeping with Aphrodite. Why would he? She was just one of hundreds of slaves available to him in Nero's court on a rainy afternoon, when woozy with boredom he could pick out any random one to revive his spirits.

Otho had once asked Epaphroditus in all earnestness and just a little hurt, "Why does your wife hate me?"

He had offered some smooth retort, navigating away from the truth. He didn't even blame Dite for it wasn't her fault. Although sometimes he wished she could let stuff like this go, like he had. No, if there was any one person to blame then it was Agrippina: Nero's mother, the she-wolf of Rome.

It occurred during those mad days at the end of Claudius' reign when the question of the succession was on everyone's lips. Nero, due to his mother's prolonged machinations, had supplanted the emperor's natural son Britannicus and there was a frantic dash among the courtiers to win his favour, with Agrippina looking smugly on.

She had won. A lifetime of scheming, of planning, of even going so far as to seduce her own uncle Claudius (which you had to admit took a certain something) in order to promote her son, had paid off. Seventeen-year-old Nero was going to be emperor: a pimply nosed youth with no governmental nor military experience. Well, it was Caligula all over again. So the freedman administrators were working overtime to secure the emperor-in-waiting's attention in the hope of gaining control over him.

His mother secured two heavyweight advisors: Seneca the philosopher and Burrus, probably the only decent Praetorian prefect in the whole history of the position. Factions were already gathering around them, if only to secure protection from Agrippina's wrath.

Epaphroditus worked for Narcissus, Claudius' private secretary. Narcissus was no friend to Agrippina. He had opposed her incestuous marriage to the emperor and had been close to Claudius' previous wife. While Claudius was alive Narcissus was safe. When he died Agrippina was expected to exact a hasty revenge.

Epaphroditus was therefore undertaking some gratuitous politicking to ensure his own survival, recognising something that Agrippina, arch politician that she was, had missed. A young boy may naturally look to his mother for support and advice but a teenage boy will look to his peer group.

Epaphroditus skidded between the factions whirling round the empress, Burrus, Seneca, and the young would-be emperor. Instead, he ingratiated himself with one Marcus Salvius Otho: twenty-one years old, charming, handsome, careless, rakish, and Nero's closest friend. Agrippina viewed him as a bad influence on her son, having the effect of making him all the more illustrious and appealing to the impressionable Nero.

Nero and Otho were typical of upper-class Roman youths: too much money and too little sense. The role Epaphroditus slid his way into was the facilitator of their jaunts. He made sure that a wild time was had by all but not so wild as to attract the attention of the vigiles or worse still Nero's mother. He managed to maintain a firm hold on the heir's dubious pleasures.

Though what pleasure was to be had from disguising themselves as plebs, hitting the Subura slums, and whacking passers-by with a cudgel was somewhat lost on Epaphroditus. Still, Nero and Otho seemed to enjoy these excursions into the city and Epaphroditus became a firm favourite of the young future Caesar, indispensable even. Where he fell down and truly earned the wrath of Agrippina was by introducing Nero to Acte.

Acte was a rather comely freedwoman at least twice Nero's age. A sex slave but of a rather different species than the usual. Solidly sensible and sweet-natured, she stroked a man's ego and offered soundly good advice when asked. Never forth-coming, she was reliable and even-tempered; the perfect foil for Nero's slightly hysterical, nervy personality.

Epaphroditus introduced them after Nero expressed inter-est in experiencing an older woman; a foolish action he realised all too belatedly. He should have chosen some golden limbed, light-brained, simpering woman. Instead, Acte's motherly affection and soft bosom transfixed the young Nero and he was soon utterly obsessed by her.

This did not please Agrippina who could feel her hold on her son slipping as he spent increasing time with his lover. Realising that it would not credit her to confront her son on the issue, she quickly assessed Epaphroditus' role and determined her revenge. She could have just had him killed, but where was the fun in that?

He was far more useful to her alive. If he could be persuaded over to her side and dispense with his foolish attempts to gain her son's favour independently. Agrippina's version of persua-sion was not to tell you what you had to gain. Rather, to show you graphically what you had to lose if you did not comply.

One wet afternoon Epaphroditus was attending Nero and Otho, sat on a stool in front of them. He was dissecting the previous night's entertainment while trying to interest the soon-to-be emperor to be in some crucial paperwork. Acte was helpfully assisting by gently coercing her lover into signing the relevant forms. Agrippina swept in all smiles and graciousness, an unlikely performance that made the hairs stand up on the back of Epaphroditus' neck.

"My dearest son." Kisses on both cheeks. "And lovely Acte, so nice to see you again."

Acte snuggled under Nero's arm, as unnerved by this scene as Epaphroditus.

Agrippina, sitting on the couch beside the happy couple murmured, "I am so glad that my son has found such a worthy companion."

She stared at Acte with an easy smile which she then turned on Otho who sat rigid with fear, well aware of how the empress viewed him.

"And Marcus, here again?"

Otho nodded, began to take his leave, but Agrippina waved him down. "No, please don't leave on my account. I have a surprise for you, Marcus."

This did nothing to placate Otho who was imagining a hit squad of Praetorians waiting for him outside the door.

"Something nice," gushed the empress showing small, sharp teeth, leaning forward in her seat. "I know how jealous you have been of my son and his wonderful Acte."

He had. Otho had been moaning for months as to why he didn't have a hot older woman like that curled up in his bed.

"So I took the liberty of examining some of the stock and I think I have found the perfect woman for you. She is rather lovely."

The empress clicked her fingers. Epaphroditus' features froze as a pale Aphrodite in her white uniform was escorted in. Otho murmured his approval of the gift.

"I thought," suggested Agrippina heavily, "that you might make use of her while my son completes his necessary duties."

Aphrodite was a beautiful woman and Otho was a horny young man. Encouragement was not needed. Agrippina smiled. It was a wide smile that lit up her violet eyes. She mouthed one word to the stunned Epaphroditus: "Enjoy."

Is there an etiquette on whether you look or don't look when a man has sex with the woman you call your wife right in front of you? Epaphroditus wondered as Otho began his seduction egged on by Agrippina and Nero, who had now lost what little interest he had in his imperial duties. Acte, alone aware of Epaphroditus' feelings, discreetly reached over and gave his hand a supportive squeeze, keeping hold of it throughout the encounter.

Should he watch? Would Aphrodite be looking for his support, silent though it would be? Or should he avert his eyes so he would not have to witness her degradation? In the end he decided to watch, to look right at her. She needed her to know that he was there for her, would always be there for her whatever took place.

It was a peculiar agony, searing in its intensity. Fist clenched impotently by his side as he watched her suffer; watched Otho complete his business with a shout of triumph.

Afterwards, dragged into a meeting with the gloating empress he was told stonily, "You work with me. Not against me. You understand? Otherwise I sell her to Otho and banish him to the provinces and you will never see her again. You understand?"

And from that delightful afternoon, Silvia, his beautiful Silvia had been conceived.

"Epaphroditus?"

"Mmm."

Mina cuddled up to him, manoeuvring under his arm so her head was on his chest. "Are you cold?"

"Freezing."

"Shall we get into the bed? Snuggle down?"

Snuggle? He was saved from having to answer by a terrific clamour. Sitting up he heard Otho directing slaves. "In the blue bedroom, I think. You will like it there. It is very comfortable."

"Where's this steam room then?" came a light, higher-pitched voice.

Mina shot up into a seated position. She looked to Epaphroditus who confirmed, "It's Sporus."

Her face shone and she jumped to her feet collecting up her hastily shed clothes. He helped her fasten her dress, using a brooch to disguise a tear in the fabric that he'd caused.

"He's alive," she babbled, fidgeting impatiently as he fiddled with the brooch.

The moment she was decent she ran out into a commotion of a courtyard. A series of slaves were dealing with Sporus' demands. The eunuch was propped up in a wicker chair, his foot elevated on a stool, a glass of cordial being handed to him. Otho was busy making arrangements in a prolonged huddle with Onomastus. Teretia, who insisted on coming along to ensure that Sporus was safe, sat on a low wall holding hands with Philo and marvelling at her luxurious surroundings.

Mina bombed in. Sporus seeing her running towards him was shocked into a smile. "Mina!"

"Sporus!" She threw her arms around him in a tight embrace. Then picking at his hair she said, "Gods, are you going to get barbered? This is rank!"

"Mina, Mina, you would not believe what's happened to me."

This was drowned out by Mina babbling at the same time, "I have so much to tell you!"

And she did. There was her and Straton's daring escape from the slave complex; Sabinus trying to persuade Statilia to marry Galba; Lysander's creepy pursuit of free women; Philo walking out of the emperor's welcome party; Daphne's pregnancy; Titus Vinius' sweaty palms; her new-found talents with a whip (which she was dying to show off). All of which she told him extremely fast and with great animation. Sporus missed most of it, talking over her with his own stories of escape and dire peril.

Teretia looked put out at having her new friend so monopolised. Philo squeezed her hand. "Let's go."

"Otho will take care of him?" she asked anxiously.

"He will be fine. Honest."

She smiled happily at him which warmed him to his toes. "They will be waiting for an update back on the Viminal."

"Oh yes, aunt Pompeia was most keen. Can I …" she paused looking at Philo shyly. "Can I visit him?"

"Of course. I'll come with you." Escort you, accompany you, and censor you, he thought.

"I didn't know they knew each other," Otho commented to Epaphroditus. Then seeing his friend's strained expression asked, "Are you ill?"

"I'm fine."

"You don't look fine."

"I'm getting too old for this."

Otho followed his eye line to where Mina sat on the stool beside Sporus' foot waggling her hands excitedly.

"Surely not!" exclaimed Otho. "You've got years left in you. Remember old Claudius? He kept at it right till the end."

Epaphroditus did remember old Claudius, far too well. He remembered the emperor's wrinkled cock having to be teased into life by a long chain of sex slaves. Special kudos given to the one who achieved the desired stiffness. He did not want to end up like that. It was pathetic.

"I should go home," he said quietly, his thoughts dwelling on his wife again.

Teretia offered a fond farewell to Sporus, hugging him tight and telling him that she hoped his foot was better soon. Sporus took the attention smugly, clinging to her and declaring her the bravest girl he had ever met, before spotting Philo's displeasure at this affection.

"Don't cast those eyes on me," Sporus told him. "You are soooo going to lurrrrve me tonight." Waggling his eyebrows and winking.

Philo, unnerved, hurried Teretia along, allowing one final eunuch embrace.

Mina waved them out sarcastically.

"Oh come on, she's a love," Sporus cried.

"It shouldn't be allowed, these mixed marriages. We girls of servitude have a hard enough time as it is without freebies like her stealing all our best freedmen. And what was all that about?" said Mina, imitating Sporus' waggling eyebrows.

Sporus, fidgety with his news, lowered his voice and divulged in a hushed whisper, "I have persuaded her to give him a Sporus tonight."

Sporus had worked for many years as a catamite, a profession in which certain skills are required in order to progress. A catamite with no repeat bookings was a failed catamite and likely to be banished to some unsavoury position washing up pots, cleaning bathrooms or, gods forbid, filing.

Sporus had one very particular talent. One in which he positively excelled. So much so that he harboured a great desire for that particular act to be named after him. From Britannia to Babylonia he imagined men gathering in the bars and the cook shops and the wherever elses they holed up for entertainment in the dour provinces, loudly boasting to their friends/relatives/drinking acquaintances of how their boyfriend/girlfriend/random prostitute performed a wonderful Sporus. No one could accuse the eunuch of lacking ambition.

Earlier that day Teretia, in full confiding mood, a mood that Sporus was all for encouraging, had told him that Philo had asked her to perform something for him in bed that she wasn't quite sure she should do. A vague sentiment that pricked the eunuch's ears, eager as he was for some dirty insight behind Philo's exterior mildness.

He was even more intrigued when Teretia told him that Pompeia had informed her daughter that it was unbecoming to her status and that she shouldn't involve herself in such slave practices. Sporus by this point was mentally running through

197

all the palace orgies he had attended trying to figure out what Philo's particular fetish was.

He was thus extremely disappointed to discover the requested act was only a Sporus, thinking that it showed a distinct lack of imagination by the freedman. Still, he told himself, he was here to aid in any way he could, especially after witnessing what passed for their love life that morning. So he told Teretia, "It won't lower your status. Why, Nero was extremely fond of it and he was emperor. Can't get more high class than that!" Which soothed Teretia's worries. For she only wanted to make Philo happy, and if this would make him happy …

"So I educated her in the Sporus ways," he told Mina. "I would be an excellent teacher. I am going to petition for Zosimus' position. I would be so much better than him!"

Mina shook her head, trying to dislodge a rather squelchy image that had stuck there.

"And I know why Philo turned you down," boasted Sporus triumphantly.

"Because of that limp thing."

"Oh no it isn't," crowed Sporus. "They weren't together then."

"Yes they were. They got together before Nero …" She stopped, not wishing to upset her friend. However, Sporus was too overjoyed by his stellar gossip to notice.

"They weren't. They only did the deed last month. On his bed. After dinner. Which I believe was rabbit stew with dumplings."

"No, no, no. You are wrong, oh half-boy. Epaphroditus told me."

"Teretia told me. My source outweighs yours. Ha!"

"You are as irritating as I remember. Outrageous behaviour. How dare you have palace gossip when all you've been doing is hiding in a cupboard for six months? Go on, spill, non-boy. Gods, he's not one of your type is he?"

"Purleeesse. They don't just make anyone a eunuch. You have to have a certain something. Philo so does not have that something."

Mina pulled her feet under her. This was so much fun, like old times.

"Spill, spill, spill," she chanted, banging her fists on her thighs.

Sporus rang a hand through his flowing locks. "I could get used to these. Much nicer than a nasty, itching wig."

"Sporus," she whined.

He waved a hand. "I know *everything*. She is very good on confidences is Teretia."

"Shame she doesn't know you well enough to know you can't keep them."

"Anyway, she told me …" He paused for effect.

Mina, warning him, hands held lightly round his blackened foot, answered, "I'll squeeze it. I swear to the Great Mother. I'll squeeze if you do not spill now."

Sporus, who was one of life's natural cowards caved. "OK, OK," he said, moving his foot away. "It is worth it though."

"Fab-o. We should send for Alex so he can bathe in this, I hope, glorious anecdote. Sporus? What is it?"

Sporus' smile had faded. He replied through clenched teeth, "Don't mention that treacherous scum to me!"

TWENTY-SEVEN

"You haven't been waiting here all this time for me?" asked Epaphroditus.

Aphrodite, sat in their atrium, placed down her sewing. "I had some needlework and it's nice and quiet here."

"Sporus is safely installed," Epaphroditus told her. "I have never seen Philo so relieved. He thanked Otho exactly twenty-seven times for taking him off his hands."

"Why, what had Sporus been up to?"

"Teasing him, I think. Philo has never had much of a sense of humour. He is far too serious for his own good. Hopefully Teretia will lighten him up."

"She's had a tough time, mind. Her father dying."

"True. She seemed fond of Sporus, I got the impression a little too fond for Philo's liking. He was very keen to separate them …" he petered out. "I'm sorry."

"For what?"

"For walking out like that."

"You're back now. That's all that matters. Will you sit?"

He sat down beside her. She put her arm around him and he settled his head on her shoulder, Aphrodite stroking his hair. "It won't make a difference. Not to me. Not to Silvia."

Epaphroditus sighed gently. "We could have got a much better match for her than Martinus if we'd known she was a governor's daughter."

"Much bigger dowry, though."

"True." He rubbed his head with the heel of his palm.

"We would have been bankrupted," said Aphrodite, continuing her gentle strokes of his hair. "We would have had to move in with Philo. He'd hate it. Five giggling girls to torment him. He would be terrified."

"True." He almost smiled at the image.

"Will you tell Otho?" she asked quietly.

"No, no. Of course not. Not if you don't want me to," he muttered, caught in a sudden thought of his own.

If Otho succeeded Galba as they planned, it could be a very useful connection. A family tie to Otho's good background, very useful indeed.

She protested at first: no, Alex wouldn't do that. He was mad, mistaken, just plain wrong. He was their friend, their best friend, always had been. If he had known about Sabinus' coup he would have told them because they told each other everything. He wouldn't have left them to their fates. He just wouldn't.

In the end Sporus had cited Epaphroditus as his witness, which swayed her, for he knew she would ask him to corroborate. Walking back to her room through the palace, Mina thought back over the past few months.

There were several incidents that stood out for her now: Alex's mysterious absence when Nero fell; his lack of excitement when she had mooted the possibility of Sporus' survival; his friendship with the Praetorian tribune. She recalled his preoccupation in the days leading up to the end of Nero. How little fun he'd been. How serious. Because he had known.

When she had gone to him the night of the party, weeping over Epaphroditus, he'd known what was coming. He'd let

202

her go to bed without warning and she had risen, innocently walking into that carnage.

She was hit by the sudden image of Juba's leering expression as he closed in on her. But more than that she remembered that first stab of terror when the guards had rounded them up, not knowing what would happen to them. He had known though. Alex had known.

He had sat there night after night in her room comforting her, watching her cry, when he had known full well that Sporus and Epaphroditus were both alive. How could he do that to her?

Reaching her room she was all prepared for a full-on rant. Until she saw Daphne sitting on the floor, rubbing her belly and singing to herself. Seeing Mina she explained, "She was moving all over the place. The singing seems to calm her down."

"She?"

"Definitely a she."

"All the best people are."

"Mina, I'm worried," began Daphne, biting her lip. "What if when she's born she's all upset. I won't be able to sing to her." And she began to cry. An all too frequent occurrence these days.

Mina threw her arm around her. "They'll let you see her in the nursery," she said softly.

"What if they don't though?" Daphne asked, panicked. "What if they don't let me see her? What if they don't let me sing to her?"

Mina hugged her close, making extravagant promises that she would get Straton to break them both into the nursery. That they would hide her baby beneath the bed roll and keep her all for themselves.

If I had known, thought Mina, if Alex had told me, I could have hidden with Daphne. We could have stayed in the empress' quarters in safety and none of this would be happening.

Over on the Viminal Hill, somewhere between the slums at the bottom and the large spacious villas on the higher slopes, Teretia raised her head.

"Did I do that right? I'm not sure that I did that right. Was that right?"

Philo, laid out on the bed gasping for air, and greatly resembling a fish left out on a riverbank, was unable to answer for some time. When he did, it was to squawk in a rather high-pitched voice, "I think we should get married."

Such was the effect of a well-executed Sporus.

TWENTY-EIGHT

The day began like any other. The usual scramble for breakfast hurriedly eaten before dashing off to their positions. Mina skipped the refectory feeling distinctly sick and sore. It had burned painfully when she peed for the third morning in a row and she couldn't face eating anything that might cause her to go again.

There was a big do arranged for the day. Statilia was to dine publicly with Galba. To reassure her family and the populace at large that she was still alive and had not, as the gossips claimed, been quietly dispatched. So they were to attend the games, in a big box at the front. All the better for the plebs to marvel at her. Then they would retreat back via the tunnels that linked the stadium to the palace for a dinner attended by the senate and their wives or mistresses.

It is worth noting that excluded from the invites were the palace freedmen, who usually would have expected to revel in such entertainment. Only those working were allowed to attend. Galba keen to demarcate between the social strata.

Philo was attending, much against his will. He hated the games and had hoped to take a day off to assist Teretia with the wedding arrangements. Though legally they could start calling themselves husband and wife, he knew that Teretia would like a ceremony and a big party for all her family. So there was much to arrange. Philo's organising abilities were proving the perfect foil for Teretia's giddy pink excitement.

He'd planned to accompany her to her aunt's home to discuss the food that Pompeia Major volunteered to provide. But Icelus, though possessed of an irrational loathing of his assistant, nevertheless found himself unable to function without him by his side. So he insisted Philo attend the games. He needed prompting on etiquette and names. Philo had an in-depth knowledge of both.

Also attending was Straton with strict instructions to keep the labour in line. "No fuck ups," as Felix had succinctly put it. There had been notable occasions in the past when slaves accompanying their masters to the games had gone slightly giddy with excitement and participated in inappropriate behaviour.

You could get away with such shenanigans under Nero. He liked to see his staff cheering for his favourite chariot team, the Greens, or loudly supporting a fine gladiator. But Galba was a different species. Felix lined them all up after breakfast, eyeing them with ill-disguised hostility.

"Fucking decorum," he told them. "That is what I want to see today. I want you in fucking position and staying in fucking position. Heads lowered unless requested otherwise. There will be silence, total fucking silence. Anyone who breaks that silence will be sent to Straton for correction."

Straton dutifully leered and fondled his whip causing a collective shudder. Mina, propped against table, yawned. A gesture that Felix luckily missed.

"Now get fucking to it!" he yelled, slamming his hand down with a bang.

"Felix, do you have a moment?" asked Philo, satchel slung across his chest, note tablet in his hand.

"For you, Philo, anything. Wot's up?"

"Erm … Icelus says he doesn't want Theseus attending Galba."

"Why the fuck not? He's a fucking emperor's attendant, ain't he?"

Philo, wiping the spit off his face, replied calmly, "Can we strike him off for today, please?" He was distracted slightly by Straton who was stood behind Felix trying to attract his attention. "Apparently he's too comely."

"Fears the competition does he?" laughed Felix. "Fuck knows what Galba sees in that bald fucker. He doesn't touch any of my boys or my girls. Galba, that is. Icelus is all over the fucking fan boys. I've had to write five of them off. Cutting into my fucking budget it is."

"Have you any body slaves who are less … well, just less?"

Felix was enraged. The whole point of a body slave was attractiveness: they were bred for it. "Righty fucking ho! I'll give him fucking Straton. Straton, you fancy handling the imperial todger?"

"No," rasped Straton looking directly and intently at Philo.

"I could ugly up Theseus."

Philo took a step backwards. "Could you just sort it Felix, please?"

Felix wasn't listening. His attention had been caught by Lysander wandering by in a lurid green tunic with yellow fringing.

"Oi, Lysander! No way, you fucker!" he yelled, running out to confront the freedman over his attire.

"Philo, need to talk," croaked Straton.

Gods, thought Philo, please don't tell me you love me again. His method of dealing with the Straton situation since the overseer's first declaration had taken the form of dashing behind doors or into cupboards whenever he heard him approaching in an attempt to avoid him. As a long-term strategy he was aware that this was unlikely to hold up.

"I am really busy today. I have lots to do. Not a lot of time. Very busy," he stammered out quickly.

Straton stood in front of the door, closing it and throwing across the bar. Philo made a quick scan of the room for alternative exits. Finding that there weren't any, he pressed his back against a wall and waited to see what would happen.

Straton had been practising his speech for days. It was very important to him that Philo understood. He worked on the words very carefully so they conveyed exactly what he felt. Standing before his beloved he felt oddly nervous; an emotion he was not used to. Straton was a man of action. He did not have the intellect for nerves or regrets.

He swallowed hard, hoping his voice would hold for all the crucial words.

"Love you," he began. "Want you. Just you. Only you. Always."

He looked to see how Philo was taking this: blankly, silently.

"Be together. Us. Always. You love me?"

Philo thought this last bit a statement. It was the sort of mad assumption Straton frequently made about him. But seeing the overseer's eager face, he realised it was a question and there was an expectation that he would answer it. He briefly toyed with the idea of replying, "No."

He loved Teretia. If Teretia had not loved him back that would have been truly dreadful. So he was not without sympathy for the overseer. But he was also absolutely terrified of him and what he might do if he replied honestly. He had an image of Straton going berserk, smashing every stick of furniture in the room and him alongside it. So with a sinking heart he said in a quietly trembling voice, "Yes."

Reaching her seat in the box, waving to the crowd who nudged each other, "Empress still alive then," Statilia decided she was cold. The shawl chosen for her was not warm enough and she was not going to sit for many hours in such a draught.

"Statilia Messalina, would you like me to loan you my cloak?" Galba asked chivalrously.

Statilia looked at the rough, brown material. She then looked at the tens of thousands of spectators who were gawping right at her.

"Girl," she addressed Mina, "rush back and get my woollen shawl. Quickly."

Then she smiled at Galba. "It wouldn't match my dress."

Highlighting one of the many qualities that Galba felt made women inferior.

Vinius, Laco, and Icelus, stood at the back, were cheered by the reception Galba was given from the crowd. There had been some debate as to whether his attendance was a good idea. The senate were all behind Galba but the people were a different story. Votives for Nero appeared regularly outside the palace walls even now.

Nero had attended every games, every chariot race, and every theatre production he was able to. He'd even participated in performances: giving his people a rare opportunity to see their leader in a most un-imperial fashion. It made him wildly popular. For who didn't want to see the emperor risk life and limb in the races for their entertainment, cheering until they were hoarse when he completed a circuit safely?

Nero's games became ever more elaborate, ever more entertaining spectacles, and it was difficult to see how they could be topped. Galba was uninterested in the details. "They're plebs. They'll watch whatever they are given."

His advisors knew the truth. The mob were picky and if unimpressed by the entertainment, they would not be slow to show their displeasure. The city was edgy. The last thing they needed was a riot. The price of restoring order could well be Galba's place in the people's hearts.

Though they didn't chant his name as they had Nero's, they at least politely cheered Galba's arrival in the stadium. The empress elicited a far louder cry, leading Vinius to wonder whether he should suggest a marriage again. He'd heard from Artemina that Statilia was fond of Otho. Which would not do.

Vinius planned for Otho to marry his daughter. It would be wise to cut Statilia's hopes before they could flourish.

Galba had no particular love for the games. He'd seen real action and considered gladiator bouts as mere play: overdone and false. Yet he attempted a tight smile and waved as required.

It appeared genial to the palace staff, who were used to their grim-faced master. But the people, accustomed to cheery, flamboyant Nero, were not so enamoured of their new emperor. Casting sly looks at him in-between the entertainment, they saw a hook-nosed, scrawny old man with thinning white hair who looked almost bored by the proceedings.

"Thing is, he's the only guy for the job," said Tadius who had shut his shop for the day. "Nobody else wants to do it."

His companion, the cobbler Damos, nodded sagely and then exclaimed, "Hey, is that Otho?" Squinting down at the seats in the lower levels.

"Yeah, think so," said Tadius and then put his considerable lungs to work by bellowing, "HEY, OTHO!"

Otho twitched and scanned the crowd for his addresser. Onomastus pointed him in the right direction. "The Viminal traders who threatened us."

"So it is," said Otho. Rising to his feet he cupped his hands round his mouth, calling out, "The lads from the Viminal steal all our best chicks by the size of their monstrous dicks!"

Tadius and Damos grinned and yelled back, "TOO TRUE!" then repeated the ditty. It chanted round and round the stadium in increasing volume. Otho laughing as it rang out took a stagey bow for the crowd which got a huge cheer. The empress stood to her feet and applauded him. Icelus' and Laco's jaws stiffened. Their faces reddened when the crowd, enthused by a good chant, started on a ditty of their own composition, singing loudly and joyfully. Though Laco didn't catch all the words he certainly caught the beginnings of the first verse: "The old man who stinks of Spanish piss …"

TWENTY-NINE

Mina ran through the subterranean tunnel that linked the stadium to the palace complex. A necessity for the emperor's safety. The plebs hated to see a favourite gladiator dispatched and were apt to blame the top man for his demise. She ran with speed, imagining the empress' displeasure if she were left chilled for too long.

"Mina!" The call froze her. She turned to see Alex, all smiles, heading towards her.

"How are the games going? Theseus has a hundred sesterces bet on that gladiator Pyrrus. He's gutted he can't watch it. Has he been on yet? Pyrrus?"

"They are still on the wild beast hunt," she told him coldly.

Catching her tone he asked, "Mina, what's up?"

She'd avoided Alex for the past few days. Unsure what to say to him. Not sure what she felt about him. She still harboured a little hope that Alex was innocent, that her friend hadn't so cruelly deceived her. It was a hope lost as soon as she told him, "I've been to see Sporus."

The colour faded noticeably from his face and the smile drooped.

"How could you?" she demanded.

"Whatever he said, it's rubbish. I saved him. I vouched for him. Honoratus was going to have him killed."

"Honoratus?"

"The Praetorian tribune."

"So you are in league with the Guard," she stated calmly.

"No. Yes. I helped make Galba emperor."

"You say that as if it is something to be proud of."

"It is. It is, Mina. Galba is a great emperor, miles better than Nero."

"How would you know? Did you ever meet Nero? No. Have you ever met Galba? No."

"Nero was corrupt, depraved. An invert."

"And Sporus? What is he?"

"He has a chance of a better life now. He doesn't have to be a catamite any more. Galba doesn't like catamites."

"Sporus loved Nero."

"Nonsense. Nero corrupted Sporus," said Alex stoically. "I freed him from that. He has a chance to better himself now."

Mina closed her eyes. She saw Juba once again before he raped her. Two Praetorians dragging Erotica away by her hair. Daphne with growing belly. Sporus terrified and shaking as the soldiers closed in on Nero. Epaphroditus faking his own death. Sabinus struck down by his own troops. Teretia's father flattened by a horse. The empress held against her will. And that moment, that heart-freezing moment, when the guards sealed off the slave complex. Remembering the fear and the terror she'd experienced.

Opening her eyes she glared at him. "You shit! You absolute shit! How could you? How could you do this to us all?"

She flew at him, slapping and hitting. Alex tried to grab hold of her wrists to subdue her but she was too mad, too angry for control.

"I did it for you," he said in-between stinging slaps to his arms and back.

"For me? For me?" she screamed, clawing at him. "How in great Minerva's name was this mess for me?"

"Listen to me. Listen to me," he said, grabbing her arm tight. "Listen to me."

She ceased her attack. "Go on then. Do tell. I can't wait to hear how betraying your friends and engaging in treason was all for me!"

He let go of her arm. This wasn't how he'd imagined this moment would be. "Because I fucking love you, alright," he said angrily. "I've always bloody loved you from when we were kids. And you never looked at me. Not once. You'd open your legs for Vinius or Epaphroditus or Lysander or Philo or … anyone you thought would help you, but not me. Never me. I wasn't good enough, important enough for you. But I was a big deal. A big deal to the Guard and Icelus and Sabinus and Galba. I was a big deal. I was the one who told Sabinus where Nero was. I was the one who hunted him down. I made Galba emperor. I stopped Sabinus when he went mad. I held Galba's throne for him. Me So I am important, very important. I am valued."

It was not at all what he meant to say, but it was at least honest and true. He stood red-faced waiting for her reaction.

Mina, swaying slightly, said quietly, "Where are your important friends now, Alex? I don't see Icelus promoting you through the ranks for your valued contribution. I think they've forgotten all about you."

"Not true," he spat at her. "Honoratus is going to buy me from the palace. He's getting the money together. I'm going to be his son." Then calming slightly he added, "He says I can still visit you, though."

"Why would I want you to visit me?" Mina said slowly. "Why would I ever want to see you again after what you've done? How could I ever love someone who could betray us so easily for his own glory?"

"Mina," he pleaded. "Mina, please." He tried to take her hand but she pulled it away from him sharply.

"You are pathetic," she spat with every molecule of bile she could produce, and turned to leave.

"Pathetic am I?" a crushed Alex, stung into retaliation, called after her. "What about you? What about you and your precious Epaphroditus? Do you know why he screwed you the other night? Do you? Because he's got a disease of the dick, that's why. He didn't want to pass it on to someone he actually cares about. That's why he sent for you!"

She turned. "That is not true."

"It is." He nodded fast. "I heard it from Otho. He's passing his magical cure round the guards."

"Not true," she said again. Knowing now the origin of the burning sensation.

"True. It's what you get for being a whore. I wonder how many you've passed it on to?"

It was too far, too far for either of them to retreat. Mina ran for him, nails bared, with pure fury in her eyes.

The wild beast hunt over, Galba and entourage were heading back to the palace for some brief refreshments. Walking through the tunnel, they heard shouting. Galba looked quizzically at Icelus.

"I shall go find out, Caesar."

Felix, coming from the other direction, also heard the altercation. "Fucking Hades!" he swore. He clicked his fingers at Straton, the two of them running to the scene.

Alex gave up trying to defend himself from Mina's onslaught. He retaliated blow for blow and it had degenerated into a proper fight with accompanied insults and yells. Despite their differences in sex they were surprisingly well matched. Alex might possess a certain wiry energy but Mina had the outrage of a wronged maiden and she could punch hard. She could also scratch. Alex's arms were a mass of red stripes.

Felix waded into the midst of this fierce battle, grabbing hold of Alex and pulling him away. Straton took Mina, lifting her off her feet with ease and with a great deal less brutality than he usually would have employed. Mina kicked her legs.

"Let me go, Straton. I want to brain the fucker."

"Whore!" screamed Alex, earning a thump to the head from Felix.

"What the fuck is going on?" Felix yelled above the squabbling slaves.

"You are nothing to me, Alex," shrieked Mina. "Nothing." She kicked her legs wildly.

Straton, holding her round the waist, told her, "Calm it."

"Why don't you listen to your boyfriend, Artemina?"

Straton frowned.

Even with Felix's arm across his throat, Alex was determined to get his point out. "She's told everyone you're fucking her. Everyone thinks you're screwing. Everyone!" he spat. Too enraged to think through the disadvantages to himself of upsetting Straton.

"Think your special friend will like that when he finds out? Think he'll be jealous? Upset by her lies?"

Straton's eyes narrowed.

The sound of running feet alerted those present that the guards were aware of the situation. Felix, keen to preserve his stock intact, pulled Alex backwards. "You're going back to the complex. Correction will be dished out there. You should both be fucking ashamed of yourselves. I said decorum, fucking decorum today. Straton, bring the girl."

Straton threw Mina over his shoulder.

And that should have been that. They would have all gone back to the slave complex. Straton would have inflicted a couple of whippings. They'd have been taken off public duties for a bit. And the whole thing would have been forgotten in a day or two. But that wasn't what happened.

215

They were halfway along the tunnel. Mina was kicking hard but ineffectually at Straton's back, who wasn't taking it personally, screaming insults at Alex. Alex, dragged along by Felix was letting loose exactly what he thought about Mina's love life when a weepy Philo came round the corner.

He looked confused at the scene in front of him. As Alex passed him, struggling against Felix's hold, he let out a kick that flicked wide. It hit the freedman on the shin, knocking him against the wall. Straton, seeing Philo hurt, responded instantly and violently. Dropping Mina he tussled with Felix for Alex, grabbing the slave by the throat and delivering one killer punch to his face, sending him a good five feet backwards.

It was unfortunate that the punch directed him back towards the stadium. Alex fell just as the emperor rounded the corner. Mina, released from Straton's grip flew at him again, and though dazed and bloodied he was not entirely defenceless. The emperor, flanked by Laco and Vinius, was treated to a display of bitter wrestling accompanied by screams of, "Whore!" "Traitor!" "Scum!"

With Straton distracted helping Philo to his feet, Felix moved in alone in an attempt to separate Mina and Alex. He managed to disable Alex with one hand round his throat, the other gripping Mina's wrist. Neither prevented the barrage of insults they continued to hurl at each other.

Galba looked down his long nose. "THIS IS A DISGRACE!"

THIRTY

"Well," said Felix, cracking his knuckles. "Right fucking mess this is."

Straton standing beside his desk nodded.

"Fucking embarrassment. Sodding slaves fighting in front of the fucking emperor. I'm not fucking surprised he's mad! What with the fucking language coming from that girl's mouth. I'm fucking mad!"

He certainly was. He'd been erupting all day, and most were giving his office an extremely wide berth. "And what the fuck happened to you?" He turned on Straton. "One moment it's situation contained and then all fuck kicks off? What the fuck happened?"

Straton, greatly reassured to find Philo unhurt, had helped him to his feet gently, brushing down his tunic where the earth had stuck to it. He'd looked rather upset but then who wouldn't be by the show Mina and Alex had put on? Philo was a nervy sort and no doubt the fight had frightened him. Still, he could take care of Philo when he moved into his quarters. He would be able to look after him properly.

To Felix's question, Straton gave a sparse justification. "Thought boy was going to escape you. Thought had better contain him."

"Thought? You didn't fucking think, did you?"

Straton shook his head. He was as embarrassed by the situation as Felix was. It made them look like amateurs, not being able to control their own slaves.

"Sorry," he croaked.

"Apology accepted," said Felix flipping open a tablet. "OK, let's get this mess sorted. Artemina." He looked down at Mina's file. "A girl with friends in high places. Vinius has placed a plea for clemency. The empress says she can't be bothered to train up a new girl."

"Good sort," interrupted Straton.

"Jupiter, not you too? I was going to throw her to the overseers for a night. Let them have their fun."

"Good sort," repeated Straton with emphasis.

Felix, amused, replied, "You carry on like this, I'm going to start believing you're screwing her. But she's good breeding stock and them fuckers would rip her terrible. She was way out of fucking line though, behaving like that! No fucking decorum at all. Not having it, Straton. Not having it at all."

"Light rod?"

"Whip. Ten lashes and I'm giving it to Xagoras because you'd be too soft on her."

Straton looked unhappy but accepting. (Later he would dash off to menace Xagoras into a lighter sentence.)

"OK, Alexander." He opened Alex's file grim-faced. "Some fucker's got to be made an example of. Sorry Alex, mate, but that fucker is you. Galba's orders."

At the back of the file he inscribed the date neatly and wrote beside it one word in capitals: *CRUCIFIED*.

Alex sat chained to a wall. His face throbbed from where Straton had punched him. He was familiar with this cell. A couple of years previously there had been uproar over a quantity of food stolen from the refectory. A steaming Felix promising stern retribution for those responsible.

Somehow, and Alex never found out how, suspicion had fallen on him. He'd been dragged to this cell and told he would be tortured for the names of his accomplices. Here he had sat, chained to a wall quivering in anticipation. When Scaveous arrived with his bag of tools, Alex had promptly fainted in a heap on the floor, tearing his fingernail off in the process.

Later he was to exaggerate this tale to some high adventure. Truthfully Scaveous told Felix it wasn't worth torturing Alex as he was unlikely to get any answers out of him if he was lying in a faint on the floor. Alex endured a thrashing though. So he sat now, chained to the same wall, not worried at all. He figured he was maybe in for another beating at most and expected Straton with his sturdiest whip at any moment.

Rather than fretting over his punishment he let his mind wander to Mina and Sporus. He was pretty sore over the whole situation. He couldn't wait to live with Antonius Honoratus. When that day finally came, Alex decided, he wouldn't bother to visit his so-called friends again. Let them wallow in their imperial degradation, selling themselves for higher positions. He was off to a whole new life, a better life. Better than they could ever hope for.

A little after dark, as Alex was watching his cell fade away in the gloom, the door was unlocked. The jailer accompanied by Felix undid his chains.

"Stand," he was instructed.

He was walked out by Felix and Xagoras, assuming he was on his way to a whipping. Alex strode along briskly, wanting to get it over with as quickly as possible. He was surprised when he was led through the palace doors out into the gardens, but still unsuspecting.

It wasn't until he saw the small party waiting for him on the Aventine side of the hill that he understood. Seeing the carpenter finishing off the cross with a mallet, he turned to Felix in panic. "No, no, no, no, no, no." Shaking his head, his knees giving way. Xagoras lifted him roughly to his feet.

"No, no, no Felix, no, please no. I'll do whatever, but no, no," he pleaded, sobs escaping from him.

Felix shook his head sadly. He hated doing this. It was a waste of good merchandise. But orders were orders and Galba was vehemently insisting. Alex was crying, trying desperately to wriggle free from Xagoras' grip but the overseer had a firm hold on him. "No! No! No!"

Xagoras dragged him to the cross. The carpenter standing back, hammer in hand, ready to nail Alex to it.

Crucifixion is not much of a spectator sport, as those who had sat numb-bummed through the execution of criminals at the games could contest. Nevertheless there was a good turn-out for Alex. If someone was going to be made an example of, you needed witnesses. So Felix had rounded up a band of grudging imperial slaves who could pass word back about how fucking horrible it was.

And it was. Philo's assistant, Talos, a reluctant presence suffered nightmares about it for years afterwards. If Mina had been there she would have instantly forgiven Alex. Just the sound of his screams as they tapped the nails in would have swung her back to his side.

Once he was up, the screams ended. It was hard enough work trying to breathe, so he concentrated on that: in and out, in and out, in and out. His head hung down staring at his swollen feet. There was a buzzing in his head which wouldn't go away that irritated and broke his concentration.

There were no last thoughts or reflections on what had led him here. No musings on Mina. No regrets about Sporus. There was nothing but the buzzing in his head and the rasping sound he made as he struggled for air. Eventually both of these ceased.

High on the Palatine Hill they kept the body positioned, letting the crows peck at it. The race followers in the Circus

220

Maximus below able to see the cross highlighted against the sky. The palace staff passing the fallen slave several times a day as they completed their duties. It was a stark and bloody reminder of the lowliness of their position and it sent a collective chill through the complex.

THIRTY-ONE

"I'm free. I can wear whatever I like, surely? That's the point of freedom. But Felix keeps telling me to tone it down."

Otho nodded sympathetically to Lysander's complaints, offering this advice. "I tell you what, Lysander. It would make more of an impact if you wear your flash gear out of hours. I mean, why waste it on the likes of Felix when you could be showing your wardrobe off to some beautiful free girl out there."

Lysander smiled. He was right. "Thanks, Otho. That's brilliant."

Otho gave a beam, leaving Lysander brightened and no doubt planning his next excursion within the freebie world.

It had been a more cheerful distraction than his last. A visit to a sullen Antonius Honoratus.

"I wanted to thank you," Honoratus had said, small wooden animals lined up on his desk. "For what you did." Correcting himself. "What you tried to do."

"I am only sorry I did not succeed," said Otho sadly.

"Not many would have even tried for just a slave. Pleading for clemency like that. Putting your own money forward to buy him for me."

"I am sorry that Galba was not willing to listen to our pleas." Otho took hold of a dangling hand and squeezed it. "It is a dreadful waste."

Honoratus nodded, overcome with emotion. "He was just a boy. He should have been playing dice or getting into trouble with girls."

"A problem that afflicts me still," smiled Otho.

Honoratus attempted to smile back. "The girl? She lived?"

"She did. Vinius threw in a word for her. I persuaded the empress to put in a word as well."

Honoratus picked up a wooden elephant, running a finger across its delicately carved trunk. "I am glad. Alex would not have wanted her to …" he broke off.

"No, he wouldn't," agreed Otho. "He liked her, I heard."

Honoratus nodded, composing himself. "You are a good man, Otho. If there is anything I can do for you, ever …"

Otho waved the offer away. "There is no need, Antonius. No need at all."

He left Honoratus with his wooden animals and broken dreams; the scene dampening his natural buoyancy. It was all so unnecessary. Yes, slaves had to be kept in line but this was an over-reaction, surely? What had the boy done? Got into a fight, cussed in front of the emperor?

Otho tolerated a lot worse from his own staff. The matter should have been resolved privately. Keeping the body trussed up like that. It was cruel to all those slaves who had known Alex, liked Alex. It reminded him of that terrible moment at the Milvian Bridge when Galba dealt with a potential riot with decimation. Yes, the law said he could but it seemed so extreme.

The issue with Alex had led to a very rare falling out with Epaphroditus. The freedman was shocked by Otho's attempts to buy Alex out of trouble.

"What were you thinking?" he had demanded. "What do you care whether he crucifies one of his own slaves? You are meant to be sucking up to Galba. Not disputing his perfect right to punish his own household. How does this forward our plan?"

"I had to try and help," he'd responded. "I couldn't just let it … could you? Would you?"

"Not my business. Not your business either."

To placate him Otho had nipped up to the palace to keep up the required presence. He came up most days, chatting with the staff, flirting with the empress, and keeping Titus Vinius on side. The latter introduced him to his daughter Vinicia. She was, Otho was pleased to note, a comely girl with black hair tied modestly back and large brown eyes which appraised him with clear regard. She was not, thought Otho, as untouched as her father supposed. Which was fine by him, for he liked them game.

Poppaea had certainly been game. She who could silence a whole room with a well-crafted anecdote to an audience who hung on her every word. Otho inevitably stood next to the drinks, watching her with pride. This gorgeous, sexy woman who was his wife and every man in the room hated him for it.

They had been quite a double act: his relaxed charm and her showy wit. They bounced off each other providing entertainment of their own. Who needed acrobats and dancing girls when you had Otho and Poppaea as guests? Touted in the highest of society they laughed and drank their way through the party scene, becoming ever more outrageous, more talked about, more in demand.

It was a madcap kind of fun. A whirl of glamour. Of killer hangovers, both of them sipping at melon juice and bemoaning that final goblet of wine. Of money lavished on clothes and jewels (Otho never able to deny his adored wife her desires). Of sitting under the table giggling as they hid from the moneylenders. Of a hundred glorious evenings that they shared together.

Then he made the mistake of introducing her to his boyhood friend Nero. And was abruptly shown to be the mere stepping stone to Poppaea's ultimate goal.

Otho shook off those memories, realising with regret it was time to see Icelus. Epaphroditus had told him to make nice to the freedman, commenting dryly, "He holds the emperor's ear, amongst other things."

Otho had done his best but he had the distinct feeling that Icelus did not like him, which was most unorthodox. In an attempt to find common ground he spoke most flowingly on the horror of discovering that his hair was receding, of the many unguents and potions he experimented with, and his absolute joy in finding his barber Menachus.

"The man is a miracle worker. I can even bathe in it!" he had told Icelus, scribbling down Menachus' details. Icelus was not amused.

Still, Otho was not one to give up. Meandering down the corridor for what was bound to be another tense encounter, he met a jovial Straton coming the other direction whistling happily.

"Hello there, Straton," he cooed. "You're a fine sight. Not much cheer here today," he confided, Honoratus on his mind again. "Bit gloomy. All very sad," he continued, for a conversation with Straton was always going to be one-sided and you just had to plough on to plug the gaps. "So what is cheering you today?"

He waited hopefully for an answer. Straton smiled. And it was a smile. Not a grimace, not a menacing grin, nor even a sadistic smirk but a genuine smile that lit all the way up to his eyes.

"Got meself boyfriend. Moving in," he told Otho. "With me." Adding proudly, "Love me."

"Well, I am very happy for you. I hope you and your fellow will be joyfully content."

"Shall," said Straton, thumbs hooked in his belt.

"I hope it works out well for you."

"Shall," determined Straton.

Otho watched him go. He'd always had a bit of a soft spot for Straton, seeing him as a protective bear of a man. The sort of view only the freeborn who'd never had much to do with the overseer could ever possibly hold. He once expressed a little of that sentiment to Epaphroditus, commenting that, "Straton was the sort of man you'd want covering your back."

Epaphroditus' response had been a look of sheer disbelief and horror.

Otho bounded into the antechamber to find Philo sat at his desk staring miserably at a scroll. Hearing the door open the freedman's head had shot up. Thinking it was Straton returning he greeted Otho with an expression of pure despair.

Philo had no idea where Straton had got the idea that he was moving in with him. He had definitely not agreed to anything of the sort but then consent was rarely something Straton sought.

Bizarrely and mystifying for Philo, Straton was seeking his opinion on some more mundane matters such as his preferred side to the bed, how many pillows did he like, was the book-case big enough for his scroll collection? Straton was appearing more and more in the antechamber. A fact that was causing Philo increasing anxiety since Teretia was doing much the same thing in relation to the wedding arrangements. It was inevitable, he thought, that their paths would cross.

He'd attempted to suggest casually to Teretia that she not visit him at work, citing Icelus as the determining factor. However, her lip had begun to wobble and she had replied in a breaking voice, "But what if I decide on the food and I choose something you don't like? Or the flowers? Or the guests?"

She looked so hurt that he'd instantly caved in and she happily trotted up to the Palatine most days with all the latest plans for his approval. Philo was thus a man on the edge, a precipice of an edge which he expected to plunge off at any moment.

"Blimey, Philo, you look like Acteon before he was torn apart by wild dogs!" Which nicely encapsulated the freedman's feelings. Otho pulled up a chair, leaning his elbows on the edge of Philo's desk.

"Are you OK? You look a bit …" pale, deathly, haunted, terrified. Otho settled on, "peaky."

Philo, busying himself with tidying up some scrolls gave a, "I am fine thanks," with as much spirit as he could muster.

"Are you sure? Is there something bothering you?" Otho asked kindly.

Philo, staring down at his desk, did not answer.

"Come now, there is clearly something eating at you. Perhaps I can help?"

A suggestion that at least elicited a, "Pah," from the scribe.

"Oh come on! Nothing can be all that bad!"

No, not bad at all, thought Philo. Just an insanely jealous homicidal maniac who had terrorised and tormented him his whole life had now fallen in love with him. Oh, and believed they were moving in together in some public declaration of their feelings (a thought that made the freedman shudder), while remaining unaware that Philo was about to marry the woman he utterly and devotedly cared for. Oh, and he was cheating on the pair of them.

It had all the makings of a terrifically messy, public catastrophe. Philo maintained a keen recollection of the time he had shockingly dared to share breakfast with a girl, which led to Lysander reluctantly covering for him as he lay trembling under a blanket wondering if he was well and truly broken this time. Jupiter knew what Straton would do if he found out that Philo had talked, kissed, slept with, Sporus-ed, and fallen in love with a girl. Jupiter did know and actually so did Philo. Straton would kill him. Literally and brutally.

Otho was looking at him with concern and kind eyes.

"Come on, try me. Let me help. I am sure there is some solution we can hit upon between us."

He sounded so sure, so positive that Philo felt a tiny sliver of hope build in him.

"You think?" he asked.

"Absolutely," Otho assured him cheerfully, with little idea of the problem he was about to blunder his way into.

Philo bit his lip, weighing it up before deciding it had spiralled beyond any feasible solution, shaking his head.

Otho was not to be discouraged. "Is it Icelus? You can always put in for a transfer. I am sure any department would snap you up. He is not worth getting upset over."

Philo did not reply.

"Is it that slave that was killed? Was he a friend? No? Not that? Alright … is it Teretia?"

Otho noted a lip wobble. "Philo, is everything alright between you and Teretia?"

Another lip wobble, then a stylus thrown down and an anguished cry of, "I've messed everything up!"

"Surely not, you've always struck me as particularly capable."

"No, I have, I've messed it all up." Then casting a distraught look at Otho, "I've done something dreadful."

Otho rather doubted this, thinking that Philo's version of something dreadful was most people's idea of an average night in. A view the freedman confirmed by blurting out, pained, "I've been unfaithful."

"Well that's nothing to worry about," Otho consoled. "You tried it and you didn't like it. You don't have to do it again. I wouldn't tell Teretia, mind."

"I just want to marry Teretia and be happy."

"You can still do that. She'll make a great little wifey. She doesn't have to know about this indiscretion of yours. Unless," Otho broke off. "Unless this filly of yours is threatening to tell her? Jupiter, Philo! Are you being blackmailed?"

Philo rubbed his eyes.

"Not a problem," beamed Otho. "I've been caught in much the same situation myself. 'Course the girl in question was claiming to be carrying my child which made it a little messier. Your indiscretion, is she …?"

He left the question open. Philo shook his head slowly.

"Well that's good. Simpler. We'll just buy the girl off. Don't you worry about the cash, I'll sort that out."

There had to be someone left in this city he could borrow money from.

"You don't understand. It's not …, it's not that simple."

Philo pulled open a drawer and placed on the desk a pile of trinkets.

Otho picked at them. There was a seal ring with an engraving of an erect phallus. A couple of scrolls of Catullus elegantly decorated with satyrs. A gold chain bracelet. And a clearly very expensive stylo set with *Philo* engraved on its box.

Oh dear, thought Otho. Poor Philo, just his luck. Epaphroditus can discard hundreds of women whilst enjoying a blissfully happy marriage to Aphrodite. Philo strays once and the girl develops an obsession with him, threatening his happiness with Teretia.

He interjected as much cheer as he could into a, "Right! How are we going to sort this out?"

Philo looked at him in surprise. "It can be resolved? Without Teretia knowing? Really?"

"We simply need to make it clear to your indiscretion that you are not available," stated Otho. "Or have you tried that already?"

Philo shook his head. "No, I couldn't. He wouldn't like it."

Otho swallowed this additional nugget of information calmly. As a former member of Nero's inner circle he was pretty much unshockable. He was surprised though. Philo didn't seem the type for that sort of philandering. He'd always thought him a bit of an innocent.

"Would it help if I were to talk to him? Explain the situation?"

Philo gave him a horrified look. "I don't think that would be a good idea, Otho. I don't want him to know about Teretia. He wouldn't like it."

"I would be very sensitive. We could work on the words together."

Philo shook his head rapidly to each sensible suggestion put forward.

"Short of faking your own death, one of us is going to have to talk to him."

"No, no, Otho. I don't think that's a good idea. It could get …, could get nasty."

"OK," he smiled patiently. "How about a letter? We could compose it together. Let him down gently."

"But when he got it he'd come looking for me," Philo protested. "And I wouldn't be able to …" he trailed off miserably, adding in little more than a whisper, "resist."

Otho, seeing his distress, whipped round to the other side of the desk and put an arm round him. Philo flinched away.

"I don't want him to be in love with me. Why does he have to be in love with me?"

"Well, let's think about this properly. Come up with a solution together," said Otho, thumb and finger pinching at his chin.

Marcus Salvius Otho was many things. He was exceptionally kind-hearted and generous. A superb drinking companion. A loyal friend. What he wasn't was practical. Faced with a problem to solve he took his own unique way. If the quickest point from A to B was a straight line then Otho's brain would zigzag its way there and then end up at F. It was why he had led such an adventurous and unpredictable life.

For sensible advice Otho relied on Epaphroditus and Onomastus. Both of whom he would happily ignore if it suited him. To Otho's cluttered thought processes there seemed to be two key points to Philo's very particular problem as he saw it: a) Teretia must not find out about Philo's indiscretion, and b) Philo's indiscretion should desist from pursuing him (without actually being told to).

Otho clicked his fingers. "Aha! I have it!"

"Really?" asked Philo a little desperately.

"Absolutely," assured Otho. "What we need is a distraction!"

THIRTY-TWO

The bookcase was lovely, thought Straton. It matched the desk perfectly. What he wasn't sure about though was the mass of cushions that lay fattening on the bed.

It was fair to say that Straton was nesting. He'd spent a great deal of his free time furnishing his quarters in anticipation of Philo moving in. To add to the desk there was now a bookcase, an additional easy chair, a couch where they could cuddle up together, and a foot stool. An actual foot stool as opposed to the human variety that Straton usually employed.

He'd taken care of the hard furnishings leaving Mina to deal with the soft. She had decided on cushions. Lots of cushions, which Straton failed to see the point of.

"Got pillows," he told her.

"But these are decorative," she replied, bouncing one in her hands. "Or to prop you up more if you want to read in bed." Correcting this to, "If he wants to read in bed," when she remembered Straton's illiteracy. "They're gorgeous," she assured him. "Feel."

Straton squeezed one, commenting, "Soft."

"And colourful," added Mina, who had purchased in a range of reds and golds and russets. Straton's room was all a

233

bit vapid in her view. It needed an injection of hard colour to stop it appearing drained.

She was spending a lot of time with Straton these days. Not just for her lessons in which she was acquiring some impressive skills, but because she recognised that, somewhat improbably, she enjoyed spending time with him.

She was avoiding the complex as much as she could. The talk was all on what had happened to Alex. She didn't want to know about that. Did not want to know that he had suffered or let her mind dwell on those endless what ifs. She hated the piteous looks and the cloying sympathy. She couldn't even bear to tell Sporus, to speak the words out loud. She was hoping that Otho had filled him in to save her the anguish.

Straton didn't ask about Alex, didn't talk about Alex, didn't sympathise with her about Alex, which made him a positive pleasure to be with. The overhaul of his rooms gave her a project to concentrate her mind on and she had thrown herself into it with gusto, touched by Straton's fretting for perfection.

"Can I still come see you when he moves in?" she asked. "I'd like to, for lessons. I'm getting good now."

Straton, testing out the cushions, didn't see a problem with this. "Lessons elsewhere though. Frighten him."

Even Straton had noticed that Philo seemed increasingly nervy. At a moment when he had been moving in for a post-coital cuddle and a discussion on when Philo would be moving his things in, the freedman had burst into hysterical sobbing. This was not a novel experience for Straton. Most people cried when he had sex with them. And it was true that during the early days of their liaison Philo had cried before, during, and afterwards, and whenever they happened to pass in the corridor.

But that was different. They were in love now and the overseer was puzzled as to whether this was normal behaviour for people in love. He needed advice. The only other people he ever spoke to were Felix, who held a dim view of him messing with the goods, and Mina. So he began a little shyly.

"Ask you something?"

"'Course," smiled Mina kicking a cushion across the room where it landed squarely on the desk. "As I intended," she told Straton, plonking herself on the bed. "Ask away."

He wondered how to phrase it. Remembering how his every attempt to comfort Philo had stoked him into more tears. He began cautiously. "You and Epaphroditus," struggling over the name which stung his throat.

"Urgh, don't. We had this mind-blowing sex, best ever. Then I find out that he's given me something! Can you believe? It burns like Vesta's flame every time I pee. Though I suppose it could have been Titus Vinius who gave it to me. I don't think Epaphroditus would be so cruel as to knowingly … I mean we have a thing going. A good thing. Mind-blowing thing. I really need to talk to him about it but Felix won't let me out after …"

After the ruckus with Alex, she was still in disgrace. Confined to the slave complex, and just a little sore after Xagoras' beating. The overseer had taken the opportunity to touch up her breasts, telling her viciously, "Bet Straton doesn't feel them like this," making a crude attempt to turn her on.

"But once I am free. In the unfree sense of the word of course," she said with a cheer she did not feel.

"Knock, knock!" Mina and Straton looked at each other.

"Can we come in?" asked Otho from the other side of the door unwilling to walk in on Straton doing something he really did not want to see.

Mina went over and opened the door, Otho hiding his surprise behind a wide grin, "Is Straton in?"

She held the door open for him. He was a patrician. What in Jupiter's name was he doing in the slave complex? How had he even found it? Otho walked past her followed by the loyal Onomastus and a small boy dressed in a blue tunic with a satchel thrown across his chest, who to Mina's mind looked oddly familiar.

Otho had been impressed by Onomastus' work. His freedman had told him, "Crap time of year for slaves. The traders don't want to sail in the winter."

Yet the dwarf wonder had managed to find this boy quivering on a block at the slave market. He was a little thing, grubby even when Onomastus had brought him home, and Otho had been sceptical that he would fulfil their very particular needs. For starters the boy was clearly southern European in appearance, whereas Philo hailed from much further afield and his skin was much darker in tone. However, Onomastus took him off for a bath, a haircut, and a change of clothes, returning with a far more presentable specimen.

There was a certain natural resemblance to Philo in that the boy too had dark hair, brown eyes, and was slender in build, Onomastus attempting to replicate the persistent curl that plagued the nape of Philo's neck by use of a pair of hot curling tongs. What aided them in the deception was the boy's clear terror and confusion, which manifested itself in a very Philolike aura of general anxiety.

"Hullo, Straton," Otho smiled at the bemused overseer. "I have a gift for you."

Onomastus pushed forward mini-Philo who stared up at Straton with fright.

"Gift?"

"For your birthday?" suggested Otho.

"Not birthday."

"Oh really? When is your birthday?"

"Don't know."

"So it could be your birthday?"

"Could be," admitted Straton.

"He is so cute," gushed Mina, patting the boy on the head. "What's his name?"

Otho and Onomastus looked at each other and improvised in unison, "Ganymede."

236

"Hello, Ganymede," she cooed. "He's sweet." She gave the newly named Ganymede a little hug. Spotting a soft touch he clung to her shoulders with tiny hands.

Otho watched Straton carefully. He was evidently confused by this unexpected generosity. "Mine?" he rasped.

"Completely," Otho assured him. "I thought you deserved a treat. I often think it is a shame you overseers fail to get the recognition you deserve. It is a dirty job but you do it so well. Work well done deserves a reward."

A speech that Straton fully concurred with.

"What does he do?" Mina asked Otho.

"Whatever you want. He's a game little fellow. Likes his books and letters," he slipped in to underline the similarity to Philo.

Mina gave the boy extravagant kisses all over his face which made him smile for the first time.

"You have him," Straton told her.

"Really? He's a sweetheart, aren't you Ganymede?" She blew a raspberry on his cheek, eliciting giggles.

Otho, who really, really did not want to explain to Philo's haunted features that his guaranteed grand scheme to resolve his problem had failed, interjected, "Artemina, he is a gift for Straton. Have you done anything singularly impressive recently? No, I thought not. The opposite from what I hear."

She put him down and he clung to her legs viewing Straton nervously.

"Where sleep?"

Otho groomed a nail between his teeth suggesting lightly, "Could he not stay here? You have a lovely large room. I like the cushions. Very colourful."

"See, I told you they were just the thing. You should keep him." She tousled Ganymede's hair.

Straton thought about it. He'd never had his own slave before. Of course he borrowed freely from the palace's large stock but it wasn't quite the same. Felix bawling him out regularly for damaging the merchandise or failing to return it on time.

He was an attractive boy. Actually, looking at him now, Straton noted his slim limbs, large brown eyes, and the extremely alluring way his little body trembled all over.

"Thanks," he muttered.

"Not at all," swaggered Otho. "An absolute joy."

Straton bent down. Picking Ganymede's fingers off from Mina's leg, he lifted the boy up and placed him on the bed where he sat feet dangling, clutching his satchel to his chest.

"Hey!" said Mina. "He looks a bit like—"

"A young Apollo. I know, uncanny isn't it?" Otho interrupted hastily.

A tiny sliver of suspicion entered Mina's mind. It did not manifest itself yet but rather sat in some dim part of her brain waiting for the trigger that would turn it into a full-blown realisation.

Cornelius Laco sat behind his desk in the Guard's office. It was a much-changed room from the days of Nymphidius Sabinus. Then it had been cold, austere, dignified. Laco had tarted it up considerably. The walls had been painted black with intricate gold swirls and scenes of the gods. There was a round table and a low couch for Laco to relax upon. He'd even installed a small bubbling fountain, which he found helped him think.

Not that the role of Praetorian prefect required much thinking. There was nothing to it. All you had to do was brief your tribunes and they did it all for you. Occasionally Laco roused himself to inspect his troops. No, his thinking this day had nothing to do with his job. He was musing over one Marcus Salvius Otho.

He could not quite work him out, which bothered Laco for he considered himself an astute judge of character. Otho seemed to fit into two distinct personalities.

There was the Neronian Otho of a thousand sordid anecdotes: dissolute, wild, full of drunken excess and brashness.

Then there was this Otho, the one he had met: a well-regarded former governor who at the palace banquets avoided wine and ate sparingly and was so keen to play a part in the political workings that he was up at the palace most days talking to the dullest administrator, charming his way onto the most boring committees (the ones even Vinius could not stomach), and ingratiating himself with Galba.

This last part Laco could understand when it related to the fall of Nero. After all, it was well known that Otho had a score to settle with his former friend. This score was settled now. Yet Otho persisted in his efforts, spouting Galba's own policies back at him in an attempt to impress.

What did he want? Did he really expect Galba to adopt him? Laco would not have that; a man like Otho in Galba's inner circle.

Icelus, he could take. He was easily influenced. A weak man with a weak stomach. Wanting only Galba's approval; Galba's love. Two things he would never receive.

Vinius, Laco could tolerate. With Icelus on his side, dear Titus was no impediment.

But Otho would be a problem. He was siding with Vinius. Evening up the factions. Interfering with Laco's plans. That would not do. He must be taken out before he truly turned Galba. Before the old man decided on his heir. If he could just find Otho's palace insider, there would be scope there. Definite scope for Cornelius Laco to triumph.

On that cheery thought he stood up, stretching his arms. Time for a little stroll before dinner, he decided. On his way to his sumptuous suite of rooms which were housed in a particularly decorous part of the new palace he witnessed a curious scene. Otho talking quietly to Philo in the corridor, pulling him to one side with evident excitement. Laco was close enough to hear the words he spoke: "It is all in place."

Cornelius Laco frowned and then he wondered.

THIRTY-THREE

It took Cornelius Laco with the help of Talos two hours to establish the facts. Irrefutable facts. Smiling at the slave he pressed a gold coin into his hand, "You have done well, boy. Very well."

Talos, unaware of the blow he had just dealt his boss, took the coin with real pleasure. It was the first towards his freedom fund.

Laco slipped into Icelus' office, slapping his gloves on the desk and telling him, "I've found your leak."

Icelus started from his prone position on the couch. "Vinius?" he asked sitting upright.

"No," smiled Laco enigmatically. "It always troubled me that Otho argued quite strenuously for the disbanding of the German Bodyguard when our dear Titus was all for retaining them. If Vinius were Otho's creature you would expect total parity, yet there is deviation. I couldn't imagine poor Titus providing Otho with information only for him to side against him. An unworkable partnership I would have thought."

"They are friends though. I have seen them dining together."

"Show me a man who isn't friends with Otho! The man is positively wanton with his amiability. A fact Vinius will discover when his pal breaks off his engagement to his daughter and marries Statilia Messalina. I had Talos dig out the minutes for every meeting he could find from the past three months."

"And?" asked Icelus impatiently.

"The same five people have attended all: Galba, you, I, Vinius, and Philo."

"Philo?"

"He has minuted every one. He's the one who has been feeding confidential information back to Otho."

Laco stood, waiting for this to sink in with Icelus. The freedman's eyes twitched nervously from side to side and then opened very wide. He stood up, rubbing a hand across his scalp. "The little shit! I knew it! I knew he was too good to be true! Didn't I say it? I am going to have him executed …"

"Woah, Icelus. Hold on," interrupted Laco.

"He's been plotting with Otho, passing information on to him! Galba will be so mad. He will be thunderously angry. This will neuter Otho, Laco. He will be done after this. Philo will be definitely done." Icelus gave a sneer, though it was a happy sneer. He couldn't wait to see Philo and inflict punishment.

"I know, I know," Laco smoothed. "But let us have a think about this?" he suggested to Icelus, who looked at him blankly. "Otho worries me. It's not just that he's trying to impress Galba. He is a courtier. It's standard form. But he has pals in every office in the city. He is tighter with the Guard than I am and I'm their commander. He's persuaded the senate that his record in Lusitania supersedes his past exploits. He's to be found gambling with Galba's legions most nights and he's wooing the former empress intently. Otho has never struck me as a patient man. I don't think he wants Galba to adopt him, I think he wants to replace him. Now. That's what all this information is for: it's a plot. It is treason. He is deliberately getting close to Galba so he can more easily replace him." Laco gave Icelus a knowing glare.

"No, he'd never succeed. The senate chose Galba."

Laco gave him a hard look. "Are you prepared to risk it? Are you prepared to risk Galba's life?"

"No, of course not. Never."

Laco picked up his gloves. "Let me question Philo. He is in on this. He will know how deep it runs. He will know all the key players. We can therefore remove them. Then you and I can take this plot to Galba. Epaphroditus once brought a plot to Nero and he was promoted by two levels and amply rewarded for his troubles."

"We take it to Galba together," insisted Icelus.

"As I said."

"Go ahead. Question him. The emperor's safety is paramount. Use whatever force is necessary to extract the information."

Laco gave a thin smile, thinking how wonderfully pliable Icelus was.

Philo awoke early. It was a cold morning and he could see his breath in the air so he hugged Teretia closer to warm him. She stirred and snuggled into his arms.

"Oi, your feet are freezing!"

She giggled, placing them on his thigh. "Warm them for me then."

He kissed her cheek before reluctantly emerging from the blanket into the chilly room. Teretia began to move but he pulled the blanket back over her. "No, you have a lie in. I'll get breakfast at the palace."

"Sure?"

"Positive."

"Good, because it is very cosy in here. Are you sure you don't want to come back in? I could warm you properly. We haven't. For a while." She lowered her eyes.

Kneeling beside the bed, he brushed her lips with his. "I'm sorry. I'm sorry for that. Soon. We will. Again. Soon. I promise."

Once Otho resolved the Straton situation like he promised. Once he had shaken off the terrible guilt that was afflicting him regarding his infidelities. Then he would be able to look at her properly again and things could be like they should be. He would make it up to her, as many times as she wanted.

Reassured by this, she wound her arms around his neck and gave him a proper kiss that he settled into happily.

"Have you written your guest list?" she asked. "For the wedding? The people you want to come?"

He stroked her hair. "I don't know really. Epaphroditus and Aphrodite but that's all I think."

"What about Lysander? Did you want to invite him?" She crinkled her nose revealing exactly what she thought about the announcer.

"No. I thought not."

Though he was Philo's closest friend, Philo had an image of Lysander attempting to chat up Teretia's many cousins, all of whom possessed strongly built fathers. He didn't want anything to ruin Teretia's day. Changing the subject he told her, "There's a lot going on today. A deputation from Germania. There's going to be a feast for them."

"How lovely. What do they eat in Germania?"

"No idea. Wild boar, perhaps? But raw, torn apart by their hands and devoured."

"Urgh. That can't be true, can it?"

He gave her a smile and a quick peck on the cheek. "I'll find out and tell you all about it later. I have to go. Sorry."

He used the walk in to get his thoughts in order. He'd decided to let Talos attend the banquet. He was hard working and it would be a treat for him to be present at such a high-profile event. It was also good training. Talos was apt to be a little giddy about the dignitaries. A thrill visible on his spotty features when the emperor was in the same room. That would have to go. The proper expression was blank but dignified.

He still had some shorthand he needed to decipher from yesterday's budgetary meeting. At least there was some joy there. The campaign to repossess Nero's favourites' loot was resulting in a healthier treasury. He'd heard a rumour that Tigellinus had decided to drink his fortune away in a series of lavish parties lest he fall from Galba's protection.

He nodded a morning to the guards on the gates as usual. A few hellos to people he knew as he walked through the palace. Lysander, sporting a pinkish tunic far more reserved than recently, stopped and they exchanged pleasantries. Lysander told him about the hot piece who worked in the bakery beneath his apartment and who he was convinced was giving him lusty looks every time he took his grain in. Philo excused himself before the conversation could slip into the lewd.

He entered his office, his mind fixed on the day's agenda, only to be greeted by Cornelius Laco flanked by two guards. His eyebrows shot up in surprise.

"Morning, Philo. Could we have a word?" the prefect smiled.

They marched him to Laco's office at the guardroom. The prefect sat behind his desk, Philo in front of him. The guards positioned themselves either side of the freedman. When they weren't dismissed, Philo became ever so slightly disquieted.

"What is it, Laco? I have quite a lot to do today. Icelus will be wondering where I am."

"Icelus knows where you are," responded Laco. "So I would not worry about that, Philo. What I would worry about is Marcus Salvius Otho."

Philo looked at him blankly.

"You know him rather well, don't you, Philo?"

"I wouldn't say that. I know of him."

"So you weren't once his scribe?" Laco unrolled a scroll and pointed. "It says so here. Philo."

Philo leaned forward and noted his own signature. "I used to work for the scribes hall. I transcribed for a lot of people," he explained.

"For Otho?"

"Once or twice. A long time ago."

"But you've stayed in touch."

"Not really."

Laco smiled. It was a false smile encompassing a lot of teeth. Philo felt himself shiver.

"You have been feeding him information, haven't you, Philo? Confidential information. Information that you had no right to share."

The freedman blinked, incredulous. "I don't know what you are talking about."

Laco nodded to a guard. "Let us help him recall."

The guard, moving to face the shocked Philo took a swing and punched him in the stomach, doubling him over with a wheeze.

"Philo, Philo," came Laco's soothing tones. "I think you can do better than that."

Philo attempted to stand up straight, an arm across his stomach, coughing. "I don't know what you are talking about," he spluttered red-faced. "I barely know Otho."

"Not good enough." Another nod, another punch to the gut, flooring him this time.

"I saw the two of you together. What was it he said?" Laco pulled at his chin, pausing for effect. "Oh yes. He said to you, *'It's all in place'*."

"That was … That was …" Philo began, stuttering.

"Oh yes? What was it? What is it that is in place? A plot? A coup? An assassination?"

"No, no, no," insisted Philo. "It was a … a personal matter."

"A personal matter?"

"That Otho was helping me with."

Laco sighed. "You expect me to believe that? I know you have been leaking to Otho. That is not in dispute." He signalled to the guard who inflicted another blow.

Philo, from the ground, head hung over, wheezing, managed, "I haven't. I swear I haven't."

246

"It is what Otho intends to do with this information that concerns me, Philo. How he intends to use it. Who is he working with, besides yourself of course?"

He managed to blurt out, "I'm not—" before one of the guards dragged him to his feet, hooking an arm around his neck to keep him upright so that the other could deliver a blow.

"Names, Philo. Dates. Timings."

"I don't know. I don't know what you are talking about, Laco, please" he pleaded helplessly. "He was helping me. That was all. Some trouble. Some trouble I was having. With Straton."

"Rubbish. Why repeat these lies, Philo? Such a loyal little thing, aren't you? You were loyal to Epaphroditus. Loyal to Nero. It is a shame that loyalty did not spread to Galba."

Another nod, another punch to his gut. This one winded him and it was some time before he managed to get his words out, Laco watching impassively as he struggled against the pain. "I am loyal," he wheezed. "I am."

"Names, Philo. I need names. Just tell me. We are going to keep this up until you do. And if Lucullus and Proculus here tire, I have thousands of other guards to take their place. This will not end until I have those names. The names of those who are preparing to overthrow our noble emperor with that popinjay Otho. So tell me, Philo. Who else is prepared to commit treason?"

At the mention of treason his knees gave way. Philo had lived through Nero's reign: he knew what happened to traitors. He made one last attempt at pleading with Laco. "I don't know. I swear. I don't know anything. I can't … I can't tell you anything. Please, Laco."

The prefect looked at him coldly. "Shame," he said, indicating to Lucullus who smacked Philo across his jaw knocking him to the floor.

THIRTY-FOUR

Sporus was enjoying himself immensely. It had taken him but a day to work out the kind of master Otho was. During that first night he was sitting on his wicker chair, foot propped up on a cushion, goblet of wine in hand, listening to the pleasant flute boys, when he noticed one particular flute boy or rather man standing on the far right.

He was fifty if he was a day and still belting out a tune and dancing like the sprightly adolescent he should have been. He should have been sold off when his beard grew; farmed off to an inferior household and position. The fact that he had not clearly indicated that Otho was soft. Very soft. This made him exploitable. Sporus was prepared to exploit.

The result: Sporus reclining on a couch in Otho's pleasant indoor garden courtyard, wearing a red silk dressing gown and bejewelled slippers, watching colourful parrots fly between branches. Beside Sporus stood a small boy holding a bowl of honey-roasted dormice which the eunuch periodically dipped into. The boy, whose actual position in Otho's household was stable lad, muttered his annoyance under his breath.

Sporus was not popular amongst Otho's staff. It was fair to say they loathed him. There had been many protests to the master regarding the eunuch. Such things did not bother Sporus; they merely encouraged him. He'd been despised by far greater creatures than these. Why, Sporus counted three great eastern kings, one empress, and the vast majority of the Senate House amongst his detractors.

He'd persuaded Otho to allow him his own team of body attendants, which he had nicknamed the Sporus Set. It was they who had produced his dazzling gold-painted eyes and fabulously flashy nails. And they who had dealt most splendidly with the issue of his hair.

He sipped at his wine, contemplating whether he would head for the steam room now or wait until after the fifteen-course lunch menu that he had devised and sent his personal taster down to the kitchens to organise, when Otho entered with a, "What ho, young Sporus!"

Sporus lifted up a knee; all the better to display his fine legs. "A fine morning, sir," he said, flashing glittering eyes and moving on the couch to display himself to best advantage.

Otho took in the dressing gown. "I asked Onomastus to sort you some clothes. Did you not find the tunics?"

"I did, sir, but I have to confess that I am not much of a tunic boy. I find them very common, drab. A Sporus needs a little shine."

Otho couldn't help but smile at this. "Come now, though, it is January. You must be freezing in just that dressing gown."

Sporus gave a small, theatrical shiver and concurred in a small voice. "Just a little, sir. If sir should have anything that would suit the Sporus …?"

The stable lad gave an audible groan. Otho in concern asked him, "Palasides, are your arms aching holding that bowl? Perhaps you should take a break. Yes, take a break. Go get some food from the kitchens."

The lad grinned his thanks and legged it before Sporus could order him into some other demeaning task.

"Good lad that Palasides. I hope he is treating you well. Now then, to your attire. What can we do about that?"

"Something pretty; glittery; gorgeous?" suggested Sporus.

A thought occurred to Otho. He suppressed it instantly but it floated back to the surface and he found he couldn't push it down again. "Follow me."

Otho swung open the wardrobe. Sporus' eyes lit up with delight as he took in the rows of glittering, shining gowns of all shades and colours. Feeling the material with shaking fingers, he truly didn't know which one to try on first.

"They are *gorgeous.*"

"So they should be. They depleted the family fortune by some hundreds of thousands of sesterces." Reaching across him Otho pulled out a gown of flaming red. "Try this one on. I always liked this one."

Sporus took the dress greedily, flinging his dressing gown onto the floor. Otho sucked in a breath at this sight and then assisted him with the complicated hooks and clasps that held the gown together.

Sporus glanced down. "It's wonderful. Your wife's?"

"Ex-wife's," Otho told him.

Sporus spun round and round on his good foot, Galli-like, enjoying the flare of the material. Coming to a halt he smoothed down his skirt, standing up straighter, his neck held back, hands splayed on slightly tilting hips. Otho recognised the pose immediately: it was Poppaea.

"I had to throw out the wigs," said Otho sadly. "They got infested." He lifted Sporus' hair lightly up. "We could pin it, I suppose."

"Do you have tongs? Tongs are an *essential.* Oh, and eye-lashes, I don't have my eyelashes!" He gave his own lashes a quick flutter.

Then seeing Otho engrossed, he ran his tongue very slowly across his teeth and then his lower lip in a gesture that Poppaea herself had taught him.

"My gods, you are beautiful," said Otho running a hand across Sporus' cheek, finding it smooth and feminine. "You are exquisite."

He moved in for the kiss, one hand cupping Sporus' chin.

"Ahem."

Stood by the door, arms crossed, and looking extremely displeased was Epaphroditus. Otho removed his hand from Sporus' face. The eunuch audibly sighed with disappointment having been all geared up for an erotic encounter.

Epaphroditus stormed through Otho's house telling him angrily, "Do you know how hard I am working for you? I spend my time assuring people that, yes, you are the one that … But that Lusitania was your making, that you have matured, that you are a reformed character of fine upstanding morals these days. Then I walk in on you cavorting with a eunuch!"

"Nothing happened."

"No, but it was about to, wasn't it?"

"A moment of weakness. It won't happen again."

"He should go back to the palace."

"Surely, that's not necessary. He's still injured and I rather like having him around the house."

"So I saw."

"A moment of weakness, nothing more," repeated Otho to Epaphroditus' suspicious glare.

"It had better be," warned his friend. "My sources tell me Galba is getting close to a decision regarding his heir. If he should find out about this …"

"Very well, if it will make you happy," Otho sighed. He had dearly wanted Sporus to stay so they could get to know each other properly. Still, this was what being emperor was all about no doubt, making sacrifices for the greater good, so he told Epaphroditus, "I shall take him back to the palace today."

Epaphroditus, arms crossed, gave him a satisfied nod. "Now let us talk politics."

"Do you own any other topic of conversation?" sighed Otho. "It's a mystery to me how you've managed to bed so many females with such dry talk."

"By my position and influence," replied Epaphroditus handing Otho yet another file to read.

"Did he talk?"

"Claimed all the way through that he knew nothing," sighed Laco, fiddling with his gloves.

Philo proved a disappointment. He'd refused to sign the scroll Laco had put together detailing his charges against Otho, no matter what the guards did to him. Even forcing a pen into his hand and physically hauling his hand in order to affect a signature had failed. The freedman determined not to put his name to the accusations.

Which was not how Laco had expected this to play out. He had assumed Philo would sign in panic whatever was laid before him. He'd been so sure he would have the list of names to take to Galba that evening. That Otho would be dead by the morning. That he, Laco, would be promoted and richly rewarded for his efforts.

"He's up to his neck in it, you said so yourself. How else did Otho come by the information?"

"You want to have a go?" queried an irritated Laco. "Be my guest." He held open the door, Icelus passing through cautiously.

Philo lay in a bloodied heap on the floor. Lucullus rubbed his knuckles commenting, "He's soft like mush."

Proculus laughed, gazing at his own grazed knuckles. "Why does my hand hurt then?"

"Silence," barked Icelus, poking a toe into Philo's form. "Is he dead?"

"No, sir. Our orders were to keep him alive."

"He is not moving."

"That happens when you get them in the head. Stuns them, like."

Icelus bent down. "Will he be able to hear me?"

Lucullus shrugged. "You can try. He weren't saying much towards the end."

"That's coz you broke his jaw," Proculus pointed out.

"Philo? Philo, can you hear me?" Icelus asked gently.

There came a slight moan.

"Good, good. You're in a lot of trouble, you know that don't you? The emperor is very cross with you, disappointed."

This hit a spot because Philo moved slightly, distraught at letting down the emperor whom he had toiled so diligently for. He tried to raise himself up on his arms. Icelus calmly watched the effort as Philo failed to find the necessary strength, flopping back onto the floor with a grunt. Icelus, squatting beside him, ran a finger down his cheek.

"Lift him up."

The guards grabbed Philo under his arms and hauled him to unsteady feet.

He is a mess, thought Icelus. Blood dripping from his nose. Eyes swollen near-shut trying so hard to focus on him. A cut, bleeding lip and bulging jaw. Still, opportunities didn't often come his way and he was determined to best the little shit.

"Throw him over that desk and hold him down."

Philo was not battered so insensible that he didn't realise where this was headed. He made a futile attempt at resistance that Lucullus swatted aside easily, before his head was smashed down onto Laco's desk, his cheek squished against the wood, held down by his neck in a vice-like grip that would have impressed Straton. Hearing Icelus moving behind him, he squeezed his swollen eyes shut and mentally chalked up yet another infidelity.

"You can't fucking keep him!" On that Felix was adamant.

"Why?" croaked Straton.

Ganymede, standing beside Straton, gazed at Felix with amazement. He'd never seen a beard before and certainly not a big red one like that. He rather thought he'd like one of his own when he was grown up.

"You can't go out and buy your own slave."

"Why?"

"Because it sets a fucking precedent. You can't have every fucker bringing in their own slaves. Big fucking chaos. Who are they responsible to? Are they palace workers or are they not? Who punishes or rewards them? Who feeds 'em? If they're not palace, I ain't paying for their bellies."

"He don't eat much. Good worker."

He was indeed. Straton had set Ganymede to cleaning his quarters which he had done rather impressively, balancing on a stool with a feather duster and clearing away the cobwebs. He'd even scrubbed the floor without being asked and spent the morning folding Straton's tunics into a neat pile. The overseer had never looked so uncrumpled.

"Not fucking good enough. Right, that's it! I'm fuckin' confiscating him," yelled Felix, slamming a hand onto the desk. Neither Straton nor Ganymede jumped. "You, boy, you're coming home with me till I work out what the fuck to do with you. Gods, what a fucking day! First it's reappearing eunuchs … Now this!"

That morning Sporus had been carried into his office using the light golden chair held on poles that Nero made use of when he was too drunk to crawl back to his chambers. The injured catamite was insisting that he had hidden himself away for the last six months in order to maintain his stock value for Felix but claimed he was unfit for work just yet.

"My foot," he sighed dramatically. "It hurts so horribly."

Felix gave it a tweak. "Ain't most of your work lying down?"

"True, but if my partner should knock it, it could well kill the mood if I yelled in agony."

Felix reluctantly signed him off duties until it healed but with the threat that if he discovered the eunuch was feigning he was for the lash. Sporus, a natural coward, shuddered, and beneath the extravagant make-up Felix thought he detected a draining of colour from the eunuch's face.

"OK, matey," he said to Straton. "I want to know where the fuck you got him because you are getting a fucking refund!"

Ganymede, unable to resist any longer reached out a little hand and gave Felix's beard a quick fondle, telling Straton in a surprised tone, "It's all soft!"

An apoplectic Felix marched them out of his office just as Lucullus and Proculus dragged Philo past. The freedman held between them, his feet trailing along the ground, head hung down.

"Minerva's arse!" swore Felix as he watched them go past.

He turned back to Straton to comment. The overseer's expression was one of absolute devastation.

Many years back Felix had worked in slave retrieval: locating and recapturing runaway stock. A role that left him with a couple of crucial skills: the ability to spot those with something to hide and damn quick reflexes—all the better to grab the exposed errant slave. Thus Straton had only got a hundred yards before Felix threw himself onto his legs bringing him to a crashing fall. "Straton! No!"

Straton struggled to dislodge him, crawling along the ground. Felix took out his cudgel and walloped him on the head. And then, because this was Straton and he had a particularly thick skull, he gave him three more blows.

The news about Philo spread rapidly round the palace, gaining a grimmer status the more people it passed between. Lysander was stunned. Not stunned into silence obviously, for he spent most of the day expressing how stunned he was.

"I don't get it," he told Theseus. "Why are they picking on him?"

"Rumour has it he was involved in some kind of plot."

"Plot? Philo? He couldn't plot his way to the end of the corridor. It's ludicrous. Madness."

"Clearly."

"What can we do?"

Theseus shrugged. "Take it to Icelus?"

Lysander considered. Philo was his best friend in the whole world and he would do anything to help him. But if he went to Icelus with a plea it might look like he was in on this plot. So he didn't. Instead he sought out as many assurances as he could that there was nothing he could do. While a guilty thought registered that when Philo died, Teretia would need a great deal of comforting.

THIRTY-FIVE

Straton opened his eyes cautiously. It was dark and his head was hurting. More than hurting. Thundering. He sat up slowly, the room swirling as he did so, putting a hand on the back of his sore skull.

"You're awake," said Felix, sat on Straton's favourite chair, a cudgel resting in his lap.

Straton's meagre brain tried to remember what had happened. Turning to Felix extremely slowly, poking at the lump on the back of his head, he croaked, outraged, "You hit me!" And then assailed by another memory, "Philo."

He tried to get up.

"Oh no you don't," said Felix pushing him back and waggling the cudgel. "You're staying right here where I can keep an eye on you."

"Philo," he croaked a little more desperately, trying to get up again, but his vision was blurred and swirly.

Hanging over the edge of the bed, he vomited noisily onto the floor.

Felix rubbed his back. "I'll get that cleared up, don't worry."

Straton wiped the back of his hand across his mouth, pleading, "Philo."

"Yeah, yeah, I get it. You've been messing with my stock again. When you're better we'll have words about that. Right now you need to rest."

Ignoring him Straton put his feet on the floor. Feeling the earth tumble, he held his head willing it to stop.

"You're not right. You need to recuperate."

"You hit me."

"Yeah, I did. And I'll do it again if you don't get back in bed."

"Philo."

"Can't think what he can have done to fuckin' upset them. Fucking excellent little scribe is Philo, best I've ever had. But it's not our business. We don't make the orders, we enforce them. That's the way it is, way it's always been. Can't have overseers taking it into their heads to disobey the emperor's advisors. Right old mess that would be."

Straton looked mutinous, if a little green.

"Look here. It's no good, alright. You're staying here. I've got Xagoras outside and in this state he'll best you."

A claim that was all too offensive to Straton who held a low opinion of Xagoras' abilities. He tried to stand up again but the floor moved and he couldn't catch his balance. Frustrated he rasped, "Philo!" with urgency.

Felix sat down beside him. "I'm sorry, pal. Real fucking sorry."

Philo knew he was on the floor because it was wet and hard. If he reached out his fingertips he could pull on the edge of a flag-stone. He wasn't sure what he was doing on the floor. It seemed a strange place to be but he thought he would stay there.

Each time he woke, he told himself that he was on the floor. It seemed a good thought to hold onto. Next he'd attempt to move an arm or a leg, a flash of pain blinding him. Then he'd decide it was better if he went back to sleep because next time perhaps it wouldn't hurt so much. So he'd drift off again.

Icelus was delighted. He'd expected some form of retribution or defiance over Philo. Instead the slaves avoided his gaze and the freedmen treated him with a wary respect. If this was all it took, he would have had Philo executed months back. Aside from Talos' snivelling, which had irritated him so much he'd sent him back to the slave complex, Icelus was on top of the world.

"They fear me, Laco. They actually fear me."

It was a noteworthy occasion. Icelus with his skinny neck and scrawny body was not a figure that would usually intimidate. He was positively invigorated by his newly discovered power. This was how it should have been from the moment he'd been made private secretary.

Laco was more pragmatic. "We still have no proof that Otho is planning a coup."

Icelus, to Laco's annoyance, had taken their suspicions to Galba, assuring the emperor that the necessary proof would be forthcoming. So far Philo wasn't talking, mostly because he was dipping in and out of consciousness. Dragging him back for further interrogation had proved a pointless waste of time; the freedman unable to mutter a single word.

"I know I am right," Icelus stubbornly insisted, forgetting that it was Laco's suspicions that had set the whole thing off. "Do you think we should bring in that girlfriend of his? Rough her up a bit? It might concentrate his mind."

Laco hissed, "Low, Icelus, very low."

"If it works though," he said, picturing Galba's gratitude.

"She's freeborn. It won't look very good for the emperor if we start kidnapping plebs and torturing them."

"These are dangerous times!"

"Just leave it to me," snapped Laco.

Cornelius Laco was not a happy man. He was a worried man. And he was mad as Medea that Icelus had gone to Galba. If Icelus had let it be, Laco could have extracted what he needed from Philo or concluded, regrettably, that he was wrong in his suspicions should the freedman persist in his stubbornness. Now Galba knew, there was pressure for actual evidence.

Of course, under previous caesars such practicalities were unnecessary. A hint, a dull suspicion, a poor turn of phrase, or a bad joke were enough to damn hundreds to opening their veins. Laco positively envied them, Galba obsessing that Otho had been the first to support him and unwilling to hound him without proof.

So what choice did Cornelius Laco have? Either he would have to lose face and favour with Galba by admitting there was no plot, which he really did not wish to do, or he could simply fabricate the evidence.

THIRTY-SIX

A wobbly Straton paced his room, pausing briefly to steady himself, just about holding back from throwing up again. This would not stop him though: Philo needed him.

He'd managed to convince Felix that he'd given up, that he was too sick to move. His boss had sat with him for some time promising him that: "When it's fucking over, we'll raise a drink to him, remember him properly."

Then he paused as he struggled to put any memories together of Philo. He was an anonymous little fucker. Just sort of always there in the background scribbling away all quiet like, no trouble at all. Felix tended only to remember the troublemakers. They were the ones he encountered in his day to day work.

This was agony for Straton. He just wanted Felix to piss off so he could go save Philo. He didn't want to lament or mourn him, not when he could still be alive. So he sat, his skin itching, while Felix droned on and on.

The moment he left Straton jumped to his feet and then nearly passed out, spots floating in front of his eyes. Of all the times to be weak! It would not do. He had to be strong.

Sticking a head out the door, he noted Felix had been telling the truth: Xagoras was lounged against the wall.

"Awright, Straton," he sneered. No doubt joyful at this assignment, for the two of them had never been friends. "Don't even think about it." He slapped his cudgel into his palm. "We've taken away your toys too. I should just go have a little snooze, till you're all better."

Straton searched his room. His toys were indeed gone: all of his whips, his cudgel, and a couple of light rods that he occasionally employed.

Not now, not when he needed them more than ever! He rubbed his head, feeling the anger build inside him at the gross unfairness of it all, letting out a roar of rage mixed with pure sorrow, kicking at the wall and knocking off a clutter of plaster. Philo needed him. Needed him now. Couldn't wait. Xagoras banged on the door yelling, "Keep it down in there!"

Straton sat on the end of his bed in despair. What could he do?

Xagoras was bored. On receiving Felix's message to meet him outside Straton's quarters, he'd been absolutely delighted. Finally Straton was going to get what he deserved after all those infractions that would have got Xagoras kicked out instantly. No one in the overseers team was in any doubt who among them ranked as Felix's favourite.

So he'd turned up with glee and a freshly oiled whip to his assignment. He had hoped Felix had Straton tied up already. Not that Xagoras couldn't take Straton down (or so he imagined) but it would certainly speed things up so he could get to the fun bit.

On hearing what his mission actually consisted of, Xagoras had said, incredulous, "You want me to nursemaid him?"

Earning a fierce glare from Felix. "You fucking questioning my orders, slave?"

Xagoras, seeing his boss hit simmer, shook his head, "No, no, of course not."

"Too fucking right you're not. He's sick. He ain't to move. He ain't to get through this door. You get it?"

Xagoras nodded and took up position. Thinking that of all the crappy assignments that were routinely given to him, this was by far the crappiest.

After he had banged on the door, Straton quietened down. Xagoras, sticking an ear to the wall, could hear him stumbling about, clearly unsteady on his feet. Well, this was interesting. An injured Straton confined to quarters. Perhaps this need not be such a dull job after all, he thought, sharply recalling all the occasions where Straton had humiliated him. Including the most recent incident when he'd smashed Xagoras' face into a wall, warning him to go easy on Mina. Xagoras, picturing that assault, prodded at his cheek and decided it was time for a little bit of revenge.

Taking out his whip, he pushed open the door slowly. He poked his head round, noting Straton's bulk lying on the bed.

"Awright, Straton? You feeling poorly again?"

Straton grunted and rolled onto his side.

"You a bit sick?" Xagoras asked, approaching the bed, whip trailing beside him. "I was going to tell you something, mate. You want to hear?" he offered in a half whisper. "'Bout your girlfriend," he added, watching Straton carefully.

Straton did not move, lying on his side beneath a blanket, eyes firmly closed. He did not look well, with a green pallor, sweaty countenance, and shivering slightly.

Excellent, thought Xagoras, edging forward. "I was going to tell you about the whipping I gave her and that other I gave her too."

No response.

"She said it were the best she'd ever had. Said you ain't much in that department. Speedy, she said. Disappointing."

Straton opened one eye. Xagoras laughed. "That got your attention didn't it, mate? She told me all about you … Unsatisfied she was. Lucky I was about. I gave it to her proper."

If Xagoras thought he was taking advantage of Straton's weakened state to inflict some brutally hard home truths, he was wrong on so many counts. What bothered Straton was that Xagoras clearly thought he could get away with such insults. That could not be allowed to stand.

Xagoras was delighted. Poor fucker couldn't even move, couldn't retaliate, so he could say what he liked. Years of resentment came flowing out of his gob. This manifested itself in a long, lurid tale of his supposed sexathon with Mina, to a very long disparagement on the size of Straton's equipment, and ending in a hefty discourse on the overseer's personal hygiene.

Straton, listening impassively with eyes closed, upgraded his plan from disable Xagoras to kill Xagoras.

Soon Xagoras tired of mentally torturing his rival. It was no fun at all when he didn't respond. Sneaking forward he gave the bed pole a quick crack of his whip. The incumbent made a small noise but otherwise did not respond. Xagoras tried out another quick crack. Finding the same lack of response, he edged forward and brought the whip down on Straton's feet. The overseer pulled his feet upwards, made a small grunting noise but again did not move.

For many a man this would have been sufficient. Xagoras had berated, belittled, and now whipped Straton. He could crow about his victory for years. He had bested the beast; the thin red slash on the overseer's ankle proof of Xagoras' triumph. Most sensible men would have left it there, given a harsh cackle, perhaps a final well-crafted insult, and then departed. Not Xagoras though, for he was a particularly stupid man, and he just could not resist tormenting his rival further.

Standing over Straton's immobilised form he held his whip back, bringing it with a crack over his shoulder. Straton reached up one hand, caught the end of the whip and pulled hard. Xagoras, caught unawares, failed to let go of the handle and found himself yanked onto the bed where he fell onto his back, staring up at a kneeling Straton.

Lifting up his bleeding palm, Straton stuck out his red tongue and licked it clean with a slurp. "Oh dear," he rasped.

Xagoras regained his senses just in time to roll out the way of the punch. He landed on the floor with a crash and then leapt to his feet ready to retaliate.

Whip held in one hand, cudgel in the other, Xagoras asked Straton, "What you gonna fight with? I'm fully loaded, big man."

Straton gave him a leer. Staring with beady black eyes he lifted up his new footstool and lobbed it straight at Xagoras, telling him, "Wotever I got."

Xagoras danced easily out of the stool's path. "Not very artful was it, big man? I expected so much better of you."

He gave a crack of his whip which hit his rival on the leg. Straton didn't even flinch.

"Clumsy," he growled. "I'd go for face."

"Wouldn't be worth it with you, big man, you're ugly enough already!"

Straton was not one for trading insults. He had one word which he felt summed up Xagoras perfectly: cock, and he felt that it could not be bettered. Also, he saw such witticisms rather like the execution of criminals at the games: a pointless spectacle before the main action took place. So he waited one beat before launching himself at Xagoras, pulling him to the floor and punching him in the face. In return Xagoras aimed a knee at Straton's groin. This distracted Straton long enough for his rival to get to his feet and whack him on the shoulder with his cudgel. This blow unsteadied the already-shaky overseer. Straton held a hand to his swirling head, leaning back against the desk.

"See, big man, you are still poorly," gloated Xagoras, using his sleeve to wipe away the blood that was pouring from his nose. "I suggest you go back to bed like a good little boy. Otherwise, I might have to inflict a thrashing on you."

Straton rubbed his head again. His palm groping along the desk hit a long, solid object. He grabbed hold of it in his fist as he imparted his one insult: "Cock."

Xagoras laughed. "Face it, Straton, you are beat. I could do this all day, I ain't going to tire. But you, you're not right. I should give up now if I were you. Have a nice sleep before Felix comes to tuck you in."

Amused at his own joke, Xagoras began to cackle. A mistake as it turned out because as he inwardly congratulated himself on his wit, he took his eyes off Straton just for a moment. A tiny moment that proved fatal. Straton jumped onto the bed, sprang to the other side, and grabbed Xagoras in a headlock, stabbing him in the throat with the stylus grasped in his hand.

Xagoras looked rather surprised at this sudden motion. His eyes opened wide, he gurgled but failed to utter any final quips.

Straton lowered his body to the ground and then rubbed the bloody stylus on his tunic before placing it neatly back on Philo's desk.

Daphne, the baby keeping her awake with all her jiggling, took one look at the creature stood in her room, his menacing face lit up by the flaming torch and let out one almighty eardrum-bursting scream.

Mina shot up rubbing her eyes. "What the—?"

Daphne, shaking and pulling her blanket around her, pointed silently to the spectre.

"Straton?"

The overseer threw her a whip. "Mission for you."

THIRTY-SEVEN

Mina was convinced that this was a very bad idea. Ignorant of what Straton's mission encompassed, she knew it wasn't good from the overseer's grim demeanour. Insistent that she had to follow him now, quickly, she padded behind him in bare feet and her nightgown, whip clasped in her hand.

"Straton," she hissed. "Straton."

He gestured for her to keep moving.

"Where are we going?"

"Mission."

Which told her diddly-squat. He did not look right to her either. Straton always moved with surprising grace but tonight he was heavy footed, stopping to lean on walls, rubbing his forehead with desperate motions. It was hard to miss the enormous lump that had formed on the back of his head. Mina assumed the two things were connected. He was determined, though. A sack on his back contained a stack of lethal-looking weapons, which she hoped would compensate for his wobbliness.

Galba kept early hours so the palace was near-deserted. A few slaves pottered about sleepily, paying them little attention. Most were too scared of Straton to give them more than the briefest glance lest they catch his black eyes. The positioned guards similarly ignored them. They had heard *that* rumour and assumed it was a lovers' tryst, though one wonders what they made of Straton's pack of toys.

However, where they were going, the guards were going to be a little more arsey. Outside their destination Straton stopped and pulled out a vicious-looking, nail-studded cudgel. Mina's eyes opened very wide, Straton telling her gruffly, "Could get nasty."

"Whack." He demonstrated a slap using both hands, taking a wide swing. Too wide, since he lost his footing and had to prop himself against the wall until the dizziness passed.

"Can we not do this tomorrow? You don't look very well. You're sort of green."

Straton went to shake his head, but realised in time that this was not a great idea given the way the floor was rocking for him. "Needed now," he said and then, "Help me. Please."

He'd never used that word before; had never needed to. It fell oddly from his tongue. Mina could see he was desperate, truly desperate. And recalling the time he had rescued her from Juba, she nodded. Because that's what friends did, wasn't it? They helped each other out.

Reading the dispatches from Germania, Galba knew the issue of an heir could no longer wait. He disliked having his hand forced in such a manner, but facts were facts. The empire craved security after the tumultuous reign of Nero and he would deliver it. That was his role, his destiny.

As a young man he watched Tiberius and Caligula diminish this great office. Even then he had known he could do better. He'd come close once before when he was put forward as a suitable husband for Agrippina. He'd not known then how important she would become and how her child, Nero, would be the last of the Julio-Claudian dynasty.

Even if he had, he could never have contemplated marriage to that witch. As a young girl she displayed those qualities for which she became so notorious. She had made such advances to him when she'd been a widow but for a day that his mother had slapped her full across the face in public. Agrippina, tasting the blood on her lips, smiled sweetly and retorted, "I should not wish for such a mother!"

So to a new dynasty. One untainted by such scandal. A chance to start afresh. And unlike those prior, he was not forced to choose an unsatisfactory heir from within his family. He would choose the best, just like Julius Caesar had chosen the young Augustus. Unfortunately for Galba, today's youth seemed much less promising. Corrupted by Nero's airs, they favoured pleasure over politics and he had no desire to raise another such creature for Rome. No, his heir must be a seasoned man, trialled and shown to be able. His advisors were advocating hard for their chosen candidates: Dolabella or Otho.

Otho seemed to be the preferred option. He was certainly popular. Such charm could well hold the edgy city together. It could not be discounted. Yet there were these rumours about him: the situation with the secretary. Although Laco had so far failed to bring forward any convincing evidence of Otho's culpability. The torturer, Scaveous, had made a private complaint that his work was being interfered with and pressure exerted on producing the correct answers whether they were there or not.

If Otho were to be appointed heir apparent it would split his advisors brutally; entrench them into hardened factions. Galba did not like factions. They were disruptive in the army and they were similarly disruptive in government. They needed unity, now more than ever.

Then Servius Sulpicius Galba made his decision.

There were two guards on the entrance to the cells. Peeking round the corner, Mina asked with a hint of horror, "We're going in there?"

Straton nodded.

The palace dungeons were where misbehaving members of the palace workforce were held. Sometimes this might only be for a night. A short, sharp shock of a lesson of what awaited them if they didn't buck up their ideas. Sometimes they would be held here after a brush with Scaveous the torturer. To recover from their wounds and mull on their behaviour. And sometimes there would be no escaping. For this was where slaves were held prior to their execution. In fact, it was here that Alex had stayed before his death.

"Won't it be heavily guarded?"

It would. There would be pairs of Praetorians on each cell door. There were ten individual detainment cells. That was twenty guards plus the two on the entrance making it twenty-two to their two.

"We'll never get in."

"Getting in not problem," said Straton evenly.

He frequently brought misbehaving slaves down, a familiar sight to the guards. If he were to drag Mina in saying she was to be detained, they would not question it. No, getting in wasn't the problem. It was getting out. He didn't, however, mention this to Mina, aware that she was jumpy enough already. What he did do was outline his plan which contained just the right amount of high drama to appeal to her.

She certainly played her part well, kicking and screaming at Straton's back as he effortlessly carried her across his shoulder past the guards who smiled, joshing, "What she done then, Straton? You gonna teach her a lesson? Need any help, mate?"

The dungeons were one of those palace corners that had sprung up according to need. In more dangerous times a room or two had been added with no particular forethought, so that architecturally it made little sense. The reason why there were two guards on each cell was partly because they packed them in tight and fights frequently broke out among the desperate inhabitants. And partly because rather than the cells being thoughtfully lined up side by side, they were spread out over quite a distance.

Straton, Mina slung over a shoulder, walked from cell to cell nodding to the guards and peering through the grills. "For space," he told the Praetorians.

Reaching cell number eight Straton slapped open the grill. Through the gloom he could see two figures manacled to a wall and another lying in a heap in the centre of the room. It was a small figure with lightly curling dark hair, clad in a blue tunic. He was lying on his stomach, head turned to one side. There was just enough of those battered features on display for it to be recognisably Philo.

Straton banged on the door, the guard obligingly opening up for him. "This one's for it?" indicating Mina.

"Punish."

"Right you are, Straton. No trouble here. A couple of fuckers but they're chained, and one other. He's no threat though. She should survive the night at least."

Mina, despite being held upside down, felt the blood drain from her face. She'd been right, this was a terrible idea. Daphne awakening to find her missing because she was dead, in a dungeon, with Straton. What a wonderfully gossipy way to die. It would keep them talking for generations.

The guard held open the door for them, Straton waited for it to close before throwing Mina down and rushing over to the prone figure. He gathered the limp body up, cradling him in his arms. His face was all mashed. His beautiful face which Straton had kissed so many times was swollen and cut. Stroking his hair, Straton was disturbed to find his hand was covered in blood. Philo's usually pristine blue tunic was marked by patches of red and brown. Putting his head to his beloved's chest he could just about hear a faint wheeze.

273

Mina, frozen by the door by the worryingly lascivious glances thrown her direction from the manacled prisoners, heard Straton talking very softly and gently.

"Get you out of here. Safe. Take care of you."

Now she gathered that the mission's object was to rescue his special friend. Trust Straton to fall for a condemned prisoner, she thought.

"Straton," she hissed, unnerved by the more rotund prisoner who was running his tongue across his teeth and crawling ever so slightly towards her. "What do we do now?"

Actually he had no idea. His plan only extended as far as finding Philo and if necessary dying with him.

"Straton," she hissed with more urgency, the tubby prisoner clawing at her feet. She hit his hands with her cudgel, the prisoner yelping and throwing himself back against the wall.

There was a bang on the door. "Everything alright in there? They giving you trouble, Straton?"

Straton, distracted by a small gulping noise from Philo, did not answer. Mina in a panic replied for him in as husky a voice as she could manage, "Fine." Then she froze, waiting for the guard to suss it out, open the door, and drag them both off for a slap-up crucifixion. Except he didn't and Mina experienced a very small sense of temporary release.

"Straton, please, we have to get out of here. Get help for your friend."

This provided the necessary effect. Staring down at Philo's battered features, watching him struggle for each breath, Straton felt the murderous anger that was his natural state rise within him. The bastards. Look what they had done to him. Turning to the tubbier of the two chained prisoners, he asked, "Wot in for?"

"Murderrrrrr."

"Who'd you murder?"

"Praetoriaannnnnnn."

"You goin' in arena?"

"Straton, really not the time for a getting to know you session. We have to get out of here," hissed Mina.

"Yerrrrrr," confirmed Tubby.

Straton dropped his bag of toys. "Want some practice?"

He beckoned Mina over, gesturing that he wanted her to take over with the injured prisoner. She cautiously stepped around Tubby and the other one (whom she mentally named Less Tubby), taking hold of the slight body. Straton set to work unpacking his toys. A fascinating if rather worrying spectacle. It certainly transfixed Mina, who wondered as to the purpose of the fierce-looking metal-studded cuffs. Feeling the body in her arms shiver slightly, she looked down and her eyes nearly fell out of her head. "Philo?"

THIRTY-EIGHT

Mina kept telling herself that this was going to make one outstanding anecdote to compete and beat Sporus' "I was with Nero when he died" tale.

She was in the imperial dungeons with two murderers; Straton, who undoubtedly ranked with them; and Philo, the world's most improbable traitor and adulterer. The plan they had cobbled together between them at speed (which explains much of what subsequently happened) was to nobble the two guards on the door as quietly as possible.

"So as not to alert," said Less Tubby sagely, rubbing an un-manacled ankle, Straton demonstrating a surprising skill for picking locks.

"We then nobble the guards on the next cell. That's the fullest cell. There are twenty of them in there. We arm them with your tricks and then the whole gang of us run full pelt at the rest of 'em fuckers. It'll be chaos and you guys will be able to slip out coz they'll be after us."

"I'm top of the bill for the next games," volunteered Tubby. "They won't want to lose me!"

"You'd do that for us?" asked Mina, touched.

"No," replied Less Tubby. "But if I'm going out, I want it to be in a good old vicious punch-up. I don't want to be no posh ladies' entertainment or that hook-nosed ugly fucker they call emperor. I'm going out screaming and I'm taking as many guards with me as I can."

There seemed to be rather a lot of flaws to this plan which would neatly fill a page or two but nobody gave them much thought. It was a shame Philo was unconscious because doubtless he could have come up with something much better.

They stood poised for part one of their action plan, Mina's heart near beating out of her chest.

"Mina, promise me summat," rasped Straton.

"Whatever."

He looked at her with those black eyes. He didn't look frightened. He looked fully geared up for action. But it was with a slight melancholy that he asked, "If summat happens, you get Philo out. Promise."

"We've got a plan," she squeaked, terrified. "Nothing is going to happen."

His big paw of a hand took hers. "Promise."

She gave a small smile. "Promise. You really love him, don't you?"

"'Course. Always."

She wondered whether this was the moment to bring up the subject of the little busty blonde that Philo called his girlfriend. But concluded that it was perhaps best to wait till they all got out of this alive. There was no need for their last moments on earth to be so awkward and emotional.

"OK, folkies," whispered Less Tubby. "Let's do it!"

Mina gave a scream, followed by a cackle from Tubby.

A bang on the door. "Straton, you awright, mate? Straton? Straton?"

The door opened cautiously. A plumed helmet stuck itself round. Mistake. Straton grabbed him round the neck and heaved him into the cell, snapping his head sharply to the right. Tubby grabbed the other one before he could react,

278

stabbing him in the throat with one of Straton's blades, dropping the body beside his colleague's.

"Let's go."

Straton led the way. The guards on the next cell would be expecting him. The others, Mina dragging the dead weight of Philo, stood round the corner waiting for the signal.

"You break her in good?" joked Proculus.

Lucullus sniggered. Straton gave a lecherous glare.

"Nice and tight," he rasped before sidling up to Lucullus and making good use of those metal cuffs that had so fascinated Mina. Straton smacked him across the nose, which exploded in a spurt of blood.

Lucullus' shriek was the required signal and they came running and yelling towards the startled Proculus. He took longer than he should to unsheathe his sword. Too long because Straton had unlocked the cell door and out came the condemned, the soon-to-be tortured, and the insanely bad of the imperial slave population; the overseer throwing them weapons.

What occurred was predictably chaotic and bloody. Mina, dragging Philo along the floor, found it a confusing mess of limbs, yells, grunts, bangs, shouts and the odd, "Urgghhhh."

Hearing the commotion the other Praetorians legged it round to help, which was when it really kicked off. Corridors, especially dark narrow ones, are not made for full-scale battles. The space was too cramped, meaning though you might be aiming for a fucker Praetorian you were just as likely to conk your cellmate on the nose during the trajectory.

Mina didn't see how she was going to get Philo through the anarchy. Though a slight man, unconscious he was a dead weight and it was a struggle to move him.

"Philo, I need you to walk for me." She shook him roughly. "Come on, wake up! Wake up! I swear to Jupiter that I will tell Teretia that you are Straton's very special friend if you don't get up right now!"

279

He didn't even stir at that. And frankly anyone who could sleep through this din was clearly somewhere else.

There was no way she could squeeze through the crush of frenzied slaves and angry guards; not without adding to the casualty list. But soon there would be more guards on their way. This was her best opportunity. Crouching down, she hooked one arm under Philo's armpits dragging him onto her lap. She started moving backwards, slowly, very slowly, chanting, "This is madness. This is madness. This is madness."

Her free hand hit upon a fallen helmet which she plonked on her head for protection. Then it came upon a cudgel and, continuing her backward shuffle, she tried to aim blows at the Praetorians' legs, hoping to trip a few up.

Straton was remaining neutral. He was no fan of the guards but on the other hand he was no fan of slaves who broke the rules. Similarly, they were not fans of his and he was a target for those he had whipped into submission or just plain bullied. Now they were armed they were keen to show him just how they felt about him.

Straton therefore was slashing out indiscriminately at whoever was nearest, protecting himself against revenge assaults, while trying to spot Mina and Philo so he could clear a space for them. While smacking a guard with steel knuckledusters, he noticed a plumed helmet wobbling along at crotch height. Looking below the helmet, he saw Mina surrounded by hairy legs, whacking at them with her cudgel to create room for her to push through. She looked like the goddess Minerva with that helmet on. Although Minerva probably didn't use the language that Mina was freely littering about.

Straton kicked his way through, grabbing her and thereby Philo, and pulled them with all his might, using splayed feet to move people inconsiderate enough to get in their way. Mina felling guards with a wallop to the back of their knees as she was dragged along, told Philo, "You had better be extravagantly grateful to me for this."

They reached the far end of the scrum. Mina jumped to her feet and looked back at the pandemonium she had somehow got through.

"Bloody Juno!"

The overseer grinned, bending over to pick up Philo. He made an odd groan, standing up suddenly on unsteady feet.

"Straton?"

Turning to his side Straton removed a dagger from his hip with something akin to annoyance. He punched its owner (a pale slave he had whipped earlier that day) in the face impatiently and gestured Mina to follow him. Mina had one thought: "What a man!" Then immediately scratched it as the consequences of spending too much time with eunuchs.

The backup Praetorians ran past them, failing to wonder what they were doing there or why Mina was wearing one of their helmets.

"I'm going to keep it. I'm going to give it to Daphne as a trophy," she told Straton.

Philo made a slight gurgling noise. They both bent down. The freedman laid out on the floor coughed, his chest racking from the effort. His eyes remained closed and soon his chest fell into a more regular rhythm.

"What are we going to do with him? Once they sort out that mess they'll notice he's gone. I can't see Icelus liking that."

Straton ran a hand down Philo's cheek. "Take him my room. Take care of him."

"Won't they look there? Surely they'll search the palace top to bottom. We'll never keep it quiet. Some git would sell us out for a sodding promotion. We need to get him out of the palace."

Straton did not look convinced. He did not want to let Philo out of his sight, not in this state, not ever. What sort of boyfriend was he to let this happen? To let them fuckers even lay a finger on him?

"He'll be safer outside the palace."

"Where?"

Mina thought hard, Straton staring at her intently. Eventually her brain, which had been just a little overstimulated recently, kicked into gear. "Epaphroditus." she declared. "We'll take him to Epaphroditus. He'll look after him."

Titus Vinius cursed himself and more particularly his companion, one Ofonius Tigellinus. He'd told Tigellinus that he needed to be up early for Galba's big announcement, his friend asking innocently, "Where's the harm in a quick drink?"

Like the fool he was, Vinius had been suckered right in. Talking over old times, those mad days of their youth when Tigellinus had dragged him into increasingly dubious adventures. It was so much fun to remember, such a delight to reminisce, that he'd scarcely noticed his cup being refilled. Until that moment when he stood up, the floor tilted, and he'd ended up on his arse, Tigellinus roaring his head off.

He had no chance of sobering up in time. His friend suggested he may as well keep at it to postpone the horrific hangover.

"All those sacrifices and speeches will be far more tolerable wasted."

Which Vinius had to admit was true. So it was with a staggering, swaying, and distinctly unsteady gait that he manoeuvred himself inexpertly down the corridors of the palace. Bouncing off walls which seemed determined to attack him and covertly vomiting into a pleasing urn outside the throne room, until Tigellinus came up to slap his back crying, "Get it all out, Titus! Don't want to throw up on Galba."

Vinius figured a quick nap and a rinse in the bath would cover up his shame. If he could just stand still, Galba need never know.

Holding onto Tigellinus' arm, Vinius staggered round a tight corner that seemed unusually hard to navigate and ran straight into Straton and Mina.

"What's going on here?" bellowed a red-faced Tigellinus at the small party.

The overseer growled at him. Mina raised their sole remaining toy, a spiked cudgel, and glared at them.

Vinius held up a palm. "Whoa, stand down, Mina."

The cudgel was lowered slightly.

Vinius, viewing the body that was held in Straton's arms, asked, shocked, "Gods, is that Philo?"

Straton pulled Philo back towards his chest protectively.

"You're trying to get him out?" Vinius asked, sobering up remarkably quickly.

Mina nodded cautiously. Though she and Vinius were part-time lovers he worked for Galba, for Laco and Icelus: he could denounce them at any moment.

Tigellinus, a palm on the wall, said, "Isn't that the little chap who works for Epa … Epa … Epaphra … the secretary? What in great Jupiter's name has happened to him?"

"My esteemed colleagues and their rampant paranoia."

"Swines! I say we should outfox them, Titus."

"Where are you taking him?"

"Esquiline. Epaphroditus."

"Good plan!" belched Tigellinus. "That nifty wife of his will patch him up."

"Not move," rasped Straton, holding Philo tighter to him.

"Can I?" Vinius asked Straton, indicating Philo.

Straton's fierce expression did not alter, yet he let his grip loosen slightly.

Vinius leaned in and said gently, "Philo, it's Titus Vinius here. We're going to get you out of here, somewhere safe. Philo, can you hear me? I'm holding your hand, Philo. If you can hear me, squeeze it."

It was a very small gesture, a tiny flutter even, but it happened all the same; Philo's fingers moved ever so slightly.

Vinius stood back and said briskly, "He's still with us. Let's get him out of here."

THIRTY-NINE

T he riot in the cells was eventually quelled by the guards with their customary brutality. Once the ringleaders were dispatched and the battle corridor cluttered with their corpses, they turned their attention to the mop-up exercise. By mop-up, we mean of course, attributing blame. The palace owned a whole legion of cleaning slaves for that other sort of operation.

It looked bad for the Praetorians. They had let the condemned run amok, causing considerable damage to palace property, and had lost a couple of their own men in the course of that chaos. Someone would have to be held accountable. Someone would have to be disciplined. To the guards who had grown soft since Sabinus' departure, this was a gruesome fate. They had no intention of submitting to an army punishment. Not when someone else could be blamed.

They cobbled a story together between them and devised a useful scapegoat. They then removed all witnesses who might dispute this tale. Cornelius Laco followed the cohort centurion along the cells.

"Everyone?" he queried.

The centurion nodded. "Unfortunately so, sir," he said in what he hoped was a suitably sad tone. "It was the only way. The jailer had gone mad, released the lot of them."

"I always thought him a sound fellow," commented Laco, recalling the ruddy-cheeked, apple-stomached keeper of the keys who assisted him so ably in his campaign to find evidence against Otho.

"It gets them like that sometimes, locked down here with them sort. Turns them, flips them. Very sad."

"So he killed himself in the end?"

The centurion adopted a fixed expression. "After he had done the damage by unlocking the cells. I guess he could not live with himself after such a dereliction of duty."

The Guard had indeed made sure he could not by dragging him out of bed and stabbing him in the gut.

Laco winced. "This is a mess. You know that don't you? There were valuable prisoners, prisoners with information we needed to extract. They all died?"

"Yes, all of them."

"Jove's white hairy bull!" swore Laco. "What about Philo? Is he dead?"

"They all died," stated the centurion.

Icelus was going to do his nut, thought Laco. The freedman was imagining a wonderfully gruesome death for his assistant. Cut down by the Guard was far too quick to sate Icelus' bloodlust. Cornelius Laco paused, thought, and asked smoothly, "You only killed those who attempted to escape?"

"Basic containment manoeuvre, sir. Unfortunate but necessary for the security of the palace. And the emperor," he added quickly, finding himself under a hard Laco glare.

"The thing is, centurion," began the prefect, "the last time I checked on the prisoner, he could barely stand. So I find it somewhat surprising that he danced to his feet unaided and made a break for freedom."

The obvious reply to this was to blame the prisoners themselves for Philo's death. After all, none of them could deny it now. However, the Praetorian Guard are not recruited for their intellect. And thank the gods for that because Juno knows what mischief they would get up to with a bit of brain power behind them.

The centurion looked blankly at Laco and muttered but one word: "Ermm."

"Ermm indeed," said Laco. "Show me the bodies. Now!"

Aphrodite was up nursing a grumbling Rufus so it was to her that Callista brought the news about the visitors.

"At this hour?"

"Men and a girl."

Puzzled, Rufus balanced on her hip, she went to greet her guests. The first she saw was a clearly drunk Tigellinus holding onto a torch sconce for support.

"Dite!" he greeted her warmly and loudly. "Lurvely to see you again. This your nipper?"

Rufus eyed him suspiciously, visibly unimpressed by the tickle Tigellinus gave his chin.

"Cutie, isn't he?" A lopsided grin, drool escaping from the corner.

A sobered-up Titus Vinius took control. "Madam, I am terribly sorry to intrude upon you at this hour," he said, lowering his head respectfully. "They said that this was a safe place to bring him."

Aphrodite followed his gaze to "they": Straton and one of her husband's lovers sitting on a bench. Laid out between them was "him": his battered face resting on Straton's lap, his hand held by the girl. They both looked at her with clear desperation.

Aphrodite's hand went to her mouth. "Philo?"

She bent down beside the bench, placing her palm on his forehead. It was cold but he gave a small wheeze to let her know he was still alive.

Standing up, she said, "Straton, bring him through. Callista, we need blankets, water, linen bandages."

Callista snapped out of the room. Straton picked up Philo's limp body ready to follow.

"Sorry, girl, I don't know your name."

"Artemina."

"Artemina, could you hold this little man for me?" She handed Rufus over to Mina.

"How long has he been like this?" Directed at Vinius as they marched through the house. Aphrodite instructing slaves as they went, possessing the useful practicality that was sadly missing in both Mina and Straton.

"I am not sure, madam." He looked to Mina who was jogging to keep up, clutching onto Rufus.

"He was very quiet before," she told Aphrodite. "We dragged him through a riot and he didn't stir at all. But just before Titus came he got like this: noisy."

Philo gave a splutter, fighting for breath in painful spasms.

"Lay him down here, Callista. Pillows now."

Straton gently laid him down on the bed. Callista and Aphrodite held the injured man forward as he coughed through a particularly brutal spasm.

"Poor little chap," commented Tigellinus, attempting to lean on a wall, missing and crashing to the ground. Vinius helped him to his feet, shooting Aphrodite an apology as he placed Tigellinus onto a chair.

"We've established that he can hear us."

"Philo?" said Aphrodite softly, rubbing his back as he groaned. "Philo, it's Aphrodite here. You are in my house and you are perfectly safe. Now, we are just going to find out how badly you are hurt, OK?" She nodded to Callista who began unbuckling his belt, Philo becoming increasingly agitated as she did.

"What happened?"

"My colleague Icelus conceived some strange idea that Philo was plotting against the emperor."

Aphrodite's expression said it all.

"I know, I know," sighed Vinius. "The emperor is not a bad man but sometimes he can be misled. Icelus and Laco presented it to him that Marcus Salvius Otho was angling for a coup and that Philo was his palace insider."

"Otho?" Aphrodite's features hardened.

She was distracted from her grim thoughts by another demonstrative fit from Philo, who was battering a limp arm at Callista as she pulled his tunic over his head. He was near black all over; the imprint of boots and fists embedded into his skin. They'd clearly thrashed him for his back was covered in red lines. And there were other injuries Callista quietly drew her attention to that suggested some sort of sexual assault.

"We need to bind his ribs, mistress."

Aphrodite stroked Philo's cold brow. He shivered, making small noises which might have been an attempt to talk.

"Madam, regrettably, I have to leave," said Vinius. "A function I cannot get out of, unfortunately. You will let me know his condition?"

"Certainly. You should take these two back to the palace before they are missed."

Straton did not move, engrossed by the grunting Philo. Mina clawed at his arm. "Straton, we have to go. They'll know we were involved if we're missing from duties."

He shook his head stubbornly, arms folded.

"Please, Straton. We have to go." Adding quietly so the others wouldn't hear, "You'll be no good to Philo if you're crucified. Who would look after him then?"

This hit a spot beneath Straton's hide, for he nodded his assent. "Come back later," he told Aphrodite. "Check on him."

"Of course," she smiled in return. "And thank you for bringing Philo here."

He gave another nod.

"Teretia will be most thankful to you."

A blank look from Straton. Mina pawed at his arm with more urgency. Partly from her fear of discovery and partly to distract him from wondering who Teretia was.

"Come on, I'm meant to be in place one hour before dawn. The empress will go nuts over arse if I'm not there." She dragged him along.

"You get me if anything …" Straton insisted from the door.

"I shall," promised Aphrodite.

Laco stood in front of a line of bodies, the humbled centurion wiping the blood off their faces to aid identification. The prefect worked his way along the line, noting the sword slashes to the bodies, ordering a chin to be lifted so he could examine the dead features. He went down the line four times with increasing irritation for this was not as simple a task as he had supposed. The bodies were in such a state that it was difficult to even determine skin colour or sex. Discounting the clearly rotund and beefy, that still left a large quantity of bodies that might or might not be Philo.

Pointing to one poor fellow, he demanded of the centurion, "How am I supposed to identify him? He has no face. No nose, no lips, no eyes."

The centurion sympathised. "Does your man have any distinguishing features?"

"If he did, your guards would have no doubt hacked them off!" he snapped back. Regaining his temper, he said evenly, "We need expert help. That man who heads the overseers' team, he will be well placed to identify Philo. Presumably he had a file at one point listing his features."

"Felix?" asked the centurion with a gulp.

So far that evening the centurion had defeated a band of marauding, heavily armed slaves; casually executed the remaining prisoners; murdered the jailer; and then lied shamelessly to his superior officer. What he was not about to do was get Felix out of bed. Some assignments were just far too dangerous.

It was a small mercy that the head overseer was not asleep. For a prematurely woken Felix possessed a bellow that could reduce masonry to rubble and young messenger slaves to wibbling jellyfish.

Tucking Ganymede beneath a huge knitted blanket, Felix told the boy, "There you go lad. This will keep you warm. That'll be why you woke up, it's a cold night tonight."

Ganymede wriggled further under the blanket as Felix tucked its edges under the mattress.

"I told you he needed an extra blanket," said Felix's wife Vallia from the door. She was wrapped in a shawl that was made from so much material it could easily double as a tent for a trio of legionaries. Such proportions were necessary to cover Vallia's gargantuan figure, which had it been rendered in stone would've broken the back of many a quarry slave forced to dig for materials.

Sitting on the bed beside Ganymede, she told him, "I got you this." Handing him a toy soldier carved out of wood.

Ganymede's eyes lit up. "Cor," he said. "Thanks." Taking hold of the soldier, he tucked it beside him in bed.

"Night, night," she said kissing him on the forehead.

Felix opted for a slightly awkward pat of the blanket as his farewell.

Pulling the door shut he asked, "Where did you get that soldier from?"

"The shops, of course," she snapped. "Where else would I get it from? You threw out all of little Felix's toys!"

Felix crossed his arms across his chest. "Well, what fucking use did we have for them, hey?"

Vallia gave a huff, the prelude to an argument. But it was an argument that never happened. For it was at this choice moment that the unlucky fool of a messenger rapped on the door.

Felix stood legs apart, cracking his knuckles with an expression akin to the emperor Augustus after he learnt that the rather careless general Varus had lost three of his legions in the German forest.

"This had better be fucking stupendous," he told Laco.

Laco, who like everybody else had given up trying to assert any authority over Felix, told him, "I need you to identify Philo."

A gathering redness on Felix's neck signified an imminent explosion.

"You what?" he began in the unnatural stillness that precipitated a meltdown, known collectively to the imperial slaves as *"the fleeing time"*.

"YOU WANT ME TO IDENTIFY PHILO?" he roared.

Laco unconsciously took a step backwards.

"Is this some sort of joke? You've fucking met him! What the fuck do you need me for? And why the fuck did you get me out of fucking bed for this fucking lunacy?"

Laco persisted, "Does he have any distinguishing features? A mole? A birthmark?"

Felix shook his head in incredulity. "Does he have any fucking distinguishing features? Yes, he fucking does. A whole load of them that put together make fucking Philo!"

Laco pointed to a doorway. Felix entered to be faced by a line of bodies. While Laco picked at an ear, Felix hollered his disapproval at the loss of his stock.

"Timon is worth 900. I only put him in the cells coz he'd taken to stealing from the kitchens. It was hardly a fucking executionable offence!"

"There was an incident."

"No fucking kidding," said Felix, eyeing up the thirty-or-so bodies.

"Which one is Philo, though?" pressed Laco, keen to clear the matter as quickly as possible.

Felix furrowed his brow, red eyebrows meeting across his nose. His instant thought was: none of them. They were all too tall, too pale. He undertook a further examination, pulling down tunic necks.

"He's got a mole behind his ear," he told Laco.

Though in reality he was searching for the silver chain holding the stationery cupboard key that he knew Philo always wore. Inspection complete, he stood back scratching at his beard.

"Well?" insisted Laco. For at this rate he was going to miss Galba's adoption announcement. Plus, the cadavers were beginning to reek horribly.

Felix's brain made the connection quickly. A missing Philo; an utter bloody massacre: Straton.

To Laco he said, "Third from the left." Adding, "I shall be submitting my expenses form later. That's nearly 15ᴋ of lost goods you fucking owe me."

Laco, however, wasn't listening. He was just gratified that the niggly issue over Philo's fate was resolved. There was no need for evidence now. No need for a trial. The execution had already been carried out.

In Epaphroditus' courtyard, Mina embraced Vinius.

"You saved us. You saved us all," she told him feeling a rush of affection. He might be a bit fumbling, a bit sweaty of palm but he had put himself out for a bunch of slaves. He was her hero. "I shall never forget this. Never!"

She gave him a quick kiss, which he responded to cheerfully. "I'll make sure you both get back safely and that there are no repercussions."

Straton, standing to one side, watched this scene with a smile. He nudged Tigellinus awake to share the moment. "Cute," he slurred and gave a belch.

Mina gave Vinius the tightest hug she could, which is what a sleepy, yawning Epaphroditus witnessed as he came to investigate what all the noise was. He was saved from any kind of response to the odd spectacle of his mistress embroiled in an embrace with another man by his wife. Aphrodite stormed over, grabbed him by the arm, and dragged him into their dining room, demanding, "What have you and Otho been up to?"

Taken aback by her anger, he stammered, "Nothing, nothing at all."

"Don't give me that. All those cosy sessions holed up in your study. What were you planning?"

Recovering himself, Epaphroditus replied evenly, "If two old friends can't enjoy each other's company … This mistrust does you no credit."

Hands on hips, she threw back at him, "So you weren't plotting to make Otho emperor then?"

Blank-faced he replied, "What a bizarre idea. I cannot think of anyone less qualified."

She grabbed him by the hand, pulling him roughly along. "Come see what your scheming has achieved."

She dragged him across the courtyard and into one of the bedrooms, pointing furiously at Philo. Callista was trying to get him to drink from a beaker, the injured man groaning and resisting the liquid. Epaphroditus' face whitened. "Oh Jupiter. Philo."

"This is your doing. How could you? How could you drag Philo into one of Otho's crackpot schemes?"

"I didn't," he protested. "I promise I didn't."

"And we all know how much your promises are worth!"

Epaphroditus knew he was on a losing streak so he stopped himself retorting. He sat on the bed beside the shaking Philo and put a hand to his forehead.

"He's so cold."

"I imagine they don't bother to heat the dungeons," snapped Aphrodite, pushing him out the way. "If you want to do something useful, I suggest you go and pick up Teretia."

"I'll send a litter."

"No, you will go personally. I am not having that poor girl travelling on her own. You will pick her up and you will spend the journey explaining just how Philo got injured."

FORTY

Lysander decided that it was up to him to break the news to Teretia about Philo's dire situation. He had dashed straight over to the Viminal after work and used his best announcing tone to inform her of the grave news, noting keenly the gasping heave her bosom gave.

"We shall go to the palace," Pompeia had stated firmly. "Demand an audience with the emperor and insist that he release him."

Seeing her roll up her sleeves with a determined air, Lysander could imagine her doing just that. Berating the aged emperor with shaking red fists.

"Not a good idea," he said. "They wouldn't let you in. Worse still, if you did get in they might consider you part of the plot. It is a very dangerous situation."

"The emperor would not arrest women."

Lysander, recalling certain rumours from Galba's time in Spain said, "He would. You'd best stay here. Safe."

This was directed at a silent and pale Teretia. Or rather, at her chest. Lysander finding it near impossible not to gaze upon those magnificent globes. He was not entirely insensitive. He would give Teretia a good month before he made his move. But there was no harm slipping in a bit of groundwork. So he said solemnly, "I knew him better than anyone. We used to share a room as boys and then later too. He was always a very good room-mate. Never any trouble between us. We were always the best of friends. Such a tragedy. I knew him so very well."

"KNOW," shouted Teretia, jumping to her feet. "Know. You *know* him very well," she yelled at Lysander before fleeing the room in tears followed by her concerned mother.

Sat at the kitchen table, Lysander listened to her sobs for a while before discreetly letting himself out.

The family quickly gathered round to support Teretia. Holing up in the kitchen there was much loud, bawdy discussion about what they could do. Uncle Gnaeus was convinced that they could get a large-enough contingent from the Viminal to storm the palace.

"You'll get yourselves killed," scoffed Pompeia Major. "You lot against the Guard? They'd cut you to ribbons before you'd even unsheathed your daggers."

"That fiend killed Teretius and now he's after Philo. I say we cut him down!"

The mention of Teretius spread a general gloom, Teretia affected more than most. It was the impotence of the whole situation. What was she to do? Just sit here until Lysander slimed his way back with his lecherous stare as he told her that Philo was dead? Was he dead? She knew that she would feel it the moment he was gone. Her heart would surely burst? A world without Philo would feel different the very instant he left it. Surely that was how it worked when you loved each other like they did?

She feared his death. But she feared his living much more. Fretting over what had happened to him. Was he all by himself? Was he in pain? She couldn't bear the thought of Philo alone without her to comfort him; without knowing what was going to happen to him. He must be frantic. He must be terrified. And here she was sitting at the kitchen table not doing anything to help. She couldn't bear it. She just couldn't. She sat fiddling with her fingers, feeling the panic rise to her throat. Meanwhile, her family argued over her as to how much of a bastard Galba was. Dreaming up schemes that were nothing but talk.

Epaphroditus had plenty of time to assess his actions on the way to the Viminal. He had thought the scheme innocent, harmless even. Galba could adopt Otho or he could not. Where was the harm if he didn't? Of course Otho would owe a lot of money to a lot of people but such was his natural state. When Epaphroditus first knew Otho he would cheerfully bet 100,000 sesterces on the roll of a dice and never seemed particularly downcast when he inevitably lost. No, it had been a game. A diverting game he'd been flattered into playing.

He should have foreseen how Galba and his associates would view Otho's cheery machinations. They'd overthrown a wildly popular emperor just six months ago, destroying a dynasty that had ruled Rome for more than a century. Their situation was far more precarious than Nero's. Far less established. Tottering even in comparison. They would be jumpy, looking for any potential dissenters. Especially after Sabinus' failed coup. Otho's politicking under his guidance was bound to irk their suspicions, particularly given his past friendship with Nero.

Rubbing his head, Epaphroditus recognised his own foolishness. He had not thought it through, had he? That was unlike him. He was usually so careful, so precise, weighing up every factor before making a decision. It was how he'd survived so many decades of deadly imperial politics. So why had he abandoned his defences this time? Because it was Otho he concluded. Marcus Salvius Otho had charmed him into taking part in his daft scheme, just as he always had.

The litter came to a halt and was lowered gently to the ground. Epaphroditus pulled back the curtain and stepped out, gazing up at a dull-looking apartment block that stood five storeys above him. This was Philo's home? he queried internally. Had Icelus cut his salary? On the wages Epaphroditus paid, Philo could have saved for a year and bought this entire Viminal street. What had made him move here?

Trudging up the stairs to Pompeia's first-floor apartment he marvelled at the drab brown walls and the smell of cabbage. He'd never been in a plebeian home before. Were they all like this?

Reaching the first floor of the block he yelled out a, "Hello?" and followed the smell along the corridor, sticking his head into the kitchen. There was quite a crowd and they viewed him with suspicion. Looking beyond the hard glares he saw Teretia shoot to her feet, her hands at her throat.

"He's dead, isn't he?" she asked in anguish, her eyes already filling with tears.

"No, no, no" he assured her hastily from the doorway. "He's at mine. He's very much alive. I've come to take you to him."

Teretia sobbed from sheer relief.

Philo opened his eyes to see a woman gazing down at him. She had one hand on his forehead and was asking him how he was.

He looked at her vaguely and asked in a croaky voice, "What day is it?"

"It is five after the nones," replied Aphrodite, helping him into a sitting position, Philo wincing with pain.

"Do you know where you are?"

He shook his head and looked at his surroundings. It seemed rather luxurious. Was he in the palace? It didn't look like the palace. Where were the slaves? Where were the guards?

"You are in my house, Philo."

Which didn't help him at all since he didn't know who this kind lady was.

He prodded at his swollen cheek. It hurt. He'd been hurt, hadn't he? And this lady had taken him in?

Seeing his confusion Aphrodite said gently, "You don't need to worry about any of that now. You just need to get better."

"What day is it?"

"It is five after the nones."

Five after the nones? He'd gone to work. He remembered that. He'd gone to work but it hadn't been five after the nones.

Aphrodite could see him puzzling over the timescale. "Do you remember how you got here?"

Another vague look, a shake of his head, hands fidgeting with the blanket. "What day is it?" he asked again, with a hint of agitation.

She sat on the bed beside him. "Philo, darling, I've already told you. Don't you remember? I told you just now for the second time."

"My head hurts," he said by way of explanation. "Is it the nones?"

"No, Philo, it's five after the nones. Can you remember that?"

She took his hand and watched him struggle with his thoughts. Eventually after a mammoth effort he said, "I've missed dinner. And breakfast."

A thought that upset him a great deal. They would be frantic, Pompeia and Teretia.

"Teretia?" he voiced, visibly troubled.

"It's alright, it's alright," she soothed. "She is on her way. Epaphroditus has gone to pick her up."

A statement that relaxed him a little, leaning back on the pillows puzzling over his lost days. "Have I been here?" he asked the lady.

"You came here last night. You were asleep. You woke up a bit earlier. Do you remember that?" Aphrodite probed.

Philo had regained consciousness an hour previously and they had shared much of the same conversation. He had been seemingly unaware of his surroundings or what had happened to him, questioning her about the day before. Exhausted from the effort he had drifted off again. The mention of Teretia was new though, which was promising.

"Is Teretia coming?" he asked.

"Yes, she is on her way."

"Good."

She stroked his brow. "Yes, that's good isn't it?" She watched his eyes close.

Before departing for the Esquiline, Teretia had been given a long speech from her mother about how she had to be strong for Philo. Epaphroditus had told them Philo was a lot better than he looked, leading Pompeia to assume it looked pretty bad.

"Now then, my dear, no matter what, you have to keep your composure. None of them tears, love, you have to be strong. Because Philo wouldn't want you to be upset, would he now?" Teretia shook her head.

"No, because that would upset him, wouldn't it? And we don't want him to be upset because we want him to get better, don't we?"

Teretia nodded.

"Good, so you be strong, my girl."

"I shall, mother," she promised.

This promise she was so determined to keep lasted approximately three beats into her first vision of Philo propped up in bed with bruised jaw, swollen eyes, and sporting a range of lurid bruises across his face. Her hand went to her mouth, her lip wobbled, and she gave a small cry. Epaphroditus put his arm around her, leading her to the bed where Philo lay resting.

Aphrodite gave her hand a squeeze. "He has been awake a little," she told Teretia. "But he is very confused. I need you to be prepared that he might not recognise you."

Teretia looked worried by this but nodded anyway, gulping back her tears.

Aphrodite gently rocked the patient. "Philo, Teretia is here to see you."

He opened his eyes slowly. Nobody could mistake he recognised Teretia, for his entire face lit up. Then he winced as his bloated lips cracked from the smile.

"Can I hug you?" Teretia asked, her eyes filling with tears.

Philo could think of nothing more he wanted than a hug from Teretia so he nodded, adding in a soft voice, "Carefully."

She put her arms slowly round him, checking that it wasn't hurting. He rested his head on her shoulder, inhaling her sweet scent and burying his face away, mumbling a sentence that was intelligible only to Teretia who replied, "I'm not angry with you. Why would I be angry with you? I am so happy you're OK. Sort of OK. But you will be OK, won't you?"

She looked up hopefully at Aphrodite who said, "In time."

Teretia told him, "There, you see, everything is going to be fine."

Another mumble. Teretia replied, "That doesn't matter. No it doesn't. We'll just put back the wedding. I'm not disappointed. Of course I'm not. I just want you to get better. What's that, darling?"

A soft mumble on her shoulder.

"You are in Epaphroditus' house," Teretia told him.

Philo looked up and took in his surroundings with bewilderment.

Epaphroditus, sitting on the end of the bed, told him, "You've probably not been in this room before. That's why you don't recognise it."

"When you used to stay we would always put you in the orange room," Aphrodite offered, "and we always found it far neater when you had stayed in it. You would even sweep the floor before you left," she smiled.

Philo screwed up his eyes. "Aeneas," he muttered.

Aphrodite smiled. "That's right. There's a fresco of Aeneas and Anchises fleeing from Troy on the walls."

Teretia gently squeezed Philo's hand. He looked down at it, squinting at his bruised knuckles and grazed fingers.

"Do you remember what happened?" pushed Epaphroditus.

Aphrodite, keen to keep Philo's mind on happy thoughts, gave his ankle a swift kick. Her husband shot a questioning glance her way.

Staring at his injured hands the patient said, "I got hurt."

"You did," Teretia confirmed. "But you are going to get better. You just need to rest."

Philo reached up to scratch his face, hitting his swollen cheek. He gave it a prod, eyes opening again in confusion.

"Yes, you hurt your cheek too," Teretia told him.

Philo gave it another prod, frowning. Something was moving at the back of his mind, a ghost of a memory. A desk. A desk in Laco's office. There was something about a desk. Then a flash: his cheek slammed hard, hitting wood. His eyes shifted uncomfortably as he struggled to fit the memories together. A hand began to fidget with the blanket.

"Philo, it's alright. It's alright," soothed Teretia, stroking his brow.

"I want to sleep. Tired," he said very definitely to his visitors.

Aphrodite stood, heaving up Epaphroditus by his elbow. "We'll leave you to have a sleep."

"Yes, you get some sleep."

Epaphroditus patted his arm. Philo flinched away and closed his eyes. Not from tiredness but rather to get rid of them. He needed to think. He needed to piece it together himself. Teretia stood to leave but Philo reached over and grabbed hold of her hand with a firm-enough grip that she understood his intention. She sat back down beside him. Once she was settled, he loosened his grip, lay back on the pillows, and began to puzzle it all out.

FORTY-ONE

Lysander was particularly proud of his assignment. It kept his mind off Philo's situation and Teretia's grief. He'd been personally summoned to see the emperor. Galba glared down his long nose at him and barked, "I've been told you are good with words."

"Yes, Caesar," he had dutifully and honestly replied.

"I need a particularly fine introduction to a particularly fine young man who I wish to bestow a very important gift upon."

Which Lysander took to mean the great announcement regarding his heir.

"Your discretion is absolutely crucial," Galba told him sternly. "This is privileged information. Highly confidential."

Lysander had burst with joy. He was in possession of the news regarding Galba's heir. In fact he had a whole biography of the man in question in order to fully compose his introduction. He was one of only four men who knew the identity of the emperor-in-waiting. A statistic he was eager to share with as many people as he could, adding, "But I cannot tell you who is it," and tapping his nose.

Sporus gave a theatrical yawn. "Like we care. Politics is so dull. I had much rather hear about that freebie girl who was so alarmed by your chat-up lines that she screamed for her father."

"That is not true," said a red-faced Lysander.

"I heard you had to flee through the streets from a baying mob."

"Not true," huffed Lysander, taking his gossip elsewhere.

Sporus laughed at his retreating back, elbowing Mina awake. "That was classic! I can't believe you slept through it!"

Mina rubbed her eyes. "I am never going to get through today."

"What were you up to last night? Is Titus Vinius keeping you active? He looks a sturdy sort." Sporus pursed his lips. "Rampant."

"Shows what you know, no-ball boy," replied Mina, jumping up and down in an attempt to wake herself up. "He is a top bloke though," she shared.

She recalled his vital assistance the previous night. Despite his shortcomings he had replaced Epaphroditus in her affections. He was a proper man. A soldier. A man of action. Not of fancy words and lies dished out at will. Mina, after her daring mission with Straton, was all about action now.

She gave the reclining Sporus a kick as she bounced up and down.

She hadn't told her friend about her adventure. He was hopeless at keeping secrets and Philo's survival depended on silence. She wondered absently if this was how Alex had justified his actions, then threw that thought clean out of her head. She couldn't think about him now. She just had to somehow stay awake. She wondered how Straton was coping with the lack of sleep.

Straton was being punished. Rolling into Felix's office, he had been roundly bollocked.

"I found Xagoras. Dead as fucking Pluto!" his boss had yelled. "Out of fucking line, Straton, you understand? Way out of fucking line! Slaves are one thing but you don't go murdering the ruddy enforcers! Brings down team spirit."

Straton wasn't aware that the overseers had any team spirit but he stood and took Felix's wrath. Watching him go increasingly purple, waving his fists about, and coming up with ever more inventive insults for Straton's unacceptable behaviour.

"He is coming out of your wages," he said, scribbling in Straton's file, which he always kept close to hand and which was ten times as thick as anyone else's. "And do you want to tell me what you were up to in the cells last night?"

Straton looked away.

"Had your name all fucking over it! Right bloody scene it was. We lost thirty-four slaves. Thirty-fucking-four! OK, fair enough, seventeen of them were scheduled for death anyway, but still way out of fucking line! Laco had me down there identifying the bodies."

Straton shifted on his feet. Felix narrowed his eyes. "Where the fuck is he?"

"Who?"

"You know who. Philo. What the fuck did you do with him? Don't fucking try to argue. Thirty-four bodies down there and not one of them was Philo. Where is he?"

"Safe," said Straton stubbornly, folding his arms across his chest.

"Well, I hope you left him with enough fucking food coz you ain't leaving my side. I got a job for you."

He indicated the pile of tablets on his desk. Straton pulled a face.

"Yeah I know," replied Felix. "But you don't need your letters for what I need you for."

Thus Straton spent an extremely dull day assisting Felix. Boxing up the files of the slaves he had helped decease the previous evening for archiving. He managed to slip out briefly, claiming bowel trouble. Rushing down the corridor to Philo's office, he found Talos sitting quietly staring into space.

Talos was a little shaky of late. He still dreamt of Alex's death. Waking up in a cold sweat, his room-mates throwing sandals at his head and telling him to shut up. Then there was Philo. Dragged off to the cells, awaiting certain death. And all those slaves Icelus imagined were plotting who he'd sent to Scaveous. So it was not surprising really that on Straton's entrance, he leapt to his feet, trembling, imagining the overseer had come for him.

Straton gave him a leer which pushed Talos into tears. The overseer rummaged behind Philo's desk before appearing triumphant with the satchel in his hands. He would take it to him tonight when Felix finally let him go. Straton imagined Philo's happy face when he beheld it.

Glancing at the wobbling Talos, he put a finger to his lips and rasped, "Ssh."

Talos nodded silently as the urine ran down his leg forming a puddle on the floor.

Otho had given particular care to his appearance. Though he naturally tended towards the dandified, he made a conscious effort to tone down his flamboyance. He wore his senatorial purple-striped tunic complete with stoically draped toga, sensible (or, as Otho felt, dull) boots, and a neatly washed toupee which gleamed with applied oil.

A little too much celebratory wine the previous night had given him a more sedate air, which Onomastus assured him was most befitting to an emperor-to-be. He walked with studied solemnity through the old palace giving sharp and dignified nods to his acquaintances, as opposed to his usual cheery hello.

He was determined to do everything correctly and so he even greeted Icelus with decorum.

"Good day to you, sir. How are you?"

Icelus glared at him and then smiled. "Oh, I am very well, Otho. Very well indeed. You look very smart."

Otho affected a tight smile when his mouth naturally wanted to beam. "Thank you, Icelus. So very kind of you to notice."

This rather dull and forced conversation was broken up by Lysander announcing formally, "The emperor requests your attendance."

They were led into a small, tastefully decorated chamber: white walls decorated with fake columns wound with green garlands. Galba sat at the head of the room on a large wooden chair. His straight-backed position reeked of authority.

"Ah, Icelus, Otho. Do sit," he gestured and they were led to their respective seats among the other senators and courtiers.

Regulus gave a supportive smile. Otho returned a regal wave.

Galba stood before them. "My friends," he began. "I am an old man."

Though this was patently true, the assembled senators and dignitaries mumbled a protest. Galba held up a hand. "No, it is truth and it is truth I speak. The issue of my heir must be dealt with and it must be dealt with now. If it were possible for our glorious empire to stand erect and keep its balance in the absence of a ruler, then I should want nothing less than to hand it over to you, our glorious senate, you fine men of standards. But unfortunately we have long passed a point where these drastic measures can be taken. Hence in my declining years, I can make no greater gift than a good successor."

Otho shifted slightly on his chair waiting for the moment when he can stand, give his "gosh what an honour" face, and then deliver the frightfully dull but worthy speech Epaphroditus had written for him.

"The dynasty of the Julii and Claudii has come to an end and the best man will be discovered by the process of adoption. The man I have decided upon is one of noble parentage."

True, thought Otho, remembering his very severe and respectable father.

"He is one who suffered great misfortune during the reign of that despot Nero."

True again, thought Otho. Lusitania was a dump of a backwater.

"He shows great promise and great loyalty. I hand to him this empire and will that he rules it wisely."

Otho gathered up his toga ready to stand when Lysander took the floor and announced in his best baritone, "Gaius Piso Licianianus, son of Marcus Crassus and Scribonia it is Galba Caesar's desire that you become his successor and his son. Do you concur?"

An extremely pale, thin man at the far end of the row stood up and walked forward. He turned to the assembly and nodded. Turning back, head bowed, he told Galba, "I do, Caesar."

The emperor took hold of his hands and shook them before announcing to the stunned senators, "Behold the future of Rome!"

FORTY-TWO

"Well, if that's the future of Rome, I suggest we move back to Lusitania," consoled Onomastus as they followed the imperial party to the Praetorian camp to announce the joyous news to the troops.

Otho attempted a smile. It failed. Staring at the blackened sky and rolling clouds he said, "The gods are angry. They knew it should have been me. I would have been a superior emperor."

"The very best," agreed his freedman, pulling up his hood as the rain began to fall.

His master felt decidedly gloomy. It wasn't just the moment pasty Piso had accepted Galba's offer that had dampened his spirits. It wasn't even the five hours' worth of speeches praising Piso's ancestry and particularly fine qualities he was forced to sit through. Nor even the glee with which Icelus and Laco had commiserated with him, offering such sickly sentiment that a hungover Otho had felt distinctly nauseous.

No, it was the senators. His noble colleagues who sped forward with sworn oaths of allegiance to Piso. When the very day before they had been declaring undying loyalty to him and telling him that they would support his claim 100 per cent. The sheer speed of their switch had left a distinctly bitter taste in

311

his mouth, which had nothing to do with the copious vomiting session of the previous evening.

"Tasty wife, though," was Onomastus' comment, indicating the noble Verania, wife of Piso.

She certainly was, with long black hair, red pouty lips, and gloriously rounded hips.

"Think she's pullable?" enquired Otho, thinking it might just cure his injured pride.

"Got to be worth a try," said the dwarf, watching her bottom with awe and feeling distinctly hot despite the damp weather.

Ahead of them, Verania gripped her husband's hand. He turned to her. "I couldn't refuse him, could I?" he asked a little desperately.

"No, of course you couldn't, darling, and you must not worry. I shall always be by your side."

"Thank you, my dear. It is a great comfort to me."

Galba watched this sweet scene with pride. He had chosen well. Piso was a decent man, untainted by scandal, with a lineage to match his own, an extremely beautiful wife, and a selection of well-behaved children who walked alongside him now: his dynasty.

Even better, just as he had hoped, his decision to adopt Piso had united his advisors. Laco and Icelus had expressed their approval. Vinius was slightly more sceptical but after chatting with Piso he had at least declared him, "a nice guy and pleasant with it."

If the soldierly Vinius approved then the guards would see Piso's fine qualities too. All these mutterings so distasteful to Galba would cease. The empire would be united and all this business in Germania would melt away.

The guards certainly gave Piso a warm welcome. Although if Galba thought this was due to the young man's star quality, he was wrong. For there was a tradition that had always been observed: when a new emperor was declared, the imperial bodyguard were rewarded (or bought, depending on your view) with a satisfactory bounty.

The Praetorians were almost gleeful at Piso's arrival. As they saw it they were in line for a double payday, for Galba had never settled his account with them. Honoratus stood grimly, arms crossed as the young man spoke in a narrow, reedy voice. He wanted his money. It was too late for Alex. Too late for his dreams of a son. But he wanted his money: he'd earned it. He'd killed his friend Sabinus to secure Galba's dynasty. He was owed.

Somewhere in the crowd Otho shuffled his wet feet as the guards cheered pale Piso to the hilt, waving their swords with enthusiasm.

"I've had enough. Have you had enough?"

"For definite," replied Otho despondently, catching Honoratus' eyes and giving him a tight smile; the tribune nodding in return.

"Otho's face!" crowed Icelus to Laco as they sat in the bathhouse, slaves oiling them up. "It just collapsed in on itself!" And he laughed, a high-pitched giggle of a laugh, his stomach rippling from the effort.

Laco gave a tight smile. "It was wonderful. He really believed he would be emperor. He was so sure."

"Poor Otho."

"Very poor Otho. I hear he is heavily in debt. The money-lenders will be closing in on him now he's exposed," Laco sneered, picturing a destitute and broken Otho and finding he enjoyed the image immensely. "It was rather special."

"We underestimated Galba, didn't we? He saw through Otho all along."

Laco stretched happily. "How about we kick a man when he's down."

"Hey?"

"Get rid of Otho utterly. Now is the time to do it, before he can wheedle his way back in." Laco did not doubt that Otho was capable of this. "We have the leverage," he continued.

Icelus, admiring a particularly handsome young slave who was sweeping the floor quietly around them, gave a lazy smile. "I want to see Otho debased, prostrate, begging me for my mercy."

"Let us do it then. Let us finish him off for good."

After the blurred haziness of his first awakenings when he had fumbled over names and days, Philo was beginning to get a hold on events.

He spent the day quietly worrying things through. Working out the sequence that had led to his bruised cheek, his broken jaw, his cracked ribs, and pulsating head.

It wasn't all clear but with some careful thought and Teretia's calm assistance, he was able to reach some conclusions that filled in the blanks in his memory. With those conclusions came a firm resolution which he delivered to his host and hostess.

"I want to go home."

"I don't think you should be moved yet, Philo. You need to rest," said Aphrodite.

"I want to go home. With Teretia," he insisted, still a little vague on who Aphrodite was.

Teretia had told him that she was his former boss' wife, but he had no clear memories of her despite Teretia's insistence that they'd met many times before.

Epaphroditus cleared his throat. "It's not safe. Icelus will be looking for you. It will be the first place he goes."

Philo looked at him blankly. "I don't understand. You pulled strings for me, at the palace. You got me released."

Epaphroditus sat on the edge of the bed. "I didn't even know you were in trouble, not until you showed up here. Do you remember what happened?"

He stared at his hands, eyes crinkling as he struggled to grab hold of the fleeting images. "The floor was wet, slimy, and Laco … Laco kept asking me questions … and I didn't know … The emperor was very cross with me … They didn't believe me … wouldn't listen when I said that I didn't know, because I didn't know!" Which came out indignant. "And I wouldn't sign because it wasn't true. What they were saying about me giving information to Otho."

Aphrodite shot her husband a hard glare.

Epaphroditus, shamed, asked, "Do you remember how you got here?"

Eyes crinkling again, a shake of his head, before saying unsurely, "There was shouting, I think. Lots of shouting."

Then a vague remembrance of someone telling him he had to wake up. A girl? It had sounded like a girl, but he couldn't catch hold of the memory and it floated away.

"You were broken out of the cells," Aphrodite told him.

Philo looked aghast. "I'm not pardoned?"

"No."

"Should I go back and try to sort it out?" he asked.

A question determined void when Teretia exclaimed loudly, "No! Look at what they did to you! You're not going back. Not ever. I don't want you working at the palace any more. It's far too dangerous."

Philo, head pounding, eyes throbbing, amongst his other injuries and pains, asked quietly, "I can't go home?"

"No," confirmed Epaphroditus.

"And I can't go to the palace?"

"No."

His resolution crumbled as he asked Epaphroditus with pleading eyes, "What will I do?"

Epaphroditus found himself unusually lost for words. Luckily Aphrodite was not so tongue-tied. "Let's not think about that now. The main thing is that you get better, don't you agree, Teretia?"

"Oh yes," she nodded eagerly.

"You are very welcome to stay, Teretia, until things are more settled."

She was about to agree when a thought struck her. "What about mother? She'd be all alone! I couldn't leave her alone, I just couldn't. She needs me."

"I need you. Please stay, please," Philo pleaded, poking at his cheek, remembering his face being slammed onto the desk, hands holding him down. "Teretia, please don't go."

It was the crack in his voice that turned her. That and the tears filling his dark eyes before he buried his face into her and began silently sobbing, begging her to stay.

"Your mother can stay too," an unsettled Epaphroditus said quickly. "Anyone else you want to, we'll send for them. Whatever."

Aphrodite grabbed his elbow. "Let's give them some privacy." She led him out.

When they were outside the door she turned to her husband and snarled, "I hope you are happy. I hope you are wonderfully satisfied at utterly ruining Philo's life."

"Don't," he warned her.

"Don't what? Don't point out that without a job he can't keep a roof over that sweet girl and her poor widowed mother's heads. Or that he is a fugitive and that his hard-earned freedom is worth nothing now!"

She would have gone on for some time in an ever higher pitch had not Callista slid in and announced, "Marcus Salvius Otho. I have put him in your study, master."

"Oh, you go! YOU go to your *friend*." That final word was spat out with venom. "I shall patch up Philo and console Teretia and make sure her mother is fine. You just GO!"

In fact she did not wait for him to go but flounced off in a high fury before he could respond.

"Fabulous," he said to the sky, hands clenched by his side.

FORTY-THREE

Felix looked down at his clear desk, rubbed his hands together, and declared "Job well done." Then, "Want to get a drink?" he asked a dusty and tired Straton. "I've got a lovely amphora at home and Vallia cooks a mean gourd pie. Only fucking thing she can do. That and whinge. She'll not mind one extra for dinner. Likes an audience for her disappointments does my wife."

"Tired."

"Well, that'll be all the fucking massacring you got up to last night."

Straton attempted to look humble. It did not suit.

"You ain't forgiven. Yet," Felix told him. "But go on, knock off for the night. Sleep it off. And tomorrow we'll have that little chat about you messin' with my goods AGAIN!"

Straton had absolutely no intention of sleeping anything off, tormented as he was by a gnawing fear that Philo had succumbed to his injuries. He headed straight to Epaphroditus' home, a slave showing him through to the bedroom where his beloved was napping.

The freedman was lying on his side, his chest rising from gentle breaths. Straton sat beside him, felt his brow: warmer than before. A good sign? His face was still a mess, though they had cleaned off the blood to reveal colourful bruises and a blackened jaw visible even against Philo's dark skin. Straton muttered a prayer to his favourite gods. Those best placed to wreak vengeance on all those who had hurt his love.

"Hullo, have you come to see Philo?"

Straton turned to see a blonde girl standing in the doorway, a pile of clothes in her arms. A slave? One of Epaphroditus' daughters?

"I've been to get his tunics," the girl told him, placing them on the end of the bed. "Aphrodite was most kind. She said she could lend him some but I knew he would be much happier in his own clothes." She smiled sweetly at him. "Is that Philo's satchel?" she asked. "Did you bring it all the way here? For him?"

Straton, hugging the satchel possessively, nodded.

"Oh, that is so kind!" gushed Teretia. "I am sure that will perk Philo up no end! Does it have all his books in it?"

Straton opened it slightly to demonstrate. Teretia clapped happily. "Oh, thank you, sir. That is so kind of you, so nice. He is a little better," she confided.

"Woken?" croaked Straton, staring down at Philo's battered face.

"Oh yes. He has been awake and talking."

"Talking?"

"It hurts him a little. His jaw is very painful. Beast, Laco."

Straton nodded approvingly.

"And he is a little gloomy but I think that is to be expected," Teretia said, more to reassure herself than Straton.

On the bed the patient mumbled a little and stretched. Teretia stroked his hair. "It's OK, darling," kissing him lightly on the cheek.

Philo opened his eyes.

"Hello there," she cooed. "How are you feeling?"

Gripping her hand, he gave a small, sad smile. "Sore," he replied quietly, moving slightly and wincing as he did.

Teretia smiled down at him, giving the sore lips a gentle kiss and rubbing his hand. "You seem happier on your side. Is it more comfortable?"

Squinting through a pounding headache Philo whispered painfully, "I think."

"Are you hungry yet? Because I really do think you should eat something even if you don't feel like it. Otherwise, you will never get your strength back."

Philo shook his head.

"A drink then. Are you thirsty?"

"A bit," struggling to pull himself up, screwing his eyes up in pain.

"Oh, and Philo, this nice gentleman has come to see you and he has brought your satchel for you," said Teretia, smiling. "Isn't that kind?"

Philo, propped upright, gazed vaguely at the large shape, his eyes slowly focusing on the bulk of Straton.

"I would have made a fine emperor," sighed Otho, sipping at his wine.

"The best," toasted Onomastus.

"Certainly better than some who've inhabited the position," supplied Epaphroditus.

The three of them were holed up in Epaphroditus' study. Their host despondently flicking a marble back and forth across his desk.

"Ahh, let's get drunk. Rolling, falling drunk. Even you, Epaphroditus. I insist upon it. Soothe my battered feelings."

"You're not going to the sacrifices for Piso's well-being?"

"It would be ever-so-slightly hypocritical of me. Besides, I don't think I could bear to look at Laco's smarmy face. I am usually such a genial fellow."

"You are," agreed his freedman.

"But I actually found myself contemplating punching him."

Epaphroditus looked up shocked.

"Yes indeed," Otho told him. "I reckon a quick jab would break that pretty nose of his."

"Tempting I know, but it might diminish your status as a senator. Make you look like a poor loser."

Otho winced at that last word. It was true though, wasn't it? He'd thought that for once in his life he was actually going to achieve something. Something tangible, something worthwhile.

Though he fashioned a casually laid-back persona, pretending it was all a game, he'd rather wanted to be emperor. Not for the glory: Otho was comfortable enough in his own skin to not need outside approval to function. No, it was something more daring, more idea-driven. He'd actually thought he could do some good as emperor.

Though he had spent the early years of Nero's reign in an alcoholic daze, he still remembered those good works of Nero, advised by Seneca and Burrus. A tightening-up of small legal matters, dull to some but fairer to the people, stamping out those lawyers' abuses. Otho fancied being that sort of emperor: a genial protector of his people.

Otho liked people, adored people. All people, whether they were senator or pleb, man or woman, child or adult. His people. He wanted to help them, help them all.

He would have been great at it. It was a desperate pity. He liked Piso well enough (he liked everyone, it was his major failing), but he doubted the young man was up to the job. Otho had been a member of Claudius' and Nero's court. He knew how the imperial system worked. He was highly qualified to be emperor. More qualified than Galba even.

"I'm getting more drinks in," said Epaphroditus, calling for a slave and instructing him. "And don't bother about the water this time. We don't care to look sophisticated."

Aphrodite stuck her head round the door. "Oh, it's you two, is it?" she sneered at Otho and Onomastus.

"Good day to you, fair Aphrodite," swooned Otho.

320

"Good day, is it? You've told him what's happened, have you?"

"Poor Philo. Yes he did. Terrible shame, poor chap. I hear he is on the mend, though."

"No thanks to you."

"Now that is harsh. Very harsh. Unfair too."

"Dite, aim your bile at Laco and Icelus if you must. They are the ones responsible."

Otho scratched his belly. "I should go see him. Check on his condition. Cheer his spirits a little."

"He tires easily and he already has visitors. Straton has dropped by to see him."

Epaphroditus gave an involuntary shudder. "Why'd you let him in? I don't want Straton in my house."

"He brought Philo's satchel for him," Aphrodite informed him. "It was kind of him, I thought. When I walked past, Teretia was chattering away to him."

"Sir!" interjected Onomastus, jumping to his feet.

Otho raised his eyebrows.

"Sir, Straton," he pressed. "Straton and Teretia. Sir."

Otho looked blank. Perhaps it was the wine.

"Straton, Teretia, and Philo."

Which was the point at which he got it, with wide-eyed horror. "Good Jupiter, greatest and best! Oh no, not a good idea. Not a good idea at all," blustered Otho.

"What are you twittering about, Marcus?"

There came a crash and then a scream.

FORTY-FOUR

All four of them ran to the source of the commotion, skidding to a halt in the doorway. Philo was stood against the wall, palms pressed against it, Teretia shielded behind him. Straton stood, cudgel raised above his shoulder, demanding in as high a volume as his throat would allow, "Who girl?"

Epaphroditus was momentarily stunned. "What in Pluto's three-headed dog do you think you are doing?" he yelled, thinking that this was contravening every etiquette on Roman household civility.

Straton, ignoring him, demanded again, "Who girl?" His knuckles were white from his grip.

Teretia stared at him over the top of Philo's shoulder with wide eyes.

"Who girl?" He raised the cudgel.

"Straton, Straton," interrupted Otho, trying to gain his attention. "Straton, Straton," flapping his hands. The overseer viewed him out of the corner of one black eye, the other focused firmly on Teretia. "Look where you are aiming, Straton," continued Otho. "Look … if you bring that club down, you'll hit Philo."

Epaphroditus was horrified. "Thank you for that interjection, Marcus, but I don't think you should be supplying him with tips."

"Straton," said Otho with gentle calm. "I don't think that you'd want to hurt Philo, would you now?"

Straton furrowed his brow.

"Because you like Philo," offered Onomastus in a similarly gentle tone, as if persuading a kitten down from a tree.

Straton's expression softened slightly, relaxing his grip. Otho let out a relieved sigh that halted halfway through exhalation when Straton rasped, "Philo here," and pointed beside him, raising the cudgel again. "Philo here," he growled with more emphasis. "Here."

Slowly, ever so slowly, Philo made his first stand against the man who'd terrorised him his entire life. He shook his head.

Straton's eyes narrowed, struggling to understand what was going on. Otho was perfectly correct. Straton did not want to hurt Philo. He loved Philo. Cherished Philo. Wanted to protect and look after Philo. His Philo. So he resorted to plan B: walking forward and reaching round his beloved, trying to grab hold of the girl.

Teretia squealed. Philo, shuffling round to block the overseer's hands, moved slightly too quickly. He slipped and fell with a howl onto the floor, leaving Teretia exposed. She looked up at the scary giant and screamed. Philo kicked frantically and impotently at the overseer's legs as he made to take hold of her.

Epaphroditus slipped in-between them, held up a palm, and glared at the overseer. "Enough," he commanded.

Epaphroditus to Straton's mind was still an important man at the palace and he halted instantly.

"You want to know who the girl is? Is that it, Straton?" barked Epaphroditus.

The overseer gave a sharp nod.

"That is Teretia. She is Philo's girlfriend."

"No," said Straton.

"Yes," insisted Epaphroditus. "They have been together for some months now and are shortly to be married."

"No."

"Aphrodite and I were very pleased to receive an invite. It should be a lovely day."

He stood slightly to the side to allow the overseer full access to the sweet scene that was developing behind him. Teretia kneeling down, gently assessing how hurt Philo was from his fall, holding onto his hand.

"No," insisted Straton. "Philo with me." He thumped his chest. "Moving in with me."

Epaphroditus raised an eyebrow. It arched high and conveyed a thousand words, nay a whole essay on how improbable that was.

"True. Said so."

"Straton, Philo lives with Teretia," said Aphrodite firmly. "They are getting married. I can show you the invite."

Straton shook his head. He didn't understand. He didn't understand it at all.

Epaphroditus took advantage of his confusion to throw a few searing arrows. "Whatever you think you have with Philo is all in your head. This is another one of your delusions. Come on, Straton. Look at her. *Look* at her. She is beautiful. A sexy, gorgeous woman. Have you looked at yourself recently? Do you possess a mirror? How could you ever imagine that Philo would choose *that* over this wonderful girl?"

Straton's face fell slightly.

Otho muttered, "Harsh, far too harsh."

Epaphroditus told him back, "I haven't even started yet," and then continued on his theme.

"Philo is a very important man. He deals with senators and emperors every day. He is highly respected, respectable. Why? I mean, in Jupiter's name, why would he ever want you? A fat, ugly, slob of a slave who can't even be bothered to save for his own freedom."

"No. No. Different this time," he rasped, rubbing a knuckle across his scar. "Different." And he attempted to explain. "Summer. Stay. All time. With me. Porridge. Two spoons. In morning. Stay."

Aphrodite, edging her way in to extract Teretia, saw the girl's face absorb Straton's peculiar statement. It clearly meant something to her. Indeed it did. Teretia remembering those hot nights when Philo was absent from dinner, absent from his bed. They had thought him working, but he hadn't been, had he? He'd been with this man. A quick glance at Philo's cringing features confirmed this. She let go of his hand.

Epaphroditus listened impassively. One hand behind his back held up four fingers. The number of slaves he wished Callista, who was hiding by the door frame, to go and fetch to expel their unwelcome visitor.

"You expect me to believe that? Delusions, Straton. Nothing more."

"No." A sharp shake of head. "Love me." Another thump to his chest. "Said so. Love me," he insisted, rubbing his scar with clear agitation. "Love me. Said so. At games."

Another statement that hit a nerve with Teretia, who remembered Philo's distraction after that day and the lack of lovemaking since. If Epaphroditus had turned round, he would have seen Philo burying his head in his hands and bearing an expression that his wife was extremely familiar with: the look of a man caught out. Instead, he barked out a laugh. "What did you do, Straton? Lock him in a cupboard until he complied?"

There was a certain amount of truth to this and it pierced the overseer's thick hide. Aphrodite, edging in while his attention was on her husband, offered a hand out to Teretia who took it willingly Ignoring Philo's silent pleadings as she was led out to safety.

"This is all in your head, Straton," continued Epaphroditus. "Just like before."

"No. Different."

"Just like before," insisted Epaphroditus. "Just like Pericles and Hespides and Arminius and Arsaces and Polycides."

Epaphroditus had not purposefully noted the list of Straton's failed love affairs. It was just, as Felix had earlier commented, that they tended to need mopping up. This had stuck them in his head. He added in one other name that he knew of: "Oh, and Ariston of course," pulling his finger across his throat.

This caused a definite reaction. Straton rubbed an eye and then his scar with more ferocious movements. He didn't like to be reminded of how he'd incurred the famous scar. "Not like that," said Straton, a slight crack appearing in the rasp as he remembered the handsome young clerk whose actions had led to his dreadful injury. "Philo love me."

Epaphroditus, seeing Aphrodite giving him the all-clear from the doorway sighed heavily, as if weary from the conversation, and said, "Let's ask Philo then."

Sat on the floor, legs spread out before him, Philo looked and felt utterly wretched. Teretia was gone. Gone for good. Straton had driven away yet another chance of happiness he'd managed to achieve.

So when Epaphroditus asked him, "Tell us, do you love Straton?"

He replied instantly and firmly, "No."

"Are you moving in with him?"

"No."

It was beginning to sink in. To penetrate. Each negative having a devastating effect on Straton. Otho felt almost tearful on his behalf. The overseer's face was visibly cracking as his beloved Philo looked at him directly and denied everything he had thought true. Onomastus screwed his eyes shut, finding it too excruciating to watch.

"Philo love me?" Straton whimpered, looking at the crumpled freedman.

Philo stared at his feet and said quietly, so quietly that you had to concentrate to hear, "I want you to leave me alone. That's all. That's all I ever wanted." Then looking up at Straton with teary eyes he begged, "Please leave me alone. Please."

At that plea, that heartfelt plea, something broke inside Straton. Perhaps it was his heart, though many would have been surprised to learn he had one. Perhaps it was merely the walls of his carefully constructed fallacy. Whatever it was, it showed visibly on his pockmarked face. Philo did not love him. Philo wanted to be left alone.

There was silence, complete silence. The assembled inhabitants of that room waiting with held breaths to see how he would react. Straton had only one way of expressing himself. Always had. Ever since his throat had been slit wide open all those years back. He raised his cudgel high above Philo's head and brought it down hard.

Luckily for Philo, four of Epaphroditus' slaves leapt into action at that sweep of the club. They wrestled the overseer to the ground before the cudgel could hit its target. They dragged him out hollering. Epaphroditus asked Otho and Onomastus, "Can you make sure he goes?" They both nodded.

"Let us get you back in bed. It cannot be very comfortable down there," Epaphroditus commented to a crushed Philo, Straton's yells still audible in the distance.

"No, it's not."

"Come on then. Let's get you up."

Epaphroditus assisted the injured freedman in standing. He helped him across to the bed, thinking that his freedom speech to his assistant had been woefully inadequate. He should've listed fully the activities that were unacceptable for a free man. Playing the woman for Straton would definitely have been in his top three.

Philo's thoughts were not on his wrecked career though. When he was settled onto the bed he asked quietly, "What do you think is best practice? Should I write to people to tell them that the wedding is off or should I visit them in person? I shall do it. It would be too cruel to let Teretia … to make her explain."

Epaphroditus, sitting on the end of the bed said, "You don't know that the wedding is off."

"No, I do. It is. I don't see how …" He gazed up at the ceiling miserably.

"She might surprise you."

"No, it's off, isn't it? Probably for the best. She can find someone nice now. Someone who deserves her. Someone decent and kind. Who will treat her properly, like she should be treated. Because she is so … She is so … so lovely."

Epaphroditus put an arm around him and gently rubbed his shoulder. "Hey, let's just wait to see what she says. You should have told me, Philo."

Philo flinched away, eyes cast downwards on his hands.

"It could have been sorted. I could have sorted it."

There was no problem Epaphroditus couldn't resolve: he was the *fixer* after all. "I have to admit to being rather offended you turned to Otho for help. Much as I love Marcus he is the absolute last person you should ask for advice. I wouldn't trust him to tell me the correct way to buckle my sandals."

"I'm sorry, sir. I didn't … mean to. It just sort of happened that Otho was there and …" he trailed off again, rubbing at his arm.

A cough from the door alerted them to Aphrodite. She stood framed in the doorway, her arm around a red-eyed Teretia.

"Teretia would like to have a little chat with Philo," she told them.

Epaphroditus stood up, brushing down his tunic. "I'll leave you two to it," he said, giving Philo a supportive pat on the arm before exiting.

Outside the door, lowering his voice, he asked Aphrodite, "What did you say to her?"

"I tried to explain about Straton. I don't think she understood," she sighed. "Do you think it's true what they say about mixed marriages not working?"

"Let's hope not," replied Epaphroditus, squeezing her hand. "It's up to Philo now."

"He's gone," said Otho, walking across the central courtyard. "He didn't look too happy," he told them. "But Onomastus is going to make sure he gets back to the palace. He had to borrow some of your slaves, though. Hope you don't mind."

"You knew about this?" asked Aphrodite stonily, glaring at Otho.

Otho blustered under her scorn, "Only recently."

"But you knew?"

"Yes, I knew. Philo told me."

"You should have come to me," insisted Epaphroditus.

"He made me promise not to. I couldn't break a confidence. The poor chap was in a right state about it all. But we came up with a workable solution."

"So we saw," said Epaphroditus dryly.

Otho looked slightly sheepish. "I may have underestimated Straton's devotion to him. Who would have thought Straton was capable of such passion?"

Aphrodite gave him a withering stare. Seeing their disapproval, the couple reunited in their condemnation of him, Otho said, "Well what would you have done?"

"Gone to Felix," they answered in unison. "He is the only one who can control Straton."

Otho gave up, saying, "Perhaps I shall go to Piso's sacrifices after all."

"Perhaps you shall," replied Aphrodite linking onto her husband's arm and glaring at him.

Otho wilted under her gaze, offering an apologetic smile before exiting.

"Fool," said Aphrodite when he had gone.

"I have never seen anyone try to reason with Straton before. You can't fault his ambition."

Aphrodite smiled, holding onto his arm tighter. "What you did, standing in-between Straton and Philo, it was very brave."

"Thank you," he smiled in response, letting his free hand roam to the small of her back. She allowing the action.

Expelling one long sigh he said, "I should have known."

"How could you?"

"He was always so nervy and anxious. Now we know why."

"You couldn't have known that Straton was the reason," she assured him.

A bitter laugh blew from his lips. "He's small, brown-skinned, boyish. He may as well have had 'Straton's toy' tattooed across his forehead. Isn't hindsight a wonderful tool?" he grimaced. "If he hadn't been so good at his job I'd have looked into it, all of it. I failed him. I totally and utterly failed him."

Aphrodite turned to face him, cupping his chin in her hand. "You could not have known," she stressed. "And Philo would never have told you. He idolises you."

"Thank you," her husband smiled and dared a kiss to her lips.

FORTY-FIVE

They were sat on the bed. Teretia, to Philo's pain, as far away from him as possible. She stared at the floor. She wouldn't, couldn't, look at him.

He cleared his throat. "Teretia, I need … I need to tell you some stuff. About … About before."

She didn't reply so he cleared his throat again and hoped that she would at least listen to him. He started at the beginning; that very first time. He thought he'd been ten or maybe eleven years old, a pupil at the imperial training school, in old Archimedes' class. His fellow classmates teased Archimedes because he was a hunchback but Philo liked him. He was a nice man and because Philo was always the first to put up his hand to answer a question and because he was top of the class in Latin, Greek, and arithmetic, Archimedes had given him a special job: he was allowed to water the plants that sat in terra-cotta tubs around the classroom.

It was a role he took extremely seriously. Staying behind after class to fill the can and pour exactly the right amount of water for each plant. Archimedes had taught him that some varieties needed more than others.

He'd just finished his round, the can empty, when the door opened. Thinking it was his teacher, he had turned with a smile, ready to announce that the bud they had both noted the previous day was now a lovely purple flower. Except that it wasn't Archimedes. It was Straton. Looking him up and down, closing the door, and telling him in that grating rasp, "Fun time."

What followed had not been fun at all. Philo limped back to his room in a daze, unable to comprehend what had just happened to him. He hadn't known then as he pulled his blanket over his head trying to make sense of it, that this was the mere starting point.

The next day Straton was waiting for him in the corridor, dragging him off to a dark storage cupboard. And then the day after that. Philo, sitting in class, could see his large, dark shadow lurking by the door, waiting for him. It was on the third day that Straton let him pass unimpeded, throwing him a snarl but otherwise leaving him unmolested.

He'd hoped the overseer had bored of him but it turned out sadly not to be the case. He couldn't work it out. Unable to understand why Straton would leave him alone for a month at a time and then force his presence upon him daily. He would lay awake at night desperately trying to work out the pattern, like the mathematical sums he was so good at. But there was no pattern. So he awoke every morning not knowing whether today he would be taken or today he would be ignored.

This gnawing state of terror filled his every moment. So much so that he rarely heard the questions that Archimedes asked and he certainly never volunteered an answer. He no longer stayed to water the plants. For it was too easy an opportunity for Straton. Rather, he would hurry from class without even saying goodbye to his favourite teacher, frantically trying to keep up with Lysander for protection.

At some point and he couldn't remember exactly when, he'd been so consumed with the Straton situation, so utterly overwhelmed, that he stopped talking altogether. He'd thought nobody noticed. Certainly nobody had mentioned it to him at the time. Subsequently he'd gathered from various Felix comments that he was not quite as invisible as he had supposed. His file had been marked with one word: mute.

This explained, he supposed, why after leaving school he'd been placed as a humble filing clerk in the scribes hall when his exam marks should have assured him something far more illustrious.

He did not like the scribes hall. It was absolutely freezing in the winter yet sweltering hot in the summer, and was populated by slaves such as himself who had been overlooked for the more glamorous positions. There was a heavy layer of bitterness that tainted everything. It was everyone's dream to escape that draughty hall. And there was nothing they wouldn't stoop to to realise that dream.

Philo, hard-working as ever, had quickly shone by completely reorganising the filing system, improving the efficiency of the scribes hall by degrees that nobody had ever thought possible. He was moved up the ranks quickly and given the job of transcribing the minute-takers' notes into hard, ink copies for the files.

This promotion earned the jealousy of one Anatolius who considered himself top scribe and therefore the man most likely to make his break from the hall. He did not need an impediment to his escape. This fact he made very clear to Philo by instigating a campaign of harassment and sabotage that made the slave's working life a misery. Philo often arrived to find his stylus missing, his tablets broken, or his filing unfiled.

Since Philo didn't speak he was forced to find more surreptitious ways to replenish his stationery. Thus thwarting Anatolius' plans to get him into trouble. Frustrated, his rival had resorted to ever more dirty tricks to ruin his career.

"I suppose I should thank him, really," Philo said quietly, staring at his hands.

For it was Anatolius' meddling that had led to the nicest thing that had ever happened to Philo. Showing himself more than capable, Philo had been given his first assignment outside the hall. No more copying or filing for him, he was off to minute his first meeting. It was a subcommittee meeting on the use of Greek dating on official correspondence. Not terribly thrilling but it was the first time he'd been trusted outside the hall and he was determined to make a success of it.

He'd taken pages and pages of notes, not knowing then the trick to minuting was to note down only the most important points. His intention was to copy them out neater and hand them to the head of the department for approval the next day. However, when he came in the next day his thick tablets of notes were on his desk, broken into a hundred little pieces.

Staring down at his hard work that he had been so proud of he felt a little sob build inside. His boss Tenarmarchus asked him, "What happened here, Philo?"

Philo looked up at him and opened his mouth, only nothing came out as usual. Glancing over Tenarmarchus' shoulder he saw Anatolius smirking and waving at him.

How dare he? How dare he ruin his work? It wasn't fair. It wasn't fair at all. It was this sense of unfairness that drove him. An anger building inside that erupted after Anatolius came over and said sadly to Tenarmarchus, "It wouldn't surprise me if he did it himself. He's not right in the head." He tapped a finger against his temple.

Philo flipped. Picking up a scroll he whacked Anatolius over the head with it, yelling, "You did this! You ruined my work!"

To the general astonishment of everyone in the hall.

The mute tag was taken off his file. And when Epaphroditus came scouting for an interpreter for a visiting Indian trade delegation, it was Philo who was recommended for the job. So competently did he complete this task that Epaphroditus decided to take him on as his assistant scribe in the petitions office.

"And that was truly the best thing that ever happened to me," he told Teretia, adding, "until I met you."

He dared to look over to her. She did not look up.

Epaphroditus was the best of bosses: kind and patient. Under such delicate tutelage Philo flourished. There was still Straton of course, because there was always Straton. But Philo's new elevated position meant he was not quite the easy pickings he had once been and he became adept at avoiding the overseer's overtures. When Straton did catch up with him, Philo found he could put his mind elsewhere. Concentrating on his much-anticipated freedom when the overseer wouldn't be able to touch him.

Except it hadn't worked out that way. Because when he'd finally saved up his coins, Epaphroditus adding a few of his own to help him, it had made no difference at all. Straton was in love with him and so there could be no end to it.

That was the most awful part of it. Sinking to an all-time low during that summer past when he realised just how besotted Straton was with him. All those nights he had stayed in the overseer's room with the hysteria rising inside him as he felt increasingly trapped.

But then something happened, something truly marvellous. He met a girl, a beautiful girl who was sweet and kind and who liked him. He'd never thought that would happen to him, had given up on that idea years back. Instead he'd concentrated on his career, his precious work that filled his daylight hours and stopped him dwelling on what his life lacked.

Now he knew what that had been. Knew that Lysander hadn't been merely boasting when he'd lectured on and on about his exploits. If anything Philo thought he'd underplayed the sensation side of it. His only sexual experience being with Straton, he'd never imagined that the act could be so pleasurable, so special.

But it was more than mere sex. It was her. It was Teretia. He wanted to wake up every morning with her, snuggle down

337

with her every night, watch her brush her golden hair and tease it into plaits. He loved every single inch of her from her pink, wriggling toes via her soft belly to her sweet smile that warmed him every time he witnessed it.

Philo lived in a merry daze. This was how Epaphroditus felt about Aphrodite, how Otho had felt about Poppaea. Wasn't it wonderful?

Until Straton, as ever, had rolled in and ruined everything. Locking him in a room and demanding that he tell him he loved him. And he had said yes, simply because he didn't know what else to do.

"I'm sorry. I am so sorry. I didn't mean to hurt you. I would never want to hurt you. Because I love you so much. You are the best thing that has ever, ever happened to me. And I've mucked it all up. I don't … I don't expect you to forgive me," he stared at his hands. "Because what I did, what I've done. It is unforgivable."

He ended it there, shooting pains whipping round his jaw into his head from the effort of saying so much. He didn't think he had ever made such a long speech. He dared to look over to Teretia. Her shoulders were shaking from the tears. He'd made her cry, hurt her, and that was the most painful thing of all for Philo, who only ever wanted Teretia to be happy.

Teretia rubbed her eyes on her sleeve. "I wish," she sobbed, "I wish I had known you back then because I wouldn't have let you be so unhappy."

Then she threw herself into his arms and cried onto his shoulder.

Though she'd crushed several festering bruises, which winded him with pain, Philo felt a stab of joy. And in return he gushed compliments all over her: his darling, his beauty, his honey, his Venus.

"So that is it. Bye-bye empress," Mina told Daphne over dinner. "She is going home when everything is packed up."

338

Statilia gathered her considerable team of attendants together, clapping her hands, bright of eye, telling them, "Well, I would say it has been a pleasure but it would be a lie. Soon I will leave this insanity, return to my real life. Then you will all be dismissed."

Statilia ignored her shocked women and turned to organise the boys to begin packing up her things. Mina had never seen her so gleeful.

Rubbing her stomach Daphne asked, "Has Felix told you what your new position is yet?"

"Nope. Perhaps I'll get to attend to Piso's wife. She looks alright and she doesn't wear much glitter so she'll be far easier to prep. Probably more reasonable too."

"She has a more natural style," agreed Daphne. "I did like her dress yesterday, demure yet stylish, and she has a nice figure."

Daphne was looking forward to getting to work on her wardrobe, telling Mina, "The empress was alright but rather difficult. She could never stand still long enough for me to get proper measurements. And to tell the truth, Mina, her measurements did change rather a lot."

"That will be all those honey cakes she used to scoff. Hang about … What's that noise?"

It was a strange, unnatural sound. A honking wail followed by a prolonged cough before another honk. It reminded Mina somewhat of the elephants in the wild beast hunt at the games. That or a donkey with a cold. Sporus, who though maintaining that he was still far too injured to work, nonetheless danced into the room telling the assembled slaves with delighted mischief and an angled thumb, "Well worth seeing. Unmissable. You'll all be noting this in your journals tonight."

There was a quick scurry of feet, Mina and Daphne being two of the quickest to the door. They were thus in prime position to note the extraordinary sight of Felix, hand on shoulder, leading Straton down the corridor. The overseer's face wet with tears, expelling that odd noise as he walked, his body racked with sobs.

Danae could not have been more thunderstruck when she was impregnated by Jupiter disguised as a shower of golden rain than the assembled slaves were to see Straton, who had whipped, raped, and brutalised them all their lives, crying like a wounded child.

It was Theseus who verbalised their collective thoughts. "Wow," he said.

FORTY-SIX

The walk to the Palatine was a wet, cold one. Otho would have taken a litter only it had been impounded by Gracius, a man to whom he owed more than a little money.

He'd spent the last few days licking his wounds, wallowing in as much self-pity as his buoyant nature would allow, and drinking down his entire wine cellar. Which in retrospect had been a wonderful idea since Gracius doubtless would have taken that too.

He awoke that morning to what he thought was a thumping wine-induced headache but what actually turned out to be Gracius and his enforcers. Staggering out of his room in a silk nightgown, toupee adrift, he watched as Gracius' buddies carried off his best plates, best art work, and best slaves. The little flute boys, who knew they would never have it so good again, cried for their master with pitiful tears. Otho could have cried too if he possessed anything to wipe his tears with, Gracius having walked off with his best linens too.

Pointing his blade at Otho's throat, Gracius had told him with menace, "This is the down payment. I expect the total sum tomorrow. By sunset."

There was greater chance of Galba discovering Piso as a pig molester than there was of the necessary funds becoming available by sunset. So it was with some relief that he received the imperial messenger: he was being summoned to the palace to partake in the emperor's private sacrifices.

Quite an honour. Clearly there were no hard feelings. Otho decided to attend for many reasons: the expectation of more of his creditors paying him a call, that he might be able to tap Titus Vinius for a crucial loan, to secure some reasonably well-paid post in Galba's administration, and partake of some low-level flirting with Statilia Messalina.

The empress welcomed him warmly. Taking in his bedraggled, damp appearance and muddy toga, she cried with real concern, "Marcus, you must come in and warm yourself."

A task she assisted with by hugging him tight and rubbing his goose-pimpled arms. Otho mentally upgraded to medium-level flirting.

She led him through to her private dressing room: a compact box of a chamber with yellow-painted walls and feminine flourishes. Sitting him down, she took his cold hands and rubbed them.

"I heard what happened. You would have made a great emperor."

Otho affected a depressed sigh. "Madam, it has been a trying few days," he injected with much gloom. The empress' face softening with pity, held his hands tighter.

"It is not all fun and parties. My late husband would often complain about all the paperwork and dreary meetings. Let Galba and Piso do all that. They probably enjoy it. Besides, Marcus," she began, "it would have taken up so much of your time, I wouldn't get to see you."

She smiled, a gracious smile that warmed Otho to his toes.

"Madam," clearing his throat and altering this to, "Statilia," and throwing her a longing gaze, "you are so kind to me. So many of my friends have deserted me in my time of need."

"Surely not!"

"Surely so," gloomed Otho with a sad little look. "It is most dispiriting. Though the sight of you, Statilia, cheers me greatly." He flipped his hands round so they now clasped hers.

Mina, watching this tender scene, was mentally screaming, "Kiss, for Jupiter's sake, just kiss."

It was by far the most excruciatingly slow courtship she had ever witnessed. It had been, what?, three months since they first met and expressed an interest in each other, mused Mina, recalling that first encounter at Galba's welcome party when her sharp-tongued mistress had melted from exposure to Otho's charming fire.

Was this how all the upper classes courted? It was no wonder that they let barbarians be senators now: the pure-bred Romans obviously couldn't produce the necessary next generation. Too busy fawning and offering fake sentiments to get down to business. Mina was beginning to see the merits of Apollodorus' breeding programme.

Otho, gazing into Statilia's eyes, stroked her cheek, and used the line he'd recently used on a certain attractive young eunuch: "Gods, you are exquisite."

It was either a killer line or it was in the earnest delivery with just a hint of husky lust. For it had much the same effect on Statilia that it had on Sporus.

She fluttered her eyelashes at him and pouted her lips. Otho indicated his head towards where Mina stood. Statilia barked over her shoulder, "Turn round, girl."

Mina shuffled round to face the wall, focusing on a small patch of discoloured plaster from where she heard a distinct slurp that had to be a snog.

"About ruddy time!" she thought.

It was therefore a much chirpier Otho who skipped between the buildings that had once belonged to that happily married couple Augustus and Livia to the Temple of Apollo. He pranced his way up the many steps, Onomastus running alongside him to keep up. Smiling at the fifty statues of the Danaids that stood stoically in the colonnade of the temple and bouncing through the ivory doors.

He was in such a good mood replaying that passionate kiss with the wonderful Statilia in his head, that he failed to notice the snarly smiles Laco and Icelus exchanged on his entrance. He didn't even notice the annoyed look Galba threw at him for his tardiness. The emperor already partaking in the reading of the entrails prior to the burning of the offering which would take place outside the temple.

Otho gave him a cheery wave and beam of a smile which he couldn't shake off his face since that glorious Statilia moment, and slipped to the back of the gathered dignitaries. He'd always envied Epaphroditus his Aphrodite. He wanted something of the like. He would marry Statilia. He would go see her relevant relative tomorrow and make it official. He might even be able to secure enough of a dowry to get Gracius off his back.

The priest Umbricius stood beneath the colossal statue of Apollo, poking at the goat's innards. His eyebrows grouped above his nose.

"The omens are good?" asked Galba.

Of course they would be good, thought Otho. No priest was going to piss off the emperor. They'd been known to forcibly cage birds and get their assistants to release them at the optimum moment for favourable auspices.

Except Umbricius did not seem to know these traditions. For he looked up at the assembled personages and declared in a deep, foreboding voice that would have impressed Lysander, "I foretell doom ... catastrophe ... chaos."

There was an awed hush for this blatant script-breaking. The priest pointed a finger at the crowd.

"There is a plot," he declared in a wavering voice. "He plots. He plots against his emperor. It says ... It says ... The gods say he will be emperor."

344

Galba, possessed of a healthy fear of the gods as all soldiers were, entreated the priest, "What is it you see? What plot? Who plots against me? Tell me, priest."

Umbricius, who appeared to have been an actor in a previous life, stood up on his toes, bearing upwards, lifting his arms up in his robe. Pulling back his lips and snarling, he reached out one bony finger and deliberately and with deadly accuracy pointed it straight at Marcus Salvius Otho. Otho instinctively looked over his shoulder before realising the prediction was meant for him.

"It is HE," pronounced the priest. "He is the one."

Cue general shuffling round of heads from the dignitaries. Otho found himself at the mercy of some very hard stares. Including one from Galba who looked downright peeved. Laco and Icelus in direct comparison had never looked happier.

"What do I do?" whispered Otho to Onomastus out of the corner of his mouth.

"I would suggest a calm retreat, sir," responded his freedman.

They began to carefully walk backwards, attempting to hold on to the cheery smiles on their faces. "We leg it at the door."

"Righty ho," said Otho calmly as he moved back, all the while keeping his eyes on the frozen spectators.

"And here's the door ..." announced Onomastus.

They turned from those stunned faces, threw open the temple doors, and ran down the steps. Otho flung off his toga, instantly regretting not spending more time in the gym. They'd never do it, Galba would give the order any second. They were one middle-aged, out-of-shape man and one dwarf against the Praetorian Guard.

Otho, heart bursting from the exertion, reached the bottom of the steps and heard his name called. Snapping to the source he saw Antonius Honoratus, sword safely sheathed, standing in a narrow lane beside the temple and holding out his hand.

"Otho, sir. Come with me. I'll help you."

Otho looked to Onomastus who shrugged and they both ran for the tribune. Pressing themselves against a wall, they bent over trying to catch their breath. There came the sound of running boots. An order barked out to try between the temples. Otho and Onomastus exchanged horrified glances.

This was it. There was no way they could outrun them. The guards ran straight for them, swords pointing. Otho felt his knees tremble. A shout of, "Ha," and then they were facing them; three ugly soldiers with their swords at their throats.

Honoratus looked at them calmly. "Guards, move on," he said.

Somewhat improbably and miraculously the tallest of the three nodded and led his comrades down the alley away from them.

When Otho had recovered from the shock he said, "I owe you. I owe you much." He stood up straight and offered Honoratus his hand.

The tribune took it and said, "I think it is time I repaid you that favour."

The emperor Galba sat straight-backed (thanks to his corset), hands placed on the arms of his chair. "The gods have spoken. I am sorry that I doubted you, Laco, and you, Icelus."

They both bowed their heads, hiding smirks. Otho's face when Umbricius had made his pronouncement. That smile, that amiable, charming, irritating Otho smile fixing and then melting away. It had taken all Icelus' self-control not to cheer. It was certainly worth the extravagant bribe and tarty concubine they had given the priest.

"Is there any sign of Otho?" demanded Galba. "I want him. How dare he plot against me! What does he think qualifies him as emperor? A man who depilates his entire body, who bathes in perfume, and who is more of a woman than a man!"

Stung at being deceived, Galba was full of righteous anger. Not necessarily a good thing, thought Titus Vinius. In this mood Galba was liable to extreme reactions that did their cause no good at all. No doubt Icelus was stirring him up in private, unaware, no, uncaring, corrected Vinius, of the consequences.

"Otho will be found soon, Caesar. He is not a natural hider," assured Laco, looking to Honoratus who confirmed,

"My men are on the hunt."

"I want him found. I want the worm found." Galba slammed a palm on the arm.

Piso, sitting nearby, jumped and gave his wife a nervous look, she taking his hand. "Sshh, it's OK," she told the shaking emperor-in-waiting.

Taking a hiss of breath Galba relaxed his shoulders, saying in a surprisingly calm voice after his outburst, "Make sure Statilia Messalina is sent back to her family."

"Excellent plan, Caesar," glowed Icelus. "She was close to Otho, we want no spies in this court."

"We are rounding up those slaves and freedmen who were close to Otho," assured Laco smoothly. "Those who repent sufficiently will be allowed to return."

If they were fit enough after their visit to Scaveous that was.

FORTY-SEVEN

"This had better be good, Marcus," growled Epaphroditus, throwing himself down, pinching the bridge of his nose between two fingers. "You got me out of bed. I was enjoying being in bed."

He had been. Aphrodite had been most demonstrative in her forgiveness these last few days and they had enjoyed a prolonged wrestle before drifting into a satisfied sleep. At least until he was abruptly awoken by Onomastus with a message from Otho to meet him now at this address.

"What's up?"

Otho, three drinks down a flagon said, "How are Philo and Terctia? What's the news?"

"Sir," interrupted Onomastus. "I think our news is more crucial, more important."

"Pish," said Otho. "I need to know the conclusion."

Epaphroditus had not seen much of his house guests since Straton's memorable visit. He and Aphrodite had left them alone to sort it out and the couple had been holed up in their room ever since. They might have been renewing their relationship or dissolving it for all Epaphroditus knew. But nobody had run out crying yet and they were sleeping in the same room, if not the same bed. So kicking up his feet he told Otho, "We think that they may have patched it up."

"Well that is good. Very good."

"Our news, sir!" protested Onomastus.

"Oh that. Not good. Not good at all."

He repeated what had happened at the sacrifice. "Curse Laco. I am sure he was behind it."

"You need to get out of the city," said Epaphroditus. "Quickly."

Otho didn't move. Instead he helped himself to a hefty refill with but-a-dash of water.

"Laco's guards will be looking for you."

"I doubt it. Guess whose house we are in."

"I assumed it was one of your random purchases."

Otho smiled. "Oh, Antonius," he called.

Antonius Honoratus, in full tribune uniform, hand on sword, stood gleaming in the doorway. He informed Epaphroditus, "My guards do not follow orders from Cornelius Laco. They follow orders from me."

Epaphroditus was starting to get a very bad feeling about this.

"Antonius and I were talking. Fine fellow of a man, aren't you? And we rather thought that it would be a terrible waste for me to flee like some criminal."

"My master has done nothing wrong," said Onomastus. "Why should he flee? Decent men have to make a stand."

Decent men? Epaphroditus would never have categorised Otho as such. "So you three have hatched a plan of your own. Want to share?"

"Exactly why I invited you over. I am sure you would love to contribute."

"Surprise me."

So Otho did. "We put a lot of work into our plan didn't we, chum?"

"It kept you out of mischief."

"Well, we thought, Antonius, Onomastus and I, that we might extend it slightly."

"Really?" Epaphroditus had a horrible suspicion he knew where this was leading.

"Shame to waste all that hard work. All that charming and winning over of man and beast."

"All that money," contributed Onomastus. He earned a hard glare from Otho who assured Epaphroditus, "Not about the money."

Honoratus sat in that spread-legged way you can't avoid in armour, leant his elbows on his knees, and explained, "Galba has made himself very unpopular with the Praetorians. Reneging on the promises he made to us when he needed our support. They are restless."

"You said it yourself, Epaphroditus. Otho for emperor!" he beamed at his friend, adding happily, "I'll be terribly good at it because I will be led by you, my number two. Come on, what have you got to lose?"

"Apart from my state-ordered death, my assets confiscated by the state, and the wonderful opportunity to damn my name for all eternity in the history books. It is treason, Otho."

"Never stopped you before. You can give me the evil eye but we both know that old Claudius didn't just choke on a mushroom."

Epaphroditus gave him a narrow look, saying lightly, "And if I offered to pay off your debts would this scheme simply vanish?"

"Not about the money," Otho assured Epaphroditus. "The groundwork is already done. I had so many commiserations, so many people whispering that I'd make the better emperor than Piso. A little nudge and they'll be saying I'd be a far better emperor than Galba himself. It wouldn't take much. Galba has made himself unpopular in so many quarters and those he

351

hasn't, Laco and Icelus have done the work for him. Come on, what do you say?"

Indicating Honoratus and Onomastus, Epaphroditus said, "Would you mind if Otho and I had a little chat in private?" Then added, "Not a question, Shorty. I was just being polite. Scoot."

Then, face to face, "Now that your freedman and hot shot have gone—"

"Hot shot?"

Epaphroditus mimed the throwing of a javelin, a reminder of Honoratus' involvement in Sabinus' death. "This is about money, isn't it?"

"It is not about money," insisted Otho. "It is about doing what is right for Rome. I thought you'd be all in after what Icelus and Laco did to Philo."

"That can't be undone."

"You supported my adoption claim. You were a primary partner."

"That did not involve men with swords. Men with swords are never a good idea."

"The men with swords are on our side this time. They will do it anyway, they're hopping mad about the bounty. Honoratus says the consensus is Nymphidius Sabinus was right."

Epaphroditus barked out a laugh. "Now that is something you don't hear every day."

"Wouldn't you rather it was me in the top role than some guard's appointee? Jupiter knows who they'll come up with. It would be no fun at all."

Epaphroditus pinched his nose, rubbed an eye, and said, "Marcus, flee the city. Hole up in some sunny spot. Wait for Galba to die and then sashay back in. Pasty Piso will have forgotten the whole thing by then."

"Can't."

"Won't."

"Can't, Epaphroditus. I may have made a few promises."

"Involving money?"

Otho shrugged, giving an apologetic smile. "I was so sure Galba would adopt me. We both did such a good job. You'd be amazed at the credit you can get if you use an imperial title as collateral."

"How much?"

"Rather a lot."

"How much?" insisted Epaphroditus.

"Ahem, two hundred million."

"Sesterces?" pressed Epaphroditus, though what else could it be.

"The men, ahem, who were so kind with their purses have rather a long reach. There is not a sunny place on earth where they or their associates could not get me. Of course if I had access to the imperial treasury … Problem solved!"

His companion groaned and put his head in his hands.

"How you remind me of my father. He often took such a stance."

"One question, Marcus. Sabinus took months of dedicated planning to bring down Nero. How long have you etched in your diary for such a scheme?"

Otho scratched his chin, furrowed his brow, and said, "I was rather hoping we could finish it off by sunset. Don't look so worried. There is no danger of failure."

"No danger? You want to overthrow an emperor in a day? An emperor with an army. With a personal bodyguard. With the blessings of the law. And you say there is no danger! You've flipped Marcus, really you have."

"Of failing, I said. No danger of that at all. The other type of danger perhaps there will be a smidgeon. Might upset things a bit, I suppose."

"I shall forgive you this because you were in Lusitania but when Nero fell it was chaos. The streets were awash with blood and that was with Sabinus' meticulous planning. With you in charge we'll be crawling over corpses till summer. What makes you think you will succeed?"

"Aha!" Otho announced. "My astrologer told me so."

Epaphroditus gave an extremely long groan, mixed in with a sigh and a dash of scorn thrown in.

"Splendid fellow. Uncannily accurate in all his predictions even if you don't want him to be. It was Seleucus who said Poppaea would leave me years before she did."

Not so much of a prediction as a foregone conclusion, thought Epaphroditus.

"And that I would lose my hair but that I would find my own way of dealing with the affliction." He gave his toupee a quick tug.

"Go on then, what did this marvel say?"

"He foretold that Nero would die before me even though he is my junior."

"By three years!" interjected Epaphroditus.

Otho ignored him, continuing stoically, "And that I would one day be emperor. He was very exact on it. None of those Delphic Oracle vagaries. He said I would be emperor. Of course when all that commotion kicked off with Vindex in Gaul I knew, just knew, he was right, and that time had come. With Galba being so old and with you being unemployed and restless, it seemed almost criminal not to strike. You don't get opportunities like that every day. Then when the old guy didn't adopt me, I confess I did falter a little. But you see, Epaphroditus, what happened at the sacrifice shows Seleucus was right."

"Please elaborate."

"He saw it, that priest. He saw it in the entrails. He saw that I was to supplant Galba. He said as much. So you see I have to go full out. It is my destiny. The gods wish it. It would be a crime against them not to pursue my claim. And you know how the gods punish those who thwart their will!"

A statement that was rendered positively ominous by a sudden clap of thunder. Epaphroditus despite himself jumped in his seat.

To Otho he stated calmly and clearly, "No. I want no part of this."

"You are in as deep as I am," said Otho, examining a nail. "It is not as if you even like Galba. What do you care if he goes? Wouldn't you rather I was emperor? I would give you your old job back, with an increased salary naturally. I would be swayed by you in all decisions. You tell me what needs doing and I will do it. No chariots, no beckoning eunuch harems, no bribery necessary of any sort. You snap and I will follow."

It was a tantalising offer. "No."

"Five days ago you thought I would make a fine emperor."

"Five days ago I didn't know your sole motivation was that bearded Greek loon!"

"Seleucus is Syrian and clean shaven," said Otho, as if this were a pertinent point.

Epaphroditus shook his head and went to stand. "Oh, come on!" protested Otho. "I need you. I need that knowledge, that intelligence, that insight."

"Just tell me one thing. Do I have time to get Aphrodite and the children out of the city before you begin this stunt?"

Otho was shocked, "You have nothing to fear from me. Nothing."

"Do I have time?" Epaphroditus pushed.

"Onomastus is gathering a crowd to take me to the Praetorian camp right now," said Otho.

Epaphroditus rubbed his head. He had no choice, did he? Otho was resolved to this madness. Damn Laco and his plotting, backing Otho into a corner. Did he imagine Otho would just roll over and die? For all his apparent geniality this was a man who had survived both Agrippina's and Nero's wrath when so many had lost their heads. If he was in on this, maybe there was a chance that he could prevent the absolute mayhem he was now picturing. So he said quietly, "I'm in."

Otho rubbed his hands together. "Excellent. You will not be disappointed!"

FORTY-EIGHT

Teretia and Philo lay face to face on the bed, Philo absently twirling one of Teretia's golden locks through his fingers. Their host and hostess had speculated a great deal on what they had been doing these past four days. In fact it could be summed up in one word: talking. There had been an awful lot of talking.

Teretia told Philo, "I think what hurt the most is that you didn't tell me. There you were all unhappy and you didn't tell me. I was banging on about the wedding and all that other stuff and you were in pain and I didn't know. I didn't know at all."

"Sorry," mumbled her fiancé. "I didn't want to let anyone down. I wanted you to think well of me."

Teretia squeezed his hand. "I would have done. It wouldn't have made a difference. It was the shock. I wouldn't … I wouldn't want any more shocks like that." She looked directly at him.

He got the hint. Knowing how close he'd come to losing her, Philo 'fessed up promptly. To anything and everything he could think of. From Mina's seduction attempt and his failure to obtain the necessary erection, to what Icelus had done to him, to his freak-out in the breeding programme, to the reason he didn't like turnip (a bout of fever, a plate of the vegetable, and a stream of sick all over the refectory table), to letting Lysander copy his work at school (because it stopped him whining), to the time he had accidentally kicked over a toddling Faustina and when she'd cried blamed Silvia (toes curling in shame as he watched Epaphroditus berate his eldest daughter for her attitude), to certain incidents that had taken place in Greece when he had accompanied the emperor Nero on his tour of the province, and onwards to every whipping, beating, and rape he could recall at the hands of Straton (Philo possessing good recollective powers, this took some time).

At the end of this exhaustive litany of shame Philo was left with a throbbing jaw. Teretia, who'd been raised by parents who adored her, been showered with pretty dresses and dolls by indulgent aunts, and all-in-all had enjoyed an idyllic childhood, was reduced to a weeping puddle.

She'd never imagined anything so awful. She'd pictured Philo's enslaved existence much like Tadius' slave boy who half-heartedly swept the floor, had a nice cosy room above the shop, and ate far too much according to the butcher. Hearing Philo's catalogue of woes she found she couldn't stop crying.

Her beloved, rather alarmed by this state, assured her that it hadn't all been bad. In fact, he once won a prize for Greek composition at school and old Archimedes presented him with a plant. He had named it Horace. He had very much enjoyed taking care of Horace: trimming his leaves, watering him regularly, and drawing his evolving appearance across the seasons.

Yes, he had loved Horace very much; the plant bringing much joy to Philo's life. This happy tale subsided the sobs from Teretia. At least until the epilogue.

"And it was because of Horace that I decided not to hang myself," Philo told her. Adding, "And I'd made the noose and everything."

Indeed he had. It was a particularly well-crafted noose. Diligent as ever, Philo had taken the subject of suicide extremely seriously. He worked out that if he could balance himself at a certain height then the fall would break his neck and speed up his death.

He had spent the whole afternoon constructing the noose, probably spending a little too much time on it, because when he was ready, standing on the cushions piled up on his stool ready to throw it over his head, Lysander had opened the door and knocked him to the floor.

"What are you doing?" his room-mate had asked, gazing down at him and then taking in the noose in Philo's hand. "Oh, Jupiter! You were going to hang yourself. Why would you want to hang yourself?"

Philo's expression did not need much interpreting. It said it all, being a mixture of despair and desperation.

"No, no, no. You can't kill yourself, you can't," Lysander had blustered. "You just can't. I won't allow it."

Then somewhat to Philo's surprise, for he was under the impression that Lysander viewed him as an irritating impediment in his life, his room-mate sat down on the floor beside him and burst into tears.

"You can't do it. Please don't do it. Please don't kill yourself, Philo. If you die, I won't have anyone to talk to. I won't have any friends …"

He broke off into noisy sobs leading to the odd picture of the would-be suicide acting as comforter. Taking a deep breath Lysander added, "Besides, you can't … You can't do it because who would water Horace? I'd forget, you know I would."

Philo glanced over to the shelf where Horace was gently blooming red flowers and knew the truth of that. It seemed unfair to make Horace suffer. So he put down the noose, moulded a determined lip, and tapped Lysander on the shoulder to allay his fears. His room-mate, teary-eyed, noted the lip, and said urgently, "You promise never to try again? For Horace's sake?" Philo gave a firm nod in response.

Lysander, reassured by this, wiped his tears on his sleeve, and suggested they do something fun to cheer themselves up. Thus, they spent a happy evening washing down Horace's leaves and giving him a nice prune.

Philo informed Teretia, "He looked much happier afterwards. Horace that is. Lysander was a bit gloomy still."

Teretia, looking rather gloomy herself, tentatively asked, "What happened to Horace?" She feared another bleak conclusion.

"You saw him when we went to the party at the palace. He got too big for my room so Lysander and I planted him in the courtyard. He's a lovely big bush now."

This story certainly cheered up Philo. Picturing Horace's flourishing state, there was a small smile (the first for some days) visible on his lips. Teretia, fiddling with her fingers, said quietly, "Philo, I have something to tell you."

The smile slipped, followed by a whimper. "It's not something horrible, is it? I don't think I could cope with anything horrible."

A pang of guilt followed for he'd presented Teretia with nothing but horrible things and she'd taken them so well. So he took her fidgeting hand and gave it a quick squeeze. "I can take it, whatever it is."

"I hope it's not horrible. I don't think it is horrible. I hope you won't think it's horrible. I hope you will be pleased."

Teretia looked up, bit her lip, and informed Philo of something. After she had repeated it a couple more times, answered a number of his questions, and after he had taken a bit of time to reflect upon it, he finally concluded it was not horrible at all.

Given leave to ensure his family's safety, Epaphroditus dashed through the streets cursing Otho, himself, and even cursing Aphrodite for being absolutely right. How could he have forgotten how reckless Otho was? Had he been swayed too by Otho's record in Lusitania? He hadn't changed at all. Not one bit.

Take the most outrageous drunken night you'd ever had and then throw in an ostrich-feathered girl, a million sesterces wager, and a naked chariot ride through the forum: that was Otho all over. He was the only man who could out-scandal Nero. His showy charm at least partly to blame for his exile; Poppaea and imperial love triangle aside.

Would he succeed? He was popular but short on time. With Piso in place as heir apparent that popular support would naturally swing. But with his creditors right now preparing to swoop, and those he had made such extravagant promises in return for their support now expecting their reward, and with his two hundred million sesterces debt … he really had nothing to lose. Do or die.

Epaphroditus found his wife sitting quietly on a couch, feet resting on a stool, gnawing on the end of a stylus and staring into space. He sucked in his panic, managing to keep his voice light.

"Hello, what are you up to?"

"I am revising the menus for the next few days," she told him. "Teretia has informed me that Philo does not like turnip. But he won't say he doesn't like turnip. And if we serve it to him, he will either attempt to hide it under the other vegetables or worse still, he will eat it and that will upset his delicate stomach."

"Oh dear, dining catastrophe. Cook pleased?"

"Ranting and raging. She had a good stock in of said vegetable and was preparing an impressive variety of dishes. Then Teretia slips in that he can't eat beef either, which did not go down well."

"Ah, this I know about. The eating of cattle offends his gods. We really don't want to offend Philo's gods."

"Don't we?" queried Aphrodite, who like most Romans maintained a healthy disregard for the barbarisms of other cultures.

"Definitely not. They have many arms holding many swords," he smiled.

She put the stylus down. "Do you want to tell me where you've been? I turned over in the night and there was a space that should not have been there."

He sat beside her. "Sorry, sweetheart, something came up. I have to nip out again shortly."

"So soon? I was hoping you would stay today. I need you to have a chat with Pollus."

"*The* chat?" asked Epaphroditus, taking her hand and kissing it.

"*The* chat," his wife confirmed. "I caught him spying on Teretia in the bathhouse. Don't laugh! She was mortified. I was mortified!"

"What did you do?"

"I smacked him across the head and told him that his father would have some stern words for him. So if you could supply those paterfamilias sentiments and then move into *the* chat."

Epaphroditus hid his smile with difficulty. "I suppose he is of the age. Though what I can tell him about girls that he does not already know from having five sisters …"

"Do you have to go out?" She cuddled in next to him.

"I need to see my banker. I am thinking that it's silly to rent a villa down at the coast each year when we could buy. That way we could invite Silvia and Martinus, his parents too if we must, grandchildren eventually."

"Gods, grandchildren!" Aphrodite pulled a hair from her head. "Grey," she told him.

"You are as beautiful as the day I met you."

A compliment that led to a very happy smooch. Aphrodite broke free and said, "The villa, though, it is a good idea. Be sure to get one with plenty of space. I am not keen on pools though, not with Julia and Rufus the ages they are. Julia particularly. She dashes about. Even the slaves lose sight of her."

"I'll consult you before I commit," he promised. "I'll go and talk to Pollus now. And the other creatures? I'd like to say hello before I head out."

"They're with the tutor. Rufus was curled up on Callista last time I checked."

"Dite, I would prefer it if you and the children stayed in the house today. Until I return."

Alerted by his tone she asked, "Why, what's happened?"

"Nothing, nothing," he smoothed. "Just rumours. The Praetorians getting a bit cocky, molesting the locals under the guise of security. I wouldn't want you or the girls …" He trailed off letting her fill in the blanks.

"We'll stay put," she assured him. "Just be back for our turnip-free dinner."

"I would not miss it," said Epaphroditus, moving in for a kiss that was far more passionate than a simple see-you-later peck should have been.

There were about twenty of them, Otho doing a quick, grubby head count. "It is not so much a crowd as a gaggle."

"Sorry, sir, it was the best I could do at such short notice."

"I was hoping for a bit more popular support, but, ah, no matter."

The leader of the group gave a gappy smile, "Awright, emperor!"

Otho preened, straightened his toupee, wrapped his toga round his arms some more. "They'll do."

PART II

OTHO
15ᵀᴴ JANUARY AD 69

"Once killing starts it is difficult to draw the line"
—Tacitus, *The Histories*

FORTY-NINE

When Nymphidius Sabinus so effortlessly took control of the city he did so overnight, when most were asleep and the necessary manoeuvres passed unnoticed. Otho's coup began in the early morning as slaves were dashing to work, traders were setting up for the day, and the forum was full of noble citizens followed by their gaggles of clients; all of whom had their own distinct take on what was going on.

The rumours flooded up the Palatine Hill, citizens keen to ingratiate themselves brought dire warnings. The petition slaves marked down their names, addresses, and a line or two concerning their news. Polyclites, who had listened with a steadily draining face, trotted off to see Icelus.

"What are they saying?" enquired Icelus, placing his tablet down very slowly.

"Well, it's a mixture," admitted Polyclites. "Otho is in the Praetorian camp. Otho has fled the city. Otho has been killed by the Praetorians disgusted by his antics. Otho has been declared emperor. Take your pick."

"How do we find out which is true?"

Polyclites shrugged. "Send someone down to the Praetorian camp? Whatever is going on, it's happening there."

Icelus stood up abruptly and banged his knee on his desk. "I have to speak to Galba," he said with a wince.

Actually, he didn't have the chance. The alarming news had already reached the emperor, who summoned his staff to his presence.

"What now?" Galba barked. "Can he succeed?"

Vinius stood to one side, arms crossed, waiting for Laco and Icelus to reply. Fools, backing Otho into a corner like that. What else could he do but fight back?

"Well?" prompted Galba.

Icelus blustered, "Not a chance, Caesar," without offering any reasoning why.

Laco was silent under the emperor's glare.

"What now?" yelled Galba. "You are my advisors. Advise me!"

"The immediate priority is the Praetorian cohort at the palace. Don't you agree, Laco?" said Titus Vinius. "Otho has done this in a rush after the sacrifice. They may not even know what has occurred. We need to secure their loyalty."

Laco didn't move.

"Now," pressed Vinius. "You are prefect. They are your men. Go talk to them!"

Laco did not reply. Vinius stared at the ceiling. He could let Laco falter, he supposed. He deserved it. But he was Galba's loyal servant and this was no time for factions. They had to work together.

"I'll do it," he said. "Perhaps Piso could join me."

Piso whitened. Vinius said kindly, "It would help rally the men to see you. Your wife also."

More the wife, Vinius privately thought. She had the demure beauty the guards would be willing to die to protect. He was prepared to hold her aloft as a fine example of Roman womanhood against Otho's debatable masculinity. Vinius did not wait for Galba to agree but sped off with a reluctant Piso.

The emperor addressed Laco and Icelus, "What now?"

"We need to, we need to …" began Icelus, petering out and looking to Laco.

The Praetorian prefect, stunned by the speed of Otho's reaction, found his thoughts jumbled. One cohort of Praetorians against the nine in the barracks did not sound good.

"There are other soldiers," he blurted out suddenly. "Outside the city. We need to send scouts to bring them in."

"Make it so."

The brief Epaphroditus gave Otho was slim: "I want charm and I want hurt. Hurt that just as they have been betrayed by Galba in relation to their bounty, so have you. That you both offered Galba support in his time of need yet now find yourselves abandoned like some lost lover. That sort of thing."

"Human drama," said Otho. "It's what I do best."

Onomastus straightened his toga. Otho fiddled with his toupee. And then, taking a deep breath, he walked out onto a platform to address the waiting guards.

It was a blinder of a speech, Epaphroditus admitted. He could not have written a better one himself. It was made all the more impressive that Otho spoke freely from memory without aid.

He implored the guards to protect him from Galba's undeserved wrath. Telling them that he considered them his friends, reminding one or two faces in the audience of the fun evenings they had spent together and the favours he had granted them. The gathered Praetorians were outraged on his behalf, huffing out chests in indignation at Otho's treatment.

He talked at length about what high hopes he had owned for Galba, just like they themselves had. How he'd risked his own life to throw in his lot with Galba, betraying his own dear friend Nero. Because he had felt, no, he had known, that Galba was the better man and that his dear old friend had been sadly led astray by such creatures as Tigellinus.

He suspected that Galba had taken against him for a mild criticism he had uttered regarding certain advisors. (Shouts from the guards naming the individuals with insults attached). Otho threw in a warning of dire peril. If even he, the first to flock to Galba's side was attacked, what hope was there for anyone else?

Not once did he suggest they should declare him emperor. That was left to Honoratus who did a neat twist on his anti-Sabinus speech of five months prior. Epaphroditus standing cross-armed at the back threw in an anonymous, "Hear, hear," which sped round the crowd with increasing velocity, complete with raised swords and oaths of allegiance.

Otho feigned shock, hesitated, until the office was forced upon him, and then accepted graciously.

"Well, that was easy," said Otho, bouncing on his feet. "Did you notice the way they were behind me before I mentioned the bounty?"

Epaphroditus did. He was secretly impressed by Otho's rhetorical skill. Who'd have thought he could be such a Demosthenes?

"They want to carry me to the forum to take up my new position."

"We might want to remove Galba first," said Epaphroditus in an attempt to dampen him down. "Piso also. When we have proof, then the senate will have no option but to ratify you as emperor."

"Proof?" queried Otho, rubbing a hand across his sweaty brow.

Epaphroditus gave him a sweet smile. "I was thinking his head. Nobody could dispute there was a vacancy that way."

Otho looked slightly sick.

"Welcome to politics," was Epaphroditus' cool response.

FIFTY

There was a sizeable crowd, or mob depending on your view, forming within the forum. The outside of the palace was similarly busy with onlookers who, hearing the rumours concerning Otho, were eagerly awaiting the next instalment. Felix, standing at the top of the old palace steps, did not like the look of them.

"One fucking word from emperor Otho and they'll be up these steps fast as fuck to break down them doors."

"Ooh," marvelled Ganymede with widened eyes.

"But don't you worry, boy. We'll put you on top of a high cupboard and they'll run straight past you. Won't we, Straton?"

Straton did not reply. Felix had been keeping him busy to take his mind off Philo. It had not been easy. Straton stubbornly sitting in his room, hugging a cushion to his chest, staring at that desk, and weeping his stony heart out. Rasping his throat raw as he tried to explain everything to Felix. Felix groaned when he heard Mina's part in the whole sorry saga. Stupid girl, what was she thinking? Encouraging him like that? Thing was bound to end tits up. All of Straton's love affairs did.

He'd even taken Straton home with him for dinner. Ganymede, balanced upon a pile of cushions in order to reach the table, had given his former master a friendly wave.

Felix had decided to return Ganymede to the slave market. It was top of his list of things to do. But somehow it hadn't happened yet.

Vallia, glaring at Straton Medusa-style, asked her husband, "Who's he killed now?"

"Never the fuck mind, woman, just feed him up. Can't you see he's hurting?"

He did look miserable. So miserable that even Vallia felt some sympathy. She sliced him a double helping of gourd pie.

"He's sad," offered Ganymede.

"Is that so?" said Vallia. She banged the plate down in front of Straton, yelling (for she erroneously thought the overseer's lack of speech was linked to his hearing), "EAT THIS!"

Straton stared down at the portion.

"EAT," shouted Vallia, miming the action. "Wot's up with 'im? He ain't usually so slow on the food uptake."

"Leave him alone, woman, he's had a fucking upset. We're fucking trying to cheer him up!"

"He's in love," supplied Ganymede, tucking into his own enormous piece of pie.

Vallia, well aware of Straton's romantic history, groaned, "Juno's arse, it's all or nothing with you, ain't it? Have you ever tried a casual fling?"

"Wish I fuckin' had," muttered Felix under his breath, earning a whack on the arm with a wooden spoon.

Rubbing this bruise now, he said, "Now then, Ganymede, shall we go organise a resistance army? Can't be too careful, hey? Straton, mate, I'll let you get out that elephant-hide whip you're so fond of. Put it into proper action."

It was meant to cheer him up, but Straton had wonderful memories of that whip. He'd used it on Philo many times. A reminiscence that broke him into fresh tears. Felix and Ganymede exchanged looks, both raising their eyebrows and shaking their heads before patting Straton supportively. Felix on his back. Ganymede, who couldn't reach that high, on his thigh.

"What do you mean I can't leave?" shrieked Statilia. "I have everything packed. I am ready to go. I have the permission of the emperor."

Lysander, head bowed, not from respect but from the memory of the last time he'd delivered bad news to the empress and she'd flung a shoe at his face, replied, "It is not safe, mistress."

"What does that mean? Not safe? I'll take some slaves with me, the burly sort to discourage street ruffians."

"Not possible, mistress."

"Not possible? Who are you to deny me my freedom, boy?"

A slave placed her cloak on her shoulders, fastening it at her neck with swift fingers. "I am going."

It was a statement delivered with some force. Lysander briefly wondered whether he should let her face the gathering mob. She might even best them in her current mood. However, he had his orders.

"You are not to leave, mistress."

Statilia Messalina pulled herself upwards, steely eyes boring into Lysander's. Mina, feeling mischievous, handed her mistress a slipper.

"Thank you, girl," she said, before flinging the object straight at Lysander.

It hit him with a smack on the nose. Lysander scurried out, telling the guards not to let her pass in a nasal whine, all the while wondering when people were going to treat him with the respect he was entitled to.

Vinius was passably impressed by Piso. He'd convinced the lad it was necessary for him to speak to the Praetorians on duty at the palace. Though Vinius had done the groundwork, whipping them up into a frenzy of patriotic fever, Piso stammered out enough words on duty and sacrifice to convince them he was the real-deal aristocrat. It was enough.

Dashing back through the palace complex he found Galba, Laco, and Icelus standing in the main entrance hall to the old palace.

Galba, finger on lips, was listening to the increased noise coming from outside the doors. Around the edges of the hall stood the white-clad imperial slaves staring at the floor respectfully.

"Loyalty assured," Vinius told Laco. "We have the full cohort behind us. Any news on Otho?"

"Much," admitted Laco. "But contradictory and muddled. The latest rumour is that the Praetorians have cut him to pieces. Wishful thinking, alas."

There came an absolute roar, the slaves exchanging worried looks but maintaining their positions.

"What now?" asked Galba.

"We appeal to the people, tell them what a grubby snake Otho is. He has not planned this, he can't have done. We would have known. He still has to win support. Let us cut him off now," said Laco with surprising passion for one so cold-blooded.

Icelus nodded approvingly. "Look how the people felt about Nero's fall. They hate a usurper," he opined, casually forgetting who that usurper had been.

"Vinius?" asked Galba, a crack evident beneath the grit.

"I agree with Laco on one point," he said, shocking the prefect for they had never agreed on anything before.

"He has done this with speed in reaction to the adoption. He will have no support. We have the advantage. However," stressing that last word, "I propose we stay here, hold the palace. Let him run his way round town trying to gain support and let him fail miserably. The thing will blow down and then he can be dealt with."

"What about them?" Icelus thumbed at the doors.

"They'll get bored and go home when they realise nothing is going to happen."

Icelus swallowed hard as an almighty clamour broke out behind the doors.

"Though if it makes you happy, my dear Icelus, we'll barricade the doors and arm the staff. There are several thousand slaves. That'll even the numbers out a little."

"Do it," commanded Galba.

So the Praetorians had declared for Otho, that was good. Onomastus was on his way to the legions quartered outside the city to secure their support. But it would be hours before they would know where their allegiances lay. That the cohort at the palace had not returned to camp signified that the news was out and that Galba was still very much in control of the Palatine Hill.

"Can't we storm it?" asked Otho. "The guards know their way around the palace, after all."

"What a lovely image, the guards running through the palace slaughtering as they go, dragging Galba out and …" Epaphroditus pulled a finger across his throat. "Do you really want the reign of Imperator Otho Caesar to start in such a fashion? It will taint your name forever."

"Even with superior numbers it would be a bloody battle. They can defend well on the higher ground," was Honoratus' contribution.

"I bow to both your superior knowledge. What do you recommend?"

"If we'd had more time I would have put people on the inside," admonished Epaphroditus.

"Well we don't," said Otho matter-of-factly.

"OK, OK." Epaphroditus began to pace the room. Otho, hands laced across his stomach, as relaxed as ever, waited for the solution. Epaphroditus, coming to a dead halt, scratched his chin. "It's crap, it's makeshift, it probably won't work but it's all I've got."

"Do tell."

"We cause a riot. Send some agitators down to the forum, the bottom of the Palatine Hill, get them to cause a stink. Once it kicks off the cohort on duty will have to come down and investigate. It will leave the palace dangerously unguarded. Galba will realise it is over then."

"You think he'll take the Roman way out?" asked Otho, meaning suicide.

Epaphroditus shrugged. "Probably. He is the noble sort. Icelus and Laco they will have to drag out screaming," adding with a smile, "Shame."

FIFTY-ONE

The overseers handed out the weaponry with extreme reluctance. It stood against everything they believed in to arm the workforce. White-clad slaves stood nervously in line as the din outside the doors increased.

"Can you hear what they are shouting?" Lysander asked Theseus.

Cocking an ear Theseus caught "— Galba," being chanted.

It could have been "Death to Galba," equally it could have been "Hail Galba." It was utterly indistinguishable, impossible to tell even whether it was a happy or angry chant. Theseus shrugged.

Glancing to his left Lysander saw Sporus holding a club by the wrong end, regarding it with evident curiosity. "We're all going to die, aren't we?"

"Oh, undoubtedly," replied Theseus dryly.

At the back of the hall, Ganymede, looking smart in the new green tunic Vallia had made for him, handed out cudgels to the panicky slaves and freedmen.

Mina queued up and waited patiently as all twittered and gossiped around her. When she got to the front, Ganymede looked at her, hands on hips. "You're a girl!"

"What's that matter?"

"No girls."

"Says who?" demanded Mina.

"Says me."

Mina gave a barked, mirthless laugh, "And who are you?"

Ganymede put his tiny fists on his hips. "I am assistant to the Head of Slave Placements. So you have to scram, right now."

Mina didn't move. She glared at him, holding her position at the front of the line.

"There is a queue," said Ganymede petulantly. He pointed at the grudging slaves behind her who looked very much like they wished they were back on towel holding, cleaning, polishing, cooking, chopping, scribbling, barbering, or announcing duties.

"I want to help defend the palace," protested Mina. "Surely the more hands you have the better."

Ganymede, having lost his trembling anxiety under Felix's brief mentoring stood firm. "Next!"

Mina shuffled to the side infuriated. Seeing Straton wrestling with an armful of clubs she dashed over and recovered a stray one that had slipped from his grasp.

"Thanks," he muttered, placing them on a table where they rolled straight off the end. Mina helped with the retrieval.

Muttering another thanks he began handing them to Ganymede to dish out.

"He won't arm me," she told Straton.

The overseer silently pulled a whip from his belt and handed it to her. Ganymede squeaked in protest, bouncing up and down on his feet. If Straton's reputation as the menacing whore-son of a Gorgon had been dented by the whole crying incident, then it was positively sabotaged when Mina threw her arms around him, kissing him on both cheeks and crying, "Straton, you are the best of men!" The overseer's cheeks turned pink with pleasure.

An outraged Ganymede demonstrated some rather gruesome language that he could only have learnt from his new father.

Over in the Praetorian camp, a similar arming procedure was taking place. Epaphroditus' agitators, easily recruited from the city plebs, were lining up for whatever they could get. In this line-up stood Tadius and his Viminal Hill crew. Hearing the rumours they'd walked up to the Praetorian camp determined to help, keen to avenge both Teretius and Philo.

They ran out of actual weapons fairly quickly. The Praetorians were extremely territorial regarding their arms (they hadn't spent so many hours polishing swords only to hand them out to grubby peasants), so the remaining ramshackle army were given kitchen knives, plates, fence posts, anything that could be used aggressively in pursuit of their aim.

In the palace, the guards on duty were placed behind the wall of slave resistance. Lysander, shoulder pressed against the door, hand gripping onto his cudgel, listened to the increasing shouts beyond and felt his knees begin to shake. Beside him Theseus was silently mouthing entreaties to the gods, any of them, all of them, Mars for choice.

Sporus, who had remarkably discovered the correct way to hold his weapon, was a quivering wreck further down the line, rambling terrified to Mina. "What are we doing? I don't care about Galba. I want Otho to be emperor. He'd be much better at it. He'd have me as his consort, like Nero, dear Nero. How I loved him. He was such a wonderful, wonderful husband. And they want me to defend the evil man who … Those plebs out there are going to rip us to pieces. I don't want to be ripped apart. Such a tawdry death. I should have killed myself with Nero then I wouldn't be here now, about to be ripped apart by plebs …"

"Oh shut up, Sporus," snapped Mina, hoping the doors would be broken so she could get in some solid whip action.

Felix, marching in-between the slave/freedmen walls and the guard wall who possessed the heavy artillery for the second offensive, yelled what he considered encouragement, while mentally calculating his potential fiscal losses. Ganymede trotted beside him waving his fists in imitation.

Far beyond the defence lines, Galba, fingering his chin, said to Vinius, "They are not quietening down. They are getting louder."

"But they have not made any attempt to breach the doors," replied Vinius. "They are all noise. When Otho fails to enter the forum as a conquering hero they will get bored, go home, hit their wives, sleep with their slaves, work it off any old how."

"And if you are wrong?" suggested Laco slyly. "The legions outside the city have declared for Otho. The navy has declared for Otho."

This was hardly surprising given Galba's decimation of them during the ruckus at the Milvian Bridge back in the autumn.

"We are sitting targets. This is not a terribly noble way to die is it?"

The word "noble" attracted Galba's attention. His head snapped round to the prefect.

"The crowd is swaying, unsure of the circumstances. A good speech from Caesar could sway them in the right direction. With the people behind him, Caesar would triumph and Otho would slink away like a kicked dog."

"Piso's speech swayed the Praetorians," was Icelus' contribution.

"Caesar's safety is not assured out there," Vinius protested, thumbing to the doors. "At least we are protected here."

"For the time being."

"Caesar needs to stay put."

"Caesar, you have won the people round. Remember at the games? The cheers? The people need to know you are still their Caesar. They need you to tell them what a treacherous fool Otho is."

"Caesar, it is not safe."

"Rubbish, Otho has probably been cut to pieces already."

"These are Caesar's people. They need to know it."

"Later, when the situation is contained."

"How can it be contained if we hide in here?"

"Juno's bastard son!" broke in Vinius. "We hold the palace. Otho does not. Otho cannot. If we open those doors, we give him the opportunity to slide in and complete his declaration."

"How do we know that there is not some back door you are proposing to open while we stand here?" Laco threw in.

"I'm sorry?" asked an enraged Vinius.

"Well, you are the one who championed Otho so highly."

"You did," squeaked Icelus. "You spoke again and again on his nobler points. Where is that nobility now?" he questioned, ending in a high indignant point.

"Are you in on this plot, Titus Vinius?" pushed Laco. "Is that why you insist we stay here? Is your protégé making his way up now to the Hill and you're just waiting for that moment to suddenly change your mind and allow us to fling open those doors? Are you a traitor, Vinius?"

Vinius was too outraged to speak which played into Laco's hands.

"It all becomes clear now." Laco pointed a podgy finger at Vinius. "You're the inside man."

Galba looked keenly at a ruddy-faced Vinius. "Titus?"

Vinius clenched his fists a couple of times before putting them to good use by punching Laco in the face. The prefect staggered some steps backwards, Icelus stepping in between them, telling Vinius, "Now we see what kind of man you truly are, Titus!"

The altercation attracted the attention of the workforce as a suitable diversion from their imminent deaths.

"Blimey, Mina, your boyfriend just punched the Praetorian prefect," said Sporus.

Mina, jumping on her toes, yelled, "Way to go, Titus!"

She earned a rod slap to the back of her knees from Ganymede, who told her, "Hold position."

Mina snarled at the boy, telling Sporus, "I've gone completely off him."

"Tick," spat the eunuch at Ganymede, who slapped him on the calf with the rod. Sporus let out a high-pitched squeal.

"Cease your squabbling," commanded Galba. "That was abhorrent, Titus."

"I am sorry, Caesar, that you had to witness that. But I was provoked." He glared at Laco, who was dabbing at his fattened lip with a cloth. "I stand by my advice. We need to hold the palace."

"We need to win the people round."

"We need to strike against Otho."

Galba was torn. As a soldier he recognised the advantage of holding the higher ground. From up here they could see any forthcoming force. But as a Roman citizen he was educated in rhetoric, in the noble gesture and the dutiful sacrifice. He saw himself as Mark Antony at Julius Caesar's funeral damning those cowardly conspirators.

The people had to know what a cunning traitor Otho was. They had to see that Galba was their rightful emperor. He would hold the empire together alongside Piso, young Piso who had a family, the necessary dynasty. They could not skulk in the palace when there was a war to be won.

"Open the doors."

FIFTY-TWO

The aim was simple. Galba, accompanied by Piso and Vinius (who'd insisted on attending as the consul elect), were to walk down the hill to the forum and secure the rostra from where emperor and heir would speak directly to the Roman mob.

As an announcer Lysander had, to his horror, been co-opted into the party. The emperor informed him that he needed a strong introduction.

"You have a powerful voice. We need that now more than ever. You need to attract their attention."

Great, thought Lysander, the attention of several thousand rabid Roman plebs all centred on him. He was regretting wearing his flashy yellow tunic that morning. Even if he legged it, he was garishly obvious in a crowd. He also regretted not bedding that saucy young baker's daughter who'd winked so suggestively at him that morning.

The great palace doors were thrown open. When no marauding army ran through, a collective breath was released. Galba gave his advisors a nervous smile.

"Now we shall see," he told them, walking forward, the lines of soldiers and slaves parting for him.

Piso gave his wife a farewell kiss, she whispering to him, "It will be fine, darling. You'll be back here in no time."

Vinius gave Mina a wink and a smile. She returned the gesture, mouthing, "Good luck."

It was agreed that the emperor should travel in a litter as was befitting his dignity. Vinius would have preferred a horse, much better for a quick getaway. But at least with a litter the emperor would be hidden from view. And if the atmosphere proved too ugly, he could be discreetly delivered back to the palace.

Galba had disregarded Vinius' suggestion of a heavy Praetorian presence. "The people down there are frightened. If we go in with soldiers, there will be panic."

So the security presence was deliberately low key. Felix watched his merchandise trotting alongside the emperor's litter with trepidation.

Settling into the cushions Galba tried to concentrate his mind, to single out what needed doing. Walking beside the litter on full alert, Vinius glared around him, his hand firmly on the hilt of his sword. On the steps of the palace Laco and Icelus watched the purple litter jostle its way down the hill.

"You think …?" Icelus began, but he could not finish the sentence.

"He is a great man, Icelus. The mob will see that he is a good, decent Roman of old versus the perfumed, toupee'd Otho. Such vanity against our nobler Galba." Laco pointed: the crowd was fanning aside to let the litter through. "See," he told Icelus, smiling.

There was a lot of people, jostling against each other, pushing, shoving. Lysander, trotting beside the litter, his heart a heavy stone in his chest, listened to the calls.

"Who's in the litter? Is it the emperor?"

"Caesar! Caesar!"

"Long live Galba Caesar."

So far, so encouraging. Galba smiled at Piso who lay beside him. "They want to see their emperor. They want assurance that he lives."

Piso attempted to smile back. He failed. He was so white that it was debatable whether any blood was reaching his head at all. His lips had turned distinctly grey.

Laco squinted, asking Icelus, "Who are they?" and pointed over to the arches of the Basilica Aemilia.

A group of brown-tunic-clad men were methodically forcing their way through the crowd. Shoving citizens aside with a careless brutality that belied their mission: these were no curious bystanders. Looking along, Laco spotted another group of brown tunics pressing along the walls of the Senate House and yet more working their way from the House of the Vestals. Flicking his head from side to side he could see more and more, creeping in from every corner of the forum. Oh, gods, it was an ambush!

It was a loud squeak from Ganymede that alerted them. The boy, sat on Felix's shoulders, pointed towards the colossal golden statue of Nero that peered over the city. Laco caught the flash of red, a clattering of hooves, and screams as the mob fled their galloping path. Scurrying to escape by any means necessary, trampling over women, children, anyone who stood in their way.

The horsemen cut their way through with swords whipping low, the bobbing heads running as fast as they could. The emperor's litter was by now at the bottom of the hill, between the Basilica Julia and the Temple of Castor and Pollux. They could see it weaving its way along as the horsemen pelted down the Via Sacre.

Galba and Piso felt the litter sway one way then another. Piso holding onto a pole, looked distinctly green.

Galba banged on the side. "What is going on?" he demanded.

The litter bearers were too caught up in the struggle to keep the litter upright to answer and pressed on with their mission with wide eyes.

Entering the forum area, the bearers were greeted by a mass exodus of fleeing bodies who ran straight into them in their panic to escape. The litter rocked in their hands and then fell under the pressure. Two of the bearers disappeared under the feet of the mob and were trampled over by panicked boots.

Thrown to the ground, Galba and Piso exchanged looks but neither had a chance to speak. There came a scream and a body fell through the curtains onto the emperor's own lap. Theseus' dead eyes gazed upwards at Galba, the javelin point sticking through his neck.

Piso, terrified, scuttled through the curtains, out of the other side of the litter. His last view of his new father was of the hands that thrust through and roughly grabbed at his arms.

The emperor taken, the slaves attending him fled for their lives. Lysander took one look at the bedlam around him and ran. "Got to get to a temple, got to get to a temple," he chanted, weaving his way round the unfolding chaos.

For now the legions were in play, marching in formation from every road, every side street, striking down anyone and everyone who stood in their way, cutting off the exits and leaving the open spaces of the forum as a clear killing ground.

Galba, lying in the dirt, gazed up at the soldiers, and in that moment his military training fell into place. He was not scared. He was not frightened. He simply pulled down his tunic, bared his throat and told them calmly, "Do it."

It was to be his last command, and as ever, it was obeyed. Sort of. The first soldier did indeed strike at his throat but the others were not so accurate and they hacked away at his body carelessly, eagerly.

Vinius, who had been leading the party, clearing a path for the litter, was outside the Temple of Julius Caesar when the horsemen entered the forum. Spun by the fleeing crowd he turned back to see the litter crash to the ground, the emperor pulled from within.

"No!" he screamed, pulling out his sword, trying to fight his way through the fleeing citizens. Thrusting, pushing, shoving, ramming to get to the fallen emperor.

Scraping past the temple he felt a sudden dig to his knee. Glancing back he saw the dagger protruding, thrust in to its handle. He stumbled, then fell down onto the cobbles. Yet still he pulled himself along by his fingers, desperate to get to Galba. But it was not to be: legionary Julius Carus unsheathed his sword and pierced him from one side to the other.

Lysander, scanning for a suitable temple to hide in, saw Piso running up the steps of the Temple of Vesta and sprinted behind him, catching up with him at the doors. They banged and banged with their fists. The door of the temple was opened very, very slowly. Lysander, glancing nervously behind, saw Vinius struck down. Unable to take it any longer he prised open the doors himself, grabbing Piso by the arm, dragging him in, and slamming the doors behind him.

The temple slave, an elderly beetle-browed creature, stared at them with curiosity as they collapsed on the floor. Lysander got his breath back first. "Help! We need help!"

"Get the fuck down there!" yelled Felix. "That's my fucking merchandise"

Straton grinned, happy to be let loose in that mayhem. He took out the double-headed axe he'd taken from Onesimus back in the spring, giving it a couple of test swings. "Excellent," he rasped happily.

"I'm coming," said Mina, flexing her whip.

Straton furrowed his brow. "Dangerous," he told her, concerned.

Mina smiled. "Like the other night wasn't?"

"Bloodbath," he persisted.

"I want to save the slaves."

Straton patted her on the shoulder. "Gonna be hard. Gonna be rough. Might not make it."

Mina formed a determined lip. "So be it," she said.

"Fucking Juno's arse," broke in Felix. "Stop fucking yapping and get me my fucking goods back!"

FIFTY-THREE

"Now then, there is nothing for you to worry about," Pompeia Minor consoled Philo, Pompeia Major nodding in agreement.

The Pompeias had traipsed over to the Esquiline to check on Philo, to check on Teretia, and to check out Epaphroditus' luxurious town house. So far none of this was disappointing. Philo, though in considerable pain, was at least awake and talking as much as normal (that is, not a lot). Teretia, after her shock over Straton, had buttoned down to making her relationship work, which had taken the form of an excessive amount of cosseting.

The house had kept the Pompeias happily chatting over the niceties of positioning your kitchens near the dining areas (perfect for the preservation of the food's temperature), the use of black marble in the main bathhouse (it doesn't show the dirt as readily as white marble), and that mother-of-pearl imbedded into the ceilings was a master touch (Pompeia Major determined to copy the effect but by using sea shells instead).

"We've been making some decisions and Teretia is in full agreement. With you two being together it makes sense if she moves into your room and we take in another lodger."

Philo opened his mouth to protest but was talked down by Pompeia Minor. "Hers is the bigger room. We can charge a higher rent for it."

"It's alright, Philo," said Teretia. "It makes perfect sense."

In the intervening days Philo had regained most of his senses, the misty confusion lifting. Following on from Teretia's recent news, the organising part of his brain had kicked back into action. It was telling him to concentrate on one thing at a time. So he ignored the fact that Icelus would be seeking him down as a fugitive, that his free status had no doubt been revoked so that his former boss could inflict further indignities on him, and that he was now unemployed. Instead he worried about Teretia's large number of animal-shaped oil lamps, which she collected avidly, and how they were going to fit into his tiny room.

"And," continued Pompeia, "we've had a think about your job."

He didn't have one.

Pompeia Major took up the tale. "I've been chatting to a number of folks on the hill and I reckon there is a market for your skills. Take Tadius. There's this other butcher who's set up shop and he's wanting to compete with his fair prices and his quality merchandise."

"Which it is," chimed Pompeia Minor.

"He could do with some help writing a sign, an advertisement to attract back his wandering customers. And then there's Damia. She's got this son in the army and he writes these long letters to her and she'd like to be able to write back but she ain't so good with her words."

There followed a long list of Viminal residents who for one reason or another were desperately in need of a scribe. Under such kind compulsion Philo could only nod his thickened head. Teretia holding his hand, told him, "You see, everything is going to be fine, darling."

Pompeia Minor stood up briskly. "Right, we'd better be going. Let you rest Philo, because that's the most important thing."

"Definitely," agreed Pompeia Major, patting Philo's hand. "You have a nice nap and get yourself fit. You've got people relying on you now."

They both smiled and made their departure, commenting as the slave showed them to the doors, "I am not sure about that fountain. The nymphs were rather sinister, I thought. Not sprightly like they should be."

Pompeia Major shook her head. "Not right at all," she hissed in a whisper.

"Nice to see you, ladies," said the doorman politely.

The Pompeias nodded their approval. "We'll be back," they promised in unison.

The door was flung open just as the first exodus from the forum began: a flowing sea of petrified citizens running for their lives.

"Oh my word!" exclaimed Pompeia Minor. The door-keeper hastily slammed his domain shut. "Best stay a while I think, ladies," he suggested, before signalling to his colleagues to start arming the household slaves as requested by their master.

In any crisis there was apt to be those who seek to advantage themselves. The Esquiline area on which they resided was known to be wealthy, a prime spot for any would-be looters, and so Epaphroditus had organised a heavy resistance.

Aphrodite, seeing her attendants walk by with a variety of weapons, was understandably alarmed.

"What is going on?" she demanded of her head steward.

Porticus, head bowed respectfully, lied, "Some trouble on the streets, mistress. Best to be prepared."

"What sort of trouble?"

"No idea, mistress. Just people moving quickly, too quickly. A riot over the bread prices, perhaps."

The Pompeias returned arm in arm. "Well fancy that, they're shouting that the emperor's dead".

"About time too," offered Pompeia Minor. "After what he did to my Teretius and now poor Philo!"

"Galba's fallen?"

Aphrodite's intelligent mind was throwing together some oddities. Pausing over her husband's coincidental absence, his desire to see all the children before he departed, the long lingering kiss he had given her, and the fact that all her slaves seemed to be suspiciously well armed.

"I imagine they have made that nice Otho emperor," said Pompeia Major, echoing Aphrodite's darkest thoughts.

From the relative serenity of her courtyard garden Aphrodite could hear the banging on the door and the frantic pleas to be let in and then the piercing screams that set in when the fleeing civilians fled straight into the approaching legionaries.

"Mother?" called Faustina, rushing in accompanied by two of her sisters. "What's happening?"

Aphrodite pulled them in for a hug. "Don't worry, my darlings, just some trouble on the streets. We're perfectly safe in here." She kissed their heads one by one and hoped she was correct.

A sudden scream from outside brought in her other children, wide-eyed with fright, running to her for comfort.

Pompeia Minor clapped her hands. "Right," she said cheerfully to the startled children. "Do you have any musicians?"

Aphrodite nodded slowly, not sure where this was leading.

"Well, let's get them in here, play a tune or two, jolly us all up!"

Over in the Praetorian camp an excited, bright-eyed pleb was granted an audience with Otho who sat in genial emperor mode behind an enormous desk, flanked by Onomastus and Epaphroditus. Otho nodded his head, permitting the man to speak.

"Caesar," he began respectfully, Otho visibly pluming at the use of the word. "I bring you the head of Galba."

He dumped a bag onto the desk proudly, waiting for his reward. "Could we see it perhaps?" asked Otho.

"Of course, of course. Sorry, Caesar."

The man flustered with his bag, placing the object on the desk and then twisting it round until it faced Otho, who squinted at its bloody features.

"I hacked it off myself, personally. Right hard work it was too. I got blisters. Hard old neck that Galba."

"That's not Galba," said Onomastus.

"Yes it is," insisted the man.

"No it's not," insisted Onomastus, turning the head back to face its owner. "That is clearly a woman."

"Womanly features maybe, but then that Galba he plays the woman with that Icelus."

"There will be no reward," stated Onomastus.

The man was dragged out protesting.

"Where do you want this one, sir?"

Otho waved a hand. "Oh, put it with the others." Then turning to Epaphroditus, "How hard can it be? I'd recognise that hooked nose anywhere."

"I did warn you about offering such a substantial reward."

"Urgh. If I see one more decapitated head today …"

"It had better be Galba's," Epaphroditus finished for him.

FIFTY-FOUR

The temple slave walked them past the burning hearth to a small back room, closing the door behind them. Lysander flopped to the floor and stared at his shaking hands, sucking the air through his teeth.

Piso sat down beside him. "You think we are safe here?" A sudden yell from outside made them both jump.

"Better than out there."

"What are they chanting?"

Lysander listened before saying, "I think it is 'Otho'."

"I am sort of glad," confessed Piso. "I never really wanted to be emperor. I would never have been any good at it."

"No kidding," said Lysander, who thought he'd never meet anyone less emperor-like than Piso. He was far too meek. The freedmen of the palace would have run rings around him. He was prevented from vocalising this by a banging. "Open up, slave!"

Lysander and Piso froze, hearing the shuffling gait of the slave and then the temple door being opened.

"Let us in, slave!"

"This is the goddess' home. There is nothing in here for you," he replied with surprising equanimity.

Holding their breaths they heard a further muted exchange and then a cry of, "You cannot bring your weapons into the Temple of Vesta!"

Then a grunt and a bang informed them that indeed they could and that they had put them to some use already.

Lysander glanced around anxiously. There was nowhere to hide in this small room. No cupboards or even furniture to dash behind. And there was no window to squeeze through either. They were trapped.

"Oh, goddess Vesta," whispered Lysander. "Please save me."

"Us," corrected Piso.

"Right, whatever."

Lysander pulled his knees up to his chest, moderating his breath to catch every noise outside the door, counting mentally to calm down his rampant beating heart. He had counted to fifty-seven when the door was flung open and three soldiers and a gap-toothed man stood in the doorway, swords unsheathed, dripping blood onto the marble floor.

"Which one of you is Piso?"

Lysander didn't hesitate. "He is," and pointed in case there was any further confusion.

They dragged Piso out by his feet, Lysander watching his pale face depart. The announcer squished his hands over his ears to block out the would-be emperor's screams.

A pause and then the door opened again. Lysander removed his hands from his ears and stared up at the gap-toothed man.

"They've taken his head," he told a cowering Lysander. "But then I thought … coz I'm clever," he tapped his temple with a finger, "I thought wot if that weren't Piso."

"It was Piso. I promise. I swear. That was Piso. You got him," blustered Lysander.

The man stepped into the chamber. "Only Otho won't pay for the wrong head. Best to make sure, hey?"

Lysander pushed his back into the wall. "I swear that was Piso. I swear. I work at the palace. I know Piso. That was him. Please … that was him."

"Best make sure," repeated the man, grabbing hold of Lysander's ankle and pulling.

Lysander was a tall man, elegantly so, well proportioned, trim. He was a pleasing addition to any room positioned by the door, with his fine voice and words. What he wasn't was strong, nor much of a fighter. He'd never needed to be. He was an announcer. All he had to do was talk and stand. You didn't need muscles for that. So although he kicked and kicked, his gap-toothed assailant had little difficulty in dragging him along. Lysander's fingernails scraped at the floor as he sought to find something, anything, to hold onto.

Where the bloody Vestals, hey? Those superior virgins. Where were they now with their rituals and direct line to the goddess when he was about to be murdered on their steps? Passing through the door, Lysander grabbed onto an edge and held on with all the wobbling strength that remained.

"Oh no you don't," said Gappy, letting go of his ankle and grabbing him by the shoulders, wrenching him off.

Lysander fell backwards onto the steps, jarring his back. He gazed up at his would-be killer who grinned, pulled out his sword, and told him, "Reckon your head's worth 10к."

Lysander's singular thought was that if he were Piso, old Gappy was being short-changed. He then readied himself for death, regretting that he would never know what a freebie tasted like now.

Then something odd happened. One moment Gappy was grasping his sword ready to drive it into Lysander's chest, the next he was staring at his bloodied empty fist with puzzlement. Lysander, lifting up his head, saw Mina, whip in one hand, sword in the other.

"Looking for this?" she yelled, waggling her prize.

Gappy looked her up and down. Though the day was plentiful in death and pillaging the one thing it lacked was the raping that usually accompanied such sport. This beauty would do nicely, though. Forgetting his aim he kicked past Lysander and pulled out a dagger from his belt. Mina gave a serene smile, cracked her whip, smacking his fist, the dagger skidding across the cobbles.

"You girl, mine!" shouted an enraged Gappy.

Left without weapons he fell back on brute strength. He ran his considerable bulk with speed straight at Mina. Though her eyes widened, she maintained her composure. Stepping to the side slightly exposing her partner: bigger, bulkier, and far meaner than Gappy could ever be.

Gappy didn't see him. He was more concerned with getting hold of Mina's assets. When he did look up and see Straton it was far too late for reaction. Straton grinned, pulled up his axe and sliced off Gappy's head in one fluid motion. The head bounced to the floor where it rolled to Lysander's feet. He kicked it away and it bowled along, coming to a halt by the Arch of Augustus, where it stared up at the sky in some surprise.

"Lysander, come on." Mina offered her hand.

"Where did you learn to do that?" he asked, indicating the whip.

"From the master, Lysander, from the master."

Straton grunted and thumbed.

Mina took hold of Lysander's hand. "Come on, we've got to go rescue the white tunics!"

"There is nothing we can do," said Laco.

Icelus, jaw fully dropped open, said, "We have to help them, Cornelius. We have to …" his voice broke, caught. "Gods, Laco, we have to …"

"There is nothing."

Laco patted his arm. Icelus flinched away, his eyes drawn helplessly towards the massacre. He could see the imperial litter overturned, crushed by fleeing feet, stained with blood. He'd lost sight of the emperor. There was too much movement, too many heads, moving too fast.

From the Esquiline side more horses were whipping into the crowd, soldiers marching in from every corner in full formation as if facing a barbarian army. Eyes flicking over the carnage, Laco spotted a familiar crown.

"Icelus, it's Galba." He pointed at the bald pate visible beside the basin of Curtius.

Icelus squinted, trying to make sense of the scene. Why was Galba waggling about like that? There was something wrong with the proportions. Galba was not overly tall so why was he towering above the soldiers? A gap formed briefly round the emperor.

Laco felt the bile rise in his throat. It was Galba's head alright, only it wasn't attached to his neck. It was stuck on the end of a spear being parading through the forum.

Icelus screamed.

FIFTY-FIVE

Without the Pompeias, Aphrodite did not know how she would have coped. Her own thoughts were a jumbled mixture of anger at Epaphroditus for doing this to her again (and for who?—for bloody Otho!), combined with fears for his safety in the erupting city. An emotion which could be summarised thus: she wanted him home alive so she could personally kill him.

Her anxiety was naturally picked up by her children who had sported pale, fixed, panicked looks as the fracas outside the house increased in volume. But the Pompeias' scheme was absolutely inspired. The musicians playing at full volume drained out the shouts and screams from outside. The Pompeias imaginatively devising ever more complicated dance steps to accompany them diverted the children's thoughts.

Rufus, sat on Aphrodite's lap, gurgled with happiness as his brother and sisters tripped over each other and crashed into furniture attempting to complete the dance, his mother clapping to the beat. Even the usually spiky Faustina had joined in despite her initial protestations that, "It was for kids."

The only ones who did not partake in the fun were Teretia and Philo who sat huddled together on a couch at the back of the room. Aphrodite could see them holding hands, clearly reassuring each other.

"And where is my husband to reassure me?" thought Aphrodite cynically. "Oh yes, he is out there causing this chaos!"

"Oh my word," breathed Pompeia Major clutching at her heart. "You girls will be the death of me. I don't think I can do any more."

A statement that was greeted by a chorus of, "Nooo!"

Pompeia Major affected a miraculously sprightly recovery, telling the excited girls, "Just one more dance then. But just the one, my heart couldn't take any more!"

Julia ran up to her and hugged her legs with great affection. Aphrodite found herself actually smiling as the pipers broke into a fresh melody and they all ran with jolly disorganisation to their positions.

In all of Straton's life nobody had ever been pleased to see him. His presence generally signified pain and terror for someone, so it was rather a surprise to him when the white tunics flocked towards him eagerly.

In the midst of all that chaos, of fallen bodies, of the heads displayed proudly on spears, of blood streaked up to the elbows, Straton represented a big solid slab of normality for the imperial slaves. They ran towards him crying and shaking. He patted a few on the head telling them, "Get you home."

A quick headcount revealed he was missing eight. He gazed about the forum trying to catch flashes of white, shielding the terrified slaves behind his bulk. Beside him Mina gave a small cry as she spotted Vinius' head bobbing along, a group of soldiers singing beneath its dripping neck. Straton gave her arm a friendly brush. "Later," he advised her. "Home now."

She nodded at the wisdom of this, biting back the pang and steeling herself for what was necessary.

"Ready?" he asked.

"Ready," she replied.

"Right."

They stood out, that was the problem. Gleaming in imperial white for every blood-hungry fucker of a soldier to see. There was no stopping them now. Otho had freely promised money for Galba's leading players without offering them any assistance on how they might recognise them. Quite naturally the soldiers were hacking at anyone who might feasibly be Laco or Icelus. Anyone in javelin-throwing distance of those white-clad imperial slaves was a more likely candidate than most.

Lysander, in gleaming yellow tunic, stood by Straton's shoulder. It seemed by far the safest place to be; all around was a bloody mess. Noting his panicked look Mina said kindly, "Do you want a club? For protection?"

"This is madness," he said, dazed by his experiences. "Can you believe it?"

"Nope, but we can't dwell now. We have to get back," she retorted tightly.

They were crouched behind the arches at the Basilica Aemilia, the home of the law courts. To get back to the palace they would have to cross the Via Sacre which was heaving with heavily-armed soldiers, earnest mercenaries, and a hefty stack of bodies. Next, they would have to dash past the rostra, avoiding the arrows from the eight archers who had positioned themselves on top of it. Then run through the arches of the Basilica Julia. And finally, round the Temple of Augustus up the Palatine Hill to where safety (probably) awaited them.

"Don't like them archers," grumbled Straton. He fiddled around in his belt, pulling out a few pebbles and rolling them around his hand. "Need more," he told Mina.

"For what?"

"Slingshots. Distract archers. Slaves run."

It was almost a plan. At least, it was all they had. Mina hissed to the crouching slaves to collect stones. Being good little slaves they scrabbled around on the ground instantly for potential missiles, handing them to Mina, Lysander, and Straton.

"Too gravelly," said Mina, handing back a pile of small stones to Thenogus.

"These OK, Mina?" asked Nyssa, crawling over on her stomach to avoid being spotted by the soldiers who stood in the Via Sacre.

"Fabulous work," Mina congratulated her, feeling the tough the little pebbles. "Watch and learn, Thenogus."

Mina handed the missiles to Straton who nodded his approval and pulled out a couple of slingshots. He threw some stones into the pocket, stood up behind the pillar and whirled the material around his head at increasing speed until it was but a blur. Then he let go of one of the handles and the stones flew out. A soldier standing in the centre of the Via Sacre put his hand to his face and screamed. When he briefly removed his palms, the slaves noted the damage to his eyes and winced.

Straton handed Mina and Lysander the slingshots, telling them, "Aim for fuckers' eyes. You cover slaves when run."

"That won't work. Surely that won't work," said Lysander, holding the slingshot. "Three of us whacking odd pebbles against a whole line of archers. It'll never work."

"You two whacking pebbles," corrected Straton. "Me whacking something bigger." Then, turning to Nyssa and Thenogus, "You get me javelins soldiers left. Yes? Lots."

The two slaves nodded and crept off to recover as many discarded javelins as they could.

Straton gave Lysander a narrow look. "You up for this?" he asked.

"Do I have a choice?"

Straton waved at the crowded and deadly Via Sacre, the road that lay between them and the bottom of the Palatine Hill. "You dead if you go alone."

Lysander paled.

Up on the Palatine Hill the mood was decidedly ugly. The single cohort of Praetorians who'd been won over by Vinius' rhetoric were fully informed of Galba's fate. They abandoned their defensive line, whipped round, and turned it into an offensive one.

A hysterical Icelus was marched off gibbering and locked in his office. Here he sat wailing, the image of his lover's bloodied head stuck in his brain, so that eyes open or eyes closed it danced before him. It was so distracting a vision that nothing else filtered in, not even any thoughts as to what his own fate might be.

Laco was not so fortunate. He was left with faculties intact. His only consolation that his guards had not cut him down there and then, as they had their former prefect.

Felix eyed up the Praetorians suspiciously, bent down, and whispered to Ganymede, "Tell the overseers to take my girls and barricade them in."

The boy nodded and sped off. Felix weren't taking no fucking chances this time.

Apollodorus swiftly rounded up the girls. Sporus decided he was definitely a girl and trotted alongside Erotica as the overseers flicked at them to get them moving quicker.

"What a way to become emperor," huffed Erotica.

"Nero had a far more dignified death. I was there you know, with him at the end. I held his hand as he slipped away."

"Think anyone held Galba's hand?"

"Would have been hacked off at the wrist if they had."

"Sir, sir," gasped Daphne at the back of the pack, doubled over at the waist.

Apollodorus put a hand on her back. "Are you alright, Daphne love?"

She tried to straighten up, a hot flashing stab of pain hitting her stomach. Seeing the colour drain so suddenly from her face, Apollodorus put an arm around her. "Let's go find you somewhere quiet to sit. Is the baby bothering you?"

Daphne, teeth gritted, hand rubbing at her stomach, grasped onto Apollodorus' hand and gripped it hard.

"Let's move you, Daphne."

"I don't think I can, sir," she squeaked as another wave of pain hit her, a cry escaping from her lips. "It's too soon. It's not time," rubbing her stomach with more frantic motions. "She won't be ready!"

Those not considered worthy enough to be barricaded away had one response: panic. A barrage of white tunics and gowns flying into the palace. A number remembered that Otho was friendly with the empress and made for her chambers, seeing it as a potential haven from harm.

The cohort of Praetorians on palace patrol with no instructions and no orders were anxious to prove themselves loyal to the new emperor lest their recent siding and defence of Galba be taken into consideration. They tried to assess what would please Otho. They'd locked up Icelus and Laco ready for his particular revenge and they'd pulled out the higher-placed freedmen, spontaneously delivering judgement on those they felt had been particularly close to those tenacious advisors.

Then one of them recalled Otho's flirtation with Statilia and a gaggle of guards rushed to offer her protection and ingratiate themselves with the potential new empress. Seeing the slaves clawing at her door, they mistook their purpose and killed the lot of them.

Behind the locked door, huddled together with her attendants in a corner beneath a table, listening to their agonised screams, Statilia Messalina sobbed through sheer terror.

FIFTY-SIX

Nyssa and Thenogus had done their job well. Straton sat with his back to a pillar, a pile of javelins beside him. Mina and Lysander each held a slingshot with small piles of pebbles beside them.

Mina addressed the group of crouching slaves. "Right, here is what we are going to do. We need to get across the road, through the basilica and then beside the temple and up the hill."

The slaves nodded.

"We are going to run one after the other so that we don't attract attention as a big heap of white for the archers to aim at. What's going to happen is that Lysander will run first with one of you to the other side. Straton and I will cover your dash with the relevant ammunition. Lysander will set himself by the columns on the other basilica and fire from that side. Then we'll go one by one quick as we can."

She gave what she hoped was a reassuring smile, adding, "We'll all be back for dinner!" Patting Lysander on the arm she asked, "You ready?"

Lysander gave a thin smile. "Not in the slightest," and then pulled Thenogus to his side. "You're first, lad. Ready?"

They stood beside the pillar. Straton raised three fingers and brought the first down. Mina loaded her slingshot. The overseer grabbed a javelin in his spare hand.

The second finger came down. Lysander readied himself, handing Thenogus some spare pebbles to take with them.

The third finger came down and they bolted, Lysander holding onto Thenogus' tunic.

Advised by Straton to zigzag to avoid being hit they found that actually this was the only way to run given the vast number of corpses they had to avoid. Lysander jumped over several, heaving Thenogus along, eyes fixed firmly ahead to the Basilica Julia.

Straton had given the slaves by the Basilica Aemilia some missiles to hurl, which took the form of discarded legionaries's helmets and shields. As they watched Lysander and Thenogus run, he gave the signal for them to throw. Which they did, somewhat inexpertly for they were a mixture of body slaves, a keeper of the emperor's cloak, a carrying attendant, and an assortment of attractive but not-terribly-useful-in-a-battle-situation imperial slaves. But the clatter they caused distracted the archers sufficiently for Straton to throw a well-aimed javelin which pierced through not one but two of them who fell to the ground in a gurgling heap.

A suitably bloody end that diverted their fellow archers' attention and allowed Lysander to get clean across the Via Sacre and throw himself behind a pillar, breathing heavily. When he had recovered, he threw an arm round the pillar giving a thumbs up. Straton nodded to Mina.

"OK, Nyssa, you next."

The girl looked terrified but nodded.

"Just run," was Straton's advice.

She certainly did, leaping over the bodies and screaming all the way as the arrows pinged off the pavement around her. Straton managed to pick another off. Mina, discovering that she was surprisingly handy with a slingshot, got one archer smack between the eyes. He rubbed his forehead and then fell backwards with a crash. Mina and the white tunics cheered, Lysander pulling the crying Nyssa to pillared safety.

"Good stuff," commented Straton and pointed to Dio. "You now."

Mina picked up a fresh batch of stones. Across the road Lysander readied his slingshot. Nyssa and Thenogus grabbed anything that could potentially work as a missile.

Three fingers held up. Dio breathing heavily. One finger down. And then another. Dio ran. Straton stood up flinging a javelin at the aiming archers. It did not fly high enough, bouncing off the rostra. The overseer was rearmed and ready to throw but that gap was long enough for Dio to be hit by an arrow which penetrated his thigh.

"KEEP RUNNING!" yelled Lysander.

Easy enough to say but the shock and pain for Dio was intense and he halted. Mina and her band of stone throwers kicked into action, flinging as much as they could in a synchronised attack so that the barrage of stones did not cease upon the archers.

"RUN, RUN," screamed Nyssa bouncing up and down. "RUN!"

Dio heard this and, limping, he dashed across the street as fast as he could, another arrow piercing his ankle as he made it to the other side. He fell with a crash just before safety, attempting to crawl. The archers fired mercilessly into him, a hand just reaching the kerb before the slave stopped moving altogether.

"Oh gods," mouthed Mina, the slaves around her in tears.

Straton rubbed his head with a palm. "They got smart."

"Yep, I think they have," said Mina. "What do we do now?"

Straton scanned the area. They were barricading off the roads now so alternative routes were severely limited. This spot was their best chance.

"We go together," he told Mina. "Only way. More targets. Harder."

"But a bigger target for them to hit," protested Mina.

"Only way," was Straton's tight response.

Up at the palace the overseers had barricaded the girls in, furniture piled against the doors. The terrified girls sat cross-legged on the floor in shaking panic. The overseers putting fingers to their lips and warning, "Sshh."

Sporus clung to Erotica, burying his face in her bosom as they listened to the sounds coming from outside: screams and yells, thuds and bangs. Every now and then someone would recognise a voice, a shout for help from the chaos and a head would shoot up. The overseers gave each a quick slap of the rod to behave and heads were aimed downwards, staring at the floor, as they heard their friends and colleagues struck down beyond the barriers.

They steeled themselves. The slaves whimpering and shaking but prepared to try anything to get home. Straton signalled across to Lysander for him to throw everything he had at the archers. He nodded, filling up his slingshot in preparation. Thenogus and Nyssa armed with bits of masonry to chuck, thumbed up that they were ready.

It felt like a moment for last words. Mina, fearing this was her end, turned to Straton and opened her mouth. Clamping it shut when she couldn't think of a thing to say apart from a strangulated, "Uhhh."

Straton grinned, patted her on the arm. "Be fine."

"Uhhh."

Three fingers held up once more. One went down. Then another. And then the final finger. They ran in a clustered group, disorganised, terrified. Straton on the side nearest the archers flung javelin after javelin to protect their flight. He was not so accurate this time, but it created enough of a diversion for the majority of the slave party to dash ahead and throw themselves into the pillared basilica, accompanied by a barrage of arrows which pinged off the columns.

Two slaves fell beside Dio's body. Nyssa and Thenogus dragged them in to safety, leaving Lysander the only one attacking the archers. One eye closed for a better aim, whirling his slingshot around his head. Straton, nearly across the Via Sacre, pushed Mina ahead as he threw his last javelin at the archers. It speared one in the foot who gave a loud and inventive curse. He pulled back his bow and fired in retaliation.

The first arrow hit Straton in the hip. He pulled it out with irritation but was instantly struck by another that entered his shoulder, then another on his hip. He pulled out as many as he could, the attack slowing his flight to the basilica. Straton beginning to stumble as the archers made their target again and again.

It was the arrow that pierced his neck the second time that caused him to fall with a crash onto the pavement. Lifting his arm up above his face for protection as they pulled back their bows and aimed again.

Mina dashed behind the pillars on the other side, doing a quick head count. Everyone was safe, if a little battered, and Tiomeges had an arrow sticking out of his arm, but it was not a bad day's work all in all.

"Fabulous," she gushed. "Let's get back up that hill and home!" And then to Lysander, "Good work. Didn't think you had it in you."

"Neither did I," he confessed sheepishly.

Mina looked around for Straton to congratulate him on another successful daring mission, only he wasn't there. Glancing into the road she saw a huge, heaped body pierced with dozens of arrows, the archers spraying in more as she watched in horror. Lysander grabbed hold of her arm to stop her running back.

"He's gone, Mina," he told her, holding her tight as she struggled to get free.

"No, we can get to him. Drag him here."

Lysander looked at Straton lying in the road. He wasn't trying to deflect the onslaught. He wasn't moving.

"LET ME HELP HIM!" she screamed, wriggling free of Lysander.

"Mina, NO!"

Mina pulled out her whip. She tried to recall every piece of advice, every lesson that Straton had given her. He'd always told her to take her time with her aim, to be sure before you cracked. This she did. She walked calmly into the Via Sacre, into the open space of the forum. Standing in front of the rostra, she eyed up the archers working out her assault.

The slaves by the basilica watched with wide eyes as she pulled back her whip and snapped it at the archer at the far end. It wrapped around his ankle. Mina gave it a tug which took him off balance. He stumbled and crashed into his colleagues, bringing them down one by one in a heap.

She ran to Straton, turning him over. He was still alive, his eyes open.

"Lysander! Thenogus! Come on, help me!" she called.

The entire slave party ran over and assisted Mina with dragging Straton's considerable weight to the basilica. They propped him up against a pillar where he sat gasping.

"Saved me," he rasped painfully at Mina. "Good work."

"We'll get you back to the palace. Felix will have to give you time off to recover and I shall nurse you with fine wines and endless bowls of nuts."

"Had some adventures. You and me," he said.

"There will be many more," Mina assured him.

Straton shook his head slowly. "Don't think so," he rasped, and closed his eyes.

412

FIFTY-SEVEN

In the late afternoon as the sun was setting, the soldiers ran out of people to kill, so they made makeshift barricades on all entrances to the forum area to ensure safe passage for the new emperor.

At around the same time the senate declared Otho emperor. For what else could they do? Perhaps it would stop the bloodshed that had whipped up all seven hills of the city. Anyone with any sense was at home: their doors locked; their slaves armed.

Otho rubbed his hands together, beaming at his companions. The messenger standing stoically, hands clasped behind his back, was rewarded for his news with a highly generous tip; he goggling slightly as the bag of coins was handed to him. It was heavier than his wages ever were, but he maintained his serious expression as befitting a servant who'd just told a man that he was emperor. He clicked his heels and departed with his clinking bag.

Onomastus found himself heartily slapped on the back. "Come on then, chaps. Let us go take up our mantle!"

Honoratus who felt that he had been holding his breath since early morning let it out slowly. "I'll send the guards ahead. Make sure everything is safe."

"Pish. It is secure. It says here." Otho waved the scroll. "The senate has ratified, the legions have proclaimed for me, the palace eagerly awaits my entrance into the city. I say we just go now, settle ourselves in, and throw a fabulous party tonight. I'll let you boys be seated by my couch."

"So kind," muttered Epaphroditus, adding, "Your Imperial Majesty."

"I cannot wait to see Statilia Messalina! I'll insist on her absolute finery for tonight! Oh, she will be a sight! What a beauty she is …" he mused, losing himself in internal raptures.

The procession from the Praetorian camp, through the city walls to the Palatine was a sober one. The streets were deserted and they saw not a soul as they passed through the city gates into the Viminal.

"Such a shame. When I rode with Galba back in the autumn we had a fabulous turnout. All cheering and singing. It was most gratifying. Such a jolly day."

Epaphroditus didn't answer. Seeing the destruction around them he was possessed of a gnawing anxiousness for his family. He'd armed his slaves; he'd threatened them with crucifixion should they fail to protect. He hoped it was enough.

"I am very disappointed by the lack of turnout," continued Otho. "I've been practising my imperial wave for months," he moaned as his chariot clattered through the empty streets.

"You could give one anyway, sir," suggested Onomastus.

"Why not?" smiled Otho and gave the city's dogs picking at the corpses a nicely judged and finely elegant wave.

"Imperial Majesty, I request leave," said Epaphroditus suddenly. "To check on my family."

Otho ceased his waving. "Really? Not good form, I think. The emperor's private secretary missing from the inaugural banquet. It looks bad."

"Please, Marcus," begged his friend. "I need to know they are safe."

Otho, seeing his desperate expression, gave him leave reluctantly, telling him, "I expect you in later, though. Work to be done and all that."

On the Palatine Hill, the second cohort of Praetorians had taken the palace, relieving the first cohort of duty. A heavy silence fell and eventually the surviving imperial slaves began to reappear from their hiding places. Sporus and Erotica gazed round an eastern corridor at the bodies that lay in twisted forms. Blood from desperate hands ruining the delicate frescos on the wall. Even the overseer seemed shocked, running a palm across a sweaty forehead and staring with horror at the carnage.

Mina staggered along dazed, walking past the bodies with only the slightest glance to check if there were someone she knew, trailing her whip behind her. When she saw Sporus and Erotica she dragged herself over to them and the three of them hugged each other tight without a word being spoken.

Lysander, his proud yellow tunic covered with red splashes, sat on the floor in the entrance hall, buried his head in his hands, and wept.

Statilia Messalina was gently persuaded to open her door. The Praetorian tribune outside offering copious reassurances that she would be safe, that the palace was calm, that everything was fine. Eventually one of her pale attendants pulled the door open. Honoratus marched in to find the empress curled up by a wardrobe, her face wet with tears, clinging onto a similarly distraught attendant.

Statilia raised her head and asked, "Are they dead?"

"Who, madam?"

"The slaves, the poor slaves outside."

"Yes, madam."

Their bodies had been removed. Taken down to Felix for inspection before being added to the funeral pyre it had become necessary to build in the grounds.

"Madam, I bring news that Marcus Salvius Otho has been declared emperor."

Statilia blinked. This news did not excite her. Instead she looked at Honoratus blankly and said quietly, "I hope it brings him joy."

FIFTY-EIGHT

They'd holed themselves up in a lounge where the Pompeias sat the children down and enthralled them with a series of ghost stories. Julia and Claudia clung to each other wide-eyed as Pompeia Minor told the tale of Varus the spectral Vintner of the Viminal Hill.

"That is not true," scorned Pollus. "You are making it up."

"Oh no, it is true," said Teretia. "When I was a girl I would lie awake at night and hear him thumping along the street dragging the amphora behind him. He would curse most dreadfully."

"I suppose he would," mused Aphrodite. "Such a terrible thing to happen. Getting your hand trapped in an amphora, being unable to let yourself out of the store cupboard and then starving to death as a result."

Perella pawed at her arm. "Mother, I think we should take the handle off our store cupboard, so you can push it open with your foot."

"Why didn't he just use his other hand to open the door?" quizzed Faustina. "Was he particularly stupid?"

Pompeia Minor told her stoically, "His other hand had been gnawed off by a cat years before."

"No way. Hold on a moment. That's bollocks!"

"Faustina!" admonished her mother.

"How did his hand get gnawed off by a cat. That's … That's so unbelievable."

"Oh no, that is true, Faustina," insisted Teretia. "He got drunk on his own wine and he fell asleep on the floor with his hand in a saucer of milk and, well, that it how it happened."

Philo, laid out on a couch underneath a knitted blanket, frowned so hard at this that a cut on his forehead began to bleed.

"Now then, kiddies," began Pompeia Major in a deep, husky voice. "Who is ready for the house haunted by the humongous hairy horse?"

Unfortunately this tale was never told for the door flew open, the more spooked of the children giving a squeal. Claudia crying out, "It is Varus the mad Vintner," and Rufus bursting into tears.

Which was not quite the greeting Epaphroditus had been hoping for.

"Hello," he said, his eyes adjusting to the gloomy light that had been deemed necessary for the ghost stories. "Everyone alright?"

Aphrodite stood up slowly, regally. Walked over to her husband, and gave his face a stinging slap that echoed around the walls.

Epaphroditus' hand went to his reddened cheek. "What was that for?"

The Pompeias began gathering up the children but Aphrodite told them, "No, it's fine. I'm done." Then turned to her husband, "I'm done."

It was one of Lysander's protégés who made the announcement. Standing in the hall with a shaking, tired voice, he pronounced the approach of Otho Caesar.

They affected a line-up: a weary, stunned, wavering line that even the overseers lacked the energy to organise. Staring at their feet, lounging against walls, the imperial workforce waited for their new master. The only one of them who'd made an effort was Sporus. With Erotica's help he'd affected a Poppaea, complete with wig, tiara, stunning fat-jewelled necklace, and a ton of make-up disguising his tired eyes. Nobody had got any sleep.

Felix certainly hadn't. He sat at his desk, two huge piles of tablets before him, methodically taking one slave file at a time, opening it, flipping to the back and scrawling, "Deceased", before placing it on the alternative pile for archiving.

Theseus—Deceased
Ligia—Deceased
Tallia—Deceased
Onesimus—Deceased
Dio—Deceased
Thetus—Deceased
Ambrose—Deceased

Felix gave his hand a shake as it began to ache from the effort.

Daphne—Deceased

He paused slightly for it was a sad one, that. Adding in "and child deceased" before placing the file on the growing archive stack.

The last file was the largest of them all, containing as it did the notorious death list and associated fiscal penalties. Flicking to the end he wrote:

Straton—Deceased

He rubbed his eyes and entered two words for posterity, "Much missed", before closing it shut.

Otho made his way up the Palatine Hill surrounded by guards. He'd made his inaugural speech as emperor to the senate. It

419

had been a wower, full of populist sentiment and heartfelt desire for peace. It was delivered well, with enthusiasm and verve. It should have brought the house down. Instead, Otho was greeted with grim silence and a look of pure fury from Regulus who regarded him with white-lipped anger. It was not the welcome he'd hoped for, but they ratified his appointment and that was what counted.

The great palace doors were thrown open before him. Otho gave a secret, satisfied smile and then walked through into the palace he had visited so many times, even lived within during the days of his friendship with Nero. Now it was his. His realm.

With this in mind he greeted the slaves warmly, "My friends. You are all my friends."

He moved his way down the line, addressing them by name, throwing on the full Otho charm, which for once failed to penetrate.

Sporus bounced on his feet, trying to attract the emperor's attention. Mina, stood beside him, leant against the wall. A thick leather belt was fastened around her waist from which hung a curled whip that she fondled absently.

"I think we shall all work together famously," Otho declared, happily ignoring the universal glum expressions.

"Cock," rasped Mina.

FIFTY-NINE

"Callista said you'd asked for a litter."

"Oh, yes," Teretia told Epaphroditus as she folded a pile of tunics. "I hope that is alright? I didn't see how else I could get Philo home."

Epaphroditus sat down on the bed beside the dressed Philo. "Are you sure you are ready to be moved?" he asked, taking in the freedman's pale face and wincing expression.

Philo gave a careful nod and said hoarsely, "I am fine," before grimacing and clutching at his stomach.

"Because there is no rush. You can both stay as long as you need to."

Philo did not look well. Further bruises had made an appearance on his face giving him a black and yellow complexion. One eye was still swollen shut and he squinted painfully at visitors as if he could not quite see them. From what his slaves had told him, Philo spent most of his time asleep and the remaining hour or so staring in contemplative silence.

"You have been so very kind," Teretia told him, "but we simply cannot take up any more of your hospitality. It would not be right."

She concluded this very definitely, allowing no room for argument. He wondered whether this decision was prompted by his and Aphrodite's disagreement. His wife had taken to leaving the room the moment he entered it, flouncing out with a hardened glare. It made for an uncomfortable atmosphere, particularly at mealtimes.

"I wanted to have a little chat with you, Philo. How would you feel about taking your old job back? Once you are fit enough, of course."

"Philo isn't going back to work at the palace. It is too dangerous."

Epaphroditus gave her a tolerant smile. "Would it be possible for me to talk to Philo in private, Teretia? Just briefly?"

"There is nothing you cannot say in front of me. We tell each other everything," she protested.

Philo reached over and gave her hand a squeeze. "Just for a moment," he said quietly to her. She squeezed his hand back, gave a nod, and kissed his forehead before exiting with the tunics.

"My offer stands," pressed Epaphroditus. "You were the best scribe I ever had."

Philo looked down at his swollen hands. "No," he said. "I couldn't do that to Teretia. She would be ever so worried."

Epaphroditus wondered whether this was a dig at him for abandoning Aphrodite and his children to help Otho. "Things are calmer now," he told Philo. "Otho might even make a half-decent emperor with a bit of help. There would be a pay increase, naturally."

"I know why I was arrested," began Philo. "I figured it out. You fed information back to Otho, didn't you? Information I told you?"

"I did," admitted Epaphroditus. "I'm sorry. If I had known what would happen, I would never …"

Philo gave a small, tight smile. "Yes you would. You would have worked out that Otho had more to offer than me."

Epaphroditus opened his mouth to protest but Philo held up a hand, telling him, "I'm not angry. It is the way it works, politics. I was never any good at that side of it. I think," he began slowly, tentatively feeling his way round the subject, "I think I need a change."

Epaphroditus could see he would not be swayed so he said with warmth, "I will keep your job open if you should change your mind."

"I won't."

"What will you do?"

"I have my first job lined up already. There is an old soldier on the Viminal who served in Germania under Tiberius. He wishes to write his memoirs. I shall be assisting him with putting his words onto papyri for publication."

Epaphroditus winced a little at Philo's talents going to waste is such a manner but he hid it well, offering a congratulatory smile. "Keep in touch. I shall still need my sounding board. I've never known anyone who has given me such consistent advice."

Philo tried to smile back but it hurt his jaw too much. "I shall," he promised. Adding in a voice so quiet Epaphroditus had to lean forward to catch his words, "I shall need you too for advice. Teretia is, don't say anything, not yet, but she's expecting. A baby, that is. Not yet, I don't think it would be yet, would it?"

Epaphroditus, marvelling at Philo's ignorance of women, told him, "It takes the best part of a year."

"Really? Gosh," said Philo smiling slightly, and then telling his boss, "I don't know anything about babies. I thought …"

Epaphroditus waved a hand, telling his former assistant, "Ahh, after the first five it is a doddle. You'll be fine. But should you ever need advice, you know where I am."

Teretia stuck her head round the door, announcing, "The litter is ready."

They took a side each and helped Philo to his feet.

"Goodbye then," said Epaphroditus.

Clinging onto Teretia's arm, Philo gave her a small kiss before saying to his former boss, "Goodbye and good luck with the new administration."

SIXTY

There was a definite atmosphere, Epaphroditus mused, as he walked through the palace to his office and his old job. Though the slaves busied themselves around, their tense backs and shaking hands belied their state of mind. Phaon, back in position at the messengers hall, gave him a warm smile.

"Good to be back, hey?" He slapped him on the back cheerfully before departing with a whistle.

Other freedmen who had been prominent under Nero were also back in their old jobs, Otho happily aligning himself with the former emperor's appointments. Nero had been wildly popular with the mob: it seemed best to get them back on side by associating with that flamboyant reign.

Epaphroditus stopped Felix and that new son of his in the corridor, telling them, "I need a new assistant."

"Have to wait," Felix told him. "We have a fucking ton of stock to replenish. First dibs are to the cleaners. Place is a fucking tip. Fucking guards killed the lot of them. Wonder what fucking deadbeats we'll get there, hey, Ganymede?"

Ganymede, thumbs hooked in his belt, nodded sagely before replying squeakily, "Waste of fucking time, papa."

"Too fucking right."

Icelus had left his office in a mess. There were scrolls lying around everywhere, most unopened. Epaphroditus began to sort them into batches: internal, external, and overseas missives, wishing he had Philo there to help him. Though on the positive side it kept his mind off other subjects, most notably Aphrodite. Teretia and Philo departed, his wife had dropped the civility telling him, "I want a divorce."

Stunned by this request he had stuttered, "No, absolutely out of the question. No. We belong together."

He'd attempted to take her hand but she snatched it away.

"You made your choice. You chose Otho over your wife. Over your family."

"That is not true," he protested, trying to explain how he had hoped to minimise Otho's madness for her, for their children, for all of Rome.

It was an argument that had fallen flat since a distraught Silvia arrived home a widow. An oblivious Martinus, nipping out to undertake some business in the forum, had been struck down. His mutilated body eventually returned for a sizeable bounty. Her mother-in-law had slung Silvia back to her family and was refusing to refund the dowry. It was a blow, both for his daughter who had grown to care for her husband and was holed up in her former bedroom hysterically crying, and for the family pride.

"Legally the children belong to you but I doubt you will stand in my way. They need their mother."

The sentiment had near snapped his heart in two. He could not believe that she meant it. She would change her mind. He would talk her round, like he always had. She wasn't going anywhere. She would not leave him, take his children away. It simply would not happen.

Piling up the scrolls he noticed a series of dispatches stamped Germania, far more than there ought to be for this time of year when the campaigning season was well and truly over. Puzzled, he began to break the seal of the most recent, distracted from his task by Otho, who bounded in complete with Onomastus, three guards, and an apparent entourage.

"So you are here!" he cried, slapping Epaphroditus on the shoulder.

The newly reinstated secretary noted the purple silk tunic Otho had readily adopted and the flash golden sandals.

"Yes, yes I know," said Otho, guessing his thoughts. "They are just for the day. Let me enjoy my emperorship for just one day, then I'll do humble."

Epaphroditus, fiddling with the seal, enquired, "Where's Straton? I want him well and truly garrotted."

"Didn't you hear? He died."

Epaphroditus blinked. Like the rest of the imperial household he'd assumed Straton was immortal. A physical bulk of a shadow that would hang over the corridors for all eternity.

"Well, that will cheer up Philo," he commented, unfurling the scroll. "Icelus? Laco?"

"Cornelius Laco was executed this morning," provided Onomastus, who had added the golden ring of the middle rank to his finger. An increase in status due to his new imperial connections.

"Icelus?"

"He is still hanging if you want to see him."

Epaphroditus had insisted Icelus be crucified, a punishment his freed status should have saved him from. In all the chaos, the old rules had been abandoned. They would be reinstated only when the city was suitably calm.

"So, private secretary, what is my schedule today?" Then, seeing Epaphroditus pale as he read from the scroll, Otho enquired, "What is it?"

Epaphroditus shoved it into the emperor's hands. "Read it."

Puzzled, Otho read, silently moving his lips to the words. It was a short missive from a scout in Germania and it read:

> *Galba Caesar, Imperial Majesty, I bring report that the legions of Gaul, Britannia and Raetia have now sided with the seven legions of Germania in proclaiming Aulus Vitellius the true Caesar. They march southwards towards Rome to fight for his throne.*

Otho, lips pursed, said one word: "Oops."

AUTHOR'S NOTE

My aim in writing *Galba's Men* was to answer one question: if emperor Galba arrived in Rome in October AD 68 and was decapitated in the forum barely three months later, what in the gods' names went wrong for the new emperor?

The Tacitus quote which introduces Part I sums it up nicely:

> *"So long as he was a subject, he seemed too great a*
> *man to be one and by common consent*
> *possessed the makings of a ruler—had he never ruled."*
>
> —Tacitus, *The Histories*

Galba was a great man. He might have been a great emperor at the right time. AD 68–69 was not that time. Right from his entry into Rome, when his troops massacred innocents gathered to greet their new emperor and his invoking of the archaic punishment of decimation, Galba wrong-footed in almost every sphere.

In more stable times his keenness to balance the books, to rebuild the machinery of government, to stamp control on the army and the Praetorian Guard might have borne fruit. Certainly Vespasian tackled many of the same problems with more than a little success.

Galba, however, suffered from the record set by his predecessor. Though Nero had not been popular with the senate and upper classes, he was wildly so with the people of Rome and the provinces. Setting himself up as the antithesis of the popular, charming, glamorous Nero could only leave Galba noticeably lacking in imperial qualities.

Most of his critics agree that Galba's fatal mistake was his refusal to offer both the imperial guard and the legions the reward they felt they were entitled to for their assistance in making him emperor. Indeed so, but none of this was necessarily fatal had it not been for the machinations of Marcus Salvius Otho.

The sources are unanimous that Otho expected Galba to make him his heir. That he didn't came as a huge shock to him, and his creditors, for Otho had built up quite a debt. Otho frankly admitted that his one chance of survival was in becoming emperor, saying that he'd rather fall to the enemy in battle than his creditors in the forum.

As to whether Otho and Epaphroditus knew each other, Epaphroditus having worked in a series of well-positioned jobs under Nero, and Otho being a close confidant of the emperor, meant their paths probably crossed. Anything further is completely my invention.

L. J. Trafford

ABOUT THE AUTHOR

L. J. Trafford worked as a tour guide, after gaining a BA Hons in ancient history. This experience was a perfect introduction to writing, involving as it did the need for entertainment and a hefty amount of invention (it's how she got tips!). She now works in London doing something whizzy with databases.

Find out more about L. J. Trafford and the Four Emperors series at facebook.com/lj.trafford and follow her on Twitter @ TraffordLJ.

If you've enjoyed this book, please let others know by leaving a review on Amazon. Let's spread the word: the Four Emperors series is a five star read!